Degrees of Survival

Nick d'Arbeloff

ISBN: 0692479694
ISBN 13: 9780692479698

1

The Ob River sparkled under a quarter moon and a light breeze. One of the longest and largest rivers in Asia, the Ob winds its way across Siberia and each year deposits over 95 million cubic miles of water into the Arctic Ocean.

It was abnormally warm. The low temperature typically averaged about fifty-one degrees Fahrenheit in late August, but tonight it was a balmy sixty-three. The temperature had allowed the work to proceed a little faster than it may have otherwise; lighter clothing allowed for greater agility; every action completed a few seconds faster than planned.

Four men quietly emerged from the building on Gur'evskaya Ulitsa, each carrying a mostly empty backpack. A beige, nondescript Lada Nadezhda minivan pulled up; the driver hopped out and opened the rear hatch, then lifted the carpeted deck. Without a word spoken, each of the men placed their pack into the compartment and climbed into the van through the sliding side door. The driver made sure the packs were properly stowed, then closed and locked the deck. As he shut the hatch and started back to his seat, he saw two men approaching from the other side of the street. One of them hollered something in Russian.

The driver tried to ignore them and reached to open his door, but one man advanced and knocked his hand down, then repeated whatever he'd said before.

"Chto vy delali v etom zdanii?"

The driver looked at the two men, who smelled badly of alcohol, cigarettes and garlic. They both were stinking drunk.

"Chto vy delali v etom zdanii?" the man asked once more in a belligerent tone. The driver turned and looked through the window at one of his colleagues, who rolled his eyes and got out of the car to assist.

"He's asking you what we were doing in the building," the colleague said, coming around the vehicle. He looked at the two men, sizing them up as best he could in the faint moonlight, then answered their question. "My fiksirovali lifta." *We were fixing the elevator.*

"Fignya. Chto zdaniye ne zanyato; ya tam rabotal," the drunk man replied. *Bullshit. That building is not occupied. I used to work there.*

The colleague turned to the driver. "We don't have time for this," he said softly, clearly annoyed. He looked the two men over once more, a hard look in his eye, before turning back to the driver. He gestured subtly to the drunks with his head; the driver nodded, resigned.

Both men from the van instantly thrust a knuckled punch up into the solar plexus of each drunk; one dropped to his knees, gasping for air, but the other fell backwards, and had enough breath to get back up on his feet. He pulled a folding knife from his pocket, flipped it open, and charged the man who'd hit him.

It was not an even match. Upon first seeing the knife, the man from the van had calmly pulled a suppressed, semi-automatic pistol from inside his coat and put a bullet in the forehead of the charging drunk. The knife fell harmlessly to the street; its owner collapsed on top of it. A trickle of blood ran down the man's forehead, black in the dim light.

As the other drunk reacted, stumbling to get back up, he, too, was laid to rest with a single bullet. Silence.

"Shit," the driver said under his breath. He walked to the back of the car and reopened the hatch, looking all around them to see if there were any other witnesses. Seeing none, they put the two bodies in back, closed the hatch, got back in the van and pulled away from the curb.

The sun wouldn't rise for another three hours. In the pre-dawn Siberian glow, they took a right onto Ulitsa Kirova, followed by a quick left onto Nikitina, and made their way out of the city of Novosibirsk and away from its 1.5 million inhabitants. Soon they were on highway P384 to Kemerovo, where their plane was fueled and waiting to take them south, over the Altai Mountains, and on to their next mission.

2

The sea of cars, eight lanes wide, stretched on as far as the eye could see—apparently well beyond the horizon. News stations had reported that the back-up was now over 45 miles long.

Drake Taylor looked down from the rear seat of the HH-65 Dolphin coast guard helicopter. Every single highway and secondary road leading out of Houston was jam-packed with traffic. Not just outbound lanes; both sides of most major roads were now filled with cars exiting the city. To speed the process, personnel and signage had been placed along all of the interstates telling cars to enter and proceed in what was normally the wrong direction. Things were going more or less as planned, and it was all moving—but very, very slowly.

The pit in the bottom of Taylor's stomach had first made its presence felt 36 hours earlier when the threat had been assessed and deemed credible. It had gotten worse when he had convinced his boss to recommend the evacuation order to the Governor. In the eyes of many, including the President, this was now Taylor's operation.

"Lieutenant Howard, how are we handling folks who run out of gas?" he asked the pilot, speaking into his microphone.

A tall African-American with piercing green eyes and chiseled features, Drake Taylor had spent over two decades in the military—including eleven years in special operations forces—before being offered his current role within the Department of Homeland Security. He still looked the part, with close-cropped hair, broad, square shoulders and a lean build. Daily sit-ups and push-ups kept his chest and stomach lean and flat. His years in the military had taught him the virtues of discipline, training and planning, but this new job forced him to be more reactive than he liked, more on his heels and less on his toes. He was accustomed to managing events in real-time, and he was damn good at it. But his role at DHS often demanded that he manage from a distance, which could leave Taylor feeling frustrated and nervous. In the military, he knew full well he was one of the best; at DHS, he occasionally wondered whether he was the right man for the job.

"We've got over a dozen helicopters dedicated exclusively to motorist support," the pilot replied, pulling Taylor back to the present. "You can see one right over there just north of the clover leaf on Interstate 10."

Taylor looked down at the reddish orange dot, and slowly shook his head, marveling at the scope of the effort and the logistical issues involved in evacuating a city of over two million people. While an evacuation of this magnitude over such a short period of time was an undertaking of colossal proportions, it was not unprecedented. It had taken place just once before in modern history, during September of 2005 as Hurricane Rita approached the Gulf Coast—threatening the exact same city. However, Houstonians did not exhibit any indication that they'd learned from experience. As was the case in 2005, different zones throughout the city had been given staggered departure times, in the hope that this would mitigate some of the traffic issues. But people panicked, and the schedule had deteriorated into mayhem.

As Taylor looked down, he noted that the support helicopter had landed where Interstate 10 merged with I-45, right across from what was called Mount Rush Hour, a bizarre set of statues, reminiscent of the South Dakota landmark, but featuring busts of George Washington, Abraham Lincoln, Stephen Austin and Sam Houston.

The pilot's voice interrupted Taylor's thoughts: "Mr. Secretary, if you want to be in Austin by noon, we should probably start heading over now."

"Okay, let's do it." Taylor always felt uncomfortable being addressed that way. He wasn't a secretary, he was an undersecretary—a very important distinction in the world of Washington. But no one outside D.C. ever got it right, and he usually found it easier just to let it go.

When he joined the Department as a senior analyst, he never imagined he'd be carrying this big a load. In fact, he'd thought that things were moving fast when he was initially elevated to manager with a small team under his direction. But his promotion to Undersecretary of Intelligence and Analysis a year ago had come as a total shock. There were many career professionals at Homeland Security who had more experience; it wasn't entirely clear to Taylor why the Secretary had chosen him for the role.

The helicopter banked hard to the left, and the late summer Texas sun streamed through the window, causing Taylor to momentarily shield his eyes.

Drake Taylor had a reputation for being clever, quick on his feet, and thorough. He'd been considered one of the leaders of his special operations unit, and many saw his rise within DHS as the logical advancement of a star performer. Others weren't so sure. At this point, he considered himself in the latter camp; he had yet to prove to himself that he deserved this level of responsibility and authority—but damned if he wasn't going to do everything in his power to get there as quickly as possible.

The mass of humanity and vehicles below gave way to an expanse of green as they passed over Bear Creek Park. The 2,000 acre reserve indirectly got its name from the Louisiana

Black Bear that roamed East Texas in large numbers in the early 1900s—but was now long gone, displaced by many decades of steady development. The park appeared as an oasis within a city that had grown relentlessly, occupying over 600 square miles, an area larger than the cities of Chicago, Detroit, Philadelphia and Baltimore combined.

Taylor sat back, opened his briefcase, and removed the DHS briefing package he'd received earlier in the morning. It began with a situational assessment which, as he skimmed it, wasn't telling him much that he didn't already know. And, unfortunately, he didn't know much: A cryptic message had been sent to Taylor and his boss two days prior indicating that incendiary devices had been planted within the city limits of Houston, Texas. The message had offered no details on location, but did include a photograph of what appeared to be the mechanical room of a sizable building in which several I-beams were expertly wired with blocks of explosives and highly sophisticated wireless detonators. All other equipment and detail within the room had been intentionally blurred to deter building identification. Whoever sent the message clearly knew what they were doing. Strangely, the message also noted that the explosives would be detonated at 8 pm on August 22nd. That deadline, now just a little over 9 hours away, had given DHS sufficient time to launch an evacuation.

Ordinarily, a threat of this nature would have been regarded with a great deal of skepticism. However, two weeks earlier, an abandoned building on the outskirts of London had been taken down using highly precise explosives and methods. The incident was under investigation, but remained largely a mystery. In fact, the only communication from those responsible had been a message received five minutes before the explosion by a senior officer in London's Counter Terrorism Command, warning of the event, and noting that other incidents around the globe would be forthcoming.

Taylor took his eyes off the papers in front of him and stared out the window without looking at anything in particular. Why a terrorist group would provide three days advance notice of an attack was baffling. *What twisted motive had driven them to remove the element of surprise?* Taylor thought to himself. *Was the stated time a decoy? Was the slowly crawling and completely exposed traffic below the real target? For that matter, why did they send any message at all? Was this massive mobilization in response to nothing other than a silly hoax?*

Taylor had no clue. His mind flashed back to the mountains north of Kandahar, and a convoy under attack, but he shook off the image. As he once again peered at his watch, the pit in his stomach deepened.

3

Lieutenant Howard rolled the throttle to idle, allowed the engine to settle at around 65%, then waited 15-20 seconds for cool-down. Finally, he rolled the throttle to off, and began shutting down the electrical systems.

As the blades slowed, he turned his head towards the rear seat. "Good to go, Mr. Secretary."

"Thanks, Lieutenant." Taylor opened the door of the helicopter and saw Tori Browne, a woman he had brought on just one month prior as Deputy Undersecretary for Analysis. She was chatting with several people wearing vests emblazoned with "FEMA," employees of the Federal Emergency Management Agency. He grabbed his briefcase, jumped down onto the helipad, and strode towards her.

The helicopter had landed in a parking lot next to a white office building in North Austin. Co-located on a small campus with the Texas Department of Public Safety, the so-called "Texas Fusion Center," or TxFC, was one of over 60 such Fusion centers nationwide; each designed to offer regional intelligence and situational awareness for any unfolding event and to provide a point of collaboration between agencies. FEMA had commandeered most of the parking lot, which now accommodated three large office trailers and several helipads. They had also staged additional emergency equipment and supplies on the athletic field of the elementary school next door.

Tori looked over as Taylor approached. She wore a plain-cut black suit, and boots with low heels. She appeared remarkably put together, given that she'd been running straight out since they'd received the threat.

"Looks like you're all set up here," Taylor said as they shook hands.

"We're close, Drake. It's been a long couple of days," she responded, managing to offer up a smile.

"Tell me about it." He attempted a smile in return, but sensed it was more of a grimace.

Tori was tall and slim, with large, dark blue eyes, high cheekbones, and a graceful jawline. She wore conservative suits with flat heels, very little make-up, and always kept her long honey-blond hair pulled back in a pony tail.

At first impression, Taylor had thought her incredibly smart and capable—but also quiet, serious, and a little hard to read. As she became more comfortable and her sense of humor had started to emerge, the two quickly formed a good working relationship, and Taylor began to depend on her as a critical member of his team.

"So, any new details?" Tori asked as she gestured for them to make their way past the trailers towards the building's main entrance.

"Nope. Nothing," Taylor said definitively. "The original message is all we've got; no progress whatsoever in uncovering who it's from or what type of group we're up against."

It pained Taylor to admit this—not only to Tori but to himself as well. This was really the first major test he'd faced as the U/SIA, and he wanted so badly to ace it. Of course his first concern was for the country; the potential for casualties here was significant. But selfishly, he also wanted to neutralize this threat to prove that he deserved the job.

"Has your team had a chance to analyze the photograph?" Taylor asked in return.

"We have, and I'm afraid there's not much to offer," Tori replied. "We analyzed it pixel by pixel, but whoever's behind this took extreme care in making sure it conveyed no other information other than the seriousness of their threat."

There had been an internal argument over whether the photograph should be released to the public—or at least to building operators around the city of Houston, in the hopes that someone might recognize their own boiler room. In the end, the decision was made to keep it confidential; the photo made it very difficult to see much of anything other than the wired explosives—and it risked creating a higher level of panic, while informing other bad guys of new techniques for setting explosive devices.

They reached the entrance and were greeted by several Texas officials, who led them to an elevator and then to a conference room on the third floor.

4

The meeting droned on. Taylor looked at his watch impatiently, frustrated by the group's inability to offer up any actionable data.

The Fusion Center team had given a detailed presentation on the ongoing effort to locate explosive devices within the city of Houston, and offered some speculation on which buildings might make for better targets than others based upon ownership, tenants, level of security, and potential casualties. However, the latter was a perfect example of why such analysis was questionable: if the situation was taken at face value, then the terrorists behind this threat apparently weren't after a high death toll, or they wouldn't have telegraphed the threat in advance—let alone include a definitive time of detonation.

That is, if the whole thing wasn't a bluff, or a hoax—or worse, a simple but clever trick through which to divert resources in the wrong direction. Taylor thought back to the ocean of traffic he'd witnessed from the air, wondering again whether that might somehow be the real target here. He leaned back in his chair and massaged his closed eyelids with his fingers. He realized that there was not a hell of a lot he or anyone could do if there were explosives within the sea of fleeing traffic; needles in a haystack. He felt so incredibly restless; with a staff of over 250 people, Intelligence and Analysis had yet to turn up even the most basic intel on what the hell was going on here.

Every building owner in the city with security cameras had been asked to review footage from the previous three weeks. If they found anything remotely suspicious, they were to get it to authorities immediately. While there had been a handful of promising leads among the thousands of hours submitted, most had led nowhere, others were still being pursued—and despite the use of the latest and greatest pattern recognition software, they were still only halfway through the footage.

Time was not on their side. Taylor knew that the effort would gain focus and momentum once they knew where to look, but that was of no help now. It was basically a Catch-22; if they could find video of these bastards planting a device, they had a shot at nabbing them and possibly preventing an explosion—but until there was an explosion, the area that had to be scanned was just too damn big.

Taylor let his hands drop to his lap, then turned and looked out the window with narrowed eyes. *At this point,* he thought to himself, *the only logical course of action is to act on the limited data we've got.* He continued to stare out the window, then had an idea. He rolled it over for a bit, then turned back to the table and introduced it to the group: "If we were to assume that death toll is not what they're after, then what might that tell us about targets?"

He didn't wait for an answer. "From the message and photograph, we've assumed that these guys intend to blow up a building somewhere in Houston at eight pm this evening. If the message is on the level, then we might also assume that their primary objective may not be loss of life. In fact, we might even presume that they're trying to minimize it."

A young analyst who'd been casually flipping his pen around his thumb and index finger during the presentation leaned forward and continued down the same thought path. "You're saying that, instead of looking at targets with a high potential for casualties, we might actually want to look at the opposite."

"Exactly," Taylor responded. "Since these guys couldn't have just assumed that we'd decide to launch a full-scale evacuation, then their advance warning may well have been designed to simply keep people in their homes."

The analyst put down his pen, grabbed his open laptop in front of him and began working the keys. "So if we eliminate all targets in densely populated areas, we're left with targets surrounded by open space." He looked up at Taylor expectantly, pushed his unkempt, light-brown hair away from his face with an impatient swipe of his hand, and repositioned his steel-framed glasses which had slipped down his nose.

"And unoccupied, non-residential buildings," added Taylor, who couldn't help but grin at the kid's energy and enthusiasm. Two others at the table grabbed their laptops to help manage the list.

Tori jumped in: "Given the explosives in the photo, let's assume that the blast radius could be in the neighborhood of twenty-five to fifty yards beyond the structure—large enough to make a point, but still small enough to avoid casualties if properly situated."

After another twenty minutes, the group—led primarily by the young analyst—had reduced the list of targets by eighty-five percent, and now had a logical set of buildings to investigate. Assuming, of course, that Taylor's instincts were correct. They spent another few minutes discussing the action plan, and how available resources would be allocated across the targets.

As the meeting adjourned, one participant, an older woman who'd introduced herself earlier as a veteran of the Texas Department of Public Safety, made it clear she was not entirely on board. "Mr. Taylor, this seems to me to be a pretty giant leap we've just made, and I'm not sure I agree with it. If I understand correctly, we're going to focus all of our resources on a handful of targets, when the logic for doing so is nothing more than an educated guess."

Taylor locked eyes with the woman. "That is exactly right," he said.

"Well," she responded, "isn't it possible that the advance warning from these terrorists is all about creating panic and confusion, and has nothing to do with minimizing casualties?"

"That is absolutely possible," he replied calmly, "but here's the deal: we've got very little time, and very limited resources. If we stick to the original list of targets, we'll get a tenth of the way through before tonight's deadline, and—unless we get incredibly lucky—have accomplished next to nothing. By using a reasonable filter, we can prioritize and possibly finish the list."

"And if we're wrong?" the DPS veteran asked.

"Then we're wrong." Taylor stated flatly. "But I'd rather follow a rational hunch and be wrong than attempt to boil the ocean and be completely ineffectual."

A few folks listening to the exchange nodded in agreement; the woman looked unconvinced. But there was not a lot more to say; Taylor was technically in charge, and the decision had been made. The group made their way out of the conference room to focus on execution. Taylor again looked at his watch and turned to Tori. "What's the latest on the evacuation?"

"I'm afraid it's not great news," she replied, looking at an email on her phone. "I just received an estimate from FEMA that the last evacuees should clear the city limits by around 8:30 pm."

Given what he'd seen earlier from the air, that actually seemed better than what he'd expected—but he also knew it wasn't good enough. "So what are our options? Can we airlift folks out?"

"We'll have to," Tori replied. "I'll work with FEMA to round up some transport helicopters from Fort Hood or Corpus Christi."

"Will that make a difference?"

"It won't solve the problem, but it'll help. At this point, we might have to create a staging area somewhere within the city for those who can't make it out. The problem is where to put it."

"And that's no small problem." He rubbed his jaw uneasily. "It's one thing to bet on a hunch when allocating resources to inspect buildings; it's something else entirely if we're betting on a safe location for gathering thousands of civilians."

"Agreed. Drake, let me work the helicopter issue and we can return to this once we have a better sense of scope." She turned to leave.

"Tori, before you go, one last question."

"Sure," Tori replied, her lips curving slightly at the contemplative look on Taylor's face. When she'd first met her boss, she'd thought him a bit intimidating, and worried that behind his impressive physicality was an ego and not much else. She'd been dead wrong; in fact, it quickly became apparent that he was extremely thoughtful—his intellect as sharply honed as his body. Taylor's eloquence, insight and humility eliminated any misgivings she'd first had about working for a celebrated veteran of the U.S. special forces.

"That kid in there," Taylor began, "the analyst. Very impressive; who is he?"

Tori swallowed a laugh. There had been several "kids" in the meeting by her standards, but she knew exactly who Taylor was referencing. "His name is... Nathan something." She opened her notebook and took out a piece of paper listing team members on-site. "Nathan Verit is his name."

"And who does he work for?" Taylor asked.

She looked back at the paper and smiled. "You. Indirectly; he's an analyst in the Office of Enterprise and Mission Support. He's considered one of their rising stars."

"I'm not surprised—smart kid."

5

The pull carts rattled noisily as the two men walked down the fairway.

The grass was a muted green, its scent and color beginning to fade as the summer months waned and autumn took the baton. The oak trees lining the course had yet to turn, but a few stray leaves had fallen, a harbinger of the changes to come.

Jack realized that he'd never noticed the steady white noise of traffic coming from the expressway on one side of the course and the boulevard on the other. This was the first time he'd played here in over five years, and the area had grown considerably.

He looked over his shoulder for other golfers, and then up ahead, and confirmed that it was now safe to talk. He turned to his companion as they approached his ball just off the fairway, about a foot into the rough and sixty yards from the green.

"Alright, CJ, give me the update from Russia," he said, standing his pull cart. He studied his clubs for a brief moment before grabbing his pitching wedge. The shorter and less athletic of the two men, Jack was somewhat pale and out of shape. Years of office work had taken their toll.

"All systems go—they wrapped things up early this morning and landed in China about an hour ago," CJ replied, looking at Jack with penetrating blue eyes. A slight breeze rustled his strawberry blond hair, and pressed his crisp yellow polo shirt to his chest. He moved with grace and an efficiency of motion.

"Excellent," Jack replied, setting up for the shot. "Everything went smoothly?"

"Not entirely. They encountered a couple of belligerents, and had to take appropriate action," CJ said matter-of-factly.

"I don't like the sound of that. What do you mean by appropriate action'?"

"They had to take them out."

"What?" Jack said, turning to CJ and forgetting about his shot. "You're saying your team killed two people? Did anyone else see them do it? And who the hell were they—what the fuck is a 'belligerent'?"

"Jack, calm down," CJ said calmly, "these guys know what they're doing. They finished their assignment, and encountered two very drunk, aggressive men as they were leaving. It was a simple choice: eliminate them or leave dangerous loose ends in their wake. They made sure there were no witnesses; they performed exactly as they should have."

Jack rubbed his face with his golf-gloved hand. "This was not part of the plan."

"Well, in my experience, things rarely proceed in precise accordance with the original plan. Look, Jack, when you recruited me and the others, I'm not sure what you were thinking. This is not a simple undertaking; it's highly complex, and we must, on occasion, expect the unexpected. It's the nature of the beast."

"What was done with the bodies?" Jack asked.

"They were released over the mountains."

"They dumped them out of the plane?"

"Absolutely. The Altai range is incredibly remote. It was a good choice."

Jack looked down at his ball, forcing himself to realize that CJ's rational calm was, in fact, an asset. Nonetheless, he hadn't been fully prepared to feel so vexed by misgivings.

"CJ, how many times a day do you stop and wonder whether this whole plan isn't the biggest mistake you've ever made?"

"Never," CJ replied quickly. "I have not once doubted that this isn't absolutely necessary to avoid a much worse fate."

"But how can you be so confident?"

"Let me put it this way: I am absolutely certain that, in the absence of our efforts, civilization will dig itself into a hole so deep we will never find our way out." After a pause, CJ added, "and while I'm not 100% confident that we will resolve the issue completely, I'm quite sure that, at the very least, we'll wake up a huge percentage of the populace who've been sitting on the sidelines."

A few moments passed in silence, as Jack considered this. Finally, he nodded once. "You're right. I just hope the rest of this goes more or less as scripted."

"We'll do our best," CJ offered.

Jack turned, planted his feet for the shot, then swung his club. The ball arced up and came down about 5 feet from the pin, then proceeded to roll forward, overshooting the hole and landing in the rough once again.

"I hate this fucking game," Jack remarked sharply. "I suck at it; always have, always will."

6

Nate Verit stood on the toilet seat, grabbed the top of the gray metal stall, and pushed up the ceiling tile in what must have been the 20th men's room he'd visited over the past several hours.

Standing on tiptoes, he stuck his head up into the plenum, in between the hung ceiling and bottom of the floor above, pulled the trigger on a 2000 lumens LED spotlight, and looked around. Dust wafted in the beam of light. Trained briefly before he left the Fusion Center, he knew to keep an eye out for anything that looked new, or for anything that resembled an explosive device (he'd been given a copy of the terrorists' original photograph for reference). Last, he looked at the top side of the panels themselves for any disturbance in the surface dust that might indicate recent activity.

Once again, for the 20th time, nothing.

Verit was in his mid-twenties, but looked a little younger— as if he had yet to fill out. He was quite handsome, in a geeky, boyish sort of way, with perpetually disheveled brown hair, and intelligent brown eyes. When he smiled, which was often, dimples on either side of his mouth became quite pronounced.

Verit had graduated from Carnegie Mellon at the age of just 19 with a dual degree in computer science and environmental studies; he'd then gone on to receive a PhD in International Relations from Princeton. At the ripe old age of 23, he was recruited by DHS for the Secretary's Honors Program, an elite rotation with the organization that offered him exposure to the inner workings of various departments, professional development courses and mentorship from some of the agency's top performers. Eventually, he landed in the Office of Enterprise and Mission Support, and rapidly became one of its top analysts.

This was the seventh building they'd inspected since they left the Fusion center with their assignments. Verit's job description typically did not include a lot of field work, but given the impending deadline, this had become an all-hands-on-deck exercise. Despite his immediate surroundings, he thought it was pretty cool to be out here hunting for devices.

Accompanying Verit was Officer Lucy Archer of the Houston Police Department; they were one of a dozen extra teams that had been dispatched once the target list was finalized. Their orders were very simple: For each target building, perform a search of the mechanical room, the elevator shafts, and the ceiling plenum in and around each bathroom on the top two floors and the bottom three. If any door to one of these areas was locked, use a ram to break it in (provided); if there was an alarm, call the alarm company if one was posted, otherwise use earplugs (provided); and last, if anyone was found inside, make sure they evacuate the city immediately. If anyone found lacked the means for evacuation, or if anything seemed suspicious, call for assistance immediately.

Verit was getting the hang of it; while he handled the bathrooms, Archer handled the rest. At first, it was taking him way too long to complete his task; after they agreed to eliminate the women's rooms—another logical hunch—they'd completed each of their last three buildings in 20 minutes flat. He'd even gotten to use the battering ram on two different doors. *Sweet.*

As he lowered the ceiling tile and jumped back to the floor, he laughed. On the wall above the toilet, with an arrow pointing down, someone had scrawled "This way to the Ministry of Magic." *Clever*, he thought to himself.

Looking around, he saw that there was a lot more where that came from—most of which had not been pulled from children's books. In fact, it dawned on him just how run-down and dilapidated this building was. Most would call it downright disgusting. Verit thought it was kinda cool; it made him feel like a private eye in some old crime movie. Except with more dust and dirt.

Houston had quite a few abandoned buildings. So many, in fact, that the City had established what was now called "Demo Day," during which contractors volunteered to help demolish a number of targeted structures. The list of those awaiting this fate was in the hundreds—but most were residential, and had been ruled out.

This particular 10-story 1950s office building on Montrose Boulevard was fairly ordinary; ugly, in fact. Over the past two decades, it had gradually lost all of its tenants except one—an iconic Houston watering hole known as the Skybar, which had occupied the top floor. It was widely reported that the bar was one of the best places in the city from which to view the Fourth of July fireworks. Clinging to life on its penthouse perch, like an alpine plant on an otherwise barren mountaintop, drawing just enough sustenance for survival, the bar eventually succumbed to the judgment of building inspectors, who labeled the building unsafe, the victim of a landlord unwilling to make necessary repairs.

Verit left the bathroom, headed back to the stairs, and hopped up to the next level. As he passed a hallway, he thought he saw one of the doors closing out of the corner of his eye. "Lucy? Is that you?" he called out. No response. He felt a little creeped out.

He walked quietly down the hall, listened for a moment, then reached for the handle. His heart pounded in his ears. He swallowed once, then opened the door to peek inside. Warm, stale air and what smelled like beef stew invaded his nostrils as he took in the scene before him.

"Holy shit," he muttered.

In the run-down open office suite were 15-20 people, many sleeping on blankets, a few sitting quietly against the wall. Two older men in the back corner, attempting to heat a can of something over the flame of a Bic lighter, looked up, as did an older woman seated against the wall with her knees to her chest. Then all eyes turned to Verit, expressions ranging from blank to hostile.

No one said a word.

After a few seconds had passed, he finally spoke: "Hi, I'm Nate Verit, with the Department of Homeland Secur—" he stopped, suddenly realizing that he had no idea what the hell he was going to say or how he was going to handle this situation. He awkwardly backed out of the office suite, let the door close and yanked his iPhone out of his pocket to call Officer Archer.

7

Taylor and Tori were huddled in one of the FEMA office trailers in the Fusion Center parking lot systematically working through a non-stop series of evacuation issues; a diverse array of people had been flowing through the trailer for the past two hours—some coming in to present problems requiring solutions, others to get briefed on solutions ready for implementation.

The trailer was a fully equipped mobile command center with half a dozen workstations and a small conference area jammed into its beige interior. A few small windows provided some natural light while fluorescents overhead bathed everything in a cool blue hue.

Tori was currently on a conference call with the Houston Chief of Police, discussing how much police presence should remain behind in the evacuated city. Taylor was in conversation with one of his DHS deputies regarding how collection of debris should be handled and by whom—assuming an explosion was forthcoming.

All at once, phones started vibrating and chirping across the small office. Taylor shot Tori a quizzical look as he reached for his phone on the table.

Before he had read through the text, a staffer turned up the volume on a television mounted to the wall in the trailer; news of the evacuation was now 24/7 on quite a few channels. A feed from a news helicopter was showing a section of Interstate 69 near the Tidwell Road interchange; smack in the center of the highway was an 18-wheeler that was apparently not only stopped, it had no driver in the cab. The traffic was still moving; it was clear that cars were now flowing around the rig. Fortunately, the reporter's voice-over was simply stating that the truck seemed to be broken down; no one was raising an alarm. But it was probably only a matter of time.

Taylor's heart sank. This was potentially one of his worst-case scenarios. Tori hit speaker on the phone, and wasted no time: "Chief, I'm assuming you're seeing the situation on I-69 that we're seeing. We need to inspect and, if necessary, neutralize that truck. My thinking is this: We could scramble a team from here, but it might be preferable to have you mobilize Special Response Team assets from your station downtown on Riesner. That would allow us to keep fresh resources on-call in case this is just the first act of a well-planned event."

That's a delicate way of phrasing it, Taylor thought to himself, marveling at Tori's grace under pressure. The possibility that the initial threat and subsequent evacuation was simply to draw large masses of people out onto highways where they would be sitting ducks for a terrorist act had weighed heavily on all involved since the drama began. The use of an initial explosion to draw responders, only to be followed by the detonation of a secondary device had become common in battle theatres across the Mideast and elsewhere. This variation on the theme was on a much larger scale; the possible devastation and loss of life would be off the charts. Taylor remained outwardly calm, but inside he was a swirl of anger, nerves, and frustration.

Once again, he was pulled back to the day at Camp Rhino when he'd heard the news from outside of Kandahar. His memories of that morning were crystal clear. The convoy had been set-up, the improvised explosive device had been detonated solely to freeze them in place—so the attack could be launched on stationary targets. He had tried many times to imagine her actions, tried hard to see the event as somehow heroic or benefitting some higher purpose, but never could. The thought of her in those last moments made his heart clench in pain. All he was left with was a simple vision of her beautiful, smiling face. Her warm, caring and intelligent eyes. Her broken body.

The police chief's deep voice responded from the desk-phone, snapping Taylor back to reality: "That probably makes sense. We should be able to get a dozen officers and two or three members of the Explosive Ordnance Disposal Unit in the air within 10 minutes. How large a perimeter are you recommending?"

Tori looked at Taylor. "I think the bigger question," he responded, "is whether we get folks near the rig to abandon their vehicles, or whether we stop traffic upstream and have it flow forward clear of the area."

"Hold on a sec, Chief," Tori said as she opened her laptop. "Let's see where our choppers are…" A few seconds of silence elapsed. "Looks like we've got one about a mile west of there. I would suggest we have them land 100 yards back, set the upstream perimeter, and allow the remaining cars to move downstream beyond the truck. By the time the Chief's Special Response Team arrives, the perimeter will likely be in place and they should be good to go."

"I think that sounds right," Taylor offered. "If any bad guys are monitoring that area, it might cause them to act sooner than planned—but so would asking people to leave their cars."

"Chief?" Tori asked in to the phone. "Are you good with this?"

"I am," came the response. "Let's do it. I'm signing off to get my team moving. Will check back in 10 minutes."

"Got it." Tori turned around and addressed a staffer: "Mary, can you contact Lieutenant Hartnett in Coast Guard 6 and patch it through to this phone?"

"Will do."

Taylor took a deep breath, realizing that there was another looming catastrophe here that could easily unfold. If that truck went up, and the news got hold of it, every car on every highway would be driving over each other to get away from any other 18-wheeler in their vicinity.

In short, total pandemonium.

8

With the Special Response Team in position around the truck, three officers approached the cab from the driver's side; one dropped down and crawled underneath to inspect the rig's underbelly, another jumped up on the runner board, opened the door, and entered the cab—the third officer covered the two men from a standing position ten feet back.

A loud "clear" came from under the rig; seconds later the same was heard from inside the cab. The three officers regrouped, and jogged to the back end of the trailer. One pulled a pair of bolt-cutters from another's backpack, cut the padlock, and then they jogged back to their position with their fellow officers.

Two men dressed in blast suits walked stiffly to the side of the rig. One used an electric drill to create a small hole, the other then inserted a gooseneck borescope camera to look inside for any obvious devices—and to see whether the back door was booby-trapped. Seeing nothing immediately suspicious, they moved around to the back of the truck, worked the latch and swung open one side. One helped the other to climb up and enter the trailer.

Two very long minutes later, an "all clear" was heard as the man emerged, removing his gloves. He then removed his helmet and shouted to his team. "Mattresses."

"Mattresses?" his captain asked, seeking confirmation.

"Yes, sir. Mattresses. Looks like mostly kings, a few queens. Did three separate tests for residue—negative. Sliced open 4 of them. Negative for explosives." A few members of the team chuckled.

"Captain!" An officer pointed to a man climbing over the guard rail towards the truck. He was wearing a pair of jeans, work boots, a t-shirt with a canvas vest over it, and a faded AC/DC hat. He appeared unarmed. Two members of the SRT discreetly flanked out and took a position on either side of him to provide rear cover.

The man seemed a little out of it, but stopped abruptly when he saw the team of officers surrounding his rig. He opened his mouth to speak, but nothing came out.

"This your semi?" the Captain inquired of the man.

"Yeah," he said slowly. "What's goin' on?"

"Why did you abandon your vehicle, son?" the Captain asked sternly.

"I—I had to take a piss," he stammered.

"By our estimates, you've been gone for over twenty-five minutes."

"Yeah, um, the traffic was almost at a standstill, so I got out to take a leak. Then I saw the Shell station and hopped down to grab a cup of coffee."

There was an awkward silence. "And?" the Captain prompted.

"The station was closed. I took a piss behind the station, then found a place to sit down for just a minute to rest. I guess I fell asleep."

"You fell asleep?"

"Yeah. I been drivin' for 2 days straight. This is my fifth load without a break."

The Captain just stared at the man; as did the other officers. Finally, the Captain reached his hand up and activated the mic on his shoulder. "False alarm. Repeat: False alarm. Wait five minutes, then have traffic resume."

Back in Austin, after the Houston Chief of Police had given them the news, Tori asked him to thank his team for their efforts, then hung up the phone. Taylor let out a breath, and shook his head in near disbelief. "That is what you call dodging a bullet."

"Perhaps. But this day is a long way from over," Tori shot back.

9

As the giant H92 SuperHawk transport helicopter rose from the strip mall parking lot across the street from the office building, it powerwashed the asphalt below, creating billows of dust and debris. It was a majestic sight, and Verit tried hard to watch, holding his hands in front of his face and squinting through the cracks between his fingers. When the helicopter had gained sufficient altitude, it turned and slowly picked up speed as it headed out of the city along Westheimer Road.

Verit approached Officer Archer and gave her a hearty high-five. "Man, you were incredible!" he exclaimed, adrenaline still coursing through his body.

As soon as Archer had arrived on the scene, she had taken immediate control. Speaking in a calm friendly voice, she introduced herself to everyone in the office suite that appeared awake and alert, then chose two people in particular who she felt could serve as messengers to the rest. She explained very simply that Houston was being evacuated, and that all of them would be fed and kept warm and safe if they would simply do as instructed. At one point, she pulled out her smartphone and showed them ongoing news coverage of the evacuation to make it real.

Slowly but surely, her chosen envoys convinced the others, and Archer and Verit ushered the group down the stairs, across the street and onto the helicopter—which had arrived shortly after Verit called the Fusion Center for assistance.

Eager for more action, Verit turned to Archer: "Shall we hit the next building?"

"Hold on there, cowboy, we actually never finished inspecting this one," Archer replied, gesturing with a nod of her head and a glance across Montrose Boulevard. Archer was strong and lean, with short dark hair, dark eyes and the self-assurance of a veteran cop. She looked at her watch and drew in a breath. "But I'm afraid we may be done for the day. It's 6:15 now, and all teams are supposed to meet downtown at Discovery Green at 6:30 to catch the last helo out."

Verit pulled the list of buildings assigned to them out of his pocket. "Of the three remaining, one is just a few blocks away on Fairview."

His energy was infectious, but Archer wasn't buying. "No go, Nate. We did good work out here today. Getting to every one of these buildings was a longshot; we inspected quite a few more than I thought we would. Let's follow orders and pack it in."

Verit pushed back. "But what if—"

"What if nothing," Archer replied sharply, shutting him down. "Even if we found something in the next building, there wouldn't be time to do anything about it—nor would there be time to bring in anyone to help us," she said definitively. "Now c'mon, we're out of here."

Verit reluctantly agreed. But as they hopped into Archer's police cruiser, he couldn't shake the nagging feeling that the next building could be The One.

10

It was now 7:45, just 15 minutes left before the supposed detonation, and there were still far too many vehicles—and people—in downtown Houston.

Still in Austin, Taylor and Tori had moved from the trailer to the Network Operations Center back in the main building, which was equipped with a dozen large, flat-panel screens set against the wall, each of which could be set to any one of hundreds of different municipal cameras placed throughout the city. At present, about half of the screens were monitoring major highways; the other half were observing major intersections downtown.

The pace of activity was manic, and tension pervaded the large room like a noxious gas. As was common with such operations, the 80/20 rule prevailed: It had required some effort to get most folks out of Houston, but it now seemed like it was requiring a hell of a lot more to evacuate the remaining 20%.

Police resources and transport helicopters that had been used sporadically throughout the day were now in very short supply. People seemed to be coming out of the woodwork and only just realizing that their bloody lives were in danger. It was infuriating to Taylor, but every single person inside of the Sam Houston Tollway had to be evacuated.

He paced back and forth in front of the monitors, not looking up, but instead concentrating on the conversation he was having on his cellphone with the stubborn manager of a mental health clinic on Long Drive in Southeast Houston. The manager was making the case that there was a half dozen overnight patients that would experience substantial trauma were they to be moved. He was offering to take full responsibility, and assuring Taylor that the odds of terrorists targeting a mental health facility were infinitesimal.

Taylor was unmoved, but he'd already tried pulling rank, followed by an earnest plea, and had gotten nowhere. Finally, he told the manager he would make a call to higher ups in Washington and explore an exception; he asked the manager to hold.

He muted his phone, walked across the Operations Center to a side table, and poured himself a black cup of coffee—probably the ninth or tenth since breakfast. At this point, he was running on pure adrenaline and caffeine. He took his time stirring in a packet of sugar before slowly walking back to the monitors.

Taking the call off of hold, Taylor sternly explained that he'd just received word directly from the Secretary of Homeland Security that the President had made it clear there were to be no exceptions. He apologized, told the manager that he was dispatching a helicopter immediately, and that the patients should be ready to go in 10 minutes. Period. He hung up the phone, walked over to a young woman running dispatch for helicopter transport, and relayed the address and details.

Taylor took a sip of coffee and looked at his watch: 7:50. The place was a madhouse—both inside and out. He looked at the screens and saw unevacuated people on five out of the six that were monitoring downtown locations, and cars still on their way out of the city on most of the screens trained on highways. He closed his eyes and rubbed a hand over his face. They were almost out of time.

* * *

At approximately 8:25 pm, a heavy duty Dodge RAM pick-up truck heading westbound on Interstate 10 was the last observed vehicle leaving downtown Houston—which DHS had defined, for the purposes of the evacuation, as the area within the city's outer beltway. The last two requested helicopter transports were now airborne, and for all practical purposes, the City of Houston was—with the exception of a brave contingent of police officers—empty.

"Well, they gave us a chance to evacuate, and we evacuated," Taylor noted, speaking loudly to all present; "I think everyone in this room—and all those in the field, deserve a round of applause." He started clapping, as the 25 or so DHS, Fusion Center and DPS staffers in the room joined in.

"Part of me hopes that it was all for nothing," Nate Verit offered into the silence following the brief applause, "and part of me hopes..." he stopped mid-sentence, realizing that whatever he was about to say was not appropriate. Sheepishly, the young analyst shut his mouth and returned his gaze to one of the screens.

"I think I know what you're feeling, Nate. Part of you hopes that our efforts saved some lives here. I think more than a few of us have had the same thought." Taylor continued to be impressed by Verit, and didn't want to let his comment hang awkwardly in the air. He'd also gotten wind of Verit and Archer's discovery and subsequent actions on Montrose Boulevard earlier, and had made a point of congratulating them both upon their return to Austin.

Tori came in and handed Taylor a brief report before passing it out to the others. It was a summary of how many vehicles and people were estimated to have evacuated over the last 24 hours, along with a summary of incidents. Miraculously, during the mobilization of over 1.9 million people, there had been four heart attacks, 45 reported car accidents with 17 people requiring attention, 33 arrests for a variety of minor crimes, five healthy babies born, and zero fatalities. Taylor stared at that last statistic, shook his head, and turned to look at Tori: "That's just dumb luck," he said plainly.

* * *

8:55 pm. Almost an hour past the supposed time of detonation.

The Operations Center had quieted down a bit. Several dozen people were working diligently at computer consoles or speaking quietly on the phone. The aging facility featured worn, dark green carpeting, and cream-colored walls that may well have been white earlier in time. The technology in the Center was, however, decidedly more up to date. Although there were some holes in the wall where older monitors once were mounted, the flat screens offering views of downtown Houston were new, as were most of the computer systems.

Most of these screens were now methodically alternating between a handful of different ground-based cameras, providing a steady, rhythmic visual of all likely targets covered by available surveillance equipment.

Two screens, however, were offering a very different view. Both were receiving feeds from DHS headquarters, which was in turn receiving data from two RQ-4 GlobalHawk drones flying over downtown Houston, each equipped with a relatively new, still-experimental camera known as ARGUS-IS.

At an extremely high resolution of 1.8 gigapixels, one ARGUS camera was capable of providing the same monitoring capability as 100 Predator drones. The technology involved an array of 368 imaging chips, and had the ability to weave images together to cover an area of 15 square miles at one time, and the resolution to clearly see something as small as a seagull flying near ground level from over 17,000 feet up.

Technicians at DHS were manipulating the feed from each drone and presenting various images of different downtown areas. Should there be an event anywhere within the inner beltway, it was likely that one of the two ARGUS-equipped drones could zero in on it within seconds.

About 20 minutes earlier, Taylor and Tori had debriefed the DHS Secretary and the President. It was a case of good news and no news. On the one hand, they had managed to accomplish what many had stated candidly was improbable: successfully evacuating Houston in a little over 36 hours. While the no news component—namely, that they had no additional information on the terrorists who initiated the threat—had not engendered a rebuke, it was nonetheless embarrassing to Taylor that they still knew almost nothing about who had threatened the citizens of the fourth largest city in the United States.

President Terrence Gilman had a long-held reputation for remaining calm under fire. It was one of the reasons he prevailed in his first run for the office against a crowd of well-qualified contenders who each did their very best to knock him off stride. And it was one of the reasons he'd been reelected to a second term, after ably guiding the country through several natural disasters, as well as a major recession.

But he was also known for asking tough questions and for being very hard on his team. Whether he was coming down hard on the Secretary instead of his underling, Taylor wasn't sure—but he knew full well that, in the absence of progress, he would feel the pressure increasing very soon.

The evacuation had, of sorts, been a distraction. While no doubt necessary given the threat they'd received, it really wasn't Taylor's job to oversee such things; he was supposed to be focused on intelligence—gathering and analyzing information. However, due to the unexpected departure of the previous FEMA administrator, the agency had been without a leader for nearly two months. As such, Taylor's boss, DHS Secretary Daniel Hawthorne, who oversaw both FEMA and Homeland Security, had asked him to partner with FEMA in formulating and executing the evacuation plan. Hawthorne was a huge fan of Taylor's, frequently asking him to take the lead on tasks that really should have been handled by others. In fact, the extent to which Hawthorne leaned on Taylor as his go-to guy had started to make life a little difficult; peers were raising jealous eyebrows, and Taylor was becoming over-extended.

Taylor was now seated in front of the screens in the Operations Center, eating a Snickers bar and reviewing a preliminary report from his team in Washington. The report was categorized by function: One group of analysts was focused on communications intelligence, or COMINT, which necessitated the scanning and processing of millions of intercepted communications from suspected groups for relevant "chatter"—typically telephone traffic, email, texts, and other forms of electronic messaging. Another group was focused on human intelligence, or HUMINT, which involved querying a range of different operatives in different agencies—both U.S. and foreign, to determine whether any specific contacts had relevant information, or if the behavior patterns of any suspect groups had changed. A third group of analysts was studying financial transactions, or FININT, to see if any money had changed hands in a way that might offer insight into whether any given terrorist group was on the move. And last, a sizable number of analysts were laboriously reviewing submitted video footage from cameras all across the city.

So far, all they had to work with was the initial email message sent to Taylor and Secretary Hawthorne, and the few details available from the detonation in London two weeks earlier—not much to go on. While they hadn't come up with anything actionable, they had made some progress in identifying some of the methods employed.

Taylor made a few notes in the margins, reminding himself to follow up on a few aspects of the analysis. Encryption and internet anonymity were not Taylor's strong suit, but he wanted to at least understand it well enough to form a mental model. In his first year on the job, it had become very apparent that there would be many topics around which he would only have time to gain a conceptual understanding—which, he firmly believed, was critical. Without it, he feared he would rapidly find himself in over his head, without any means for challenging the recommendations and conclusions of his very diverse team.

All around Taylor in the Operations Center, the quiet chatter continued as people worked the phones and sought to resolve a continuing set of issues related to evacuation sites, supply logistics, and police activity downtown. Several people were also assigned to watching the monitors.

"Right there, screen eight, what was that?" one person asked abruptly. The individual turned in her chair and addressed one of the Operations Center technicians: "Hey, can we go back a bit on screen eight?"

Tori jumped up from her chair nearby and pointed to one of the drone-fed screens: "Right there!" she shouted.

The image on the screen enlarged as the technician at DHS had obviously seen the smoke and was zooming in. Clear as day, as if the camera were just a hundred yards overhead, everyone in the room watched as a sizable apartment building or hotel fell in on itself, reduced to rubble in what seemed like no time at all.

Then, just a moment later, on the other drone-fed screen, what looked like a large parking garage suffered a similar fate, imploding and then free-falling to the ground in seven seconds flat.

The room was silent; all watched in disbelief as dust from the surgical demolition of the two buildings billowed up into the night sky, obscuring the camera's close-up view.

11

"Coffee? Dessert?" the waiter asked.

They had just finished dinner and were one of only two remaining tables at Threadgill's, a decidedly authentic, southern style restaurant and bar in Austin. The place was filled with knickknacks, posters and photographs of famous Texans, including athletes, politicians and musicians. This was supposedly where Janis Joplin got her start in the early 1960s. But far more important, it was just a block or so from the Texas Fusion Center, and the restaurant had agreed to stay open late as their way of pitching in. It had been just over 24 hours since the explosions, and Taylor and Tori—exhausted after another busy day—had walked over to grab a bite to eat after activity in the Fusion Center had died down.

Taylor gestured to Tori, who ordered coffee; he asked for decaf. Any more caffeine and his system might go on strike.

Somehow, Tori seemed alert and ready to go. Taylor eyed her suspiciously, a small smile playing along his lips. "I know the hours you've been working; how is it possible that you look so bright-eyed?"

She blushed ever so slightly. "Oh, I guess it's training. Over the years, I've taught myself to get by on five hours of sleep—

and I'm pretty careful about what I eat." Realizing that might sound a bit sanctimonious given that she'd just consumed a salad while Taylor ate a burger and fries, she quickly added, "Besides, given what went down last night, I don't think giving in to exhaustion is really an option at this point."

"Tell me about it," Taylor replied.

As it turned out, three buildings in all had been brought down the previous evening—all of them near-perfect controlled demolition implosions.

The first to go and largest of the three was a Houston landmark—but certainly not one that anyone was anxious to keep; it had been abandoned and sealed shut for over a dozen years. Having first opened as a Holiday Inn in 1972, the 33-story, 600-room hotel on St. Joseph Parkway had gained notoriety 20 years later when it was purchased by the Guru Maharishi, founder and leader of the 1970s Transcendental Meditation movement, and spiritual advisor to many celebrities, including the Beatles. His goal was to create a sanctuary and learning center for his followers. He renamed it the Heaven on Earth Inn.

The vision failed to materialize, and the building was converted into a residential shelter for the homeless. With no incremental investment, the building devolved further, until—in 1998—the City of Houston demanded its closure for safety reasons. With no interested buyers, owing in part to an asbestos issue, the building had stood as an empty shell ever since.

The next to go was the long-vacant parking garage at Central Square Plaza, just a few blocks away at the intersection of West Gray and Milam Streets. The third building to drop, a good 15 minutes after the others, was none other than the office building on Montrose Boulevard that had been evacuated the previous afternoon by Nathan Verit and Officer Lucy Archer—immediately elevating them to hero status. Once the news media had gotten their hands on it, they'd run hard with the story; both Verit and Archer had been doing interviews for much of the day.

Taylor was fine with that. It was good PR for everyone involved in the evacuation, and gave some cover to the fact that, as teams began sifting through the rubble of all three implosions, two bodies had been found. All in all, a very low number, but it was not clear whether that number would rise over time.

Aside from these fatalities, it was not lost on Taylor or anyone else involved that the perpetrators had essentially done a favor for the City of Houston. With the possible exception of the parking garage, the demolished structures were well beyond repair. The permitting and process necessary to authorize such demolition would have been a dizzying ocean of red tape—not to mention quite costly. Although Taylor did not think it would bear fruit, he nonetheless requested that Deputy Undersecretary Browne and her team take a closer look at the real-estate developers involved with the properties.

In fact, it wasn't clear whether they would derive many clues at all from the devastation. Whoever planted the explosives knew their stuff; even some of the better demolition firms would have probably caused more collateral damage. Whoever was behind this were extremely capable and well-trained—and were certainly not leaving a lot of evidence behind.

Which happened to be the topic of conversation as the waiter arrived with their coffee. The original email message received by Taylor and Hawthorne had come through Hotmail—which didn't exactly winnow the field, since the service processes and sends nearly 10 billion messages every day. Of course, step one in identifying the sender is to force the email service provider to give up any data they have on the account holder. What Tori's team got back was also not helpful: The account belonged to a Susan Jones, with a birthdate of 1/1/2001 and a zip code of 10111—which happened to be New York City, for whatever that was worth.

Though it could well be gibberish, Tori noted that her team had been wrestling with the sender's email address, which was goc2dc@hotmail.com.

"Any theories?" asked Taylor.

"Well, nothing that's really worth much discussion at this point. We've run the strings through a number of descrambling programs, and what we've gotten back isn't much to work with."

"Try me." Taylor took a sip of decaf.

"Well, the logical parsing is goc and 2dc. Any other combinations bring back virtually nothing."

"Okay."

"So, for goc, we've got 'Greek Orthodox Church,' 'government of Canada, Cuba or the Congo,' and 'God's own country.'"

Taylor snorted, covering his mouth so as not to spit out the sip of coffee he'd just taken. "Tori, are you being serious? You're screwing with me, right?" Taylor asked, eyebrows raised.

Tori smiled broadly. "What, you don't think it could be Cuba?" They both laughed.

"Yes, I'm screwing with you," Tori continued: "The only two that make any sense at all are almost as bad. One is 'gun owners of California'; the other is "Guardians of the Cedars."

Taylor narrowed his eyes. "That last one—I've heard the name before. Who are they?"

"The Guardians were an ultranationalist militia in Lebanon."

"Were? They're no longer?"

"Not really. They gave up their arms a number of years ago and became a political party. But really haven't been active in some time."

"Muslim?"

"No, mostly secular. Christian, if you had to pick. And it's worth noting that they really had nothing at all to do with America."

"And what about '2dc'?" Taylor asked.

"Well, 2dc could, of course, stand for 'to Washington, D.C.' Other than that, it's anyone's guess. As I said, nothing I'd stand behind, but we'll keep moving the pieces around the card table and see what we can come up with."

"Okay then, that was productive," Taylor remarked with less than subtle sarcasm.

"Look, acronyms are very difficult without context. These letters could stand for virtually anything. Until we have motive, or discern a few basic facts about who we're dealing with, we are not going to get much out of the terrorists' email address." Tori sensed her comeback was a little too defensive, and swallowed the urge to apologize.

Taylor shrugged it off. "Alright, so let's talk encryption and anonymous messaging."

Tori sighed. "Look, Drake, everything we know was in the report I sent you—"

"I know. We're still in the starting gate. What I want to know is the basic science behind this."

Tori paused, and looked at her relatively new boss for a moment. "How much detail are you looking for?"

"Just give me the basics on how and why these guys are untraceable."

"Okay, where should I start—do you understand why the Hotmail account information is useless?"

"Yes, I get that. I want to know why we can't track back to the computer from which they actually sent the message."

"Okay, here goes." Tori took a sip of coffee and placed the mug back on the table. "Whoever sent you and Secretary Hawthorne the original threat message used a special internet browser that is capable of engaging in what's called 'onion routing.' Instead of taking the normal path to the Hotmail website, it invokes the services of special servers that encrypt the message and addresses at each step, and also uses an unpredictable and untraceable path. The notion here is that each server understands how to peel back a layer of the onion—but no single server understands how to peel all layers. This makes it incredibly hard for anyone to eavesdrop on the user's traffic. But most important for whoever threatened Houston, there is virtually no technology currently available that can de-encrypt the chain and tell us what machine sent the message—let alone where they were located when they sent it."

Tori looked at Taylor. "Have I totally confused you?"

"A little. But this is helpful," Taylor noted. "I don't think I could write a paper on it, but I definitely grasp the concept. I do have one question."

"Shoot."

"Who the hell operates this special network? It seems to me we ought to shut the whole thing down."

Tori smiled at him as she tucked a stray piece of hair behind her ear. "Well, it's actually called the Tor network, and it's backed by a consortium of NGOs, corporations, universities— and the U.S. government, through the National Science Foundation. In fact, the original project was sponsored by the Naval Research Laboratory, with subsequent funding from DARPA."

"We funded this thing? Why on earth would we create a network that allows terrorists to operate undetected?"

"It certainly wasn't created for terrorists—it was built to protect legitimate parties."

"Such as?"

"Oh, there are all kinds of people who wouldn't want to reveal their identity, or reveal what sites they're visiting. It could be an investment firm who doesn't want competitors snooping on future investment targets; it could be a celebrity who doesn't want the paparazzi looking over their shoulder. And, of course, it could be the U.S. government discreetly gathering intelligence on a whole range of bad guys—or any one of thousands of U.S. military personnel trying to hide their identity and activity in a hostile country."

Taylor drained his cup of the last swig of decaf. "So, I think I'm hearing that the message isn't going to help us much in our efforts to find these bastards."

Tori sighed. "I'm afraid that's exactly what you're hearing."

"And the photograph they attached—is there a signature of any kind within the image file?"

"Often there is," Tori replied, "but in this case, it's been scrubbed. There's really nothing there but the bits that comprise the image."

Over above the bar, a news channel was returning from commercial, flashing a cross-haired "Target: Houston" logo, then quickly transitioning to a replay of the Heaven on Earth Inn coming down. They watched it once again, and Taylor wondered why the hell the terrorists had targeted empty buildings. Consistent with the advance notice, but still baffling.

The video, provided by DHS to the news media, had been edited and its resolution reduced. Taylor was ambivalent; but he'd done as he was ordered. On the one hand, he'd wanted to release full resolution, so that every armchair pseudo-expert could closely study the footage—crowdsourcing could be a powerful means to turn up new ideas on motive and method. However, he also understood that they simply could not telegraph to the outside world just how brilliantly the ARGUS camera had performed; so much so that footage of the parking garage and the office building had been suppressed.

"You almost ready to go?" Taylor asked, anxious to get back to the hotel. He caught the waiter's eye and motioned for the check.

"All set," Tori responded. She reached around and grabbed her bag off the back of her chair.

The waiter came by with the bill and Taylor handed him a credit card.

"Drake," Tori said, leaning towards him, her eyes dark and serious, "we certainly don't have to make the call tonight, but FEMA wants a timeline soon for telling people when they can return to their homes. As I mentioned earlier, we can proceed outside in—that is, we can let residents between the beltways come back first, and hold off on the downtown area."

So far, the evacuation had been fairly smooth, with roughly half of all evacuees finding their own way, and the other half staying in FEMA-supplied housing and temporary shelters north and west of the city. But Tori had been told by her FEMA colleagues that people got impatient very quickly once they'd been away from their homes for more than a night or two.

Taylor drew a breath and exhaled, running a hand over his head. "Yup, you're right. I think it's possible that by tomorrow night, we might have clearance for letting folks return to the area outside of I-610. However, the downtown area may be a different story. I'll try to connect with the Governor and Secretary Hawthorne in the am and get you some clarity."

"Good. Thank you." She sat back, the subject closed.

"Tori, now that we know exactly where to look, I assume you'll dig in first thing on any available footage in and around these buildings?"

"Already on it, boss. A dozen members of my team will be working well into the night on exactly that."

"Good. I think it's quite likely that these guys aren't done. In fact, they may just be getting started, and I'm very worried that next time we won't be so lucky with the body count." Somehow Taylor felt a modicum of relief vocalizing the fear that he'd been carrying around since the threat first appeared.

"I have the exact same feeling," said Tori.

The waiter returned, Taylor signed the bill, and they headed out.

*   *   *

Back at their hotel, after bidding Tori goodnight, Taylor walked out of the elevator and took a left towards his room. The long, dimly lit hallway was quiet. He altered his footsteps slightly so as to eliminate any noise from his shoes on the maroon carpet—force of habit. He passed door after door, separated by expanses of faded floral wallpaper. His mind should have been on the day's events and the unfolding terrorist plot, but instead it drifted back to Rachel. *Why today?* he asked himself, wondering why, after nearly two years, she was once again crowding out other thoughts.

Rachel Freeman had been the love of his life. Up to that point, Taylor had behaved like many others in his unit. As a good looking guy, in peak physical condition, he could stop women in their tracks, and often did exactly that. He bore the confidence of a man who was extremely well-trained, and was recognized as one of the best operators in his battalion; as such, meeting attractive women and enjoying their company in short bursts in between missions was not difficult.

Rachel, however, had taken him by surprise. They'd met one grizzly afternoon at Camp Rhino, where both were stationed, when two V-22 Ospreys brought back a dozen wounded men from a firefight in Helmand Province. They found themselves on opposite ends of a stretcher carrying one of the wounded to the medical facility. Later, after the commotion had died down, they chatted outside the mess tent. She took his breath away, and Taylor felt like a kid in middle school—self-conscious and tongue-tied. She would later say his awkwardness on their first meeting was adorable, one of the reasons she fell in love with him.

She was a Senior Airman in the Air Force, serving as a vehicle op—or vehicle operator dispatcher. That meant lots of long, fairly tedious drive missions where the objective was to move supplies from point A to point B, occasionally punctuated by the horror of an improvised explosive device or an ambush. As a member of the 75th Ranger Regiment, Taylor's job was very, very different. His comings and goings were extremely unpredictable, and usually classified. He and his unit were trained to seize airfields and other facilities, capture enemy combatants, and eliminate high-value targets.

Romance on the base was not an easy proposition. For starters, it was frowned upon, and the regulations around fraternization meant that they had to be careful. That, however, made the relationship an adventure, where every rendezvous had an element of secrecy and suspense; their time together definitely did not want for passion. And unlike a number of Taylor's fellow operators who had girlfriends or wives back home, both he and Rachel knew the drill; neither was on the outside looking in. Rachel understood when he disappeared at a moment's notice; they fully appreciated the loyalty each felt to their comrades. Their chemistry together was magical and effortless; they made every second count.

Taylor slid his key card into the doorlock, entered his room, and dropped his briefcase on the bed. He hung his suit coat in the closet, pulled off his tie and put it on the dresser.

He rubbed his neck, relieved to be free of the noose that men wore into the workplace; no matter how long he'd been out of the army, he would never feel fully comfortable in a suit. He reached for the TV remote, then thought better of it; he didn't need to spin his brain up again by rewatching the explosions in Houston. Instead, he kicked off his shoes, threw his shirt next to his bag in the closet, and went to wash up.

Rachel was stunning—perhaps not to everybody, but to Taylor, she was a goddess. She was also smart and funny—and made him laugh at himself and lighten up in a way few others could. She kept him in check, reminding him that, while he was a highly-trained and well-respected star within his unit, he was also her boyfriend. Every now and then, she playfully admonished that he needed to grade himself not on his prowess in the field, but on how well he catered to her emotional and physical needs. All in all, she would say, with a mischievous sparkle in her eye, he deserved around a B+, but she could be persuaded to give him some extra credit, if he earned it. And he did: during long lazy afternoons between missions, they would be completely wrapped up in each other arms for hours, alternating between sensual massage, bouts of passionate sex, and intimate pillow-talk. It was the small moments, the jokes and the quiet conversations, that he missed the most. Those were probably his favorite—and now most painful—memories of her.

As he pulled a towel off the rack next to the sink and dried his face, he inwardly chuckled at the recollection. *A B+*, he repeated to himself with a spontaneous grin. *Not bad for a guy who knew next to nothing about committed relationships.*

He pulled his phone's charging cord out of his briefcase, plugged it in next to the bed, then set the alarm. He then got under the covers, turned out the light, and forced his body to give itself over to badly-needed sleep.

12

The glow from the headlights got steadily brighter. As the light passed through the mostly glass-less windows, it created intricate spider-webs of shadow in and around the creeping ivy that half-covered the old, square brick building. Despite its advanced age, the structure still maintained a certain grace, sitting peacefully along Suzhou Creek, just west of Zhongtan Road.

The Volkswagen Santana pulled to a stop about thirty feet from the door they were about to exit. The team leader, watching from inside the structure, swiftly altered the plan, signaling two men to exit out two back windows, drop to ground, hold, then circle back around to the front.

One car door opened, then another; they both shut at roughly the same time; the headlights remained on. All good; unlikely that they'd called for back-up, and no flashing blues and reds. The three men remaining inside the building silently adjusted their night vision goggles, and pulled weapons—two had suppressed H&K Mark 23 semi-automatic pistols, the third held a suppressed MP5 submachine gun.

Over the modest 3 am background noise of the world's largest city, the men heard the footsteps of the two officers approach, and two weak flashlight beams preceded them through the door. The first officer entered, then the second. After a quick inspection of the first room, which covered half of the ground floor, they moved into the second, which covered the remaining half. There was a fair amount of debris throughout. In the many years since the building had been abandoned, the city's less fortunate had brought in clothes, sleeping bags, even some make-shift furniture.

Finding nothing, the officers headed up the cement staircase to the second level, which was open with the exception of several crumbling wall segments, what appeared to be a standing cabinet or wardrobe, and a small cement alcove in the far corner. The flashlights bounced around the large open room. One officer went to the alcove and took a closer look; it had apparently been boarded up for quite some time. He turned, took a step over some ivy which had grown over the threshold and down onto the floor, shined his light around for another 10 seconds or so, saw nothing, and turned back to his partner.

"Zhèlǐ méiyǒu shé me," the first said flatly. *There is nothing here.*

"Hǎode. Wǒmen zǒu ba," the other replied. *Okay; let's get out of here.*

The first officer headed back down the staircase. The second paused, shining his flashlight on what looked like a relatively new pair of boots on the floor next to the old wardrobe. As he walked over and bent down for a closer look, he suddenly realized the boots were not empty. In a split second, before he could react, a quick metallic sound signaled the release of a round from an M23 and the end of the officer's life. The man wielding the weapon and occupying the boots immediately grabbed the officer around the chest before he fell and then laid him down quietly. The first officer, now on the ground floor and almost through the exit on his way back to the car, stopped short and listened.

"Chongan, nǐ lái?" he shouted up the stairs. *Chongan, are you coming?*

Silence. "Chongan!" he shouted again. Nothing.

He started to move back towards the stairs, then stopped. He called once more with no response. Reconsidering, he turned and headed briskly to the door to call for back-up.

As he exited the building, another metallic sound was heard; the suppressor did its job perfectly, the sound just the M23's bolt racking back. Less than 90 seconds later, the two officers were lying side by side in the closed trunk of the police car, the headlights had been extinguished, and the 5 men were standing in a close circle just inside the door of the building.

The team leader spoke very quietly: "Sandman, Trevor: You two have the bodies and the car; at least two miles distant and preferably undiscoverable for twenty-four hours. Ryan, Wolf: The three of us will finish up here. We will reconvene at extraction point Echo at 0430 as planned."

All men nodded and moved quickly away to execute their tasks.

13

As the black, late model Cadillac XTS cleared the North-west gate of the White House and took a left onto Pennsylvania Avenue, Taylor gazed up through tinted windows at the Old Executive Office Building—now called the EEOB since it was dedicated to Dwight Eisenhower in 1999.

"It's a monstrosity, isn't it?" Tori offered, following his gaze.

"Actually, I've always thought it was pretty impressive," Taylor replied with a self-conscious grin.

"Mark Twain called it 'the ugliest building in America,' but I've always liked it as well. It's called Second Empire architecture, a French style popularized in the mid-19th century during the reign of Napoleon the 3rd." Tori wore a dark gray coat dress, a single strand of pearls, and black low-heeled pumps. Taylor cleared his throat.

"Are you serious? Where are you getting all this?" Taylor asked, laughing gently.

"Architecture minor at NYU," she replied. "Don't remember much, but somehow that little tidbit was retained."

"So what was your major?" Taylor asked, suddenly realizing how much he didn't know about her.

"Poli-Sci."

"Of course," Taylor said, failing to hide a smirk.

"What's that about?" Tori asked teasingly, narrowing her eyes.

"You just seem like a Poli-Sci major," said Taylor. "You just always seem to know exactly how to work the organization, and how to get it all done without pissing anybody off." He smiled, subconsciously adjusting his green and black striped tie, which offered bold contrast against his black pinstripe suit and white shirt.

She laughed. "Oh, so is that what Political Science is all about?"

"Sort of. Isn't it?" Taylor asked with a crooked smile.

Tori let it go. "And you? What did you study?"

"Economics. A foolish choice."

"From where?"

"University of Wisconsin at Madison."

"Huh. Why was it foolish?"

"Because at the time I didn't have a clue what I wanted to do in life. Economics was boring as hell; I chose it to please my father. I should have studied history."

Taylor had been raised in Naperville, Illinois, a middle class suburb of Chicago. His father had been a popular Earth Science teacher and a football coach at Waubonsie Valley High School; his mother a nurse at Northwestern Memorial. But Taylor's childhood was far from idyllic. While on the surface his family looked perfectly happy, behind closed doors it was a different story. His father, well-liked at school and considered a terrific teacher, was very controlling and quick to anger with Taylor and his little sister. While he never put a hand on them, he would berate them constantly, criticizing everything they did and belittling their achievements. When they were in grade school, Taylor's mother would intervene, but eventually she became worn down by years of verbal abuse from her husband. As the kids grew older, she often stood silently by while her husband raged, cowed by his presence. As a result, Taylor and his little sister would spend hours together outside in the backyard, even after darkness had fallen—or huddled in their rooms upstairs, remaining as quiet as possible so as not to offer their father any excuse or opportunity to turn his attentions upon them.

As a kid, Taylor was somewhat of a loner—a condition which only got worse in college. But social life aside, his years at Madison taught him a lot; away from his old man's toxic influence, Taylor gained self-confidence and discovered he was every bit as smart as his peers. He tore into his subjects, and became an excellent student; his young mind soaking up facts like a sponge. To pay for school, his father had pushed him to enroll in ROTC. He got a full-boat scholarship, and found that his education at Madison had every bit as much to do with officer training as with his classes.

It was in the service after college that he eventually hit his stride. Initially, the obligation of three or four years on active duty seemed like a good way to escape his home life—but it also scared the hell out of him. There was no question whatsoever that he'd simply do his time and get out; he certainly didn't expect it to become his career.

But that's not how life unfolded.

"So that was pretty heady stuff back there," Taylor said, changing the subject. "That's not a place I expected to be at any point in my life."

"Nor I," said Tori. "I thought you handled yourself well."

"Thanks."

The two had just come from briefing President Gilman and Secretary Hawthorne in the Oval Office. The President had been magnanimous in his praise of the two of them, and noted how pleased he was that the evacuation—and subsequent return of Houston residents—had proceeded so smoothly.

The media, along with hundreds of pundits and talking heads, seemed to agree. The President had clearly gotten a boost from his administration's response to the event.

However, the meeting was not a total lovefest; predictably, the President had made it very clear to Taylor that it was now time to dig deep and get some intel on who was behind this; he wanted a full progress briefing on his desk by the following morning. It was not lost on any of them that this whole episode was more than likely just a prelude to something bigger.

"So any luck with the video?" asked Taylor.

"Actually, yes, but it's not clear how helpful it will be. The building on Montrose had no surveillance whatsoever. However, a camera focused on the Heaven on Earth Inn and another focused on the parking garage both show people entering and departing—but the video for both is extremely fuzzy."

"Can't you enhance it?"

"Ordinarily, we could, but we believe the terrorists may have actually used a spray on the camera lenses that make the image unreadable. It looks like the spray was applied at two different points in time, and each time the picture was further degraded."

"Clever. Why would they spray it twice?"

"Perhaps because they're damn clever. My analysts believe that they applied it in two stages so that anyone monitoring the cameras wouldn't see the degradation in one fell swoop, and thus would be less likely to address it."

"Sounds like these guys know what they're doing." He shifted restlessly, frustrated by the picture that seemed to be unfolding. Taylor hated the feeling that he was simply reacting to the terrorists' well-laid plans.

Tori sighed. "Yup, I'm afraid so. We also now know that, whatever the explosive used, it appears to be a relatively new technology, which may limit the number of possible perpetrators—but given how careful these guys seem to have been, I'm not holding my breath." Tori paused for a moment. "Speaking of which, you've got a meeting with the Science and Technology folks this afternoon, don't you?"

Taylor looked quickly at his watch. "Yes. In 45 minutes, and I'm going to lock the lab doors until we have at least a few concrete answers."

"Well, I wish I could go with you, but I've got too much else on my plate."

Taylor looked at Tori, and realized what an incredible hire she'd been. "Tori, I want you to know that having you in Texas was…" His voice trailed off and he cleared his throat, surprised to find himself at a loss for words. "Well, let's just say I'm pretty sure the only reason I'm not in deeper shit with Hawthorne and President Gilman is because of you and your amazing work in Houston."

Tori looked honestly surprised by Taylor's comments, her face a bit flushed. "Thank you, Drake. I really appreciate that."

"I'm serious, I deserve only a fraction of—" Taylor's phone had started buzzing. "Hold on a sec." He answered the call with his thumb and brought the phone to his ear. "Mr. Secretary, what can I do for you?"

As he listened, Tori could see his features tighten as he absorbed what was obviously very bad news.

"Understood. I'll be right there." Taylor hung up and looked at Tori, his eyes hard and grim. "They're about to call for the evacuation of Novosibirsk—a Russian city in southern Siberia. Looks like the exact same MO as Houston."

14

Inside a leather portfolio tucked under Taylor's arm was a carefully organized set of briefing notes related to every topic his team had anticipated. He brought the back of his hand to his brow to wipe away the sweat, but his hands were moist as well; it didn't do much good.

"Drake, they're not expectin' us to have all our ducks in a row," Secretary Hawthorne said matter-of-factly in his subtle South Carolinian drawl. "The most important thing we can do is just convey confidence—show that we're engaged, that we got a process, that we're movin' ahead."

Hawthorne was a straight-up southern gentleman, who always appeared comfortable and confident—rarely stressed. He wore a crisp charcoal suit and a bright red tie. His rich, dark blond hair was parted cleanly on the left and held perfectly in place by a modest amount of gel.

"Yes, sir," Taylor replied with a grimace. In truth, he wasn't all that nervous; the problem was that he'd been late leaving the lab, had practically sprinted across the Nebraska Avenue campus to his office to grab his notes, then ran back to Massachusetts Avenue to get an Uber. He was still cooling down. He thought of explaining this to his boss, but thought better of it and remained silent.

They were in the Entrance Hall of the White House, waiting for the President to return from an event at Treasury.

Hawthorne turned back to Taylor, and spoke quietly: "As I think you saw in my note, the President will make some openin' remarks, and will likely take a handful of questions. I'll follow with a quick summary of where we are in the investigation and how we'll be collaboratin' with the Russians. Assuming some of the questions call for more detail on our analysis, I may signal for you to come up and handle whatever I can't. You got that?"

"Yes sir, got it," Taylor replied.

The White House Entrance Hall was an impressive affair. Beautifully polished white and gold marble floors; the Grand Staircase off to one side; and large, imposing portraits of past Presidents—a tradition started during the presidency of Ulysses S. Grant.

Through the window, the two men and a few aides watched as the President's motorcade pulled up under the North Portico. President Gilman breezed in and firmly shook hands with the two men.

The President was a zero-bullshit, highly focused man who didn't like drama and hated incompetence. With steel gray eyes, a tall, broad frame and a receding hairline, he was an intimidating presence, a capable chief executive who liked to get things done—so he could move on to whatever was next.

"We all set?" he asked, briefly holding the eyes of both men in turn.

Taylor let the Secretary speak for the two of them. "We are, Mr. President," Hawthorne replied.

"Then off we go."

President Gilman led the two men across the Entrance Hall to the Cross Hall, a red-carpeted corridor that led directly down into the East Room where the press conference was being held.

* * *

The Secretary picked another name off the list on the podium: "Uhh, Pete Osprey, AP."

A young reporter in his mid-20s with a shaggy mop of brown hair stood up. "Mr. Secretary, what can you tell us about the motive behind these explosions?"

"As the President noted, we don't yet know who the perpetrators are, nor do we—at this point—understand what's drivin' their activities," the Secretary responded. "We're guessin', of course, that one objective is clearly to grab the world's attention; in this regard, I daresay they've been successful. However, what they intend to do with all that attention is still unknown."

The press conference had so far not offered many headlines. The President had refrained from making any statements about specific military actions—only that he'd placed the armed services on high alert. In fact, when a reporter had asked him whether he considered this an act of war, the President was somewhat restrained, stating that it was hard to view it as anything other than an act of war, but that, until he and his team had more information, he would withhold any official characterization.

The previous day had seen two large buildings in downtown Novosibirsk, Russia, reduced to rubble in very much the same manner as had occurred in Houston—both structures dropping to the ground as picture-book case studies in well-executed controlled demolition. Once again, Russian authorities had received a heads up in advance, leaving sufficient time for an evacuation. However, while the actual explosions did not claim any lives directly, the death toll from residents fleeing the city was much higher—with 37 dead. Their President was far less reticent, describing the event as the first salvo in a conflict that would ultimately see this enemy hunted down and vanquished by Russia's considerable military might.

Over the past 25 minutes, Taylor had watched the President—and now the Secretary—with a somewhat detached fascination. Like everybody else, he'd seen his share of such press conferences on television. But to be there in person—let alone standing up front and facing out onto the sea of reporters—was something else entirely. Between the flurry of shutters that erupted every time one of them made any movement, to the bright lights that ensured each photo was properly exposed, to the sheer mass of reporters—whose job it was to take what was said in that room, massage it, and beam it out to newspaper, television, radio and online audiences all over the world—Taylor had rapidly developed a respect for this transfer of information that he'd never had before.

"Lyn Persky," the Secretary looked up after reading the name and focused on a tall woman in the second row who had just stood up.

"Secretary Hawthorne, Could you comment on any specific evidence your team has uncovered during its investigations thus far? Specifically, have we learned anything by studying the rubble from the explosions in Houston?"

"I know y'all are well aware that our investigation is classified," the Secretary began. "As such, it wouldn't be appropriate for me to comment with any specificity on the results of our analysis thus far. This is jus' the way it has to be if we are going to ensure that we don't tip our hand to those who'd seek to exploit our methods in the future."

Before taking the helm of DHS, Hawthorne had been a congressman from South Carolina, a state with eight military bases. He'd also served as ranking member of the House Armed Services Committee; in short, he was quite comfortable holding cards close to his chest in front of the press corp. He looked down at the podium to grab another name, but the reporter was persistent: "Sir, if you can't share what you've learned thus far, can you at least comment on the types of things you're looking for? What are the basic elements that make up the investigation at this point?"

Hawthorne paused, as if to consider whether asking Taylor to jump in at this point would add or detract from the impression reporters would be left with at the close of the event. "If you'll allow me, I'm going to have Undersecretary of Intelligence and Analysis Drake Taylor come up and offer a few thoughts on this subject. Drake?"

Hawthorne stepped aside and made room for Taylor to approach the podium. As he placed his leather portfolio in front of him and flipped it open to reveal his notes, he thought he saw his boss inwardly wince a bit—which, to Taylor, made it crystal clear that this was not about detail. Taylor realized that the tremendous pressure he had felt since the initial threat was received would be compounded several fold if what came out of his mouth in the next 30 seconds or so in any way displeased his boss or the President.

A loud roar of camera shutters swept forward from the crowd like a powerful ocean wave. Taylor stood firm as it passed over and around him, then cleared his throat to speak.

"As Secretary Hawthorne noted, there is not much I can say about our findings thus far," Taylor began, thinking to himself *which is fortunate since we really haven't uncovered a goddamn thing.* "However, I can provide a very quick overview of the basic components of the investigation."

Taylor resisted the temptation to look over at his boss for reassurance, and continued. "For starters, we do everything we can to gather intelligence surrounding the messages that have been received—this includes both their source or point of origin, as well as the actual make-up of the messages themselves; the language and word-choice can often be quite instructive, while their method of transmission and encryption are revealing as well. Second, we scan all available video surveillance, which—in this case—may provide a few clues but not a smoking gun. Third, we look at the explosion, starting with execution. It's no secret that in both Houston and Novosibirsk, the terrorists demonstrated considerable expertise with controlled demolition—this helps us narrow the field of possible perpetrators. Then there's the explosive itself; the chemical signature can, of course, be very revealing with regards to where the bomb ingredients were obtained, while the level of sophistication and style of the device further helps us to limit the field."

Taylor felt the rush of owning the microphone and podium; like a user in the thrall of an addictive substance. But after two decades in the military, he understood self-discipline better than most, and closed with a little truthful humor: "I think if I were to offer any further thoughts, the hot seat I currently occupy would get a whole lot hotter." The remark drew modest laughter from the press corps, and Taylor used it as cover to grab his portfolio and cede the podium back to Secretary Hawthorne.

15

The Chevy Malibu slowed and turned right off Honeycutt Road into a sandy parking lot. CJ grabbed the satellite phone off the passenger seat and got out of the vehicle. He walked over to the edge of the lot and looked out across the small pond.

He startled a Great Blue Heron, which took flight from the shallows along the tree-lined bank, and flew out and away towards a forested wetland at the very far end of the pond. He watched, silently, as the magnificent bird covered the distance with deep, powerful strokes of its black-tipped wings and disappeared amidst the ghostly gray trees sticking up out of the green and brown swamp.

CJ looked at his watch, and placed the secure call on his phone.

"Is this this still a good time to talk?" he asked when Jack answered.

"It is, and right on time. So let's get to it: Are you and your team good to go for Phase Three?"

"For the most part, yes," CJ reported, turning from the pond and walking slowly towards a spillway that carried water under the road. It was a warm, bright, sunny day. Though their golf game was only a short time ago, it seemed as if months had passed in the interim.

"What was the final outcome with General Sheng?" Jack asked.

"He's scared shitless; the information we've got on him worked like a charm. He's definitely on board."

"Excellent; that's good news."

"Yes, but here's the bad news: I learned that he has less authority than we'd assumed. He cannot make the call regarding the operation."

Jack was silent for several long seconds. "Which means that, when the news hits, he will have to make the case for our involvement in real time?"

"That's what it means."

"I've got to tell you, that's adding a huge element of risk to this part of the operation."

"I'm well aware of that, Jack. Worse, he not only has to make the case for our involvement, he has to recommend that we take control—and be successful in getting his colleagues to sign on. Frankly, I'm not sure I want my men participating unless that's cleared in advance."

Jack ignored the last comment. "If Sheng argues for our lead role in the mission after the threat is received, and the idea is rejected, then they end up with the device, and it's probably game over—but we can still walk away."

CJ sighed. "Yes, I think that's probably true."

"If Sheng's recommendation is accepted, then his men will be expecting us to lead, and we should be in good shape."

"So we're just going to leave it like this, and hope for the best? I'll tell you, my men are not going to be pleased."

"Well, I'll tell you what, CJ," Jack said in a low stern voice. "I'm assuming that they will follow your fucking orders, no matter what the circumstances. And if that's in doubt—in any way whatsoever, I want to know right this goddamn minute!" Jack's voice had risen to a controlled shout.

"Back off, Jack," CJ answered with equal determination, "I signed on to this entire plan—and helped to develop it—because, like you, I firmly believe that what we're doing needs to be done. But that does not mean I'm going to automatically accept every turn of events. If there's a way to lessen the risk, I'm going to push for it!"

"You knew this thing had risk written all over it from the start!" Jack yelled back. CJ could practically feel the spray from his colleague's mouth come through the phone. The stress on both of them as the plan had unfolded had been palpable.

CJ did not escalate, knowing that this kind of interchange was beyond unproductive. Instead, he steered the discussion towards some kind of solution. "Let's think this through. If Sheng committed to direct participation in the mission, it could potentially make a big difference."

Jack recognized that his colleague was intentionally ignoring his outburst, which actually pissed him off all the more. But he did his best to control his anger. "You're right," he said matter-of-factly, his voice tight. "It would make a huge difference. Have you had that conversation with him?"

"It came up, but he was non-committal, and I didn't push it."

"To what extent would it break protocol?" Jack asked.

"Not sure. My understanding is that it would not be highly unusual. But I'll have to work it."

"Agreed. The more I think about it, the more I realize that his presence on the ground is critical insurance."

"Okay. I'll reach out and report back."

"Roger that."

The two men hung up. CJ put the phone in his pocket and stood motionless for a minute or so, watching the water rhythmically flow through the cement trough. He pondered the series of decisions and actions that had led him down this path. There were days when it all seemed absolutely foolish: recklessly putting his entire career on the line for what might well be a lost cause. Other days, it seemed the only sane path forward.

He looked up from the water, breaking the trance. As he walked back to his car, he reminded himself just how important this effort was. *If we don't do this, then who the hell will?*

16

O ver a thousand miles east of Samar Island, warm, moist air rose unobserved from the warm equatorial waters of the North Pacific. Though not an unusual occurrence, the flow of warm air was amplified by the heightened temperatures of the sea surface.

The rising air created an area of lower pressure below. As surrounding air pushed its way in to resolve the low pressure, it too became warm and moist, causing more air to rise and yet more surrounding air to swirl in and take its place. The elevated temperatures of the ocean waters served as an engine, delivering more and more fuel to a system that grew ever larger.

Up above, the top of the system began to cool, its trapped moisture forming clouds, which slowly started to spin in conjunction with the swirling moist air below. A cycle almost as old as the planet itself had been triggered; more often than not, the small tropical depression would play itself out and dissipate. However, over the decades, as inputs had been altered and variables reshaped, the odds of dissipation had been reduced.

Only time would tell.

17

"When you were a kid, did you ever take Silly Putty, and press it into newspaper, so the putty would actually pick up the ink from the paper, creating a mirror image?" The analyst asked.

"Yeah, I vaguely remember doing that," Taylor replied. He thought back to his childhood, and distinctly remembered getting his baby sister to eat Silly Putty just to see if it would do any harm—but decided to leave that part out. "My little sister and I also used to press it into door jambs and crevices to create an impression—like plaster in a mold."

"Exactly, even better!" said the analyst. "Except, in this case, we don't care much about the shape of the impression. What were after are any chemicals which are hiding in the nooks and crannies—or that may have actually been absorbed into the substrate itself."

"And the substrate would be...?"

"I'm sorry, the substrate is whatever we're analyzing. In this case, the rubble, the concrete fragments from one of the imploded buildings."

Taylor was back at the Science and Technology Directorate, working with an analyst named Olaf Henriksen. They were in a corner of the forensics lab, a large, brightly lit square room with a dozen or more long, black resin countertops mounted on gleaming, blue-gray epoxy-coated cabinets. Taylor was seated on a lab stool, Henriksen leaned against the counter.

About half of the countertops were covered by a diverse assortment of lab equipment, every unit sporting an array of buttons, knobs and stainless steel fittings. There were somewhere between 15 to 20 analysts and technicians, all in white lab coats, going about their business. Taylor was impressed; the place was not new—nor the equipment, but it was immaculate. And Henriksen appeared to know his stuff.

"Okay, but Olaf, how do you extract chemicals that are actually inside the cement?" Taylor asked.

"That's the beauty of this technique," Henriksen replied. We use what's called a self-curing polymer as the Silly Putty; it doesn't just form an impression, it actually seeps into the porous substrate material. Any chemicals within that material will have transferred to the polymer when we peel it off."

"I think I get it. And so what happens when you put it into the machine?" Taylor gestured to a large, complicated, gray and blue box with rounded edges.

"That's what's called a mass spectrometer. It vaporizes the sample, analyzes it, and tells us the base ingredients."

"Analyzes it how—using light?"

"No, you're warm—that's how a normal spectrometer or spectroscope works. A *mass* spectrometer actually uses high-energy electrons. It's like…" the analyst paused, searching for a metaphor.

"You know what—I don't care," said Taylor, waving them off the topic. "I don't need to know how it works, I just need the results."

"Okay, let's look at what we've got thus far. Follow me."

Taylor hopped off the stool, grabbed his briefcase and followed Henriksen; they turned left towards a row of offices along the wall.

Inside his office, Henriksen picked up a short stack of paper off the desk and flipped through the pages, Taylor reached over and picked up a framed photograph of a child—a young boy probably eight or nine years old—in front of a poster at a school science fair. The poster proudly displayed a blue ribbon.

"Is this your son?" Taylor asked.

Henriksen looked up. "Yes."

"I guess the apple doesn't fall far from the tree," Taylor smiled.

Henriksen returned the smile. "I guess not. I was hoping he'd grow up to play in the NFL, but I don't think that's going to happen."

Taylor chuckled, and put the photo back in its place.

"So, Mr. Taylor, each of these graphs offers a look at the chemical signatures of the most common explosives," Olaf said, placing a number of sheets of paper on the desk. "And this is the signature of what we believe was the explosive used in Houston and Novosibirsk." He placed a final sheet down next to the others.

Each graph had a handful of spikes of different heights and at different intervals along the x-axis. Taylor picked up the signature in question and compared it to the others.

"I assume each spike represents an ingredient?" Taylor asked.

"Of sorts, but it's the pattern that counts most. It's the combination of spikes that determine the signature."

"Interesting…" Taylor leaned forward for a closer look. "Doesn't look like there's a direct match, but to the untrained eye, I would say this one comes pretty close." Taylor picked up a sheet off the desk and held it next to the one in his other hand.

"Yes. The graph on the left in what's called HMX—also known as 'homocyclonite.' We ran the new signature against our database of every known variant, but it is subtly quite different from each one.

"For the record," Henriksen picked up a different graph and held it next to the other two, "the most common explosive used in controlled demolition is RDX, or cyclonite."

Taylor studied the three as Henriksen continued. "Our thinking is that someone—or some organization—has come up with a new formulation that combines these two in a new way. I'll say this: if their intent was to make it harder to derive a sample for analysis, they did a pretty good job. It took quite a bit of work to find any trace at all. Fortunately, the good guys have a few new tricks up their sleeve as well."

"Silly Putty," Taylor dead-panned.

Henriksen couldn't help but laugh. "Yes, Silly Putty."

Taylor grabbed his brief case and pulled the strap over his shoulder. "Well, Olaf, let's keep at it. If I can be helpful opening any doors for you in other labs or even in other countries, let me know. I want you to have access to whatever data you need to get the answers. This is top priority."

"I fully understand, Mr. Taylor."

18

Taylor walked back to his office across the 38-acre campus that served as the current headquarters of the Department of Homeland Security. The site had once been a naval facility, but now provided office space for one of the fastest growing agencies of the U.S. Government. It was a bright, sunny day—but incredibly hot and humid; Washington usually took its time cooling down as September unfolded, but it definitely seemed as if the city was adding a few extra days of oppressive heat each year. As he walked, he loosened his tie and took off his suit coat, slinging it over one shoulder.

The Nebraska Avenue complex—or the NAC, as it was known to insiders—was just one of roughly 60 DHS locations around Washington, and part of a sprawling organization that was, as a result, increasingly difficult to manage. There was a plan afoot to consolidate all DHS facilities into a new, $4.1 billion headquarters complex in Southeast Washington which would house over 14,000 DHS employees, but the project had stalled—the victim of deficit concerns and related budget cuts.

The NAC campus was, on its exterior, somewhat quaint. It was made up of red brick buildings and well-maintained grounds, and had the feel of a small liberal arts college. On the other hand, the impression one received from inside many of the buildings was quite different. Moldy carpeting and flaking paint was not at all uncommon; the joke around town was that the other cabinet secretaries were all going to chip in and buy the DHS Secretary a Home Depot gift card with which to fix up the place.

But worse than the physical plant was the fact that the complex might as well have been in a different state from downtown Washington; it was truly exasperating when traveling to meetings at other agencies—the trip could easily waste much of a morning or afternoon. The complex was also cramped, bursting at the seams with many more employees than it could reasonably support. As a result, there was always a chronic shortage of meeting rooms, and employees had to share offices or even double up in cubicles.

All in all, however, Taylor didn't really care. His time in the military had taught him to make do in whatever surroundings he found himself. Besides, on most days he was just too busy to notice.

He crossed the parking lot next to his building, entered through a side door and hopped up a flight of stairs. As he walked around the corner to his office, Sherry Tasker, his assistant, caught his eye as she was finishing a call. She held up a finger, wordlessly asking him to wait a sec until she was off.

Like many at DHS, Sherry was overworked. She supported Taylor, as well as three other managers on his team—and, indirectly, several of their reports as well. After the initial threat, she had cut short her maternity leave for her second child, and come back in to lend a hand. Taylor had wanted to send her back home, but he knew how much he needed her; instead, he'd discreetly filed the paperwork to get her a raise—but in the current budget crunch, he wasn't all that hopeful.

"Yes sir, he just walked in. Yes, I understand completely. If he has any questions, I'll have him give—" she paused, obviously interrupted by the other party. "Yes, Understood." She hung up and turned to Taylor. Sherry was short, about five feet four inches, and full-figured—with straight reddish brown hair that curled at her shoulders. She wore a simple red and white print dress, with white shoes. Sherry was fun to work with, but her bright green eyes were currently signaling that fun might not be on the immediate agenda.

"Hey Sherry, what's up?" Taylor asked, assuming that his plan for three or four hours of uninterrupted work time was about to slip away.

"Drake, that was Secretary Hawthorne. He wants you at Dulles airport in ninety minutes."

Taylor let out an exasperated sigh. "Why, where am I going?"

"He wouldn't say. But I believe he's going with you, and it sounded like others may be joining you as well."

"Who?"

"He wouldn't say."

"And why Dulles, for chrissakes. Why not National?"

"He didn't say."

"Okay, let me call him and find out—"

Sherry interrupted him: "Drake, he specifically said that you wouldn't be able to reach him, and that he'd see you there." A silent moment passed, during which Taylor accepted his fate. "Tell you what," she offered, in an upbeat voice, "how about if I head over to your apartment, grab your bag and some clothes, and have a car here waiting when I get back to take you to Dulles. That should give you about forty-five minutes to get some work done before you go."

Taylor looked at her, knowing full well he should insist that she stay at her post and that he could pack the bag himself. But he really needed the forty-five minutes—plus, she'd done this a number of times before, and was as good or better at packing his bag than he was. He looked at his watch, and looked back at her, sheepishly biting his lip.

"Sherry, that would be unbelievably helpful; you are a godsend. Seriously, Thank you."

"Don't mention it, Drake." She started to quickly put a few things away on her desk.

"Is there anything I can do for you while you're doing this for me?" he asked, feeling a bit guilty at the extra work he was loading onto her already full plate.

She looked at him and grinned. "Yes, there certainly is! Get your butt behind your desk and get some work done!"

He smiled and shook his head. "Yes, Ma'am." He gave her a teasing salute, and headed into his office to do just that.

19

The Pratt and Whitney engine whined as the U-28A turboprop gained altitude over Centreville, Virginia.

The plane was headed to Fort Bragg in North Carolina; that much Taylor had been told—but little else. Accompanying him was Secretary Hawthorne, Assistant Secretary of Defense John Morgan, and General Henry "Hank" Williams, Commander of the United States Special Operations Command.

The men had chatted briefly on the tarmac before boarding; while Taylor had never met ASD Morgan, he had served under General Williams in the 75th Ranger Regiment for several years—including two tours in Afghanistan. The General had been a Colonel at the time, and was probably five or six years older than Taylor. He liked and trusted the man, but had frankly been a bit surprised when he'd been elevated to Commander of special operations forces. It wasn't that he thought Williams unfit, only that the promotion seemed to come awfully fast; experience mattered in Taylor's book, and Williams hadn't racked up as many operations as he thought appropriate for someone assuming the top leadership post. All such thoughts, however, had never left Taylor's mouth. And besides, given his own promotion to Undersecretary, he didn't quite feel like he had the right to judge.

The four men sat in comfortable seats in the main cabin. Taylor and Morgan facing forward; Hawthorne and Williams facing back. Taylor had flown in a few U-28s in his day, but never one like this; the plush configuration was clearly reserved for those above his pay grade.

As the plane started to level off, the engine noise subsided and Secretary Hawthorne produced three briefing books from his bag; he gave one each to Morgan and Taylor, keeping one for himself. Williams reached down and pulled his own out of a briefcase by his seat.

"Everything in these books and everything I'm about to tell y'all carries a classification of Top Secret," Hawthorne said in a serious tone. "Alright then—open 'em up and let's get at it."

Each of them opened their packet. Taylor noted at the top of the first page the designation "1.4(h)" in bold. He knew these codes well: when classifying information, a reason must be chosen, each of which carried a designation of 1.4 followed by a letter from (a) to (h) in parentheses. The letter (h) indicated that the information was related to weapons of mass destruction.

"At approximately 1330 this afternoon," Hawthorne began, "General Williams and I each received an encrypted message informing us that an active nuclear device had been planted within the Chinese city of Shanghai. It appears to be from the same individuals or organization that detonated explosives in London, Houston and Novosibirsk.

"The message—the full text o' which you'll find in your packet—also makes it clear that the Chinese government was similarly notified. It indicates that the precise location of the device, as well as instructions for its deactivation, will be forthcoming."

Taylor flipped forward to the next page, and located the message text. His first thought was to get this to his team immediately—provided that he'd be allowed to share it.

"We made the assumption that the Chinese had been told we were in the loop, and decided to initiate contact. At approximately 1400, we engaged our counterparts in Beijing. We offered our assistance, explaining that our Special Operations Forces have considerable expertise with a range of nuclear weapons technology. They were courteous, and said that they would give the matter consideration—and specifically requested that we apply the highest levels of confidentiality to the message and the situation as a whole.

"The purpose of our trip today is to develop a set of contingency plans for managin' possible outcomes from this threat, and to work with the Joint Special Operations Command at Fort Bragg to mount an operation to assist the Chinese with the deactivation and removal of the device, should they decide to accept our offer."

There was momentary silence save for the drone of the engine.

Hawthorne turned to his left. "That's about it. General Williams, anythin' you want to add?"

"No, Mr. Secretary, I think you covered it," Williams replied.

Taylor jumped in. "Mr. Secretary, a question if I may."

"You know, gentlemen, this may be a long couple of days. How about dropping to first names as we work all this through?" Hawthorne's suggestions elicited nods all around. "Drake, by all means, fire away."

"I'm wondering about the message language, as well as its path and encryption. Any chance I could get clearance to have a couple members of my team take a close look?"

"Absolutely. Let's work that through as soon as we land."

"Dan, Hank: do either of you have any feel for whether the Chinese will see our involvement as valuable?" Morgan asked Hawthorne and Williams.

Williams spoke. "I just don't know. The interaction was brief, and, of course, flowed through translators. It's very hard to say."

"I'd say it's a flip o' the coin at this point, John," Hawthorne added.

"We have no idea how sophisticated this device is," Taylor offered, "my thought is that, if these guys are capable of something more advanced than a dirty bomb, then we really need to know about it. And if we're looped out of the deactivation and retrieval operation, we will remain squarely in the dark."

"Drake has an excellent point," said Morgan. "I'm not entirely sure how we lobby for inclusion here, but it's probably worth some effort to think through how we might make a strong case to the Chinese to leverage our expertise."

"Well, on the heels of our recent joint training exercises with the Russians in Colorado, we did receive an overture from a high-level officer in the People's Armed Police," said Williams. "We could certainly try to work that connection."

"Or, for that matter, we could contemplate initiating a President to President outreach on the issue," Morgan suggested.

"All good ideas," said Hawthorne. "I think we need to look at the pros and cons on each, and come up with a recommendation."

"I fully realize that our immediate and most important objective is dealing with this imminent threat in Shanghai," Taylor offered. "Yet every one of these events begs the question as to what the end game is here. Maybe I'm stating the obvious, but—"

"You are statin' the obvious," Hawthorne cut in, "but it's worth stating. With this latest threat, these guys are escalatin' their activities substantially. I don't know where the hell it's leadin', but you can bet that Shanghai—assuming we are given the instructions to deactivate the device—will not be the final chapter."

Hawthorne turned his gaze squarely to Taylor: "And Drake—we damn well better get some information on who these guys are before the other shoe drops, because if we don't, we're sittin' ducks."

20

Little Myla patiently looked for ripe coffee berries, picking them off the plant with each hand, placing them in a basket by her feet, and returning for more. It was hot, as the tropical afternoon sun filtered down through the canopy above, creating a blanket of warm moist air that settled over the forest floor. Myla took only the ripest berries, as she'd been taught, leaving the others until they were ready. Since the fruit took up to nine months to mature, there was a long harvesting period during which different berries on a given branch would be ready for picking.

The small mountain village of Pula, where she lived with her family, depended entirely on the forest for their survival. They were members of a clan that belonged to the Kalanguya tribe, a people that had inhabited and farmed the region for centuries. The village of Pula was located about a mile and a half above sea level in Ifugao Province, on the Island of Luzon in the Philippines—itself an archipelago of over 7000 islands, of which only about 2000 were inhabited.

Luzon was the largest island in the chain, and had undergone tremendous transformation over the past several decades. Manila, the country's capital city on Luzon's southwest coast, had doubled in size to just under twelve million people, and the Philippines had become one of the largest countries on the planet, with over 96 million inhabitants. Even tiny Pula, with one dirt road connecting it to other faraway villages, had been significantly impacted by industrialization and the global economy.

Although the survival of the tribe's farming practices were highly dependent on the forest, there was significant economic pressure to clear forest land and enable greater productivity, which would allow the local tribes to sell more of their crops. The problem was that such productivity gains would be very short-lived. The region produced a range of products, including rice, avocado, coconut, chili, papaya, banana, pineapple, ginger and wild honey. While clearing the forest for open farming would indeed trigger a larger harvest initially, the soil—no longer nourished by the forest ecosystem—would lose its nutrients after only a few years and the harvest would eventually crash, leaving the village with little means for survival.

Myla picked up her basket, now about half full, and moved down the path she was on to get at a fresh patch of ripe berries. As she put her basket down, she saw a sizable clump of civet scat, and called out to her older brother.

"Manong Ignacio!"

"Ano ito?" he yelled. *What is it?* The voice came from somewhere up the path to her right. She looked, but saw nothing other than dense, green leaves dappled with sunlight.

"Heto; aking nasumpungan ang ilan!" Myla yelled back. *Over here. I found some!* She started to pick ripe coffee berries in her new spot.

A few moments later her brother arrived. At age twelve, he was three years older than his sister, and much taller. His job was to collect the civet scat and harvest the coffee beans within. This was now an important money-making resource for the family. While much of the food they produced was simply to feed themselves, they sold the coffee beans for income. While regular coffee was susceptible to sizable swings in the market, the civet coffee—though harder to collect—sold at a substantial premium, and held its value.

The story told was that, in 18th century Indonesia, indigenous farmers under Dutch Colonial rule were forbidden from harvesting their own coffee beans directly, but they discovered that civets—also known as Asian palm cats—would eat ripe coffee berries and pass the beans through their system. As they did so, stomach enzymes broke down proteins within the beans, and the resulting coffee was extremely smooth and luxurious. As more and more people tried the civet coffee, it gained popularity and emerged as a delicacy in a number of Asian countries, with wealthy consumers paying handsomely for it. Eventually, markets developed elsewhere around the world, including the United States.

In Ifugao Province, the civet had once been considered a nuisance by farmers, a pest that ate the ripest berries off of their coffee plants and was hunted aggressively as a result. But eyeing opportunity, the Kalanguya put an end to such hunting, and now actively harvested and exported the coffee to markets worldwide.

Ignacio soon arrived and scooped the scat into his basket.

"Manong Ignacio, that is all from this morning?" Myla asked incredulously. His basket was nearly full.

"Yes," he said proudly, knowing his father would be very pleased.

And he was off, grabbing his basket and running down the path back to the village. Myla listened as his footsteps and the rustling of leaves faded into the distance—and then heard nothing but the native sounds of insects and birds as she continued picking.

* * *

As the sun dropped in the sky, and the forest light dimmed, the family returned to their hut. Myla's and Ignacio's parents had been out on the mountainside tending to their rice terraces for much of the day. The terraces—some relatively new, some many centuries old—were located in lowlands and valleys, receiving run-off from the forests above. They were built into the hillside like the steps of a pyramid. Each level contained a pool of water, held in by a stone wall, and reinforced with mud, rocks and sand. The terraces not only produced multiple varieties of rice, but the villagers also used them to cultivate mollusks and fish—while the sides of the terraces were used to grow vegetables and legumes.

The mother, Rowena, had the children lend a hand preparing the evening meal. The family was extremely poor by western standards, but well-fed and content. The father, Dabert, walked over to some neighboring huts for a discussion regarding some cattle he had seen grazing on his way back from the mountainside. Dabert had worked very hard to protect their way of life. In the 1970s, cattle were introduced, and land was cleared for grazing and farming. But the erosion that resulted, and the poor fertility of the open fields led the local tribes to decide that this new approach was a poor choice if they wished to sustain their region's ability to feed their families. Recently, a number of large agricultural companies—even several government bureaucrats from Manila—had again sought to convince the locals that their productivity and ability to grow food for sale was most important, and that they should clear the land for modern farming. However, Dabert and others were successful in convincing the tribespeople that this would lead them down a dangerous path.

Such pressures were now a constant, requiring daily vigilance on the part of Dabert and others. Left to their own accord, it may well have been possible for the Kalanguya to maintain their culture and practices, but changes in rainfall and soil quality had already occurred that were far beyond the control of the villagers. Changes that would irreparably reshape their lives.

21

The USS George Washington sat at anchor in the East China Sea, just north of Hangzhou Bay and 15 miles due east of Shanghai. While the massive Nimitz-class carrier was less than a two-day sail from her home port of Yokosuka, she hadn't been there in quite some time, spending most of her days at sea, engaged in either military exercises or active deployments. The ship's twin A4W Westinghouse nuclear reactors allowed the ship virtually unlimited range; technically, it could travel the globe for over 20 years without refueling.

While the carrier's complement of aircraft were mostly fixed wing airplanes, her mission today focused solely on a single, MH-47 Chinook transport helicopter, which sat on the deck of the carrier at mid-ship, engines on, rotors spinning—moments from takeoff.

"Traffic Control, we have engines at speed. Final clearance requested."

"MH-917, you are clear."

"Roger. MH-917, clear and away."

The large, green dual-rotor airship slowly lifted itself off the deck of the George Washington, tilting back ever so slightly as it gained approximately 30 feet of altitude, then dipping forward and accelerating up and off the edge of the carrier and out over open water.

*　　*　　*

As they drove south on Zhongtan Road, Lieutenant Colonel Greg Hering, the leader of the American unit, could just make out the lush gardens of Mengqing Park—obscured by several recently erected skyscrapers and the ever-present smog. It was said that breathing the air in Shanghai was the equivalent of smoking two packs of unfiltered cigarettes a day. The city's air quality monitors frequently indicated hazardous levels of microscopic particles, as well as ozone, carbon monoxide, and sulphur dioxide—essentially, poison. Hering felt the irritation in his lungs and swallowed—an irrational instinct. There was nothing he could do about it but get the job done and get out.

Hering was a smart, thoughtful leader who made a point of working harder than any of the men on his team. His thick black hair was shaved on the sides and flat on top. He was not particularly handsome, with a large nose and narrow eyes, but he was streetwise and very competent. A few inches shy of six feet and weighing in at 205 pounds, he was compact and agile, ready to engage equipment or the enemy at all times. LTC Hering was all about the mission.

They approached a bridge and the lead car stopped, exchanged words with several police officers protecting the perimeter, then proceeded across Suzhou Creek and took a left onto Moganshan Road. As Hering's car passed the checkpoint, he noticed that the police were wearing nasal air filters, and silently considered the notion of a growing city in an increasingly powerful nation requiring that of its inhabitants. He also wondered whether his team should be wearing them as well.

The convoy consisted of seven Xiaolong XL2060L military vehicles; the first five contained eight men apiece, the last two contained gear. The team was comprised of six American SOF operators, and 34 Chinese—all specially trained members of their respective countries' special operations forces. As they prepared for the mission, Hering had thought the giant vehicles a bit inappropriate for the task, but kept his mouth shut. If the objective was to keep the threat under wraps and not raise any alarms with the residents of Shanghai, the armor-plated oversized clones of the U.S.-made Humvee did not seem especially subtle.

Hering had heard a rumor that, in China's mad rush to consume on par with his home country, there would soon be a civilian version of the beast—available to Chinese consumers for a mere $160K. Given the smog in Shanghai, it seemed a bit ironic. But it was certainly not lost on him that criticizing the Chinese on such a topic was clearly throwing stones from an American glass house.

Hering was more introspective than many of his comrades in arms, and made a point of staying up on the news and politics of the countries he frequented most often. In between missions, he kept a low profile reading newspapers and books, or just playing his guitar—a necessary escape from the stress of the job.

The convoy pulled into the vacant lot along the creek, each vehicle going to a pre-designated position around the building. The men had practiced together for the previous 12 hours and knew their assignments. As they exited their vehicles, each wore an earpiece and microphone; several had helmet-mounted lipstick cameras as well. The Chinese soldiers who would be providing security all carried automatic weapons, but four Chinese soldiers, along with Hering and a member of his unit, donned rucksacks they'd pulled from one of the gear vehicles. The remaining four Americans pulled equipment from the other.

* * *

The Americans sent to Shanghai were some of the best and brightest within the Joint Special Operations Command, hand-picked by Lieutenant General Charles Jerrick, JSOC Commander at Fort Bragg. As the team set up shop and began working different aspects of the Shanghai situation, Jerrick had become intimately involved, ultimately taking ownership of the actual operation.

Taylor and Hawthorne had been amazed that the Chinese military had not only allowed American involvement in deactivating the device, they had gone further, offering their approval for the Americans to transport the bomb off the mainland. Morgan noted that he was a little less surprised by the Chinese acquiescence; he explained to Taylor and Hawthorne that these concessions by China were likely a form of posturing, part of a more elaborate quid pro quo relating to some upcoming arms sales to Taiwan. Regardless, the end result meant that the United States stood to gain tremendous intelligence from the device, once safely secured. Or so they hoped.

Taylor, Hawthorne, Morgan and Williams remained at Fort Bragg, patched into the operation via satellite. LTG Jerrick had traveled with his troops to Asia and was currently monitoring activities from the joint operations center inside the island— or deck tower—of the USS George Washington. It felt odd for Taylor to be watching the operation from afar; he couldn't help but feel a bit of longing, a yearning to be one of the men on the ground. Like a sled dog trained to pull a heavy load with its comrades, Taylor had a deep urge to be part of the action.

Just 24 hours prior, they had received another message from the terrorists—once again sent to Hawthorne, Williams and the Chinese. The message had offered the precise location where the device had been planted, along with instructions for how the bomb could be deactivated. The building where the device was located, along with the surrounding site, had immediately been cordoned off by Chinese police, while LTC Hering had visited the site with General Jian Sheng, his Chinese counterpart, to perform basic surveillance. Otherwise, the building had essentially been left alone—until such time as the team of special operations forces was ready to execute the operation.

Taylor, along with his colleagues, was confident that they had the resources necessary to handle the situation properly, but he was worried about what would come next. While their time at Fort Bragg had mostly been consumed by preparations for the Shanghai operation, there had been more than one discussion about precisely what the hell all of these threats were leading up to.

Feeling somewhat confined and claustrophobic, Taylor stood and walked over to a side table and poured himself a cup of coffee. It was probably the last thing he needed; a better remedy for his restlessness might have been a ten-mile run—or better yet, an invitation to join the operation in progress. He walked back to the others and remained standing, as they all watched the events starting to unfold near Suzhou Creek.

*　　*　　*

The Chinese team formed a perimeter around the abandoned brick building. Four of them—and only four, entered the structure with the six American operators. Hering realized that his Chinese counterparts couldn't be too happy with how the operation had been structured. The Chinese soldiers were all Snow Leopard Commandos, an elite unit within the People's Armed Police. Trained extensively in counter-terrorism, and having established their reputation providing near-flawless security during the Beijing Olympic Games in 2008, they were quite capable of handling this and more complicated missions without any help from outside sources. The involvement of the U.S. forces, let alone their lead role in the operation, could not be an easy pill for the Chinese soldiers to swallow.

But that was not Hering's current concern. The politics of who was in charge and how such decisions got made were not worth a second thought once a mission was underway; it was all about following the prescribed plan—and accomplishing the objective. He hoped his Chinese colleagues operated under the same maxim.

They entered the first level of the building in practiced formation. The first operator in gave the all clear sign. Hering then led his ten-man team up to the second level. While the ground floor comprised two rooms, the second floor was wide open, with the exception of some stray debris, a few pieces of furniture, and what they knew to be their target: a boarded up closet in the far corner. The interior of the building was mostly cement, which allowed it to stand strong despite decades of neglect. However, cracks were starting to show in the smooth, cool gray walls.

"Building is clear," Hering said flatly into his microphone. The Chinese soldiers all spoke limited English, but had, of course, trained on the commands they would be using. Listening in, and watching through the less-than-vivid video feed from the helmet cams, was the team at Fort Bragg, the joint operations center on the USS George Washington—which was also managing communications traffic, and the People's Armed Police headquarters in Beijing. The transport helicopter en route to Shanghai had audio only.

Hering gave the signal, and the Chinese commandos, along with two U.S. operators, advanced to the alcove. Although it gave the appearance of not having been touched in several years, it was clear to the trained eyes of those present that one side, comprised of dirty, graying plywood, had only recently been cemented in place.

The men with rucksacks took them off and placed them on the floor. Hering looked over at the leader of the Chinese commandos: "General Sheng: full perimeter cut," then at one of the U.S. operators: "Lieutenant Epstein – handgrip." In accordance with last night's surveillance and subsequent rehearsal, both men knew exactly what to do.

The appropriate tools were removed from the rucksacks. Two commandos used modified, battery-operated reciprocal saws to begin making cuts down each side of the plywood sheet from floor to ceiling. Lieutenant Epstein placed a template in the center of the panel, while another operator marked locations for drilling. The tension was palpable, but the team moved with focused confidence. They knew full well what was at stake, but each had learned to thrive under pressure, converting stress into energy and heightened concentration.

In less than two minutes, the Americans had installed a large handle in the center of the panel, while the Chinese had successfully cut the entire perimeter with the exception of two small spots at the top. The Americans, holding the handle, gave a final signal for the remaining perimeter cuts. The panel was freed, and the men walked the three-quarter inch plywood over to the far wall, placed it carefully on the floor, and returned. While non-descript in appearance, it was not lost on any of them that the device standing in the center of the alcove was a nuclear bomb.

"Device is now exposed and accessible," Hering reported, although the helmet cams had already conveyed as much. For a moment, no one moved; from here on in, the consequences of even one small mistake could mean widespread destruction— and all of their lives.

Finally, Hering took a few steps forward and stood in the mouth of the alcove. "The device is a gray, corrugated steel box. Dimensions are approximately four feet tall by two feet wide by two feet deep."

Hering took a deep breath and ran a finger along the edge of the device. It looked a little like a miniature shipping container standing on end. Bolted onto each side were lift rings. Embedded in the lid of the box was a small black plexiglass console.

Hering stepped in front of the device and studied the console, and again spoke into his mic: "controls consist of an LCD timer and three sets of DIP switches." These were three small black rectangular boxes, each with a row of tiny white switches, numbered one through eight, where each white switch had an up (off) or down (on) position. "The first DIP is labeled LOCK, the second TIMER, and the third ACTIVATE. Underneath the timer are two LEDs, one green, one red; the green one on the left is lit." Since the instructions provided by the terrorists spoke to three required codes with similar labels, what Hering was seeing was very much in line with expectations.

His eye noted the timer jump from 09:24 to 09:23. He assumed this was hours and minutes—which was not good news; per the terrorists' message, they'd been operating under the belief that at this point they would have in the neighborhood of 15-20 hours before detonation. If the timer was to be believed, they had much less than that. "Timer appears to be counting down from 9 hours and 23 minutes." He took a deep breath, centered himself, and turned to the man positioned on his left: "Sergeant Scott, get me the smallest screwdriver you've got."

The soldier knelt, reached into his pack on the floor and pulled out a jeweler's screwdriver. He handed it to LTC Hering.

"Perfect."

Hering reached into his thigh cargo pocket and removed a laminated five by seven inch card. He handed the card to Sergeant Scott: "Ready for the Unlock sequence."

"Yes sir," Scott replied, then read LTC Hering the appropriate sequence as they had practiced: "1 on, 2 off, 3 off, 4 off, 5 on, 6 on, 7 off, 8 on."

As he read off the numbers, Hering used the screwdriver to ensure that each of the small switches was set to the proper position; only three of the eight had required re-positioning. "Good. Say again."

Sergeant Scott repeated the sequence as Hering checked the string. "Okay. Ready for the Timer sequence."

"Yes, sir."

Scott read the next sequence, and again Hering checked each numbered switch in turn to ensure that it matched the instructions the terrorists had provided in their message. Once again, Hering requested that it be repeated for final confirmation. There was no allowance for errors—there would be no second chances.

There was silence as Hering stared at the timer, which now read 09:21. According to instructions, having unlocked the device, then stopped the timer, the LCD display should now hold at the current reading. Hering marked the time on his watch; they all said nothing, as he observed the passage of 90 seconds.

Finally, Hering broke the silence: "Timer appears to have stopped at 9 hours, 21 minutes. Sergeant Scott, proceed with the deactivate sequence." Sergeant Scott read the last sequence, as Hering set the switches. Upon moving the seventh switch from the on to off position, the green LED light went off and the red came on. Nonetheless, Scott repeated the string and Hering confirmed.

"Deactivation is complete," Hering said, exhaling audibly.

*   *   *

Back at Fort Bragg Taylor let out an audible sigh of relief as Hawthorne turned and, with a smile on his face, gave Taylor a high five. Morgan and Williams toasted the success with their coffee cups.

The operation still had a ways to go, and—with the terrorists' motives uncertain—they all knew that an unpleasant surprise was entirely possible. Nonetheless, the successful deactivation of the device deserved at least a small celebration.

Hawthorne pulled his blackberry from its holster and typed a quick, secure text to President Gilman.

22

Now came the hard part. Lieutenant Colonel Hering, along with three Americans and two Chinese commandos, worked methodically to assemble a floor crane, dolly and floor track. Across from them, on the other side of the small building, General Sheng and the other three soldiers set charges.

The men worked in silence for several minutes. When all was set for the next phase of the operation, the men assumed crouched positions within and around the alcove. Hering nodded to Sheng.

"Stand by. Ready, set, execute!" General Sheng commanded. The charges detonated, opening a hole in the ceiling of the structure approximately 12 feet in diameter. Debris rained down onto the floor below.

Immediately, the men split up into three pre-designated teams. One group began clearing major pieces of the cement ceiling out of the way, another laid track from the alcove to the far corner underneath the opened ceiling, and the third attached a sling to the nuclear device and, using the floor crane, lifted it very slowly off the floor.

The assembled dolly was placed underneath, and the device was lowered into place inch by inch. Once detached from the crane, the men moved the dolly and device slowly and carefully along the track. About halfway to its destination, the low, powerful sound of the dual rotor Chinook could be heard on its approach.

Responding to Hering's signal, each of the men pulled goggles down from their helmets over their eyes.

As they moved the device into place along its track underneath the hole in the ceiling, the entire building started to vibrate in concert with the transport helicopter positioning itself overhead. The lift hook was lowered, and the men stood by, with Sergeant Scott reaching upward to grab the hook and Hering lifting the top ring of the sling up to meet it. The noise of the rotors was deafening, while the tremendous downwash through the open ceiling created a dust storm within the second floor of the building, severely limiting visibility.

With two to three feet to go, Scott caught the Chinook's lowered hook. During mission planning, there had been discussion around using a winch to pull the device up into the cargo bay of the helicopter, but the lift capacity was insufficient for the expected weight of the device, and the chance of having it bang against the entry hatch too high. As a result, they were using a lift strap that could only be lowered by gradually decreasing the helicopter's altitude—a much more difficult maneuver.

A foot and a half to go. As Scott steadied the hook and aligned it with the ring at the top of the sling, he felt a strange sensation underfoot and noticed the ring drop about an inch. Looking down, he saw a half-inch crack running next to his feet and under the track on which the dolly and device rested. The cement floor was giving way.

Scott looked up, and it was clear that Hering had seen it as well. Hering immediately waved his hands and yelled into his mic: "Back off now! Scott, you too. Get out of here."

The device dropped another inch.

Hering hollered: "917, I need you lower—now! Come down 3 feet immediately!"

The floor started to give way and Hering slipped, dropping the ring. He recovered, altering his stance with feet wide, as far from the growing crack as possible. A second crack now intersected the first, and the first floor was visible below. Hering's adrenaline spiked; he was almost out of time.

As the Chinook dropped down, it created excess slack in the lift strap. With the device now tilting and starting to drop through the floor, Hering had two options: The first was to get the hell out of the way and let the device fall. He chose option number two.

He had just one shot, launching himself forward as the floor crumbled beneath the device. Time seemed to slow, the survival of the team and a good percentage of the city hanging in the balance. All watched as Hering lunged, grabbing the ring and the strap and jamming the two together, fighting to hook the ring in time.

As the floor started to fall away, He yelled the final command to the helicopter above: "917—ascend!" With a loud rumble, the floor gave way completely and the track, dolly and device—with Hering clinging to the upper half with his legs—began to free fall. Finally, the ring and hook caught, jerking the device back and forth, but holding steady as the dolly and track smashed loudly on the cement floor below and broke into pieces. An immediate wave of relief was cut short as a horrible low scream reverberated deafeningly through their sensitive mics. In the heavy dust-laden light, it became clear that something was wrong. Although Hering had successfully attached the device to the lift strap, he'd been unable to pull clear before the tension caught, trapping his hand in the process.

There was nothing the other men could do but watch from the far side of the floor as Hering winced in agony, his right hand mashed between hook and ring. The Chinook gained altitude, with Hering atop the device, his left arm hooked around the strap. Pushing the pain aside, he commanded the chopper through clenched teeth: "Up and out, you have the device!" before surrendering to unconsciousness.

The Chinook rose above the building, device hanging securely below. Sergeant Scott, as designated back-up, took control. "917, you have the device and LTC Hering, who is injured. Proceed to northeast of the building and hold."

On Scott's signal, the men clambered down the stairs and out of the structure, gathering in a group on the bank of Suzhou Creek underneath the holding Chinook. Six of them grabbed wrists and formed a human net, then instructed the helicopter to descend. Hering, having regained consciousness, held his injured hand to his chest as he looked down at his colleagues. When the device and Hering were a few feet over their heads, Scott instructed him to drop; Hering did so, and was caught cleanly in his colleagues' arms, blood streaming from his now deformed right hand—several of his fingers just a short stump of ripped muscle and exposed bone. Despite the mishap, Hering still managed to grin faintly at his team. Mission success.

"917, you are clear for return."

"Roger, we are away."

The Chinook rapidly ascended, the deadly device securely hanging from its belly. Gaining speed as it reached an altitude of 4,000 feet, it left mainland air space and headed out over the East China Sea to rendezvous with the USS George Washington.

23

Once the Chinook reached the USS George Washington, the payload was placed inside the helicopter, which was refueled and immediately flown to Kunsan Air Base in South Korea. From there, it was loaded onto a Hercules C-130 transport plane and flown to Guam, where it was unloaded and placed in a secure laboratory for analysis.

And then all hell broke loose.

Taylor, Hawthorne, Morgan and Williams—along with their counterparts in China—all believed that the existence of the nuclear device in Shanghai was their secret to keep. The messages they'd received had been closely guarded as Hawthorne and the Chinese government had instructed in order to avoid mass panic. But somehow, the information got out nonetheless.

This wasn't a leak; it was a re-release of the information by the terrorists themselves. They'd sent word of the device's existence, and its subsequent removal from Shanghai by U.S. and Chinese authorities, to several major news outlets worldwide, who'd snatched up the story and run with it. The news had spread like wildfire, igniting terror and hysteria across the globe.

At first, there had been a gleam of hope that the story could still be contained. Editors at the New York Times and the Wall Street Journal both contacted the Department of Homeland Security to discuss the situation before anything was published. But the terrorists were smarter than that, having also sent it to several other outlets who had no intention of sitting on the story. And as soon as the first report surfaced, the dam broke.

London, then Houston, then Novosibirsk. News of these events had occupied center stage within the public domain for some time, and had been all-consuming. Newspapers, cable news networks, news sites, social media, blogs—all concerned themselves with nothing else as the events unfolded and for a period of time thereafter. Massive coverage of lives interrupted and intense speculation on who might be responsible. But the news cycle is relentless; without additional fuel—in the form of new information—the media engine moves on, and the stories moved to second tier status. There were updates from appropriate government officials, mostly assurances that everything that could be done is being done. However, in the absence of direct casualties or someone to blame, the world lost interest with astonishing speed.

But a nuclear device in Shanghai changed everything. Not a lot of detail, since the retrieval and removal of the device had been achieved under a veil of secrecy. But once the word was out, it brought all three events back onto center stage, with a much brighter spotlight. The central and baffling question of where all this was leading resonated loudly from every corner of the civilized world.

Talking heads with barely a scintilla of relevant knowledge or expertise were everywhere on cable news and talk radio, only adding to the growing confusion and panic. Speculation regarding the terrorists' identities and their motives was all over the map and often outrageous—everything from anarchists to Islamic fundamentalists to unemployed Russian nuclear scientists. The theory that seemed to have actually gained traction, despite virtually no supporting data whatsoever, was the notion that some new global terror organization, comprised of shadowy figures from various intelligence agencies, had come together with the express intent of shaping a new world order. The exact meaning of this term depended entirely, of course, on what station you were watching, and what theories might be "trending" on any given day—or within any given hour.

Taylor at first monitored the media circus with some interest, believing that, within all the chaff, there might be a few grains of valuable speculation. After a day or two, however, it was clear that there was literally nothing to be gleaned from the noise, and he stopped listening altogether.

Although the distributed nature of the threat meant that the United States was in no way the sole target of these activities, this did not lessen the pressure on Taylor and his team. Even though Novosibirsk and Shanghai were halfway around the world, controlled by governments over which the United States had very limited influence, there was still a feeling that the most powerful nation on Earth, with the best-trained military and most evolved intelligence services, simply must take the lead in chasing down the perpetrators.

Taylor felt all the pressure, and then some. He felt like he was failing, and there were plenty of people in the administration who did not wish to disabuse him of that perception. The talking heads would rarely miss an opportunity to pound DHS for their "slow and cumbersome" response. In fact, media from countries all over the world lambasted the Americans—*the United States, with all of their sophisticated technology, can't seem to get out of the starting gate in solving what could well be the most serious terrorist threat modern civilization has ever encountered.* Taylor had become more and more frustrated, throwing himself headlong into the investigation, forgoing sleep, exercise and even meals in order to find answers. He was no stranger to stressful situations, but never before had he felt so ineffective—never had he worked so hard with so little to show for it. Despite their best efforts, his team was quickly running out of new information and possible leads, and Taylor was at a loss as to where to go next.

The truth was that a remarkably high percentage of terrorist acts, estimated by some at over 50%, never got solved. In the case of suicide bombings, the perpetrator is executed along with his or her victims, and there's no one to apprehend; the organization held responsible is frequently the one who merely claims responsibility—while evidence supporting such a conclusion is often in short supply.

The other 50% are often solved as a result of stupid mistakes on the part of the terrorists. When the World Trade Center was first struck in 1993, the bomber had rented a truck to carry the device, and was apprehended shortly after attempting to get his $400 rental deposit back. In 1995, following the Oklahoma City bombing of the Alfred P. Murrah Federal Building, Timothy McVeigh got pulled over for driving a car that had no license plates. The bomber who left a car loaded with explosives in Times Square in 2010 thought he could elude investigators by filing the vehicle identification number off of the car's dashboard—oblivious to the fact that most modern vehicles carry the VIN in multiple locations. In addition to revealing themselves to multiple surveillance cameras, the Boston marathon bombers were ultimately located when the driver of the vehicle they'd carjacked reported to police that he'd left his phone in the car; police tracked it and zeroed in.

Unfortunately, whoever was behind these recent events were—so far—making no such mistakes. But pointing that out would be all but useless in the face of the media onslaught. The brief feeling of accomplishment Taylor had felt after the successful deactivation and retrieval of the nuclear device in Shanghai had vanished virtually overnight. Now back in DC, he felt downright despondent.

And to make matters worse, he felt very much alone. Ever since Rachel, there had been no one else. What was left of his family offered little solace. His father had died years ago, and his mother was in a nursing home in Seattle, not far from where his sister lived with her second husband and their two kids. They spoke now and again, but rarely saw one another except for the occasional holiday. They had not really been close since they were kids; Taylor was not entirely sure why, but he had his suspicions. Growing up, he'd always tried to protect her, taking the brunt of their father's tyrannical attacks, and allowing his sister to escape. But once he'd left for college, he had never really come back. It didn't occur to him until too late that his absence meant that his sister had been forced to bear the full burden of their father's psychological torture for years.

Of course, while in the military, the camaraderie Taylor felt with his fellow soldiers had given him strength—a level of emotional and spiritual support that most humans couldn't comprehend. Simply put, they had been his brothers. They offered him the unwavering acceptance that he craved, and the immutable friendships he'd never had. But since leaving the military and entering the rough and tumble world of Washington, he felt cut off and a world apart from his comrades in arms, and now found himself more alone than ever: no family, no lover, no close-knit band of brothers.

As a Ranger, in return for giving his regiment his very best, he had received tremendous nourishment from the team's collective efforts and many successes. The feeling he missed most was being one piece of an expertly-trained, highly collaborative whole; the feeling that, in the heat of the toughest situations, he was one gear among many, working in concert to drive a powerful engine that could prevail in extraordinarily difficult conditions. And when they failed, they failed together, and could lean on each other for support.

As an undersecretary, he had a solid team, but there was no such collaborative support among his peers. Without his fellow soldiers, and without Rachel, Taylor often felt like he was a very small boat aimlessly adrift on a very lonely ocean.

24

Typhoon Duty Officer James Ling looked closely at the radar data, the satellite image, and individual sensor data. It was time.

He drafted the warning, including links to all publicly available source data, and emailed it to his supervisor at the Joint Typhoon Warning Center for approval prior to release.

The tropical depression was not especially ominous, but met established thresholds, and was within their jurisdiction—an area of responsibility that now included most of the North and South Pacific, as well as the Indian Ocean. This was where typhoons were born, and it was the Center's job to monitor the area, and issue warnings when appropriate. Run by the United States Navy out of Pearl Harbor, Hawaii, the Joint Typhoon Warning Center had been launched in 1959 as a means to protect Department of Defense assets in the region.

Typhoon Duty Officer Ling and the Center's team had observed that sea surface temperatures had remained elevated longer into the season than usual; since storms derive their energy from warm water, they were expecting the emergence of several more tropical depressions before the season ended. This one, now exhibiting sustained winds of 42-44 miles per hour, had just crossed the line and was about to be named a tropical storm.

25

The small Sailfin Dragon sat motionless on the wide central beam of the family's hut.

Myla lazily clicked her tongue several times to get its attention; the lizard twitched slightly, but otherwise remained stationary. *It's just a baby*, Myla thought, as she turned over on her sleeping mat. She curled her hair behind her ear and closed her eyes.

She could hear her mother preparing soup by the outside fire. A minute passed, and she heard the cooking pot touch a wooden bowl; then listened further as her mother climbed the front steps and walked over to where she was resting.

"Myla, some soup for you," her mother said, kneeling by her side and reaching for a pillow with her free hand. "Sit up, if you can."

Myla slowly pushed herself up on one elbow, then leaned back on the pillow.

"Are you hungry, iha?" her mother asked.

"Not really," she replied, yawning.

"Eat just a little." She carefully handed her daughter the bowl.

"I'll try, Nanay."

"Are you feeling any better?" Myla's mother asked, placing her hand on the young girl's forehead. She was still slightly feverish, but definitely not as hot as the previous evening.

"I think so," said Myla, in between sips of soup.

Her mother smiled and gently stroked her hair. She was clearly hungry, another good sign.

The two were alone in the hut. Father and son had left early that morning to work on the rice terraces. The harvest had concluded in July, and they would not begin planting for another two months or so, but the steady rains had eroded the terraces, and much work remained to get them in shape for the coming season.

Filipinos referred to the rice terraces of Ifugao Province as "the eighth wonder of the world." Some were 2,000 years old, and had been productively farmed throughout modern history.

Now, however, many believed that their future was in doubt. Some blamed deforestation; as trees were cleared to make room for open farming, the nutrients in the forest run-off that fed the terraces decreased. Others blamed the use of commercial, inorganic fertilizer; while helpful in temporarily increasing crop yield, the fertilizer added nothing to soil structure, and could actually burn the roots of plants which were critical to preventing erosion. This contributed to the more frequent mud-slides that, following a good-size rainstorm, could wipe out an entire hillside of terraces in no time flat.

Both of these were direct causes of rice terrace deterioration, but there was another, less visible culprit that played a substantial role as well. Global warming had increased the temperatures of the North Pacific, creating a greater number of more intense typhoons, which in turn flooded the forest and terraces with much more rain than they could absorb. At the same time, dry season was often dryer than ever, leading to droughts that starved the terraces of both nutrients and moisture, and made them less stable when the rains returned.

Myla's parents were much more knowledgeable than most of the villagers with regards to these phenomena, but it wasn't clear how much such knowledge would help them in the years ahead.

Holding the bowl with both hands and her head tilted back, Myla finished the last of her soup. "That was yummy, Nanay," she said, handing the bowl back to her mother. "Could I have a little more?"

Her mother laughed. "Of course, iha. I will get you a little more. Then you must sleep."

"But I'm not tired anymore!" Myla protested.

"How about this," said her mother, as she tapped Myla on the nose. "If you sleep for an hour or two, then when you get up, we will make biko for dessert."

"Can we Nanay?"

"Yes, iha. But you must promise to rest."

"I will; I promise."

Her mother left the hut, and returned a minute later with more soup for her daughter—only to see that she'd fallen fast asleep.

26

Taylor didn't get it, and neither did anyone else in the intelligence community.

Three major incidents, any one of which could have been catastrophic, but each defused by advanced notice from the terrorists.

In fact, every intelligence agency in Russia, China, and in every allied country of the U.S. had essentially no qualified theories as to who was behind this, what their motives might be, or—most important, what they were planning for their next act.

As far as Taylor was concerned, the lack of theories from other countries was irrelevant anyway; the gum had been placed on his shoe, and he was the one carrying the burden of responsibility for figuring it out.

He knocked firmly, turned the knob and stuck his head into Tori's office. "You ready to go?" he asked.

Just finishing up a conversation with a member of her team, she looked up and gave a small smile. "I am. Just give me one sec." She searched the desk for her phone, found it, and put it in her bag as she slung it over her shoulder. "Kim, have you met Mr. Taylor?"

"I have not. Very nice to meet you, sir," the young woman said, rising from her chair.

"Likewise," replied Taylor, shaking her small hand. While he had no doubt she was smart and competent, she looked like she might be a sophomore in college. "What are you focused on, Kim?" he asked, a question he often used as a more polite form of *what do you do around here?*

"Oh, well…" Kim paused, blushing, clearly not expecting the Undersecretary to make conversation. "I'm currently cross-referencing the components observed on the Shanghai device against our full database of terrorist incidents."

"Anything so far?"

"No, sir. We still don't have the full report from Guam." She swallowed audibly.

"You're using just our database? Any others?"

Kim looked at Tori, then back at Taylor. "Um, we've initiated requests to query the records of a number of different allies, but they're all still pending."

"Well, good luck with it—we certainly could use a break here." Taylor smiled in a half-hearted attempt to reduce the woman's nervousness. It didn't work.

"Yes, sir." She turned and fumbled for her pad and papers on Tori's desk, her face bright red, then nodded to them both in farewell as she left the office in a hurry.

"Aren't there labor laws about hiring children?" Taylor joked once the woman was out of earshot.

"Oh stop," Tori replied, elbowing him lightly in rebuke. "Kim was the top student in her college class, and spent six months after graduation interning at Langley. I was lucky to get her."

"I'm just giving you a hard time," Taylor replied. He gestured for Tori to head out ahead of him, and he closed her office door as they started down the hall. A moment later they were outside on the walkway to the Science and Technology Directorate.

"She was a bit nervous meeting you though, wasn't she?" Tori said with a smile.

"Just a bit. Must be my striking demeanor."

"Well, you jest, Mr. Taylor, but you can be downright intimidating. Your authoritative voice, those eyes of yours—you have to know the effect you have on people, especially women."

"I certainly do," he replied, keeping his face perfectly straight. "I practice in front of the mirror every morning."

Tori laughed loudly, her eyes shining, and shook her head. He snuck a glance at her, pleased.

Taylor turned to business: "Tori, where are we on the Houston video analysis? Any progress?"

Tori frowned, shaking her head. "Oh, I wish there was, Drake. We've cleaned it up as best we can, but all it tells us is that three or more people entered the Heaven on Earth wearing khaki-colored clothing, and then departed seven hours and 22 minutes later. One was blonde and two had dark hair."

"That bad?"

"That bad. It's incredibly frustrating."

"And what about the footage from Novosibirsk?" asked Taylor.

"Virtually nothing. The one working camera on one of the two buildings may indicate that the perpetrators left the scene in a beige Lada minivan, and we have a partial view of one of the men's' boots."

"Why isn't that helpful?"

"Because there are a zillion Lada minivans in Russia, and we've really got no distinct characteristics; no numbers, no letters, no dents. The boot may—I repeat may—help us understand nationality. If we can properly enhance it, we may be able to figure out the make and country of manufacture."

Taylor thought this over for a moment, as they kept a brisk pace across the campus. "Do you think the Russians are giving us everything they've got?"

"Good question. Hard to say, but I think so. My counterpart has been pretty forthcoming; he seems to want to collaborate on this."

They walked on in silence. In response to a persistent buzzing in her bag, Tori pulled out her phone and looked at a text. She sighed, tapped out a quick response, and put it back.

"Anything important?" he asked.

"Nope," she replied. Then, after a pause, "just cancelling my evening plans—again."

Taylor let it go. He knew full well that he asked too much of Tori and her team, but there was simply no way not to. The circumstances simply didn't offer anyone much of a life outside of the investigation. Plus, he liked having her around. Grabbing sandwiches or a salad together as they worked into the night had become one of the highlights of his day.

Tori changed the subject back to the business at hand. "Drake, I'm not sure I'm suppose to be in the loop on this, but have there been any findings from the lab in Guam?"

"I want you squarely in the loop, Tori—and I'm actually glad you asked. I just saw an email from the analyst-in-charge, and meant to forward it before leaving the office. The short answer is nothing yet; he said that disassembling the nuclear device is a delicate operation, and will take some time. It may be several days before they really start to analyze parts and techniques."

"Hurry up and wait."

"Yup. That about sums it up," Taylor said flatly.

Nonetheless, he refused to get deflated. In fact, his spirits were a bit higher than they'd been in several days. He'd received a call from Olaf Henriksen an hour earlier noting that there was some new information worth discussing with regards to the explosives used in Houston and Novosibirsk. When he'd pushed for more detail, Olaf indicated that they'd identified the specific explosive employed, but that he'd rather present the findings in person. Taylor always felt that the "classified information" card was played a little too often in Washington, but since he didn't think Olaf was the type to engage in melodrama—and his lab was just a short walk away, he said he'd be there in an hour and decided it made sense to bring Tori with him.

* * *

"You're saying this is of Chinese origin?" Taylor asked

"We think so, yes. But it's not quite so cut and dry," Olaf explained. "We believe that the formulation used in both incidents is identical to an explosive used by China's People's Liberation Army."

"And why do we believe that?" Tori interjected.

"Well, from what I understand, U.S. human intelligence assets retrieved un-detonated samples of the explosive while on a mission in Guangdong Province."

"What can you tell us about that mission?" asked Taylor.

"Absolutely nothing," was Olaf's reply.

"Okay. Can you tell us who led the mission?" Taylor persisted.

"I'm afraid not."

Taylor, Tori and Olaf Henriksen were in a conference room down the hall from the forensics lab that Taylor had visited a week earlier. On the table in front of them were three graphs from the mass spectrometer showing the signatures from the bombs in Houston and Novosibirsk, and the signature from the samples that Olaf had referenced. They were all identical.

This was a secure room, swept regularly to ensure that any discussion within would be completely private. However, so far, Taylor didn't feel he'd heard a single thing that couldn't have been said on the phone when Olaf first called.

"Then who recovered the samples and sent them to your lab?" Taylor asked, a slight edge in his voice.

"I'm sorry, Mr. Taylor, I can't tell you that either."

"Okay," Taylor took a deep breath. "Just to clarify: you are telling me that you do not know the answer to these questions, not that you know and can't divulge the information, correct?"

"Correct. I have no idea as to who, specifically, recovered the samples. I'm sorry if I'm making this difficult."

Olaf seemed uncomfortable, and Taylor wondered whether he'd somehow walked into an Abbott and Costello routine.

"Then how do you know the samples were actually used by the Chinese Army?"

Olaf was silent for several seconds, then spoke: "I had heard from a colleague that an explosive recently brought back from a mission in China was very similar to HMX and RDX, the two explosives we discussed when you were last here. I asked my colleague if he could send me a sample for testing against the Houston and Novosibirsk signatures, and he agreed."

"And your colleague works where?" Taylor asked.

Olaf again hesitated before responding: "His lab is in a facility across the Potomac in Arlington."

Taylor began to understand what he was hearing, why Olaf was being so tight-lipped, and why, if even if the man revealed everything he knew, it wouldn't amount to much.

Among those in the Special Operations Forces community, it was common knowledge that certain units were now directly conducting their own intelligence gathering and analysis, often doing so without any real oversight from anyone. When you were in the field, this was incredibly convenient and efficient; you could use internal resources to get critical information for a mission, and no longer had to wait for another agency to step in and assist.

There were now an increasing number of unassuming facilities around the nation's capitol where dedicated staff was discretely housed to receive data from the field, analyze it, and rapidly respond with results—without any bureaucracy, bloated process, or interference whatsoever. An SOF team could thus move from one target to the next with very little delay, allowing them to penetrate an enemy in much less time and with far less resistance. The problem was that all of this intelligence was highly compartmentalized; no one dared share anything with other agencies or groups for fear of reprisal.

"Olaf, if you know, please tell me: what department or agency does your colleague work for? I need to know in order to track down the original source of these explosives."

"I understand, Mr. Taylor, but I honestly do not know."

"Okay, I get it. I want you to know that I truly appreciate your efforts; this is good work, and it took some guts. The samples you've just compared, and the lead that you may have uncovered, could prove quite valuable." Taylor looked straight into the man's eyes with a hardened expression. "But Olaf, without additional data, it's useless. We're running out of time, and I need something more to go on. Look, can you at least give me your colleague's name and contact information, and let him know that Tori or myself need to speak with him? Maybe even encourage him to cooperate?"

"Yes, I can do that," Olaf nodded.

"Thank you" Taylor said, breathing out heavily. There was a long moment where no one spoke. Taylor looked at Olaf expectantly.

"Now?" Olaf finally asked.

"Yes, now would be ideal," Taylor stated patiently, offering a tight smile.

"Just one minute. It's in my office." Olaf left the conference room, closing the door behind him.

Tori turned to Taylor with a small frown. "Drake, what the heck is going on here? Am I the only one who's completely confused?"

"Well, I can understand your reaction. I'm happy to explain in detail later, but the short of it is this: U.S. Special Operations Command is rapidly becoming one of the biggest intelligence-gathering agencies on the planet. Yet it operates by its own rules—one of which is that properly processing evidence for use by anyone else is completely secondary to the mission at hand. What you're seeing is a perfect example."

"But then how are we ever going to—" Tori's question was cut short as both of their phones simultaneously started vibrating noisily. Each took a look.

"Holy shit," muttered Taylor, feeling as if every atom of oxygen had just been knocked out of his lungs. He took a deep breath, then slowly let it out. "We were waiting for the other shoe to drop; there it goes."

They both looked at each other in weighted silence. Squaring his shoulders, Taylor stood up and grabbed his brief case. Tori watched him, biting her lip nervously, then followed suit. He opened the door for her just as Olaf came around the corner, holding a sheet of paper.

"For us?" Taylor asked curtly, using his foot to hold the door as he reached for the paper.

"Yes, I—"

Taylor took the paper, folded it against his chest and slipped it into the pocket of his suit. "Thanks, Olaf. Something's come up. We will get back in touch as things unfold."

Tori slid through the door and strode briskly down the hall, Taylor right behind.

27

Everything on the desk jumped—several mints in a small lead crystal dish spilled out, a few onto the floor.

President Gilman wasn't a slam-the-desk kind of guy, but considering the circumstances, it seemed a modest reaction. He leaned back heavily in his chair, the black leather creaking in protest.

"The world is not going to hell in a hand basket on my watch, Dan," the President growled angrily. When he spoke again, his voice was more controlled, but no less intense. "I need you to get to the bottom of this, and do it very fucking fast."

"Yessir." Secretary Hawthorne thought it best not to engage until his boss allowed at least a portion of the anger out of his system.

The two men were alone in the Oval Office. Although the afternoon sun was streaming in through the floor to ceiling windows behind the President's desk, and trees could be seen swaying gently in the breeze, the terrorists' latest message had placed the White House and the entire city on high alert. Even through the bullet-proof glass, sirens could be heard crisscrossing the city.

"Is Taylor on his way over here?" President Gilman asked.

"Should be walkin' through the door any minute."

"By the way," the President continued, slightly calmer now, "is he the right guy to be running Intelligence and Analysis?"

"I'm not sure what you mean, Mr. President."

"It's been nearly three weeks since we were first told of the bombs in Houston, and we have nothing, not a single goddamn shred of insight as to who these guys are and what they're up to."

Hawthorne remained silent. In fact, it had been a little over two weeks, and Taylor had just texted him that they had a lead on the explosives used in the bombing, but Hawthorne didn't think either worth mentioning.

"What's your take on this guy?" The President persisted.

Hawthorne spoke slowly, knowing Taylor's job might depend on his response. "He's solid, sir. Drake Taylor is what you might call a dragon slayer. Everyone who's worked with the man will tell you that, if you point him in the direction of the lair, he won't come back 'til the dragon's dead and he's got the head to prove it." He looked the President in the eye.

"I assume you're talking about his time with the Rangers."

"Yessir, I am. But also 'bout his time as a DHS analyst. You remember Hassan al-Atwah and the New York City subway bomb? It was largely Drake's doing that enabled us to nab those guys."

"That was a big win," the President offered.

"Yessir, it certainly was. In fact, when Taylor first arrived at DHS, I think he might have been thinkin' it'd be a good place to hide after the death of a woman he was involved with in Afghanistan, but it didn't work out that way. Within six months or so, his supervisor was transferred to a new role, leavin' him with responsibility for the subway bomb investigation. Drake nailed it—rose to the challenge, uncovered the plot and identified the perpetrators."

The President was listening, so Hawthorne continued. "O' course, the public never heard a word about it, but Taylor's success drew massive praise within the agency. It was a few months after that when I asked Taylor to head up Intelligence & Analysis."

"Well, that's all fine and good Dan—and the guy may well be a dragon slayer," the President said, shifting in his chair, "but the problem is we don't even know where the dragon's lair is yet. Is he capable of finding it?"

"I believe he is, Mr. President."

"I'm not sure. Maybe he's risen to his level of incompetence. Is it possible that this job's too big for him? Hell, it took a week—one week—to wrap up the Boston marathon bombings in a bow."

Hawthorne weighed his words carefully. "With all due respect, sir, while they did a fantastic job in Boston, that was essentially two kids with hundred dollar pressure-cooker bombs. What we're up against here are extremely well-trained experts who not only brought down five large buildings with surgical precision, they appear to have built a fairly sophisticated nuclear device."

The President leaned back, rubbing his eyes, and sighed loudly. "Make that four nuclear devices."

The terrorists, now calling themselves the "Guardians of Civilization," had just thirty minutes earlier sent messages to key officials and numerous news outlets—and put up an official, single-page website—notifying the world that nuclear devices twice the size of the one in Shanghai had been planted in three unnamed cities around the globe. They made it clear that the "GOC" will not hesitate to detonate these devices in thirty days unless their demands—to be communicated within twenty-four hours—are met.

The President's phone beeped; he hit a button to open a line with his secretary. "Yes, Andy."

"Mr. President, Drake Taylor is here."

"Thanks. Show him in."

A moment later, the door opened and Taylor entered. "Good afternoon, Mr. President, Mr. Secretary."

"Not really," the President rejoined sourly. "Have a seat, Drake."

Taylor sent a sharp look towards Hawthorne before taking the other chair in front of the President's desk.

The President looked Taylor squarely in the eye. "So what do we know, Drake?"

An obvious question, but certainly not one for which Taylor had an acceptable answer. And both he and the President knew it.

Hawthorne did not quite see the point of this exercise. "Mr. President, at this point, I don't think there's anything you don't already kno—"

The President shut him down: "Thanks, Dan, but the question was addressed to Drake." He continued to look directly at Taylor.

Taylor had opened his folder when the question was first asked, but he realized there was nothing in there that was going to help him. He closed the folder and stared straight back at President Gilman. "Mr. President, we know that the terrorists behind London, Houston, Novosibirsk, Shanghai and now this latest threat are some of the most sophisticated actors we've ever encountered. From their development of a nuclear bomb, to their cutting-edge use of conventional explosives, to their inventive manipulation of video surveillance cameras, these guys are in a different category from the majority of folks we've encountered over the past decade."

President Gilman took this in as he sized up the man in front of him. "Fair enough, but I was under the impression, Mr. Taylor, that the methods we employ on our side are also well ahead of where we were a decade ago—or even five years ago."

"I believe that's correct, sir. And using those methods, we will identify and apprehend the individuals responsible."

"How confident are you of that statement, Drake?" The President asked abruptly. There was a brief, heavy silence. In the absence of a response, he pushed the point: "By this time tomorrow, we will have their demands in hand, and you know what? Whatever the hell they are, the odds are awfully high that the world is not going to comply. So," the President said slowly, "just how confident are you that we can crack this thing before these lunatics detonate nuclear bombs in three different cities around the globe—at least one of which, it could be assumed, will be somewhere within the United States?"

That was certainly the 64,000 dollar question, and frankly, Taylor was nowhere near as confident as he wanted to be. Not being one for false bravado, he simply offered an honest assessment. "Mr. President, I am confident that my team is smart, hardworking, and innovative in how we are pursuing this case. I firmly believe that, like most terrorists, they will make a mistake at some point, and open a hole for us to crawl through." He leaned forward, his voice deepening. "When that happens, I am confident that we will be prepared to exploit it and build on it until such time as they are identified and caught. But to answer your question directly, I can not tell you when that will be."

Again, silence. Eventually, the President leaned back in his chair, put his hands behind this head, and stared up at the ceiling. "Drake, many are suggesting that I find a different quarterback for this effort." He brought his eyes down and leveled them at Taylor. "I don't think I need to tell you that our lack of progress here has generated a lot of pressure—on me, on the Secretary, on the U.S. intelligence community as a whole, and, of course, on you. But Dan believes you're the right guy to take point, and—for the time being—I'm going to defer to his judgment." President Gilman then rocked forward and leaned on his elbows. "But let me be clear, gentlemen: when pressure builds, it eventually needs an outlet." He was now directing his words at both men. "If we don't start to get traction—very soon, I will have little choice to make significant changes in how we're managing this investigation. Do you both understand what I'm saying?"

The two men facing the President replied in near-unison. "Yes, Mr. President."

28

E ven after a major global event, it takes some time for the clamor of voices to spin itself up into a frenzy.

Not so when the "Guardians of Civilization" released their demands. The world was waiting, and the multi-billion-piece orchestra that is the internet reached a crescendo in about seven minutes flat.

It's possible that it might have spun up even faster had the GOC not put most onlookers into at least a temporary state of shock with the paradoxical nature of their quid pro quo.

Though the full message was bit more verbose, the terrorists' demands were essentially this:

Unless the developed world immediately places an appropriate price on carbon, thus promoting a migration away from unsustainable practices that threaten the viability of future generations, then the devices will be detonated in 30 days. In short, unless the world acts to save itself, then the GOC will accelerate its destruction.

A call for all nations to address climate change was hardly what everyone expected. In fact, among the confused jumble of what many so-called experts had been predicting, a "price on carbon" had never made it onto anyone's list.

Included in the GOC's communication was a five-page treaty that it expected leaders from the 20 largest developed nations—the G20—to sign by the deadline. The document laid out a timeline for action, and specified economic penalties, to be enforced by all participating nations, should any one country fail to uphold their commitment.

29

Taylor was blindsided—but so was the entire intelligence community, not only within the United States, but also within every other nation with whom Taylor's team had been communicating.

Bottom line: Not a single agency or agent had suspected an environmental motive.

Traditionally, "ecoterrorists" had operated on a fairly small-scale, with most incidents perpetrated by a handful of individuals with very limited resources. Blowing up cars; burning down a ski lodge; spiking trees in old-growth forests; blocking whaling ships. These were all very focused actions involving a very specific cause or a very specific target. While DHS took ecoterrorism seriously, the truth was that many events attributed to this form of terrorism amounted to little more than petty crime or even civil disobedience. Most organizations were "organized" in name only; they were usually nothing more than a modest number of cells operating independently—with no specific leader, and no members. Never in modern history had there been a terrorist threat that sought to strike such a grand blow on behalf of a global environmental cause.

Immediately after the demands had been released, Taylor conferred with Secretary Hawthorne, suggesting to his boss that, in light of recent developments, they had to rethink the profile of who they were after. Instead of classic terrorist networks in the Middle East, Asia and Africa, the team needed to think quite differently about suspects. Hawthorne agreed, and made it clear that, for both their sakes, there was no time to lose. A very real countdown, with cataclysmic consequences, had officially begun.

Taylor was also well aware that he needed new personnel. To his knowledge, there was no one in his inner circle with deep knowledge of the murky, leaderless world of ecoterrorism. As it so happened, upon returning to his office, there were two emails in his stack which offered possible assistance in this regard.

The first was a note from Nathan Verit—the impressive young analyst from Houston—explaining that he had done his doctoral thesis on climate change and its impact on national security, and asking if he could be valuable given the focus of the GOC's demands.

As Taylor read the email, he smiled broadly. There were established channels and protocols for reaching out to someone several levels up within a government organization, and Verit had ignored them completely. This, of course, only made Taylor like him all the more. He fired off a reply, copying his assistant Sherry, telling Verit to get on his calendar as soon as possible to discuss.

The other email was from Tori, noting that—interestingly enough—a friend of a close friend had actually spent eight or nine years as an operative with Earth First! before switching sides and proving herself invaluable to the Counter-Terrorism and Special Operations Bureau of the Los Angeles Police Department. She asked Taylor if he had any objection if she reached out to pick the woman's brain.

Taylor replied emphatically that, at this point they could use all the insight they could get. He suggested flying her to

Washington and having an afternoon session to explore what she knows and how she might be able to help.

Once he'd battled the stack of new email down to a few remaining non-critical messages, he was about to log off and head to a meeting at the office of the Deputy Director of National Intelligence, when a new message popped up from Elon Dorsk, the contact Olaf Henriksen had given him two days prior. Taylor opened the message, and pursed his lips. Whoever this guy was, he told Taylor very succinctly that he could not offer any additional information on the sample's source without revealing the identities of Special Operations Forces operatives, which he was not authorized to do.

"Goddamnit!" Taylor said under his breath. Here he was, under ridiculous pressure from the President of the United States to make some progress in this investigation, and he was being stymied by lab technicians who somehow believed their security clearance superseded his own.

He hit reply, and started banging out a terse response informing this clown of the authority under which he was making the request, and then stopped and reconsidered. He knew very well from his SOF days that threats don't get you very far—unless you're prepared to use force in backing them up.

Instead, he sent a quick note to DHS legal counsel asking for clarification on the lab's ability to share the desired information, marking it urgent. He knew counsel understood how to move quickly—and once he'd confirmed legality he'd pay this guy a visit in person.

He logged off and stood up, stretching. He winced as his body complained about too much sitting, not enough doing. Since the start of this whole incident, he'd been neglecting his exercise regime, and it was adding to his tension. He'd kill for a long run or an hour in the gym to sweat out some of his frustration. Well aware that neither was in the cards, he grabbed his briefcase and headed out.

30

I *sabel.*
Drawn in alphabetical order from a list prepared in advance of each cyclone season, the name seemed too delicate for a severe tropical storm that now had sustained winds of 58 mph and was growing more powerful by the day.

Typhoon Duty Officer Ling huddled with his team members at the Joint Typhoon Warning Center, as they compared notes and looked at data that suggested how big the storm might become, and the path it might take across the Western Pacific.

There was a very specific process in place for releasing information, mandating four sets of eyes on every forecast or warning. Once the Duty Officer presents findings, the Best Track Officer reviews all data and confirms or adjusts the predicted storm track. Thereafter, the Operations Officer reviews the package and submits approval; finally, the Technical Advisor does the same.

There were still quite a few unknowns, and everyone present knew that a storm could start to dissipate just when they thought otherwise, but at this point the data looked a little ominous.

This could be a big one, Ling mused.

After resolving some differing opinions by more or less averaging the best estimates of the experts in the room, they moved through their process and agreed to release a warning that severe tropical storm Isabel would likely become the 18th typhoon of the season, with a 60% chance of making landfall in the Philippines within seven to ten days.

31

The media circus in response to the planted nuclear devices and the terrorists' demands was in full gear, but it was clear that, at the same time, it had only just begun. Reactions to the unfolding crisis were strong and varied, falling mostly into three basic groups.

Most people felt that we should all but ignore the demands, believing that terrorism—defined as harming or threatening innocent civilians—was the highest of crimes, regardless of motive or circumstance. The Guardians of Civilization, or "GOC" as they'd come to be called, should be apprehended and brought to justice swiftly, preferably in a military court with the death penalty as punishment.

Some within this majority felt obliged to go further, pointing out that the terrorists clearly display their ignorance in proposing such a basic solution to a very complex problem. In short, a tax on fossil fuels is simply unworkable. Industries and entire economies are at stake; their demise would wreak havoc on people across the globe, causing massive disruption and hardship. In short, the terrorists, along with so many other "enviros," just didn't get it; the risk of a carbon tax was excessive—especially when some still held that global warming was just a theory.

Another camp was more circumspect: Yes, the terrorists must be caught and punished, and no, we shouldn't even begin to consider compliance with their demands—or any other form of appeasement. But completely ignoring their motive was not entirely logical, they argued; this is a problem that must be addressed, and a price on carbon may be the best approach. But many also pointed out that the terrorists had likely set back the cause of global warming considerably, since now any action on the issue would appear to be caving in to the terrorists' demands. They argued that, once the perpetrators are in custody, the issue they highlighted is one to which we must give further consideration.

The last camp did not aggressively express their views. In fact, many of them were quite possibly ashamed to acknowledge what they were thinking: Incredibly frustrated for years by the world's inability to deal with the issue, these were people who were ambivalent regarding the terrorists' demands. Of course they didn't want nuclear devices detonated in major cities—and of course they believed that leveling such a threat deserved harsh punishment. But at the same time, it crossed many minds that perhaps such gruesome threats were the only way to get the world to acknowledge the severity of what was to come if carbon emissions were left unchecked. Namely, the rapid deterioration of what we consider to be normal life on Planet Earth. Silently, they perversely lauded not the terrorists' methods, but the fact that the world was finally getting the wake-up call it deserved.

Frankly, Taylor had not spent a hell of a lot time giving the issue much thought. During his years in the military, he'd been forced to confront a wide array of very serious threats that most people would never see or even hear about. Quite simply, climate change had never made it onto his radar screen. At present, all that mattered to him was the nuclear threat. He'd been in situations with mass casualties, and it was the most wretched form of man-made hell. So far as he was concerned, avoiding that outcome should be his only focus.

As such—if he had to choose, Taylor was in the first camp: The terrorists' eco-centric demands were irrelevant; they needed to be caught, tried, and—if found guilty—executed for their crimes. Period.

Of course, that didn't mean that he could ignore their motivations. In fact, one daunting element of this new turn of events was that he had very little time in which to climb a steep learning curve—starting pretty much at the bottom.

If he didn't understand their thinking, he'd have a much harder time unraveling their methods and plans.

32

Taylor looked at his watch, wondering how long this would take, and whether he should play tough guy or nice guy. He knew full well that, despite the stakes involved, playing Army Ranger hard-ass was not an option—and as a civilian, he could only go so far.

"Mr. Dorsk," Taylor said patiently, choosing nice for the time being. "I fully understand your desire to keep the identities of those you work with confidential. In fact, I thank you for your vigilance. I was with the 75th Ranger Regiment for eleven years, and truly appreciate your efforts to keep our operators safe."

As planned, Taylor had personally made the trip across the Potomac to the non-descript facility where Elon Dorsk worked. In advance, he'd confirmed with counsel that disclosure of the identities of any SOF operators to the Undersecretary of Intelligence and Analysis was well within acceptable legal parameters. He'd given Dorsk a heads up that he would be arriving promptly at 9 AM, and brought along two military police officers as a contingency, but asked them to wait in the car.

When they'd arrived, Taylor was sure he'd made a mistake on the address. He entered what looked like a run-of-the-mill office building, with a pleasant receptionist and a basic sign-in log. But once Taylor requested an audience with Dorsk, the receptionist's tone changed, and from there on in it became clear that this was a very high-security facility. As he was being escorted to Dorsk's lab, he wondered how many buildings like this existed throughout Washington—let alone throughout the world. He found it interesting that, when he was in the field waiting for intelligence to be processed, he couldn't have cared less whether the lab had proper oversight. Now that he was part of the bureaucracy, he felt otherwise; the place seemed very much "off the books," and somehow inconsistent with his now evolving vision of how a well-organized, well-managed military-intelligence organization should behave.

Dorsk was a short, beefy little man in his mid 50s with sloping shoulders and wispy, curly brown hair. He wore a stained lab coat, under which he had on a rumpled blue button-down shirt and a poorly-tied bowtie.

Taylor, wearing a crisp navy blue suit with a crimson tie, swallowed his derision and continued calmly. "While your discretion is admirable, I've got to tell you that, first, revealing the name to me is perfectly legal and proper; and second, as I'm sure you're well aware, my investigation into these matters is of critical national importance and backed by the explicit authority of the President. Now, one more time, who gave you the samples that you passed on to Olaf Henriksen?"

Dorsk seemed to carefully consider Taylor's question, then responded yet again with something other than a straight answer. "Mr. Taylor, sending the samples to Olaf was a breach of procedure to begin with. I really don't think—"

"Breach of procedure?" Taylor barked back, losing his temper. "This whole goddamn facility is likely a breach of procedure! Don't tempt me to spend precious time I don't have figuring out how to shake this place until I get the answers I'm after. Because if I have to, I will." He glared down at the small man, his green eyes ablaze.

Dorsk swallowed and looked down at his feet in sullen silence. Taylor again looked at his watch. What should have been a five minute discussion was now going on fifteen; he wondered whether he should just ask the MPs to come in, put Dorsk in cuffs, and they could all go back to DHS headquarters together.

"Okay. I'll tell you what," Dorsk said with a pinched mouth, looking up at Taylor. "Let me make a few phone calls, and I should be able to get you the information you're after sometime this afternoon."

"No, Elon." Taylor's voice was calm, but hard. He was done with this bullshit. "I am fully prepared to take you into custody, if necessary. I have the authority to do so, and I have MPs waiting outside. You can give me the name I'm after, or you can come back to Washington and we can draw this out." He watched Dorsk carefully, waiting for his response.

In his defense, Dorsk seemed truly conflicted. He closed his eyes as if to give the decision further deliberation. When he opened them, he had made up his mind: "Alright, alright," he said finally, "Colonel Levon Plummer, AFSOC."

"Based at Hurlburt Field in Florida?"

"Yes, sir." Dorsk grumbled.

That's more like it, thought Taylor. "Is Plummer the only individual you know to be connected with those explosives?"

"Yes. I received them directly from him."

"Were there any fingerprints on the explosives—or any markings that could be helpful in identifying their source?"

"There was one partial print, but it was useless. We ran it and got over 20,000 possible matches. As for markings, both blocks were in plain, white casing."

"Can you send me a report supporting those findings?"

Dorsk straightened, clearly ready to be done with the whole ordeal. "Yes. I can do that. I'll get it done this afternoon."

"Okay. Thank you." Taylor realized this was the best he was going to get. *Was that so hard?* He thought sourly. Still, he reached out and shook hands with the man, glad to be done with the task. "If I have any further questions, I will be back in touch." He started to leave, but Dorsk stopped him.

"Mr. Taylor, I guess I am fully prepared to suffer the punishment for leaking this information to Olaf. I just want to know—"

Taylor cut him off for the third time, fed up with the whole situation: "Elon, you are not going to be punished or reprimanded. We are investigating a global threat here, and you just aided the investigation."

Taylor didn't wait for an escort to show him out.

33

"It's what's called a 'Pigovian tax,'" Ellie Alder said plainly.

"I'm sorry; say that again?" Taylor requested.

"A Pigovian tax," Verit eagerly interjected. "It's named after a guy named Arthur Pigou, an English economist who, in the early 20th century, put forth the idea that certain products carry social costs. Since these are not included in the cost of production but are still incurred by the public—he called them 'externalities.'"

"Externalities; I'm not sure I get it," said Taylor.

Ellie thought for a moment. "Okay, one of Pigou's original arguments concerned the sale of alcohol. Let's assume that a number of new bars open in a town where previously there were none. Pigou would reason that the bars will inevitably lead to some people behaving badly, and as a result, the bars will create a need for additional policemen and prisons. The costs of maintaining the peace—as well as the impact on the area's quality of life—are considered externalities, and a tax on alcoholic beverages helps to offset those costs."

"So externalities are sort of like 'collateral damage,' yes?" Taylor asked.

"Yes," Ellie considered, "not a bad analogy. The notion is that, since the bar has very little incentive or responsibility for dealing with the externalities of alcohol, the Pigovian tax makes sure it's not underpriced. When a tax is applied, the product becomes more expensive. In turn, consumer demand is reduced, as is the 'collateral damage' that consumption of the product can cause. And the monies collected can be used to address the remaining social costs."

Taylor, Nate Verit, Tori Browne and Ellie Alder were huddled in a small conference room near Taylor's office. He had "borrowed" Verit from his current job in the Office of Enterprise and Mission Support, while Ellie was the ex-ecoterrorist that Tori had brought in from the LAPD for a day or two to help them better understand the terrorists' viewpoint.

The conference room was classic DHS: None of the chairs matched, and many were broken; the whiteboard had been written on so much that it could no longer be fully erased; the table was too big, meaning that anyone entering or leaving could barely get around other attendees; and while it was usually fairly warm and stuffy, today it felt like it was about 60 degrees.

"Okay, that makes sense," said Taylor, "so you're saying that the price on carbon that the GOC is demanding is essentially to reduce demand for fossil fuels and pay for the damage done by carbon emissions to the atmosphere."

"Yes, exactly," Ellie said, speaking through a pencil she'd placed between clenched teeth as she wound her thick black hair into a knot behind her head. Holding her hair with one hand, she grabbed the pencil with the other and jabbed it through the knot to hold the hair in place.

"But it's not just the atmosphere and global warming," Verit offered, pulling his eyes from Ellie's hair. He flipped his pen around his thumb subconsciously, and glanced back at Ellie before continuing. "There are lots of different costs associated with fossil fuels—including the health impacts of air pollution from cars and power plants, the environmental damage caused by their extraction and production, and the costs incurred by our country and military to ensure that we have secure access to supplies around the world."

"The subject of your thesis," Taylor confirmed.

Verit leaned forward eagerly, looking hopeful. "You should read it, Mr. Taylor; I'd be happy to send you a copy."

Taylor couldn't help but smile at Verit's earnest expression. "Someday I may take you up on that, Nate. But right now, I only want to know what I need to know to catch these bastards."

"By the way," said Ellie, who had turned her attention to the briefing packet that Tori had given each of them, "the terrorists' email address is obvious; 2dc means two degrees Celsius."

"I don't understand," said Tori, sounding a little put out. "How do you know that?"

"Well, I'd be shocked if it stood for anything else," Ellie replied with a small shrug. "There's fairly strong scientific consensus that two degrees C is the upward limit of warming before we start to find ourselves living on an entirely different planet. There are some who argue it's even less than that, but two degrees C has become a proverbial line in the sand."

"Okay," said Taylor, "assuming you're right, does that help us in any way?"

"You mean with regards to finding these guys?" Ellie asked.

"Yeah."

"Not really. But it's directly related to our discussion. A carbon tax is typically designed to ratchet up over time, so that the demand for fossil fuels—and corresponding emissions—accelerates downward to a point where we are no longer witnessing an increase in average global temperatures. The goal is to do this in such a way as to limit warming to two degrees Celsius, or 3.6 degrees Fahrenheit."

"And if we don't?" Tori asked.

"If we cross that line, things could get real ugly real fast," Ellie answered.

Verit couldn't resist jumping in. "Scientists generally agree that we'd start to see a breakdown in the Earth's climatic systems, with—"

"Time out, folks," Taylor said, stopping Verit mid-sentence. "I appreciate your expertise on these topics, I really do. But we need to focus. I'd like us to spend some time on the actual treaty these guys provided, okay?"

No one responded, so Taylor continued in a patient voice. "If we look at the five-page treaty independently of the GOC's threat of nuclear destruction, do we think it's a reasonable document?"

Taylor waited for someone to speak, looking at each in turn. Tori shrugged and gave a look that said *I'm certainly not the right person to ask.*

Finally, Ellie said "Yes, it strikes me as a very clear, concise framework for the implementation of a carbon tax."

"Okay, why the hesitation."

"Because, Drake, I—" she stopped, and cracked a slight smile. "Am I allowed to call you that?"

Taylor laughed. "Yes, you are. Now go on."

"I want to get one thing on the table. I'm in law enforcement, and very much want to help you apprehend these guys— and make damn sure they don't hurt anyone," she said, lifting her chin and meeting his eyes straight on. "That said, I am a huge fucking advocate for exactly what they're proposing."

Taylor was a bit taken aback, but also realized he was starting to like this young woman. "Understood. I can't hold that against you. So say more."

"Well, the treaty is fairly open-ended. It allows each nation within the G20 a fair amount of latitude in their approach to implementation, including how best to manage the use of funds."

"You mean the monies raised through the tax," Taylor asked, leaning back in his chair.

"Yes."

Verit jumped in. "One of the big issues with a carbon tax is what to do with the proceeds. There's the notion of 'tax and rebate,' which typically means the consumer pays more for any carbon-based product, but gets the money back. That way, it's 'revenue-neutral,' and won't hurt lower-income consumers."

"But if you get it back," Taylor asked, "then what's the point?"

"Ahh, good question," Ellie responded. "This is where the whole thing gets interesting. Let's say that, with a tax in place, I'm now paying six bucks a gallon at the pump, but I will get half of that back through a tax rebate or some other mechanism. The theory is that, even though I'm not actually spending more money, my behavior is going to change significantly. I will still find it painful to fill up my car, and will likely start buying higher mileage vehicles, and maybe even drive less. When I get the rebate, I'll find something else to do with it."

Tori stepped in to the conversation with a question: "But if we're all still driving, albeit a little less, how does that really solve the problem?"

"Another good question; and the answer is simple. If gasoline costs more, then the alternatives become much more competitive and attractive; we still need to get from point A to point B, but we will start using hybrid or all-electric cars, or public transportation." She paused, gathering her thoughts. "And a very important point here is this: Without a price on carbon, the average driver may shrug when the price of gas goes up, assuming that, in time, it will likely come back down. However, if carbon is taxed, and that tax is structured to rise over time, then the average driver knows that they have to start thinking differently; behavioral change is forced."

Verit couldn't stand letting Ellie get all the air time. "The beauty of the carbon tax is that—"

Taylor held up a hand to silence him. "Hold on, Nate; this is all extremely helpful, but I'm not asking to be converted, I just need a foundation for—"

"But Mr. Taylor, let me offer just one last thought." Verit was like an over-eager kid in science class pleading with his teacher.

Taylor rubbed his brow, chuckling. "Okay, Nate. Go ahead."

Verit, now a little embarrassed, continued, "As a market-based price signal, a carbon tax fixes what is really a distortion of the market."

This got Taylor's attention. "Explain that to me."

"Well, since the mostly hidden costs of oil, gas and coal are borne by consumers—and the government, it could easily be said that the major energy companies currently enjoy massive subsidy—which distorts the free market. Once these subsidies are eliminated, it will cause a significant free market response, forcing everyone, including big energy companies, to pay much more attention to cleaner, cost-competitive alternatives."

Ellie agreed. "I think Nate is right on the money here. The costs that fossil fuel companies currently transfer to the consumer are staggering. One example is home insurance. There have been more than four times as many weather-related disasters in the last 30 years than there were in the previous 75, and—as a result—insurance companies are starting to limit their coverage, raise premiums and increase deductibles. Most of these added costs are incurred as a direct result of burning fossil fuels—yet the energy industry walks away scot-free, sticking everyone else with the bill."

Taylor was impressed. "Thanks. I think you guys actually managed to get some important points into my small brain."

Tori rolled her eyes, knowing he could keep up with the best of them just fine. "Okay, can we now move on and discuss the terrorists' mindset? As much as you two think their demands could save the planet, I—"

Ellie abruptly interrupted: "Tori, sorry to cut you off, but there's one thing that eats at me constantly with regards to the climate issue, and the world just doesn't fucking get it." Ellie had become quite serious; the others all froze, realizing some internal switch of hers had just been tripped. "This is not about saving the planet; the fate of the earth is not in the balance here. In fact, the earth is going to be just fine; in a million years or so, the planet will shake itself off and barely remember what happened here. What's at stake, literally, is the earth's ability to sustain life as we know it."

No one spoke, and Ellie added one last note for emphasis: "It's our human asses on the line here, not the planet's."

34

J ack took a seat on a park bench nestled within a thick stand of trees between a soccer field and two baseball diamonds.

He put the piece in his ear, plugged it into his phone and placed the secure call. Around him he could hear acorns dropping from the oak trees, as squirrels began the long process of gathering food for winter. Summer was at an end.

The call was answered and the two men chatted briefly about the security of the communication; both parties had no interest whatsoever in being intercepted. Finally, Jack focused on the topic he'd called to discuss.

"I'm assuming that the pressure is building a bit, and I'm wondering where things stand," Jack said.

"You're darn right the pressure's building. I'm getting calls from DHS almost every hour on the hour asking for details."

"And what's your response?" Jack asked.

"That the disassembly of a nuclear device is a dangerous process; that the tests take time; that it's very difficult to match material to a specific source; and, of course, that whoever's behind this is awfully damn good given the lack of trace evidence they're leaving behind." The man on the other end laughed gently.

"Let's hope they're damn good," Jack muttered, more or less to himself. "So what's your thinking, here? Can you stall for at least a few more weeks?"

"Frankly, I wouldn't advise it," The other man stated simply. "I'm starting to believe that our best foot forward would be to get them something—something preliminary, but in writing. Otherwise, we run the risk of making them impatient and pissing them off, which in turn could make their actions unpredictable."

Jack considered this. "Do you think a preliminary report will get them off your back for a while?"

"Well, I'll have to be clever about it, but yes."

Jack looked up through the trees of Virginia Highlands Park. Clouds were moving in, hopefully bringing some rain and cooler temperatures to what had so far been a miserably warm September in DC. He weighed the repercussions of letting DHS become increasingly impatient versus the possibility that they might immediately question some element of an initial report.

Jack believed he was protected on both counts; *after all,* he thought to himself, *this guy doesn't even know my real name.* He quickly decided, however, that the guy was right—simply stalling invited disaster. The worst outcome would be for DHS to stick its head too far into this piece of the investigation. If that happened, things could start to unravel much too quickly.

"Alright," Jack said finally. "Let's play it your way. What's the timeline?"

"I should be able to have something prepared within a day or two," the other man said.

"Good. Do it. I'll call you again in two days at the same time."

Jack ended the call and pocketed the phone. At that moment, a group of high-school boys in running gear jogged past, clearly training for the upcoming track season. Jack watched them go and thought of his own children, who lived in southern California with his ex-wife. His son was just entering the eighth grade.

I'm going to miss them, he thought, a sudden lump in his throat compounding his stress.

35

The U-28A rolled right halfway through its steep ascent out of Dulles and locked into its flight path, this time on its way to Hurlburt Field, home to the Air Force Special Operations Command—or AFSOC. Taylor had decided it was worth the better part of a day to meet Colonel Levon Plummer face to face instead of over the phone. In his efforts to find the original source of the explosives, Taylor didn't want anything coming between him and the airman who supposedly found them—even a phone line. This guy could offer him one-word answers, or possibly give him details and nuance that may well matter when the pieces were all put together. A trip to Hurlburt therefore seemed like the right approach.

Taylor had decided to bring Ellie Alder with him to Florida. He had no intention of having her join his meeting with Plummer; they'd agreed in advance that she would find a quiet place to work, and then would join him for the return flight later that afternoon. His intent was simply to use the flight time to learn more about her experiences with Earth First! It struck Taylor that, based on their meeting the prior afternoon, Ellie's rigidly-held beliefs offered a lesson for him and his team. If the terrorists were similarly-minded, he needed to better understand the lens through which they looked at the world.

"So, pretty fancy way to fly," Ellie teased as the plane started to level off.

"Not really. The 757 I normally fly is in for repairs," Taylor deadpanned.

"Seriously, you get your own 757?" She asked, wide-eyed.

"Just a joke, Ellie," Taylor admitted with a grin. "I normally fly coach. But given the circumstances, and the fact that this plane was headed to Hurlburt Field with us or without us, I thought it might be more convenient—especially if we want to have a private conversation."

In fact, Sherry had made all of the arrangements; when it came to travel, Taylor just followed her instructions. He'd been a bit surprised himself when she'd told him how he was getting to Florida; he usually only enjoyed such privileges when accompanying bigger fish. But he sure as hell wasn't going to turn down a private flight.

Taylor looked over at Ellie and studied her. She had thick, chaotic black hair framing an exotic, somewhat mysterious face. Big dark eyes were shadowed by thick lashes, topped by dark eyebrows. There was an inner strength about her; though fairly petit, she packed a punch. Taylor enjoyed sparring with her intellectually. She had a quick, dry wit, and a sharp mind.

"I'm curious," he said, kicking off the conversation, "you strike me as being pretty dedicated to your beliefs; what led you to leave Earth First!?"

Ellie looked out the window, gathered her thoughts, then leveled her dark brown eyes at Taylor. "Well, I guess it had begun to bother me that I was spending all of my time trying to figure how best to perpetrate silly crimes instead of thinking more deeply about how to really solve the problem."

"But I thought that the 'silly crimes,' as you call them, were the whole point, No? Each one draws more attention to the cause."

"That was the theory," Ellie said with a hint of exasperation, absentmindedly pushing several strands of long, black hair away from her face. "In truth, I think the net effect was to draw applause from a small number of radicals like ourselves, and completely piss off everybody else."

"That seems like a pretty stark assessment."

"I guess it is. Our primary focus was on the destruction of property that represented the excesses and wrongheadedness that we perceived in society. But over time, it struck me that we weren't waking anybody up or changing any minds, we were—if anything—doing the opposite."

Ellie was raised in a small town north of San Francisco by hippie parents who seemed content to simply turn their back on what they perceived as the hypocrisy of civilization. She couldn't turn her back; she felt that "tuning out" as her parents had done was a form of complicity. Like Taylor, she'd been extremely restless during college, and dropped out of USC at the end of her sophomore year. She worked odd jobs, became an environmental and animal rights activist, and eventually joined Earth First! Unfortunately, life as an ecoterrorist did little to resolve her anxieties.

"It was never lost on me that, in contrast to the immense damage that some corporations and certain policies do to the environment, what we did barely moved the needle. But none of that mattered; we were always the bad guys. The problem is that the vast majority of environmental degradation is hidden from the average citizen—or occurs slowly over time so that it's never properly acknowledged. The difference between blowing up a few Hummers and knowingly allowing factory toxins to destroy a nearby river is twofold: One, the destruction of the Hummers is an event whereas toxins leaking into a river is a slow, mostly unseen process; two, the Hummers are someone's property in a way that the river is not. The day after the Hummers are destroyed, cops and insurance companies are out in force—yet it's possible that no one will ever do a damn thing about the river, since no one really owns it."

"I am, of course, speaking hypothetically here, but your example begs the question: Why not blow up the factory that's polluting the river?"

"Well, I didn't mean to imply that blowing up SUVs might have been in response to river pollution. But let me answer your question: Let's instead say that we blew up the guard shack at the factory's entrance. The point—"

"Wait, let me stop you for a sec. It's the factory that's polluting the river, not the guard shack. Why not eliminate the actual cause of the problem."

"Ahh, I see what you're asking, and the reason is very simple. Our intent was always to make a statement that would draw attention to the cause. This is important: We always went out of our way to ensure that no one ever got hurt, and that actual damages were minimized. Within the ecoterrorism world, with a few exceptions, that's pretty much the blueprint. Don't hurt anyone, don't bring about massive financial damage—just destroy enough property to draw attention to the cause. Besides, blowing up a chemical factory would, in all likelihood, create a shitload of environmental pollution; that would have been unthinkable."

Taylor leaned back and considered Ellie's words. "From what I've read over the past couple of days, many so-called ecoterrorists think that humankind has overstepped its bounds, that every living creature should be protected on par with humans. Is that what you believe?"

Ellie tilted her head and studied Taylor. "Oh, I guess so. To an extent. It's definitely what many of my old colleagues believe."

"That just seems crazy to me. Humans are at the top of the food chain, and wild animals kill each other every day as a matter of survival. So, we're supposed to behave differently, and treat all other creatures as sacred?"

"No, Drake. That's not it." Ellie's tone cooled considerably, and she narrowed her eyes. "The point is simply that we should think more about our actions, and give consideration to the notion that a balance may be better for the world's ecosystems, and ourselves, than a world in which humans just take, take, take. In my mind, it's much more about respect than it is about equality."

"But we've declared that humans have a fundamental right to life, liberty and the pursuit of happiness." Taylor pushed her a bit more, "how do you square that with limiting what we can and can't do to better our lives?"

"Wow. We're miles apart, you and I," she replied, shaking her head. "First off, life and liberty can be had without the type of resource consumption that we've seen over the past century. So it all boils down to the pursuit of happiness, and if you somehow believe that we're justified in—"

"Ellie, I know you feel strongly about all this, but please don't treat me like your enemy. I'll be honest here; I've never given this anywhere near as much thought as you. I'm wrapping my mental arms around much of this stuff for the first time."

They looked at one another without speaking; the drone of the Pratt & Whitney turbo-prop engine the only audible sound.

Ellie finally spoke. "Okay, that's fair." She exhaled audibly and turned to look out the window.

Taylor raised his eyebrows in response. "Glad to hear it."

Her gaze still directed at the clouds outside the plane, Ellie spoke again, but this time with less emotion. "You know, Drake, there's a disconnect here, and it's an important one that may be relevant to your investigation. Right now there's seven billion people on the planet, and by mid-century, there may be as many as nine or ten billion." She turned to face Taylor. "Here's a fact: Without fossil fuels, we might never have made it past three billion. Fossil fuels, and the immense energy they have unleashed, are what allowed us to explode as a species. They have greatly inflated what's referred to as the 'carrying capacity' of the planet. If there were no downside, that'd be one thing; but the downsides are everywhere—and perhaps the biggest of them all is that the CO_2 generated by our burning of fossil fuels is changing the climate of the planet in such a way that we face the possibility of literally exterminating our own species—in addition to millions of others."

"That sounds like a page right out of the GOC handbook."

Ellie looked at him straight on with a small, serious smile. "Maybe so, but it's not terrorist propaganda. It's the truth."

36

Taylor had enjoyed the last forty-five minutes immensely. At the appointed time, he'd found Levon Plummer down by the water, hanging out on the beach with several comrades. Hurlburt Field was on the western end of the Florida Panhandle, and looked out on the Gulf of Mexico. The water off the beach was relatively calm and a stunning azure blue. Rather than pull Plummer away for a private chat, Taylor pulled up a folding beach chair and spent some time with half a dozen men who were living a life that he suddenly missed terribly.

A sharp pang of desire to return to the 75th Ranger regiment was not something he experienced all that often, but he sure did on this morning, trading crazy stories with some of the world's best-trained soldiers, and thinking back to the incredible experiences he'd shared with his squad.

It just felt so damn comfortable. He'd noted that the small group of men was extremely diverse, but race, socioeconomic status, title—none of it mattered. As a soldier, Taylor had always felt that being African American made little difference. There was racism in the military; he'd encountered a few operators who made small-minded comments—sometimes under their breath, sometimes to his face. However, such incidents were rare, and within his unit, the color of his skin was all but irrelevant. They fought together, they bled together, they survived by trusting and looking out for each other.

In Washington, bigotry was a very different affair. In the nation's capitol it was more subtle. It was the unspoken assumptions that bothered Taylor the most. As an individual holding a position of authority within DHS, he often felt that certain people—even some colleagues—looked upon his status as unearned, as if he'd been promoted to fulfill a quota, and not because it was deserved. At the end of the day, he knew there was only one response: ignore it all and get the job done.

Among these men—his fellow soldiers, that was the primary metric; the only thing that mattered was performance in the field; doing your very best to accomplish the mission and ensure the safety of your colleagues.

The day was brutally hot, in the high 90s with a healthy dose of humidity. The guys were all in shorts or bathing suits, some just lying back and enjoying the sun, a few others were playing hacky-sack; Taylor was amazed by their acumen—and their ability to calmly keep the small ball in play and aloft indefinitely. He had abandoned his suit coat and tie, but still felt greatly overdressed in a white cotton dress shirt and slacks.

Eventually, most of the men peeled away, leaving Taylor, Plummer, and one other airman. Plummer immediately grasped Taylor's silent facial gesture, and asked the other soldier if he might give them some space. Once it was just the two of them, Taylor didn't waste much time.

"Hey, I appreciate you taking time out to speak with me, Levon. As I think you know, I'm here regarding the explosives you submitted to Elon Dorsk for analysis."

"That was my understandin'," Plummer replied. He was a country boy, raised outside of Greensburg, Kentucky, and wore it like a badge of honor. "Whaddya need to know?"

"For starters, I'd like to know where you found them."

"Well, don't normally offer up this kinda info, but it's pretty clear that—even if you were once one of us, you're now a DC bigwig. So I guess I better cough it up, eh?" Plummer offered a wide grin; he had thick eyebrows, a sun-battered, ruddy face, and teeth that likely hadn't seen a dentist in a while.

Taylor chuckled. "Something like that." He unbuttoned his cuffs and rolled up his sleeves.

"Alrighty then. This must have been the tail end of August. Had a mission that took us through Mongolia into southern Russia." Plummer paused for a second. "You don't need to know anythin' about the mission do ya? Cause if ya do, I think I may need to get some kinda special clearance."

"Nah. I don't think so, but I don't want to rule it out either."

This was, of course, an elaborate game. Taylor had already gotten full clearance from Plummer's commander, and had been assured that no subject would be off-limits. He also knew that Plummer, like most SOF operators, held no special respect for DC bureaucrats. Hopefully, he'd proven his bona fides over the past hour, and would not have to force the man to give him the information he was after.

"So, it was 'round about 0200, and we were re-boarding our V-22, when somethin' caught my eye; turned out to be a rucksack right near a landing strip where we were loadin' the bird."

"And where was the landing strip?" Taylor leaned forward, his forearms on his knees.

"In Kemerovo. As I said, southern Russia. Actually, southern Siberia may be more accurate."

"I had heard that you were on a mission in Guangdong Province in China. No?"

"Naw. I jus' offered that bullshit to the lab to cover our tracks."

"Why did you need a landing strip if you were riding an Osprey?" Taylor was well aware that a V-22 Osprey, with its tilting rotors, could land like a helicopter just about anywhere.

"Yeah, well, there was a C-130 transport plane involved. And now were getting into the mission..."

"Okay, understood. Let's leave that alone for now. Can you tell me more about the rucksack and what was in it?"

"Two blocks of that explosive—sent it back to the lab."

"And where's the rucksack?"

"Didn't take it."

Taylor cleared his throat, and narrowed his eyes at the man. "You just left it there?"

"Yeah. Had some kinda shit all over it; might a' been run over. Just left it pretty much where I found it."

"Any identification or markings of any kind?"

"On the rucksack?"

"Yes."

"Not that I could see. Remember, we're talkin' 0200 and we had no intention of using any lights we didn't need."

"Understood. So, just the explosives; that was the only item in the rucksack?"

"Yup."

"So, as far as you know, there's absolutely nothing else of any kind that would help us zero in on the guy who dropped it?"

Plummer paused. "How important is the guy?"

"Very." Taylor leaned forward in his chair. "Levon, I think you know that I'm now the Undersecretary for Intelligence and Analysis within the Department of Homeland Security, and that this matter is directly related to the terrorist threat from the so-called Guardians of Civilization."

Plummer stiffened a bit. "I'm aware o' that."

"Okay," Taylor had played the credentials card, and now softened his tone and almost pleaded: "Then I gotta ask you, man, if there's anything else you can tell me, now would be a real good time."

Silence. Taylor's heart started pounding—partly because he sensed there was something Plummer was leaving out, and partly because he dreaded getting back on that plane with nothing more than the location of where the explosives had been found.

"Okay," Plummer finally relented. "I'm lyin'." He reached down into a pack behind the bench he was sitting on, and pulled out an object. "There was one other thing in that rucksack—this totally bad-ass knife."

Plummer offered up the sheathed knife; Taylor took it carefully by the edges of its case.

"Have you cleaned it?" Taylor asked.

"Nope. It'll prob'ly have my prints on it, but I didn't wash off anyone else's."

Taylor studied the handle: Ornately carved antler with inlaid silver and tiger's eye. The grip was clearly custom-fit to the owner, notched to hold each finger in place. "Levon, you have a rag of any kind?"

"Sure." Levon reached back into his pack and produced an army issue, green cotton cravat. Taylor took it and carefully placed it over the grip and pulled the knife from its sheath. The carbon blade was chemically etched top to bottom with a beautiful design that looked like topo lines on a map. Taylor pushed the blade back into its sheath, and wrapped the entire knife in the cloth.

He looked at Plummer. "Thanks. I appreciate this more than you know."

"It's cool, man," Plummer replied. Then he added, "what are the odds I'll ever see that again?"

Taylor looked down at the knife, then back at Plummer, and cracked a smile. "Not out of the question, but it'll be a while."

"I guess that's okay."

"I appreciate the help, Levon."

"Glad I could help."

"And this is it," Taylor said firmly, looking him in the eye. "You're sure there's nothing else?"

Plummer held up both hands. "I swear to God almighty."

Taylor smiled once more, shook the man's hand and said goodbye, once again noting that he'd be back in touch if he had any other questions. After Taylor had taken a few steps back towards the parking lot and his car with knife, coat and tie in his hands, Plummer called out.

"Kemerovo is what—about 200 klicks due east of Novosibirsk?"

Taylor turned. "About that; maybe 250."

"So you think those explosives and that knife might really have belonged to one o' them eco-freaks?"

Taylor looked Plummer in the eye. "I do."

"Well, hell, man. Go get 'em."

"That's the plan, Levon. Thanks again."

Plummer grinned. "If you need any help…"

"I know, I know. 'Any time, any place,'" Taylor said, reciting the AFSOC motto. They both laughed, and Taylor turned and walked slowly back to his car, nostalgia for his old unit flooding his brain.

*　　*　　*

As Taylor drove back to the airfield to meet up with Ellie, he drove through a cozy community of small ranch houses available for married soldiers and operators, and felt a mild twinge in his heart.

His mind again wandered back to Afghanistan. As his relationship with Rachel had matured, and weeks turned into months, he had started daydreaming of a time, stateside, when they might actually take a shot at a normal life together. A modest home like those around him, a couple of kids. At first, it seemed like a wistful daydream, but eventually it started to seem less distant, less crazy, less of a long shot. His relationship with Rachel was real; it was good, and it was right. She was his, he was hers, and he wanted everyone to know it. Hell, they'd even started using the M-word and making silly plans about where it would be and who they'd invite. Once, late at night, when they were all wrapped up in one another, sated and sleepy, they actually traded their favorite names for a son or a daughter, dreaming aloud in soft whispers about their future, giddy with possibility. He'd told her all about his father, and swore to her that he would be a much better dad to their kids. She told him in her no-nonsense way that he was nothing like the father he'd described, and that she knew he'd be a fantastic dad. At that moment, something started to heal inside him that he hadn't fully realized was broken.

He made his way through the small neighborhood. Up ahead he could see a younger man teaching his pre-school daughter how to ride a bike in the driveway, as the girl's mother watched from the porch. He winced as the memory came flooding back, the one he tried to bury deep inside, the one that continued to fester and poison his dreams. The worst day of his life.

Not unlike this day, it had been blistering hot. Taylor had returned to Camp Rhino very late the previous evening on the heels of a grueling mission. After breakfast, and after re-acclimating to life within the relative safety of the base, he set out to find Rachel with vague plans to sweep her away somewhere for a lazy, romantic afternoon. He passed two soldiers who he knew to be in her unit, but rather than acknowledging him, both seemed to avoid eye contact. He tried to shake it off, but developed a sinking feeling in the pit of his stomach. By the time he finally tracked down her commanding officer, he was holding back a full blown panic attack. And then his world dropped out from under him. Her CO informed him that, the day prior, she'd been part of a convoy delivering fuel to a forward operating base in the mountains north of Kandahar. The convoy was attacked, and Rachel—along with 4 other soldiers—had been killed. She was gone. The CO's report was calm and factual, and Taylor vaguely remembered how furious he'd been at the man for his lack of emotion; he was told later on that he'd actually thrown a punch or two at the officer, but no one blamed him.

In the aftermath of her death, Taylor was shattered, paralyzed. He felt as if he'd lost his equilibrium. But then it got worse: Intelligence revealed that the rebel leader responsible for the attack was a man who Taylor's unit had allowed to slip away in a firefight just three months prior. In Taylor's eyes, he was at least partially responsible for her death. If he'd done his job, she would still be alive.

The raw pain of her loss and the guilt surrounding the circumstances of her death ate away at him. It felt as if his insides were being consumed by the torment. For a few dark moments, he'd even thought of going with her. But the structure and routine of the army, along with a few of his close friends, brought him through. Days slowly became weeks, and weeks slowly turned into months.

Although the pain remained, he was no longer drowning. On the outside, he might have even seemed normal. But inside, Taylor was left with a large, open, aching hole in the center of his torso that he was simply unable to fill or resolve. Ironically, although Rachel's death had ripped him apart, his performance as an operator actually improved. He'd always been a star within his unit, but Rachel's loss removed any remaining fear of death, and for the remainder of his tour, he was indomitable—or at least behaved as if any oncoming threat was irrelevant. Just on the sane side of recklessness. Looking back, it was a little surprising that he was still alive.

Taylor drove on, passing the man and his daughter in their driveway. He briefly squeezed his eyes shut both to push out the tears, and to shove the memory back down into the depths of his consciousness. *One day at a time*, he chanted to himself.

He came to a stop sign, took a left, and could see the airfield in the distance. He drew a deep breath and exhaled, trying to resettle his emotions. *This was a very good day*, he thought, forcing his brain to refocus on the possible break that Plummer's knife might present. *Time to hunt these bastards down.*

37

Ignacio scooped clay from a bucket and rolled it into a ball between his hands, then pushed it in between several stones in the terrace wall. He then meticulously spread the clay into every crevice and crack, making sure that no air was trapped inside. Sometimes he used a wooden pestle to tamp the clay firmly in place. He had worked steadily all morning, reinforcing areas where the wall was cracking or stones were loose. Where the damage was more extensive, he would have to pull several rocks out of the terrace wall, scrape some of the hardened clay away, and rebuild the section. This was the first year he'd been given responsibility for this type of repair.

His father, who had been rebuilding a collapsed terrace two levels down, climbed up to check in on his son.

"This is very nice work, iho," his father said, mussing the hair on his son's head.

Ignacio gave his father a warm smile. "And look over here, Tatay." The boy excitedly ran down the wall to a section he had earlier rebuilt. "The damage was this big!" he held his arms wide.

"Very, very nice, Ignacio." His father bent down on his haunches and put his hand on the newly repaired section. "The stones are well-positioned, and you have done an excellent job with the clay—nice and smooth."

The child beamed.

"One thing, iho. See here where these two stones stick out? If you can, you want to create a curve, so that the wall is bowed in. This makes it stronger." He looked at his son, who was nodding, clearly a little disappointed that his work had not been perfect.

"Tell you what: go get a stone to use as a hammer—one that fits well in your hand." The boy quickly complied as his father waited. "Now, tap these two stones gently until you have moved them inward five or ten centimeters."

Ignacio knelt down and gently tapped each stone several times, until the wall was shaped precisely as his father instructed. He looked up with wide eyes at his father. "How is that, Tatay?"

"That, Ignacio, is just right! Soon, you will be a master builder." He grasped one stone and wiggled it a bit to make sure it was firm, then did the same with the other. He looked at Ignacio and nodded firmly. "That looks good and solid, iho. Now, what should you do to finish this off?"

Ignacio tilted his head and looked at the section, then ran a hand between the stones. "I should add some water and fresh clay to make sure it is all smooth again?" he suggested tentatively.

"Exactly!" his father said, putting a hand on his son's shoulder as he stood up.

His father returned to another terrace to finish his work, and Ignacio completed the section and continued with other repairs. It was still the rainy season—not a good time for wall construction, since the soil is loose and unstable, and the structure never gets a chance to dry out and harden. However, since the annual damage was increasing, they had little choice but to begin repairs earlier to ensure that everything was ready for planting season at the end of the year.

*   *   *

After the family had cleaned up from dinner, Ignacio and Myla worked on their lessons for an hour or so, and were then put to bed. With the children now asleep, Rowena and Dabert sat peacefully outside their hut, watching the embers of the cooking fire slowly die out.

They chatted about their day, and the list of things that needed attention in the days ahead—including a part of the roof that was letting rain in, and the need to hunt or barter for some meat. The conversation paused, and Dabert could tell that something was bothering his wife.

"Dabert, this afternoon I heard that a typhoon warning might soon be posted for Luzon," she finally offered.

"Yes, I heard this as well," he replied.

Typhoons were always cause for concern, but usually did not cause extensive damage in the highlands of Ifugao Province; even Typhoon Haiyan, one of the largest ever to hit the Philippines, passed well to the south of their mountain village in late 2013. However, there were exceptions, including Typhoon Pedring in 2011, which badly damaged the rice terraces, and triggered widespread landslides.

"Rowena, we know very little right now. You should not worry yourself," Dabert could see that his attempt to comfort his wife was not successful; tears formed in her eyes.

So far, there had been no warnings posted, but there was little chance that warnings would not be forthcoming. Tropical storm Isabel had tracked west, and gained strength. It was now headed directly for Luzon, and was now officially a typhoon, with maximum winds of 136 kilometers per hour, or 84 mph. It had entered what was called the Philippine Area of Responsibility, or PAR, a square area on the map that included all of the Philippines, Taiwan, Brunei, and over half a million square miles of the Pacific ocean east of Samar Island, and west of the 135th meridian east. Once this occurred, PAGASA—the Philippine Atmospheric, Geophysical and Astronomical Services

Administration based in Quezon City, began monitoring the storm, tracking its progress, and would issue official warnings when appropriate.

PAGASA also gave each storm a local name; in this case, Benito. Though confusing to many, the theory was that, by re-naming the storm, it emphasized that it was now within the PAR, and that it might garner more attention from the local populace—and be more easily remembered—if it had a Filipi-no name.

Dabert put his arm around his wife and pulled her close; she let her head rest on his shoulder. "Rowena, we will be fine. If the storm comes to Pula, we will find suitable shelter."

Rowena and her husband had spent their whole lives in the mountains of Ifugao Province. Life had not been easy, and storms had always presented difficulties. But they had been happy, and had built a life and a wonderful family together. However, over the past decade, Rowena had become more and more afraid. As typhoon season neared, she prayed daily that her family would survive the fury that might be brought down upon them. When the children were young and small, they seemed somehow easier to protect; as they grew older and more independent, her fears grew worse. She felt like she had less control, and that her precious family was ever more at the mercy of nature's wrath. It was just that *she loved them so much.*

She buried her face in his neck, as he enveloped her in his arms. "I'm sorry, Dabert, I know I'm just being silly."

38

W*hen it rains it pours,* Taylor thought to himself, grinning as he read the email, then grabbed the phone and hit the appropriate speed dial.

Tori answered a moment later.

"Damn, it's about time," Taylor said, the celebratory grin on his face making its way though the phone line along with his words. He was in his office, his tie loosened and his suit coat on one of the chairs in front of his desk. The office was a mess—with reports and documents piled high in squared-off stacks along a side table, and across much of his desk. Several dozen sticky notes of various colors framed his monitor.

"I had a feeling all of this news might make your day."

"My day? This is the best goddamn email I've gotten since joining DHS!" Taylor bellowed. "This is great stuff, Tori. Now: details, please."

"Okay, I'll just click through them in order," Tori began, excited that her hard work had invoked such a positive reaction from Taylor. She felt a rush of pleasure at his praise, glad he wasn't there to see her blush like a school girl. "We received word about an hour ago that Chinese authorities just pulled a police car out of the Huangpu River in Shanghai, with the bodies of two officers in the trunk."

"How close to where the nuke was extracted?" he asked.

"Uh, I've got that right here… Roughly six miles. Looks like the vehicle was run into the river right near the Dandong Road Ferry."

"Okay," Taylor said tentatively. "So I assume there's a connection?" He picked up a mug of old coffee next to his monitor, and inspected it for mold. Finding none, he took a healthy sip.

"I was hoping you'd ask; the last known interaction with these officers was a dispatch call for them to investigate a disturbance at the exact same building where we extracted the device."

"Holy shit. A little annoying that we didn't know that a little earlier. What about evidence? If these guys have been underwater for two weeks, we're not likely to get much. How were they killed?" He took another sip and put the mug back on his desk.

"That's the clincher. Both killed by precision headshots."

"Do we know the weapon?"

"We should have it within a day."

"Tori, if they're willing to accept our assistance, let's get two of our best forensic analysts over there as soon as possible to see what else we might find."

"Already on it. Just sent the authorization to Sherry; once you sign, a team is on its way."

Taylor silently shook his head; *this woman is incredible*, he thought to himself. "Tori, you're amazing—thank you. But you've got more here. What's next?"

"Well, let me dispense with some bad news, and then I'll get to the other good stuff. The video that shows one of the terrorist's boots is useless. We did everything we could, but just couldn't enhance it in a way that conclusively told us anything at all."

"That's too bad. So we've got nothing at all on video?"

"Absolutely zip."

"Have we exhausted all relevant footage from all three locations?"

"Exhausted is the right word. I think over 20 members of my team probably spent close to 300 man-days surveying video. With nothing to show for it."

Hearing that made Taylor tense. "Okay. Let's move on."

"Next up is the knife. Good news here; we've got a few decent partial prints, with the database offering only about 65 possible matches."

Taylor said nothing, unsure whether that was good news or bad.

Tori sensed as much. "Drake, how much do you know about fingerprints?"

"Some. Why?"

"Well, I would say 65 is a pretty low number. If you have a clean print, and the owner of that print is in the AFIS database, it'll score very high, and you'll have your match. With partials, and with latent prints, you occasionally get lucky, but far more often just don't have enough data to get any substantive score at all. In fact, even if someone of interest leaves their prints all over an object or crime scene, there's still only a one in ten chance that one of these will be of real value. As I'm sure you know, what we see on TV is complete crap." Tori waited for a response, but got none.

"What I'm telling you is that there's a good chance that our guy is actually one of the 65 hits in the database. I've got people on it already; we've opened files on every potential, and will also cross-reference them with INS, DMV—every database we've got. Once that's done, we'll execute full background checks and perform limited surveillance of the likelies. I'm guessing we can have this down to 15 or so fairly quickly."

"And the knife itself?" Taylor asked.

"Yeah. Well, here I'll confess some ignorance. I had no idea how many custom-made knives there are in the world. But this one's pretty distinct. Give us a couple of days, and we may well whittle it down to just a few vendors. And if we find the person who made this thing, we should be able to use his records to zero in on the owner fairly quickly."

"I know I don't have to tell you this, Tori, but I want to see that happen as fast as possible."

"Believe it or not, Drake, I knew that already."

"So, item last: You said something in the email about getting results back from the folks in Guam studying the nuke."

"Yes. I'm sending you a copy of the preliminary report now. Not much detail here, but it's a start. In brief, the design is similar to what's called a 'suitcase bomb,' an actual device created during the cold war; I believe both the U.S. and the Soviets created different versions. It's comprised of a tube containing two pieces of uranium. When they're brought together with force, it creates a blast. This one has a fairly simple firing unit, governed by an arming switch which in turn is governed by a timing device. The special operations team in Shanghai deactivated both of these, using the instructions provided by the GOC. All of the electronics components appear to be intentionally generic—chosen specifically because they could have been sourced anywhere—in dozens of countries and on virtually any continent.

"From a design perspective, the report notes that it's impossible to match the style to any other devices, since there just aren't really any points of comparison. There remains some hope that we might get somewhere with the casing and screws, but the team lead in Guam seems to feel this will take some time; it's needles in a handful of very large haystacks.

"The big takeaway here is probably just the existence of the thing. Bear in mind that only three countries on the planet are believed to have the technology for a miniaturized nuclear device: The U.S., Russia, and Israel. That this terrorist group managed to build such a bomb is both impressive—and very, very scary. I wasn't giving much credence to the possibility that this threat was state-sponsored, but I think we now need to give that more consideration."

Taylor paused for a moment, digesting the information she'd just shared. "Tori, when you say state-sponsored, do mean it might have been one of the countries you mentioned?"

"No idea. I guess it's possible, but my thinking was more that every country in the nuclear club deserves further scrutiny."

"Agreed. Next steps?"

"I've already got a few folks looking into whether there's been any breach of security within their nuclear programs over the past two or three years—and whether there've been any firings or conspicuous departures of highly disgruntled scientists."

"Good. Keep me posted if anything comes of that."

Taylor had brought the report up on his screen and had been skimming as Tori spoke. He kept scrolling in silence for a few moments to look at the report's final conclusions.

"Drake, you still there?"

"Yes, sorry, just taking a look at the report myself." He was a bit distracted; as he looked it over, he just couldn't shake the sense that it was somehow... cursory. "Tori, do you think we ought to send a team over there to have a look for ourselves?"

"Hadn't thought about it. What's your concern?"

"I'm not sure. I don't know shit about nuclear devices, but somehow the report seems a bit light. I guess I was expecting much more to come out of this; with technology this sophisticated, I'm hard put to believe that it doesn't create a trail of breadcrumbs to follow with regards to the uranium and other components."

"Well, it's your call, Drake. I don't think we have the expertise to second guess these guys from within our own ranks at Intelligence and Analysis, but I could definitely research and organize a secondary team from other departments if you think it makes sense."

Taylor leaned back, holding the phone to his ear and staring at his screen. "Tori, I know you've got a hell of a lot on your plate, but I'd like you to do it. A second set of eyes on this thing may not produce any breakthroughs, but at least we'd know we're harvesting all the data we can."

Tori felt a pang of stress as she thought of the time required for this task—time she physically didn't have, given all the other irons in the fire. "Okay, Drake. I understand your concerns; I'll take care of it immediately."

"Great. Thanks." He changed the subject. "How are Ellie and Nate progressing on the ecoterrorism front?"

"Well, I spoke with Ellie this morning, and it seems that they're collecting some good intelligence, but no smoking guns. They make a good team: Ellie's contacts in the world of eco-activists have proven highly valuable, while Verit is a machine when it comes to cross-referencing the activities of suspect groups against those of the GOC. I really don't thing we could have covered those bases anywhere near as quickly or as thoroughly without them.

"That's great. I'm glad to hear they're working so well together."

Tori chuckled. "I'd even go so far as to say that Nate seems a little smitten."

Taylor laughed. "Yeah, I noticed that as well. He doesn't hide it very well. And there was no problem getting Ellie cut loose for an extended leave?"

"None. The LAPD was happy to oblige; It gives them bragging rights to have one of their own on our team in DC," Tori replied. "I didn't realize just how well-regarded she is; apparently, Ellie was instrumental in solving a number of high-profile cases, and has become one of their top counter-terrorism agents."

"That's good to hear, though it doesn't surprise me," said Taylor. "But there is one thing that bothers me a bit."

"What's that, Drake?"

"I'm not quite sure how to put this," he hesitated for a moment. "During our trip to Hurlburt Field, I very much got the sense that Ellie was—well, if not sympathetic to the GOC's cause, then certainly not strongly opposed. What's your take; do you think that's an issue?"

"Frankly, Drake, I think it's a huge asset. Were it not for Ellie's strong views, she wouldn't be getting the traction she's getting."

"That's probably true," he mused.

"And I'm not sure how much time you're spending online these days, but there are many more people who share Ellie's views than you might imagine. I think it's incredibly important for us to have someone on our team who can speak their language."

"I guess that makes sense. When can we expect a report from those two?"

"Good question. I'll check with Ellie and have her shoot you an email."

"Great."

"Well, that should do it. Long way to go yet, but at least I don't feel like we're still stuck in the starting gate." She sighed into the phone.

"Tell me about it. And Tori, I want you to know how much I value your hard work. I think I'd probably have been fired by now had it not been for the results you and your team have started to produce. You are a godsend."

"Thanks, Drake, that's really sweet," Tori replied, blushing once more. "It's nice working for someone who shows some appreciation now and again."

Taylor paused for a moment. It hit him that Tori had become not only the most valuable member of his team, she had also become a confidante, a friend, and—well, someone he cared about a great deal. "I find it hard to believe that someone with your talents has been underappreciated."

"Let's just say I've had some pretty tough bosses over the past decade or two, and working with you is a whole lot more fun than what I'm used to."

Taylor felt his face flush a bit. "Wow, I'm flattered. But, Tori, I also know that I'm pushing you awfully hard. Are you doing ok?"

Tori smiled to herself, twining the phone cord around her fingers, "I'm fine, Drake—honestly; I can handle it."

39

During the months of July and August, the sight of cars loaded to the gills with luggage, bicycles, and other gear is a common sight. Summer is vacation season in the northern hemisphere—home to roughly 90% of the world's population, and most people typically find time to get out of town for some basic R&R.

But it was now mid-September, and such vehicles were still quite prevalent. In fact, with the send-off of young adults to schools and colleges now mostly complete, the rental truck business should have been well off its peak—but it was still booming.

This wasn't some anomalous uptick in the normal migration of humans from one location to another; it was the beginning of something much less benign. It was the early indications of a growing, worldwide panic.

Around the globe, the media had been unrelenting in their coverage of the terrorist threat. Detailed explanations, coupled with fancy visuals and simulations, had helped the public gain a graphic understanding of the effects that a nuclear blast within a major city would have.

Many urban inhabitants were in denial. Others firmly believed that the authorities would catch the terrorists long before the threat materialized. Quite a few felt that bowing to the threat of terrorism was something humanity must not do; everyone should go on about their lives. Period. But a sizable number of people had decided to get the hell out of Dodge.

The Guardians of Civilization had noted that, if their demands were not met, then nuclear devices would be detonated in *three major cities* around the globe. No definition for *major city* had been given—but if Novosibirsk had been on their list, then the field was wide open, since there were now over 250 cities around the world with populations greater than Novosibirsk's 1.5 million inhabitants.

Of course, the media had been helpful here as well, sorting global cities by any number of different criteria, including downtown population, metro area, total emissions, emissions per capita, growth in emissions, and many others. Some of the bigger, more obvious targets—such as Tokyo, Jakarta, New York, Seoul, Manila, Mumbai, Beijing, Mexico City—took the threat extremely seriously. Mayors and city leaders were not only developing evacuation plans, they were also privately, and in a few cases publicly, urging their national leaders to actually comply with the terrorists' demands. The logic was simple: Unlike determining an appropriate response to a catastrophic terrorist strike, this specific catastrophe could be avoided altogether through simple, straightforward action by fewer than two dozen governments. The downside to compliance was capitulation and the precedent it created; the downside to non-compliance was nearly unthinkable.

Publicly, among the Group of 20 developed nations called out by the GOC, there was a fairly unified front: *We will not acquiesce to the GOC's demands.* However, behind close doors, there was a flurry of communication between various parties that took its cue from city leaders and directly discussed the how and when of a compliance strategy.

President Gilman, unbeknownst to some of his top advisors, had engaged a few world leaders in confidential conversations regarding the best path forward, with compliance squarely on the table. His particular position was more difficult than most; since most countries looked to the U.S. to expose the terrorists and bring them to justice, the mere occurrence of any such discussion could trigger a landslide of doubt around the United States' ability to get the job done. The truth was that the President had no way of handicapping the race to find and stop the GOC before the deadline. And in the absence of any data to the contrary, he was doing what he felt he had to do to protect U.S. citizens.

Those city-dwellers who were packing up some or all of their belongings, and heading out to points more remote, were operating on a fairly similar principle.

40

A rhythmic cacophony of insects and wildlife emanated from every direction; it was as if the entire floor of the jungle was one massive, high-fidelity speaker pumping a symphony of sound into the humid night air.

The nine men crept through the dense brush, using machetes to clear their way when necessary. The sounds of their blades and careful footsteps all but inaudible under the blanket of otherworldly sounds. Each scanned the underbrush and trees with night vision goggles; in every direction was a bonanza of non-human life forms engaged in various nocturnal activities. At the prescribed GPS coordinates, the leader raised his hand. All held position as he pointed into the jungle in front of them where a small clearing was visible. He signaled for three soldiers to flank right, and three to flank left. They immediately moved out, as instructed.

Taylor was sitting in a dark room at the Pentagon monitoring the operation. Next to him was Tori Browne on one side, and his old CO, General Hank Williams of Special Operations Command, on the other. Once identification had been confirmed, things had moved very quickly. But the process that led to identification seemed to take its time.

As Tori had predicted, they had whittled the possible fingerprint matches from the knife down to a dozen candidates with relative ease—mostly by the simple process of elimination. Simultaneously, her team had sent pictures of the knife to roughly 40 custom craftsmen whose website offered products with similar features. Within a day, they had four men claiming the knife looked like their work; after transmitting additional photographs, the number dropped to two—one in Idaho and one in Mexico City.

Both of these men were then sent names and photographs of the 12 possible suspects. Hours later, the man in Mexico identified one of the suspects, noting that a man had purchased several custom knives over the past decade, but not under the name DHS had attached to him; according to the vendor's records, the man's name was Ben Alcott; he'd met him on two different occasions when he'd come to pick up his order in person. DHS had him as Fred Ramirez; their print match had come from a drunk and disorderly conduct arrest in New York City three years ago.

In return for his cooperation and assistance, and in accordance with the age-old axiom that "no good deed goes unpunished," the knife-maker was immediately picked up by local intelligence agents—along with his computer and files—and brought to the Office of Bi-national Intelligence on Paseo de la Reforma Avenue in Mexico City, approximately 250 meters from the U.S. embassy. The OBI, which housed a number of U.S. intelligence agencies, had been created through a collaboration by the two countries ostensibly to enable U.S. Intelligence agents to spy on organized crime syndicates and drug cartels. The man would be held until the suspect was in custody, to ensure that information regarding the suspect's identification would not be leaked.

Using the now-confirmed photo of "Ramirez," along with both of his supposed names, they tracked the suspect to Costa Rica, where he owned a small tree house, due east of the village of Guacimo and just on the edge of La Amistad International Park.

It was this tree house that was now being surrounded by members of the 1st Special Operations Wing of AFSOC. In fact, one of the three men who'd first been dispatched to cover the right flank was none other than Colonel Levon Plummer.

All nine men slowly closed in on the clearing where the house was located. Once in position, the team leader gave the go ahead. Five of the nine, assigned in advance, moved into the exposed clearing, and began ascending a ladder that brought them up to the first of two levels.

The house was comprised of two octagonal platforms, each built around the tree with the trunk at its center. Both levels were screened in; the upper floor was topped by a corrugated metal roof. Two men entered the first level through a hatch in the floor; roughly 10 seconds later, one of the soldiers whispered "first level is clear."

Three of the men immediately began ascending the ladder to the second level, with Plummer in the lead. Halfway up, there were sounds from above, it was clear that Ramirez had gotten wind of their approach and was on the move.

One of the four men on the ground guarding the perimeter barked into his mic: "Suspect is on the roof." Then, seconds later. "Look's like he's clipping into some kind of zip-line."

Not good. A cable from the top of the house could possibly take Ramirez fifty to a hundred yards away from the house, where he knew the terrain and the SOF team did not. They were all under specific orders to take the suspect alive. The mission's success depended on it, since the information he could provide was invaluable. Bringing back a dead body would constitute total failure.

Plummer redoubled his speed of ascent, made it to the top level, blasted through an open loft with an unmade bed off to one side, and shortly thereafter emerged onto the roof just as Ramirez had shoved off and sailed clear of the house.

Two soldiers on the team had tranquilizer rifles instead of semi-automatics; one soldier was still ascending to the roof. The other was on the ground, and took aim through trees. A fraction of a second seemed like an eternity as Ramirez gained distance away from the house. Taylor, Tori and Williams heard the shot, followed by Plummer's voice: "Miss."

Taylor turned to Williams. "We can't lose this guy, Hank."

Williams quickly gave the order: "Plummer, take the shot."

Kneeling on the sloping corrugated roof, Plummer steadied his Mk 12 marksman's rifle and took careful aim down the cable of the zip-line. He fully understood the mission parameters—that this man had to be taken alive. Unfortunately, a leg shot was not possible, given the tree cover and the man's movements. Three loud shots rang out, followed by a shout, then the sound of a body landing. Last, the sound of a man wincing in pain. Taylor breathed a sigh of relief; *he's still alive.*

Plummer had not aimed for the suspect directly. He had taken aim at the truck, or pulley housing, that was carrying him down the wire. The truck was blown apart on the second shot and fully dislodged by the third; Ramirez had fallen about 35 feet from the zip line to the jungle floor below.

When the men got to him, the lower half of his left leg was splayed out to the side, his broken tibia protruding through his calf; his right shoulder was badly distorted, likely indicating that it had been dislocated.

Other than that, he was just fine.

41

Bernardo Andrada returned to his desk after a late lunch and began to sort through the latest downloads from various radar stations, sensors and data feeds monitored by the Philippine Atmospheric, Geophysical and Astronomical Services Administration. Some of the most valuable data was derived not from the latest high-tech gadgetry—but from weather balloons. Throughout the western Pacific, small, island weather stations would release balloons twice a day; the data captured by these balloons was critical in tracking and estimating the strength of tropical storms.

As Bernardo surveyed all of the available information, it was not good news; virtually every measure of the storm was trending in the wrong direction. Turning to look at the satellite imagery, his stomach sank. Benito had gained considerable strength, and was now exhibiting winds of nearly 110 mph.

In the Atlantic, a storm of this magnitude would be labeled a category 3 hurricane on what was known as the Saffir-Simpson scale. However, even though a typhoon and a hurricane were essentially the exact same meteorological phenomenon, PAGASA's categorization of typhoons was not as precise. The only additional classification to apply to Benito would be if it grew into a "super typhoon," when the winds reached a devastating 157 mph. Given the speed of Benito's growth, Bernardo suspected that this could not be ruled out as a possibility.

Despite the less definitive classification scheme, PAGASA's warning system was quite specific. Instead of classifying the storm, the agency issued warnings that informed individual localities across the Philippines of what they could expect. The system offered four Public Storm Warning Signals: a PSWS 1 for a given area warned residents that they could expect winds of 19-37 mph within 36 hours; PSWS 2 warned of 37-62 mph winds within 24 hours; PSWS 3 was 62-115 mph within 18 hours; and a PSWS 4 was pretty close to an evacuation order, warning of winds in excess of 115 mph within 12 hours.

Bernardo catalogued the data in front of him in accordance with PAGASA procedure, noting that the storm was currently tracking to make landfall in roughly four days' time in Baler Bay—essentially a direct hit on the big island of Luzon. The winds, however, would start to impact the area in advance of actual landfall; he therefore recommended a PSWS 1 be issued for all of Luzon, including the capitol city of Manila, knowing full well that other warnings would follow.

Typhoons were a fact of life in the northwest Pacific, and had been for generations. However, larger typhoons late in the season—let alone super-typhoons—were a relatively new phenomenon. At the same time, the path of typhoons was changing as well, bringing the point of landfall to areas that had rarely borne the brunt of such storms in the past.

The island nation of the Philippines faced a difficult reality: As the prevalence of intense storms increased, their people and their economy would have to pay a greater and greater price. Ultimately, the question lingered as to whether it could realistically remain a suitable home for its 100 million inhabitants.

42

Fred Ramirez lay in a hospital bed in the sick bay of the USS Bainbridge, a guided missile destroyer engaged in training exercises off the coast of her home port of Norfolk, Virginia. Following his extraction in Costa Rica, Ramirez had been flown to a hospital ship for treatment. Although the operation on his leg had gone smoothly—his tibia having been reset with a titanium rod, it would likely require three to four months to fully heal. Once the operation was complete, he'd been transferred to the Bainbridge.

The use of a ship for detainee interrogation was fairly standard. By placing Ramirez in international waters, 12 miles or more off the U.S. coast, he could be secretly held in extralegal detention and interrogated with his Miranda rights withheld—until such time as Taylor and others made a determination as to how to proceed with his prosecution.

Taylor had worked aggressively through Hawthorne to get clearance for the visit. Ordinarily, what's known as the High-Value Detainee Interrogation Group would have immediately intervened and taken responsibility for questioning Ramirez. The HIG was created in 2009 specifically to interrogate terrorism suspects, and was comprised of representatives from the

CIA, FBI, Department of Defense and State Department, under the supervision of the National Security Council. Since this effectively transferred decision-making in such matters to the White House, Taylor's request simply required the President's blessing, which Hawthorne successfully obtained.

The detainee sick bay facility on board the Bainbridge was modern and well-staffed. Ramirez' left leg was in a full cast and elevated; his right arm in a sling. He also had some brightly colored bruises along his torso and left hip, along with a few minor cuts on his face and hands. Though he was restrained with leather straps and a leg-iron which anchored his right leg to the reinforced bed rail, he was otherwise treated as would be anyone else on board the ship, his care overseen by qualified medical personnel.

The man was in very good physical shape; clearly someone who made a point of keeping his body well-tuned. His thick dark hair was cut short, accentuating an angular face with a square jaw. He looked up, seemingly alert, when Taylor entered the modest cabin.

Taylor and Secretary Hawthorne had decided to try a cooperative approach to start; it was a given that the HIG would employ much more aggressive methods if Taylor was unsuccessful. In advance of any heavy-handed treatment, he wanted to meet this man in person, and get a feel for who he was and where he came from. In doing, so, he believed he might gain valuable insight into the overall motives and makeup of the GOC. No use busting in on an unarmed man with guns drawn.

"Good morning, I'm Drake Taylor," he said to Ramirez, trying to sound friendly—despite his sincere desire to immediately choke the man until he told him who the hell was behind all of this. "How are you feeling?"

"Okay," came the one word response.

"In a lot of pain?" asked Taylor.

"I guess not too bad, considering."

Considering what, wondered Taylor, *perhaps that you should probably be hanging upside down by your ankles in a damp, moldy cell for the global panic you've caused?* "Good, glad to hear it," he offered, once again rising above his thoughts.

Taylor took a seat next to the bed. He was casually dressed in a pair of jeans and a polo shirt, offering no indication of his role or title. The two men looked at each other for a few moments, each taking the other in.

"We actually have a number of different names for you. Maybe you could tell me your real name."

The man's eyes wandered to the foot of his bed where a package of patient information was encased in a plastic sleeve. "My name is Fred Ramirez."

The guy didn't look like a Ramirez, but Taylor really had no way of knowing the truth. The identification he'd used when arrested could well have been bogus. Plus, Taylor's team had already confirmed that there was no Fred Ramirez on any flight manifests in the weeks prior to or following his trips to Mexico City to pick up his knives.

"Okay, if you say so. Where were you born, Fred?"

"I was born in Brooklyn."

"Really. A New York City boy."

He didn't answer.

"Do you speak Spanish, Fred?

"Nope."

"Any other languages?"

"Just English."

Taylor thought there was something strange about the man's accent. It didn't sound Hispanic; it sounded flat, without any regional dialect, but was somehow unusual. Taylor filed that away for later consideration.

He decided the best approach might be to get straight to the point: "Do you know why you're here, Fred?"

Ramirez responded quickly: "I don't know where here is. I'm guessing it's not Costa Rica."

Despite the thinly veiled sarcasm, Taylor was encouraged by the relatively verbose response. "I'm surprised you haven't guessed given the motion of the ship. You're in the Atlantic Ocean—on board the USS Bainbridge."

The man looked around the compartment, as though this information made it somehow new to him and he was now seeing it for the first time.

"Do you know why you're here?" Taylor asked again, keeping his tone even and non-abrasive.

"Because a bunch of soldiers chased me out of my house and shot me off my zip-line?"

A smart-ass response was better than a one-word answer. "And do you know why they came looking for you."

"I have no clue."

"Have you ever been to Kemerovo, Fred?"

"I have no idea where that is."

"It's in Russia. Have you ever been to Russia?"

"Not that I can remember."

"Not that you can remember? What the hell kind of an answer is that?"

There was a knock on the cabin door and a doctor stuck his head in. "Mr. Taylor, may I see you for a minute?"

Taylor turned his head to the door; "Sure. I'll be right out." The door closed, and Taylor looked at Ramirez: "Fred, or whoever you are, you strike me as being smart enough to know that your detention can be a miserable experience, or just really tedious. I promise you the latter is better than the former. Please give that some consideration."

Taylor got up and left the cabin; the doctor was waiting in the passageway. Once the door was closed, the doctor spoke in a low voice: "Mr. Taylor, I wanted to tell you that, very early this morning, I was in the patient's room and observed that he was having a pretty bad nightmare. He was even shouting a bit, although I couldn't make out any words."

"Okay. Is that so unusual?"

"Well, given the pain meds he's been on, I would have expected nightmare activity to be muted. The fact that he had them gives me a suspicion that it may—and I emphasize may—be related to PTSD."

"You mean he might have seen combat?"

"Well, post traumatic stress disorder can result from a wide range of different events, but my thought was combat as well—especially since he has the physical conditioning of a soldier."

"Interesting. And very helpful."

"I'll keep you posted if I observe anything else, and will keep his records updated as well."

"Okay, please do. Thanks, Doc."

"There's one more thing." The doctor paused. "I'm a little hesitant to offer this since it was just an impression, but—when the patient was yelling in his sleep, even though I couldn't make out any words, I was fairly certain he was speaking with an Australian accent."

"Australian?" Taylor asked, surprised.

"I suppose it could be New Zealand—and it could be I'm wrong entirely, but that was my impression."

"Well, I'm glad you mentioned it. We'll be sure to check that out."

The doctor nodded, and turned to go.

"Doc, please tell your entire staff to make note of any other similar issues."

"I will, Mr. Taylor."

The doctor walked off down the passageway, and Taylor headed in the other direction. He located the communications officer, who set him up on a secure satellite phone in a private stateroom. He called Tori in Washington, instructing her to have the man's fingerprints matched against both civilian and military databases in Australia and New Zealand, and to report back as soon as she had the results.

He then found the chief medical officer, mentioned the detainee's nightmare, and asked him to see to it that the recording equipment in Ramirez' compartment be engaged at all times.

As he gave further thought to the Doctor's observations, he was torn by two conflicting thoughts: The first was that, should Tori be successful and get a hit off of a new database, it might give him much better leverage in getting the man to talk; the second was that, if indeed he was out of the military, getting him to talk might be very difficult indeed.

43

Tell me this isn't happening, Jack thought to himself.

He was in his car, heading out of town for a weekend at his cabin in the Blue Ridge Mountains. Actually, not for a weekend, but for one lousy night, since he had to be at the airport at the crack of dawn on Sunday. It had been months since he'd had any real chance to get away, and receiving a call from Guam just after crossing the beltway was not exactly conducive to the type of quality downtime he'd anticipated.

"So when are these folks expected?" Jack asked.

"I was told they'd be here on Monday night, and would expect access to the device on Tuesday," the caller responded.

"Shit!" Jack said under his breath, hitting the steering wheel with the palm of his hand. "The whole point of that preliminary report was to make sure that this didn't happen!"

"I know, but the lack of specifics must have raised eyebrows. I'm sorry, I thought it would have the opposite effect."

Jack was furious. He had not reviewed the report personally, so he had no idea whether it had been glaringly sparse, or whether the people calling the shots at Homeland Security were simply so impatient that they would have sent a second team regardless. Either way, he was officially pissed off at the man on the other end of the phone, and pissed off at the impatient bureaucrats. Most of all, since he didn't have internet access at his cabin, he was pissed off that he had to turn his car around and head back to DC to deal with all of this—especially since there were a few items in that cabin he had to retrieve, and postponing the trip added significant stress to the days ahead.

Anger, however, wouldn't solve the problem. "So what do we know about the people they're sending," Jack asked, as he signaled to take the next exit off of Interstate 66 and reverse direction.

"Oh, I have that right here... Looks like one guy out of Homeland Security in Washington, and the other two out of Los Alamos National Lab in New Mexico."

A couple of possibilities raced through Jack's mind, none of them even remotely legal; each one just digging the hole deeper.

"And have you got flight information—are they flying commercial or taking a government plane? He took a left under the highway, and stopped at a light.

"Looks like commercial."

"Do you have their flight info? Connecting through where?" The light turned green and Jack accelerated his BMW up the ramp and onto 66 eastbound.

They chatted further; Jack provided the caller with specific instructions on how to send him the information he needed.

Finally, the caller asked, "so how are you going to deal with all of this?"

A stupid question. Jack had gone to great pains to ensure that different people involved in this adventure each knew only what they had to know. In fact, no one except CJ and himself had a full understanding of the entire operation—and even CJ was not privy to certain details.

He ignored the inquiry. "If the bureaucrat from DC was the only one to show, how hard would it be for you to make him feel like he'd been given access to the weapon, and that he'd received some answers about its design and composition?"

"You're saying the guy is a civilian with no nuclear expertise?"

"That's what I'm hoping."

"Then I'm guessing it would be pretty easy to convince him that he's looking at the real thing."

"Don't guess. We both know there are risks here, but you'll need to think long and hard about how to approach it so that he goes home happy."

"Understood. But how will you prevent the other two from wanting answers?"

Jack fought to keep his temper. "Look, that's not your concern. I will see to it that the guy from DC shows up on your doorstep. Alone. That's all you have to know."

There was a pause on the other end; Jack almost didn't want to know what the son of a bitch was thinking—he just wanted him to do as he was told.

"Are we clear?" Jack finally asked.

"Yes, we're clear. I'll figure out a way to make this guy feel convinced."

"Good. Send me the information we discussed and I'll be back in touch before anyone arrives."

Jack hung up the phone, dropped it on the passenger seat, and took a few deep breaths. Making this plot more complicated than it already was made him incredibly tense. His brain was racing with what now had to be done to make sure that this didn't blow up in his face. His primary concern was to create a clear path to at least getting them beyond the stated deadline, which was all that was required for his own purposes. The first step, he realized, was to call CJ.

Just as he reached over for his phone, it started vibrating—CJ was calling him. He answered, trying to sound upbeat as he broke the news.

"Hey! I was just picking up the phone to call you. I'm afraid we've got a situation."

CJ ignored Jack's words, and said simply: "Jack, they've got Ryan Walker."

Silence.

"What do you mean?" Jack responded. "How do you—"

"He's in custody—probably at a black site or somewhere in international waters."

"Oh, fuck."

44

It was a glorious sunny afternoon. The temperature was still 15 degrees or so above average for September, but a front had moved in, bringing dry air and chasing the incessant humidity out of town for at least a few days. The sky was a striking blue, and for a moment, Washington D.C. seemed like the perfect place to be. Ellie and Verit were seated at a small table outside an upscale café near Dupont Circle, making the most of the gorgeous weather, as they waited for the third member of their party to arrive.

Ellie's colleague was late, and she was clearly on edge in anticipation of the meeting. Verit watched as she tapped her fingers on the white-table cloth, the sound muffled by the thick fabric; he wiped his own sweaty palms on his pants as he snuck another glance at Ellie's profile. *Be cool,* he mentally reminded himself. "So, you think this guy might actually be involved?" he offered, trying to break the somewhat awkward silence.

Ellie's nervous trance broken, she turned to Verit and took a sip of ice water. "Oh, I doubt it. But there's a chance he's heard something that could be helpful."

"Then why so nervous?" Verit asked.

"I don't know Nate." She paused to give it some thought. "Maybe because I tried so hard for so long to leave this chapter of my life behind me, and it just makes me uneasy to willingly dive back in."

"Oh, Ellie, I wouldn't worry about it. You're not diving back in—you're just collecting some intel."

"You're right." She smiled back. "I guess I'm being silly. Thanks, Nate."

Ellie had been unsure about working with Verit in the beginning. But he'd grown on her. In fact, the two of them had become fairly close as they'd dug into the ecoterrorist angle. Taylor had made it very clear that the two of them were to leave no stone unturned in understanding whether any of the established groups had any responsibility.

"Besides," Verit added, "I've heard you on the phone with any number of supposed bad guys from your past, and you've been confident and to the point. Why should this be any different?"

"Well, for one thing," said Ellie, tucking several wayward strands of hair behind her ear, "Alan isn't just another bad guy. He was my mentor. And after learning more from him than I care to admit—after he changed the way I look at the world, I walked away." She shook her head in thought, causing the multiple earrings she had on each ear to jingle. "His disappointment has haunted me ever since."

Verit decided not to pursue it. Ellie was complicated; there was a lot going on in there. Perhaps that was one reason why he liked her so much. He also admired her. He leaned back in his chair and thought about his own efforts. He'd never even considered taking drastic action in response to any of his views—on climate change or anything else. He had always taken the passive route. While pursuing his PhD at Princeton, he'd researched and written a number of technical papers in the hope that the right people would read them and take action. While his family and friends admired him for his dedication to a cause, he often questioned whether he'd had any impact at all.

Never once had he truly put himself at risk in any way to defend or further his beliefs as Ellie had.

"Ellie?" A deep voice snapped him back to reality. A plain but well-groomed middle-aged man had just approached their table and was looking at Ellie. She stood up and extended her hand, then thought better of it and gave the man a hug.

"Alan, it's so good to see you."

Alan smiled guardedly. "You too. You look terrific; your new life has clearly agreed with you."

They held eye contact for a few seconds; Ellie's smile seemed quite genuine.

"Oh. Alan, this is my colleague, Nate Verit; we're working together on the investigation. Nate, this is Alan Stewart."

"Great to meet you." Verit stood and shook Alan's hand. "Ellie has said very nice things about you."

"I'm pleased to hear it. It's all the horrible things she's told you that worry me."

Verit looked suddenly uncomfortable.

"Nate. He's kidding," Ellie said in a half whisper. She motioned for Alan to take a seat, and her and Verit followed suit.

"Well, I confess," said Alan, speaking to Verit, "I didn't know there'd be three of us, but if Ellie trusts you, then I certainly do as well."

"Thank you," was all Verit could think to reply.

"Ellie, it's been a long time. Never thought I'd be sitting across from you at fashionable restaurant. Across an interrogation table, perhaps."

Ellie laughed easily. "I was looking forward to that interrogation, Alan," she teased. "But it sounds like I wasn't the only one to change my ways."

Alan chuckled. "Well, unlike you, my decision wasn't entirely my own. Six months in prison gave me a lot of time to think. And, truthfully, your words from our last meeting echoed in my ears many times: Blowing things up and angry protests wasn't getting anything done. By the time I got out, I had become more than a little disillusioned. So I hooked up with an old buddy of mine doing residential solar, and we became partners. We'll do over 100 houses this year, and I'll actually make enough money to pay real taxes!"

"That's fantastic!" said Ellie "Look at you: Alan Stewart, businessman."

Alan blushed a little. "I know. Who'd have thunk it?"

"Wow," said Ellie, smiling broadly. "A counter-terrorism agent and a solar energy entrepreneur; our parents would be proud."

Alan laughed gently. "Indeed."

Alan was a tall man. Lanky, but graceful. He wore an old blue-striped oxford shirt that was worn at the cuffs and collar. His face was warm, with creases and wrinkles that clearly conveyed the character of a man who had embraced all that life had put before him.

The waiter came by and took orders all around. Once he'd left, Ellie shifted her chair slightly to keep herself in the shade of the café umbrella.

"Do you want to switch seats?" Alan asked.

Verit immediately wished he'd thought to ask her. *Damn.*

"Always the gentleman. No, I'm fine. Thanks." There was a brief, awkward silence, and Ellie took the opportunity to dive in to the topic at hand. "So, Alan, after we traded emails the other day, you offered to make a few calls. I'm curious if you got anything back."

"I did make some calls. In fact, I admit that I'd already done a little digging before I'd heard from you. As soon as those guys released their demands, I'm sure we all had the same reaction."

"And?" Ellie prompted, holding her breath a little.

"Well, I managed to connect with a couple of people—including Bella Knobloch—remember her?"

"I do. She was… out there."

Alan chuckled. "That's a kind way to phrase it. Anyway, it seems that everyone I know is as baffled as we are—I should say, as baffled as I am. You know this is far too organized and on too large of a scale for most of the organizations we've ever worked with. Some of these folks—Bella included—openly praise the GOC for taking bold action, but they seem genuinely clueless as to who's behind it. Bella said she'd poke around a bit and get back to me, but I really don't think she'll find anything."

"What about Elroy Lincoln? You and I spent two days with him in Belgium one summer. He seemed to have more resources and contacts than anyone we'd ever worked with. We've recently established that he lived at a London address up until about five years ago, but then he seems to have vanished—which further raises my suspicions."

"That guy had more money than God," Alan reflected, "but there's no way Elroy is behind this, Ellie," he stated flatly.

"Are you sure?"

"Yes, I'm sure. He's dead—of pancreatic cancer."

Ellie offered a somewhat skeptical expression. "Alan, we found no records of him dying. Isn't it possible that he may have faked his death as cover for an operation like this?"

"That's good thinking; I admire your instincts. But he's dead. Once he knew he had the disease, he left London and headed to a small cabin in the Austrian Alps to live out his last days—like an animal walking into the woods when they know the end is near. I'm sure because a close friend of mine actually visited him at the cabin a month or so before he passed away; apparently there was not much left of him. Trust me Ellie—he's not your guy."

"Okay. I trust you, Alan." Ellie paused. "So I guess I'm hearing that you don't think anyone from our old network had anything to do with this?"

Verit looked over at Ellie; he couldn't decide if she was disappointed or relieved. He knew they both wanted desperately to get a lead in the investigation, but he also sensed that Ellie still had a modicum of allegiance to her old "ecoterrorist brethren," and wanted to clear them as suspects.

"I can't guarantee that everyone I spoke to was telling the whole truth, but I consider myself to be a pretty good judge of character, and I'm confident that no one I spoke to was involved."

"Thanks, Alan. I appreciate your efforts and candor. I'd be doubly grateful if you could shoot the names of those you spoke with, so we could cross them off the list. Your identity as a source will be held in complete confidence."

"Of course it will," Alan smiled, shaking his head. "Hard to believe that Ellie Alder is now a bigwig in the intelligence community."

"Hardly. I'm sure I'll be back in my cubicle at LAPD very soon." She smiled, clearly pleased with his praise.

"So would your questioning imply that you guys still don't know who's behind this?" Alan asked.

"Well, we're actually starting to make some progress, but that just means we have a few puzzle pieces on the table. No clue yet where they go or how they connect."

"I'd have thought that, with all your fancy methods and techniques, you'd at least have a shortlist of possibilities by now."

Ellie said nothing.

Okay, fair enough. You always were the professional, Ellie. I certainly don't want you to share anything you shouldn't."

"Thanks."

Alan steered the conversation elsewhere. "So, what do you two think of all this? You've got to admit that, whoever the hell they are, the GOC's planning and execution is damn impressive."

Ellie hesitated, and Verit filled the gap. "It's mind-boggling; the fact that they've gotten the world's attention with almost no casualties is unprecedented."

"I wouldn't say there haven't been casualties, Nate," Ellie said. "The terror they've caused among millions—billions—of people can't be written off as harmless."

"Listen to you!" Alan exclaimed. "Just a short time ago, you and I spent every waking hour trying to get people's attention. These guys have managed to get everyone on the planet thinking about a carbon tax—without intentionally harming a soul. Hats off to them."

"But Alan, they're threatening to detonate nuclear devices in major cities!" said Ellie. "Can you just imagine the devastation? The death toll? The number of people who will die a slow death from radiation sickness? The millions of people who will have to be relocated?" It was not lost on Ellie the extent to which she was sounding more and more like Drake Taylor.

"I hate to be a hardass, Ellie, but we're going to have to deal with a shitload of casualties no matter how you slice it. You know that as well as I do. Just for starters, if the world doesn't act—and soon, the number of climate refugees around the world will be off the charts. And while the U.S. may be better protected than many other countries, our economic losses will nonetheless be staggering."

"I'm well aware," said Ellie, "but you can't honestly believe that the GOC's approach is the right way to deal with this."

Alan suddenly looked very serious. "Then what is the right way, Ellie? This seems to be the first time that Joe Sixpack out there is actually engaging in conscious thought regarding this issue. Up to this point, everyone has hidden behind the lame excuse that taxing carbon or taking substantive action would bring economic ruin. That's bullshit." Alan leaned forward and spoken in a steady, even voice. "The world—or certainly the U.S.—has convinced itself that we couldn't possibly survive without fossil fuels. Well, the truth is that, given time, we could not only survive, we could thrive! The 1990s saw one of the greatest periods of wealth creation in world history; why? The internet. Clean energy could be bigger. Energy is a six trillion dollar market on its way to ten trillion, and if we were smart, we would embrace the need to leave coal, oil and gas behind and think about the incredible opportunity that energy transformation represents."

"Alan, I completely agree with you, but that doesn't mean that the GOC is somehow justified in threatening the global population."

"Ellie, I no longer commit illegal acts. But that doesn't mean I'm not allowed to be inspired by others that do. Yes, these guys, whoever they may be, are threatening humanity. But as far as I see it, we're already threatened, and are just too ignorant to see it. I don't want to see nukes blowing up in American cities—or in any city, for that matter. But I definitely believe that someone had to do something to wake the world up."

Ellie stared at Alan, considering his words and convictions, and offered nothing in response. She felt so mixed up about all of this, as if her past and present were clashing inside her head. She could see both sides, and was struggling to resolve them within herself. It was starting to give her a headache.

As if on cue, the waiter arrived with their food, allowing all three of them to take at least a temporary break from the conversation.

45

Ramirez jerked in his sleep, then winced from the resulting pain and slowly opened his eyes. He immediately saw Taylor, who was seated next to his bed.

"How are you feeling?" Taylor asked, really wanting to forego the bullshit and get to the point.

"I need some water," was the reply.

"No problem, I'll get you some water, but first I want to chat for a bit."

The man seemed to accept his fate, and waited for Taylor to say more.

"How about we begin again with your name?"

"You know my name. It's right there on the chart."

"As a matter of fact, it is." Taylor got up from his seat, pulled the plastic sheath of papers off the hook at the end of the bed, and threw it at the man's chest. He turned his head instinctively and winced again, then reached over with his left hand, picked up the chart and took a look. He dropped the chart and let his head rest back on the pillow, staring up at the ceiling.

"So, Ryan, let's dispense with the crap."

Tori and her team had hit pay dirt almost immediately. Using new prints taken upon the suspect's capture, they got a hit in Australia's CrimTrac NAFIS database within minutes. It was then just a question of pulling various files to create a complete picture of the man's background. There were two very interesting elements, however: First, according to the Australian government, the man was a soldier, and had been killed in action in 2007; second, he had served in special operations for his native country, and had been involved in a well-known operation in Afghanistan shortly after the war began—an operation in which Taylor had played a role as well.

This last fact had thrown him for a loop. After getting over the shock, the question became how he might use this in his interrogation efforts.

"Here's what we know," Taylor began. "Your name is Ryan Walker, and you grew up in Sydney, Australia. I'll pass over the details on your parents, your dysfunctional childhood, your less than stellar high school career, your brief marriage and subsequent divorce to a Tasmanian girl at the age of 20, and get to the interesting part. Instead of attending university, you entered the Australian Defence Force, and eventually became a decorated commando within the Special Air Service Regiment."

Taylor noted that the Walker seemed to be taking all this in calmly, but was also well aware that the man couldn't be too pleased that the truth had surfaced. "How am I doing so far?"

"So far, so good," came the unenthusiastic reply, wrapped in a distinctive Australian accent.

Taylor was glad to hear it; maybe he wasn't yet letting down his guard, but he was at least letting go of pretense.

"How'd you like serving in the SAS?"

There was no immediate response, but Taylor waited, hoping that Walker might open up a bit.

He lay there, still staring up at the ceiling. Taylor was about to give up and try another tack, when Walker finally responded: "Best bloody thing I ever did."

Taylor smiled. "I've got to tell you, Ryan, the same goes for me." That seemed to get Walker's attention. He tilted his head forward as Taylor continued: "I was in the 75th Ranger Regiment. Incredible experience."

Walker's eyes narrowed a bit as he took in his newly revealed interrogator.

"That's right. 75th Ranger Regiment. Deployed to Afghanistan shortly before you arrived. You and I have more in common than either of us ever could have suspected."

Walker was circumspect. "Oh yeah, how so?"

"For one thing, you and I both did some pretty crazy time in the Shahi-Kot Valley."

"You weren't—"

"I was."

"Anaconda?"

"Yup."

"You're telling me that it was your bloody ass we saved that night?"

"I'm afraid so," Taylor confirmed. He remembered every damn detail like it was yesterday.

"That was one doozy of a shitfight."

Taylor chuckled. Not an expression he'd heard before, but apt just the same. "It sure as hell was."

Although the four-star general in charge at the time had called Operation Anaconda "an unqualified and complete success," it was, in truth, just short of a fiasco. During the evening of March 3rd, 2002, multiple Chinooks came under heavy fire in their attempts to land atop the mountain peak of Takur Ghar; one lost a man off the back ramp, another crash-landed in an attempted rescue. Poor communication, due to a poorly-timed change in satellite radio frequencies, caused confusion and prevented AC-130 gunships from blanketing enemy positions in advance of the landings.

Taylor and 23 fellow rangers were in the last of these landings. The Chinook was badly damaged as the soldiers made it off the helicopter and into cover under a barrage of heavy fire atop the mountain. Had it not been for a group of Australian SAS soldiers—including Walker—who'd earlier infiltrated the area, Taylor and his comrades might have been overwhelmed by enemy fire. Instead, Walker and his fellow SAS commandos held fast in an undetected location and called in and directed numerous air strikes which routed the enemy and prevented them from advancing on the soldiers and the downed aircraft.

In short, as Walker had inferred, his efforts had indeed been pivotal in saving Taylor's ass that night.

The two men spent the better part of the next 30 minutes discussing the battle, the mistakes made, the heroics displayed by various comrades, the marginal victory snatched from the jaws of what could have been a devastating defeat, and the aftermath—those lost, and the thoughts of futility that haunt soldiers following such battles.

Taylor was a little ashamed to realize that, as their conversation unfolded, he was beginning to like this guy—and the feeling seemed mutual. At the same time, he was smart enough to realize that this could be put to good use. He decided to play the next card in his hand.

"So Ryan, how the hell did you manage to pull off your disappearance? The ADF has you down as killed in action in 2008."

Walker hesitated only briefly before responding: "So, I was redeployed back to Afghanistan in 2007 as part of a special operations task group. Wasn't real happy about it. A few months later, in June, my unit was involved in the Battle for Chora."

"In Oruzgan Province."

"Yeah, that's it. But once again, the whole thing got all screwed up. We were supposedly under Dutch command, and were on our way to Chora from our base in Tarin Kowt, and then—literally one goddamn klick from coming to the aide of Dutch troops—we're called back. Some bloody squabble among the four-stars having to do with differing rules of engagement."

"The mysteries of management," Taylor offered, surprised to hear all this coming from his detainee. He guessed that, now that the jig was up, this was a story that Walker had been waiting a long time to tell someone.

"I was mad as a cut snake. The Dutch eventually pushed back the Taliban without us, but not before 70 civilians lost their lives. The whole thing really got to me. After Chora, something happened; totally disillusioned, incredibly depressed. I just wanted to get the hell out of there.

"Then, about three weeks later, a couple of massive IEDs hit our convoy as we were heading to Kandahar; it was an ambush. Two or three of our vehicles were literally incinerated; I assume those inside were burnt beyond recognition. I was taken prisoner, but two days later, myself and another bloke made a break for it; he got hit, but I managed to escape. Just before I made it back to Kandahar Airfield, I heard that I'd somehow been identified as one of the burnt bodies from the ambush."

Taylor was fascinated by the story. And it was certainly not lost on him that the disillusionment Walker described was very likely the seeds of whatever led him to join up with the GOC. "So you just vanished?"

"I wandered for a bit, then decided to head for the States. Crossing borders in the Middle east and finding the credentials to enter the U.S. wasn't easy—but blokes like us know how to make do."

"Yes, I guess we do," Taylor responded, recollecting a life that seemed like a long time ago.

Getting that story out of Walker seemed too easy. However, he knew that what he was after next would be much more difficult; in fact, he expected to hit a brick wall fairly quickly—but there was no harm in trying.

"So Ryan, I get the disillusionment. I think all of us have had it at some point in our fighting careers. But in your case, it must have been pretty overwhelming to cause you to join up with the Guardians of Civilization."

Walker looked at Taylor, his face offering no visible expression. "What makes you think I'm a part of that outfit?"

Taylor had already decided to play this straight, and answered the question directly: "We found your fingerprints on a knife in a rucksack along with two blocks of special explosives that directly matched what was used in London, Houston and Novosibirsk."

Walker said nothing, his face unreadable.

"The rucksack, as I think you probably know, was on the side of an airstrip in Kemerovo, not too far from Novosibirsk."

Walker leaned his head back and stared at the ceiling. Taylor wasn't sure if that signaled the end of the conversation, and a return to the interrogation, but he waited in silence to see if Walker would offer any indication. In the silence, Taylor could hear the very faint creaking of the ship's structure as modest ocean swells rolled down the length of the hull. He looked about at the flat gray walls and floor as he patiently waited to see if Walker would respond. Aside from the bulkhead door and lack of windows, the small room seemed as well-equipped as any hospital room.

After nearly a minute, Walker finally spoke: "That bloody rucksack. I watched it fall off the side of the bird as we pulled up and away, but there was no chance of going back to get it. Two different vehicles were already closing in on our position. It's haunted me ever since. As soon as your boys came up to grab me out of my tree house, all I could think of was that damn rucksack."

Taylor was certainly not a professional interrogator. He'd done his share of questioning bad guys in the field—and certainly witnessed well-trained colleagues work their supposed magic. But he was truly surprised to be getting so much from this guy on the first go. His colleagues might call him crazy for it, but he decided to confront Walker on that very issue.

"Ryan, you're a smart guy; in fact, we've both been through similar training. I don't pretend that I've got the power to magically pull information out of you—so I've got to ask a straightforward question: Why are you being so forthcoming?"

Walker tilted his head, and seemed to give the question some thought. "I like you, Taylor. I wasn't expecting to; I certainly wasn't expecting to be handled by a fellow special ops guy who happened to be on top of Takur Ghar with me in

March 2002. If you'd walked in here and started abusing me or demanding information, I would have sealed my mouth shut. As it was, I enjoyed having a normal conversation with a fellow soldier.

"And here's the thing: I'm not a bloody terrorist. I'm not some bloodthirsty radical who wants to kill as many westerners as possible. I'm a guy pretty much like you. Except I'm also a guy who started to see what the hell all this fighting was about, and when the opportunity presented itself, decided to do something about it."

No matter how friendly their conversation, Taylor knew the definition of terrorist, and this guy—and his organization, fit the bill. In Taylor's mind, they had a lot less in common than Walker might think. But that was certainly not an argument worth having at this moment in time. "Say more, Ryan; I'm not sure what you mean when you say you saw what it was all about and decided to do something."

"Look, the number of wars that guys like you and me are going to fight will increase exponentially unless we change our behavior on a couple of key fronts. One is our insistence on consuming the planet's resources like it's a fucking all-you-can-eat-buffet. But the most urgent is our insane obsession with fossil fuels. It absolutely defies logic for all of us in the developed world not to aggressively pursue a different strategy when it comes to energy."

"And that's the true motive behind the GOC's threats?" Taylor asked.

"Of course it's the bloody motivation!"

"But you can't really believe that threatening nuclear mayhem is the right solution to the issue. It crosses a line so distinct that there's no chance in hell that it will have the effect you're after."

Walker stared intently at Taylor, and said in a measured tone: "Don't be so sure of that, mate."

Taylor was sure of it. In fact, the very existence of the GOC's threat almost guaranteed that governments would refuse to take action. *How can this guy not see that?* he wondered.

As if hearing Taylor's thought, Walker continued: "I fully understand that governments and their citizens react badly to being threatened, but someone's got to shine a light on this issue. Otherwise, we'll end up spending every bloody nickel we've got trying to save ourselves from the final result."

"But how is detonating nuclear devices in major cities around the globe going to solve the problem?" Taylor asked, seeking to bring the conversation back to the GOC.

"By waking people up. We don't expect the twenty largest developed nations on earth to sink to their knees in the face of our demands, but you'd better believe that there's a whole lot more people out there who now know what a carbon tax is, and who are starting to understand just how high the stakes are. Blimey, I don't spend a hell of a lot time in front of the telly, but I do know that coverage of all this is playing twenty-four seven on every goddamn channel and half the websites in the free world."

"Waking people up." Taylor repeated the phrase as if it was a language he didn't understand. "But you're threatening to murder innocent people! Tell me how that can possibly be justified."

"Innocent people are already being murdered! Right now, millions of people die every year from the impacts of fossil fuels. Dying, mate. From respiratory diseases, weather-related disasters, hunger caused by drought. By 2030, the number of deaths will increase substantially. If we keep injecting our filthy carbon into the air, life expectancy will backtrack to levels not seen since the 19th century. No: those who do nothing, those who actively block action on this issue—they are the murderers. The GOC is simply giving the world a chance to save itself before it's too late. No one has to die here; if leaders do the right thing, we'll fade into the woodwork and soon be forgotten."

"Ryan, it's not going to happen. To acquiesce would be to invite others to blackmail us all over again. You can't honestly believe that we'd be willing to give in to the GOC's demands."

"You literally can't afford not to. Right now, the world is losing well over a trillion dollars a year because of climate change. That's nearly 2% of the world's GDP! Google it; it's true. Wealthy corporations and obstinate politicians sit back and say it's too damn expensive to put a price on carbon. Well, guess what, you can sit on your arses and lose double that by 2030, or you could spend a measly half a percent of your GDP and solve the whole damn thing—and address your damn deficit at the same time. Now from where I'm standing, that doesn't seem like a very difficult choice. We are simply helping you to make it."

"And who's 'we,' Ryan?"

"Beg pardon?"

"You said the Guardians of Civilization are helping the world make this tough decision. What do you want the world to know about your organization?"

"Not a hell of a lot—other than that we're deadly serious."

"Are you all from Australia?"

"Don't take me for a gallah, Mr. Taylor. I'll talk about the issues we're fighting for 'till I'm blue in the face, but I'm certainly not going to tell you anything about my comrades."

"I'm sure you're aware that not everyone who enters this room is going to be as cordial as me."

"That thought has crossed my mind."

Taylor got up to leave. He'd never expected to have a rational conversation with a member of the GOC, and he wasn't sure how he felt about it. He was, however, sure of two things: First, whether Ryan Walker—or Ellie Alder, Nate Verit or anyone else who shared such views—was right or wrong in how they looked at the world was completely irrelevant. The end does not justify the means. Second, finding Walker's colleagues before the deadline and bringing them to justice was not going to be easy, but he would do everything in his power to do exactly that.

46

The concourse was bustling with travelers as half a dozen flights were deplaning and re-boarding for other destinations. Two electric carts carrying the infirm, the elderly or the just plain lazy were beeping incessantly as they pushed their way through the crowds. Various announcements regarding flight status and boarding instructions added to the commotion.

The two nuclear scientists from Los Alamos navigated their way to the food court; one got himself a Greek yogurt and a banana, the other a hamburger and fries.

The flight from Albuquerque had been uneventful and on time, leaving them with a two and a half hour layover in Honolulu before they would have to board their connecting flight to Guam.

They looked around for a free table, but all were occupied. Rather than consume their meal in a busy gate, they decided to walk back towards the terminal in the hopes of finding a quieter place to sit. One saw a sign pointing the way to the "Cultural Gardens," and they agreed to investigate. They soon discovered that there were three to choose from, and they selected the Japanese garden. There was also a Chinese and a Hawaiian garden, each an uncrowded oasis within the busy airport. The gardens had been part of the original design when the airport was constructed in 1962—but for reasons not fully understood, they were rarely used by travelers.

Leaving their bags off to one side, they each took a seat on an elegant stone bench. In front of them was a pond filled with bright orange carp; just beyond the pond was a small pagoda. Surrounding them were a number of carefully pruned and sculpted pine trees, and several weeping willows.

They ate their lunch in relative silence, making occasional small talk. After about 15 minutes, the larger of the two men finished his burger and crumpled up the wrapper. He brushed most of the crumbs off his lap, then threw a few sesame seeds into the carp pond. It took a minute or so, but eventually a large carp circled underneath the seeds, snapped up each one and moved on.

A woman approached, wearing the distinctive blue and white flower-print shirt of the airport's hospitality staff, along with a black skirt and a pink and white lei around her neck. She had a folder in one hand.

"Good afternoon," she said, "by any chance are you Mr. Chenworth and Mr. Poirier?"

The two men looked at each other, then back at the woman. "Yes, we are," Jason Poirier answered, putting his empty yogurt container back into the bag at his feet.

"My name is Katy. I'm here to tell you that you have a secure call from the Department of Homeland Security. If you'll follow me, I'll bring you to a conference room where you may take the call in private."

Stu Chenworth collected his burger wrapper and other trash, consolidating it into one paper bag. Poirier was a bit hesitant. "How in God's name did you know it was us?," he asked.

"Oh, we have our ways, Mr. Poirier," she teased. "Actually, it was pretty simple." She opened the folder, pulled out two pieces of paper and handed them to him. "We were given photographs of each of you."

Chenworth looked at the photos, printouts from the Los Alamos website, and handed them back. "Who from the Department of Homeland Security is trying to reach us?"

"Oh, I have no idea; such information is well above my pay grade. I was simply told to find you."

They each grabbed their shoulder bags and pull-behinds and followed the woman out of the garden. After they re-entered the concourse, they took a right and walked through the food court.

"It's just up here on the left." They passed an airline lounge and a sunglass boutique and came to a plain door marked Conference Rooms. Inside, they walked by a small unattended reception desk and directly into a room marked Conference Room C. Katy followed them in, and closed the door behind her. Two men, also in blue flower print shirts, seemed to be troubleshooting the video conference set-up.

"Sorry, folks. We should have this ready to go in a sec," one of the men offered.

Katy instructed Chenworth and Poirier to take a seat. The room was set up specifically for videoconferencing, with a large screen at the front, and a table roughly 10 feet back with chairs on one side only, facing the screen. In a corner of the room, next to a side door, was an assortment of odd junk: some additional video equipment, a podium with a faded airport logo on its front, and two folded up wheelchairs.

Momentarily, the two technicians seemed to have completed their task and came around behind the now-seated Chenworth and Poirier. One of the technicians spoke: "Now, if both of you will focus on the screen, we'll give you some instructions and help you initiate the call.

No sooner had they complied than both technicians reached around and tightly clamped what appeared to be a padded surgical mask over each of the men's nose and mouth, while bringing their other arm around to firmly hold each man in a headlock. Both Chenworth and Poirier offered muted cries and struggled desperately to free themselves; at one point, Chenworth grabbed the table and tried to tip it forward, but the woman who'd introduced herself as Katy lunged forward and held it down.

Meanwhile, Poirier was trying to reach the face of his attacker, with some success—the technician now had a jagged scratch running from his left eye down to the corner of his mouth. However, the technicians were simply too strong; after 20 seconds or so, both Chenworth and Poirier had succumbed to the chemical incapacitant, become groggy, and eventually unconscious.

The woman and two men then went to work, dressing both scientists in different coats, and placing them in wheelchairs. After using a simple brace that attached to the chair and—using a headband—held their heads up and facing forward, they then added wigs, hats and wrap-around medical sunglasses to cover the headbands and complete the disguise.

The scientists' bags were consolidated into larger pieces of luggage, and—last—each was injected in the calf with a longer-lasting sedative.

Now ready to go, each of the two "technicians" manned a wheelchair, as the woman held open the side door.

Within several minutes, the five were exiting the main terminal building of the Honolulu International Airport, where a white wheelchair van was waiting to pick them up.

47

Preparations in Manila were now in high gear.
Storeowners and homeowners were boarding up their windows; trash cans, newspaper boxes and other loose objects were removed from city streets; cars in flood zones were moved to higher ground; and sandbags were placed in front of every building that could afford them. Evacuation centers across the city and region, expecting a massive influx of Manila residents, were busily re-supplying their stores with drinking water, instant foods, canned goods, rice, clothes, footwear, pillows, blankets, sleeping mats, toiletries, and—of course—medicine.

On the heels of Typhoon Haiyan in 2013—known as Yolanda locally, the number of these centers had grown considerably; all in all, they could now accommodate over three quarters of a million people. However, most of the newly-built centers would not offer much help, since they'd been built on the southern islands where typhoons were most prevalent. The northern track of this storm meant that many Filipinos would not have access to such shelters.

The Philippine Atmospheric, Geophysical and Astronomical Services Administration had issued a level 2 public storm warning signal for the entire island of Luzon, indicating winds of 37-62 mph winds within 24 hours, but everyone knew that this would soon be replaced by a PSWS 3 and then a 4.

Benito was now officially a super-typhoon, packing winds of over 163 mph and still gaining strength. Heavy rain was already pelting the region, and minor flooding of very low-lying areas had already begun.

Thus far, only a few Western news outlets had run stories on Isabel/Benito. While the storm was very large, it was not sufficiently unusual at this point to justify much global coverage—especially given the high incidence of storms in the region.

The Philippines experience an average of 20 typhoons a year. Although the number of storms had not increased appreciably, the intensity of storms was on the rise. Of equal concern, super-typhoon Bopha/Pablo, which developed off the Philippines in early December, 2012, hit an area where typhoons are all but unknown. From an economic impact, the rising storm intensity was of critical concern: In 2009, Typhoon-related costs amounted to 2.9% of GDP, and had risen each year since.

*   *   *

In Ifugao Province, rural Filipinos were also preparing for the storm. Huts and other structures were inspected and reinforced; farm animals were moved to higher ground; and, where possible, crops were harvested early and stored.

Rowena, Dabert and their children worked very hard to secure their hut and belongings, reinforce the rice terraces, and to help prepare a storm shelter in the village for themselves and other residents of Pula. Stocking the shelter was now complete, and the men in charge believed that the shelter was good and strong—"strong enough to withstand the strongest of typhoons" one of them had said in response to Rowena's questioning; she wasn't so sure. But when Myla had asked whether they would be okay in the storm, her mother ignored her own uneasiness.

"Of course we'll be okay, iha," she replied calmly, squatting down to look at her daughter's face. "The storm will make lots of noise, but soon it will be over and you'll be out picking coffee berries in the bright sunshine."

Rowena brushed Myla's hair out of her face and gave her a smile. She then hugged her tightly. The young girl trusted her mother's words, but could also sense her fear.

Once the shelter was set, Dabert & Ignacio returned to the terraces to prepare them for the storm. The heavy rain prohibited any wall repair, but the two of them used logs as wooden braces to shore up critical areas where a wall collapse looked possible.

After an hour or two of work, the intensity of the rain was increasing, and they decided they were finished for the day. Each collected a handful of tools, and they started back to the village. Seconds later, they heard a heavy thud through the driving rain.

"Tatay, look!" Ignacio yelled, dropping his tools and running to the base of the rice terrace. A brace had given way, and two or three rocks had come loose from the top of a wall about five levels up. The boy began to climb towards the breach, and his father followed with a rake in hand.

By the time they got there, water from the enclosed terrace was pouring out to the level below, and several more rocks had come loose. They wedged two of the larger rocks back into place and Dabert told his son to hold them firmly as he used the rake to bring mud from the bottom of the terrace pool up against the wall to form a buttress.

After ten minutes, the rain was now coming down so hard that they could barely see what they were doing. Nonetheless, they somehow got the log brace back in place, and—for the moment—it held.

"I don't think this will last long, Ignacio, but it is the best we can do for now," Dabert yelled to his son over the noise of the rain. Dabert did his best to hide his frustration. He had tried so hard to preserve these terraces, as so many generations had done before him. But he feared he might be losing the battle. He knew that there were many factors, most beyond his control—but that didn't diminish his own sense of failure. These terraces were ancient and a key part not only of his people's heritage, but of his own identity. It pained him that he did not have the power to save them. "Let's head back. But be very careful climbing down."

"Okay," agreed the boy.

Ignacio turned around and slowly found the first foothold in his descent, when the breach suddenly reopened. Rocks fell forward, along with a torrent of mud and water. One of the rocks hit Ignacio's finger and he yanked his hand away, putting himself off balance. The mud and water pushed him back, and he lost his footing, falling down to the next level, where he bounced off the stone wall, and fell two more levels before splashing into a terrace pool.

Dabert raced down, slipping several times himself in the process as he finally jumped into the terrace pool and pulled his frightened son from the water. He stood chest-deep in the terrace pool, holding Ignacio in his arms.

"Are you hurt, iho?" Dabert yelled over the rain. Ignacio was trembling, and blood was running down his left arm. He hugged his father very tightly.

"I—I'm not sure," he replied.

"Ignacio, let me see you wiggle your toes and fingers."

The boy complied, and seemed to regain some composure.

"Do you feel pain anywhere?"

"I don't think so." The boy put a hand on his right hip, then reconsidered. "My back hurts, Tatay."

Dabert lifted his son's shirt and saw that he had a very bad scrape the size of a mango. It looked painful, but would heal.

"Let's look at your arm." He wiped Ignacio's arm using the rain to temporarily wash away the blood, and saw that something had punctured the skin. But again, it did not look too serious. "I think you're okay, iho. Let's get you back to the village. We'll leave the tools here."

They descended the last two levels very slowly, Dabert going first in case his son slipped. When they reached the bottom, Dabert put his arm around Ignacio and they walked through the downpour back to their hut.

When they arrived, Rowena was putting out bowls for soup that she and Myla had just prepared. She looked up, saw Ignacio's bleeding arm and rushed over as the boy extended his arms, and they embraced. "Are you okay, Ignacio?"

"Yes, I think so, Nanay."

"I think he's fine," Dabert chimed in. "A terrace gave way and he fell several levels right into a pool. He was very brave." Dabert put a firm hand on his son's shoulder; Ignacio smiled.

"Well, let's get you cleaned up, iho"; his mother led him over to a pail of water, and began to clean the cut. Myla came over to inspect as well.

"I also got hurt here," Ignacio said to his mother, lifting his shirt to show her the scrape.

"Yuck!" exclaimed Myla, looking at the scrape, which was now a little swollen.

"It doesn't hurt much," Ignacio said to his sister proudly.

Rowena cast a glance at her husband, as they both silently acknowledged the wondrous power of sibling rivalry to quell pain.

"Alright, boys—both of you," Rowena spoke sharply but teasingly to her son and husband, "I want you out of your wet clothes immediately. Myla, help me clean up the mess they've brought in; once they're dressed, you and your father can prepare the soup while I bandage your brother's wounds."

All did as they were told.

Although the torrential rain continued unabated, and the family would soon have to leave their hut for the village shelter, they still managed to enjoy a nice family dinner—a warm, pleasant calm before the storm.

48

Tori Browne, Nate Verit and Ellie Alder sat at one end of a long, well-polished mahogany table, each in a sumptuous black leather chair. Around them were wood-framed, high-resolution photographs of U.S. cities, beautifully accentuated by LED track lighting that ran the length of the conference room. An overhead projector, that retracted into the ceiling when not in use, was currently beaming the title slide of their first presentation onto the automated, drop-down viewscreen.

Talk of renovations in and around the Nebraska Avenue Complex had been a running joke for years; occasionally things got fixed, but very few employees had actually seen refurbished office space. In fact, it was hard for these three to believe that such a swank conference room could even exist in the same complex as their own offices. Evidently, rank had its privileges.

The DHS Secretary's office suite was located in the main building of the complex, on the second level overlooking an enclosed courtyard. The three of them had walked over 15 minutes earlier and were waiting for Taylor and the Secretary to join them for a briefing.

Tori was a bit apprehensive. She had previewed Verit's and Ellie's presentations with them in advance, and they had just zipped through them once again to make sure all was set for the meeting, but she was still somewhat nervous given the audience. At this juncture, however, there was nothing more she could do, so the three of them made small talk, chatting back and forth about office politics, the incredibly hot weather, and their non-existent social lives.

Finally, the heavy, thick glass doors of the conference room swung open and Taylor, Secretary Dan Hawthorne and ASD John Morgan entered the room. Taylor made the introductions, noting that Morgan had been at the NAC for other meetings, and had agreed to join them. All shook hands, and they settled in for the briefing.

Ellie kicked it off, providing a brief history of ecoterrorism and its emergence as radical elements of the environmental movement of the 60s and 70s sought to generate greater attention to the issue. Clicking through her slides, she outlined all of the organizations that had been identified to date, discussed their techniques and patterns, and offered an analysis as to whether each group might have the potential to mount an operation as sophisticated as what they'd witnessed from the Guardians of Civilization.

As she started to wrap up, she made it clear that, in her opinion, there was a wide gap between ecoterrorist activities over the past decade and the GOC's ambitious plan.

ASD Morgan, who had been listening with interest, posed a question. "Ms. Alder, I get that, given the history of the movement as you've presented it, it would seem unlikely that a known ecoterrorism group is behind the GOC's actions, but I'm wondering why we're discounting the possibility that one outfit or another somehow found the resources to break away from the pack." Morgan seemed a bit restless; he shifted in his chair, and adjusted the collar of his somewhat wrinkled khaki suit

"It certainly can't be ruled out, Mr. Morgan, but I think if you add in the data that Nate Verit is about to present regarding the recent activities and whereabouts of these groups, you'll see that the odds are extremely low."

"Okay, fair enough," Morgan replied. "But I guess I just keep thinking that some eco-radical—with or without his old accomplices, might have developed a grander vision and partnered with a more sophisticated terrorist organization to pull all of this off."

"Again, it's possible," said Ellie, "but unlikely. And here's why: One of the primary drivers of ecoterrorism is the idea of biocentrism, a philosophy that promotes 'biospheric egalitarianism,' or the notion that all life on the planet is of equal value, and that humans have no greater right to thrive than their animal counterparts.

"As we've all seen, the GOC has made no mention whatsoever of this premise; in fact, every communication to date has centered solely on the issue of global warming—with absolutely no reference to other species. This is one of three major discrepancies between what we might call 'traditional' ecoterrorism and the GOC's activity.

"The second is scale. On the one hand, ecoterrorism is fairly prevalent. There are 50 to 60 events each year—hundreds if you count smaller incidents of vandalism. But that is precisely the point. The vast majority of ecoterrorism involves damage to housing developments, forestry equipment, automobile dealerships, animal research labs, fur farms and restaurants. The weapons employed are often crude, and—to our knowledge—have never included controlled demolition of any sort, let alone nuclear devices.

"The third discrepancy is violence—or threatened violence. The number of deaths that have resulted from eco-terrorism is extremely low; in fact, only a handful of perpetrators have ever sought to inflict injury. Obviously, the GOC has been fairly methodical in their avoidance of casualties thus far, but the idea of threatening a nuclear explosion just doesn't fit the MO of any ecoterrorist group we've seen thus far. Not only is the loss of life, both human and otherwise, counter to their philosophy, but the environmental degradation that would result from a nuclear bomb is unthinkable; they just wouldn't do it."

Secretary Hawthorne, wearing a tan linen suit that somehow looked wrinkle-free, along with a dark purple tie and a white pocket square, leaned back in his chair. "That's a helpful foundation, Ms. Alder. Nice job," he said, nodding to Ellie.

Taylor gave Ellie a discreet thumbs up.

Next up was Verit, who enthusiastically dove into his slides, a combination of maps, graphs and spreadsheets which amounted to a very thorough compilation of data indicating that most of the key actors currently monitored by the intelligence community were simply not capable of perpetrating the bombings in Houston or Novosibirsk, and even less likely to have been involved with any nuclear technology.

He stood at one side of the screen, with the sleeves of his tie-less white shirt rolled up to just below his elbows, gesturing to components on his slides as he worked his way through the presentation. Using recent surveillance on the known whereabouts of these players, Verit made it clear that many of them were so geographically removed from these events that their involvement was almost physically impossible.

"While we're still waiting on some additional data from the NSA and several police departments, the picture is unlikely to change," Verit stated firmly.

Morgan sat back in his chair and seemed to consider the young analyst's conclusion. Hawthorne was impressed.

"Mr. Verit—and Ms. Alder: I want to commend you both on a solid and convincing presentation. On the one hand, it's disappointin' to drill a dry hole; on the other, our efforts often advance through the process of elimination. To be fairly certain that we can now rule these groups out is a big step forward."

Taylor looked at both Ellie and Verit. "Good work, both of you." He then turned to Tori. "Since we have the Secretary and Assistant Secretary with us today, perhaps we might offer an update on a few other fronts. Tori, why don't you begin with a summary of our findings from Shanghai."

"I'd be happy to, Drake." She pulled a document out of the stack in front of her, and addressed Hawthorne and Morgan. "I believe you're both aware that two police officers who had been dispatched to the abandoned building in Shanghai were recently found in a submerged police vehicle several miles away."

"I was not aware of that," Morgan interjected coldly, "how long ago was this?"

Tori looked at her notes. "About a week ago. We—"

"John, I don't believe you're receiving all of our updates," Taylor interrupted.

"No, I'm not," Morgan replied with a slight edge.

"I think we can probably rectify that moving forward." He looked at Hawthorne for approval, who did not respond. "Sorry Tori; continue."

"Right. We dispatched a team to Shanghai to participate in the investigation, and now have confirmation that the bullets that killed each man—both headshots—were from two separate H&K Mark 23 semi-automatic pistols."

"Mark 23s? Our boys use those, I believe," Hawthorne noted.

"Everyone uses those, Mr. Secretary; it's a very popular weapon," Morgan stated, somewhat dismissively.

"Yes, very popular, and very easy to acquire," Tori agreed, a little distracted by Morgan's tone, "although each of the weapons involved in these shootings used a newer version of the standard suppressor."

"Which tells us what?" Morgan asked, pulling a kerchief from his pocket and patting his forehead and upper lip before putting it back.

"I'm afraid it doesn't tell us much," Tori replied. "There aren't that many of these newer suppressors out there, but there are enough to make them difficult to track. However, considering that both police officers received a single shot directly to the brain, I do think that we are looking at actors with considerable training."

"What else did we learn in Shanghai?" Morgan asked pointedly.

"Very little. Due to the fact that the bodies were submerged, we took no additional evidence off them whatsoever. That said, we did match tire tread material back to the site where the device was found, and also noted that, whoever drove the vehicle to its final destination was probably around six feet tall—or taller."

"Why's that?" Hawthorne asked.

"Because the seat had been readjusted to its farthest back position. Which implies that the driver was very likely not Chinese. Anyway, I wish there was more evidence, but we know these guys are good, so I guess I'm not surprised."

"Let's switch gears for a second," Taylor said. "John, I'm not sure you're aware of this, but we sent two nuclear experts from Los Alamos to Guam two days ago to help evaluate the nuclear device extracted from Shanghai."

"Why? Was the team in Guam dragging their feet?" Morgan asked.

"Not explicitly," Taylor responded, sensing a slight pique; he wanted to be diplomatic here, since the lab was a DoD facility. "But let's come back to that. The bigger issue is this: It seems the guys from Los Alamos never made it Guam. We've confirmed that they landed in Honolulu, but never boarded their connection—and haven't been heard from since."

"That's a little odd. You mean no one's heard from 'em, not even their families?" Hawthorne asked.

"Nope. So far, it's been handled as a local police matter, but I wanted to get both your opinions as to whether you think we should escalate."

"It seems awfully far-fetched to think their disappearance is somehow related to the GOC, don't you think?" asked Morgan.

"I'm just not sure," said Taylor, "for two people to simply vanish from an airport just doesn't makes sense."

"Maybe I can help," Morgan offered. "The FBI's Special Agent in Charge in Honolulu is an old friend; how about I give her a call and ask her to look into it—at the very least I'll make sure the investigation into their disappearance is being given the right priority."

"That'd be terrific, John," said Hawthorne.

"That would be very much appreciated," Taylor agreed. "The next question is whether to send another pair of experts in their place."

"Drake, with all due respect," said Morgan, "why are you second-guessing the lab in Guam? They're very well-qualified to evaluate that device; they don't need any help from outside experts."

Taylor was expecting a little pushback from Morgan, but his tone seemed almost combative. John Morgan held a very long title; he was officially the Assistant Secretary of Defense for Special Operations/Low Intensity Conflict & Interdependent Capabilities. Though a civilian, he was considered a principal advisor to the Secretary of Defense, and had oversight responsibility for a range of activities which fell under his title's domain; these included counterterrorism; special reconnaissance; foreign internal defense; information and psychological operations; and counterproliferation of WMD. While the org chart and reporting structure was complex, Taylor suspected that sending additional expertise to Guam was somehow an affront to his territorial sensibilities.

He attempted to explain his reasoning, without getting defensive himself: "I think my intent was simply to make absolutely sure that we're harvesting every shred of evidence we possibly can from the nuke. The preliminary report was—dare I say it—a little light, and I've got to believe that there are signature elements to that device that could be critical to the investigation."

"Tell you what," said Hawthorne, "I agree with you, Drake, that the device in Guam is awfully important to the investigation—but I'm also skeptical that Los Alamos is going to send additional scientists until we know what the hell happened to the first two. John, if you're willin' to apply some pressure to the lab in Guam, that'd be mighty helpful. If that's a burden, I'd be more than happy to work it myself."

"No, it would be my pleasure," Morgan offered, clearly satisfied by the outcome. "I will work this, and will keep you both in the loop."

Taylor let it go. He decided not to mention that Tori had also sent a representative from her team in DC, and hoped that she wouldn't mention it either. At the very least, they'd get their own set of eyes on the device.

Hawthorne took the opportunity to change the subject. "So Drake, what's the latest on our Aussie detainee? Any new progress?"

"The short answer is no. He's had a number of visitors since I saw him four days ago, and so far no one's gotten anything from him. Like our SOF operators, he's well-trained to endure harsh interrogation, but at the same time—just like me and almost everyone else who's been through resistance training, it's just a question of time. If we apply enough force, we'll get something back—whether it's true or accurate is another question."

"Is he still under medical care for his injuries?" Hawthorne asked.

"Yes, which is part of the problem. But he's been moved out of sick bay and into a detention cell—so doctors no longer have primary responsibility for his care."

"Got it," Hawthorne said.

"We do have some background that may prove helpful," said Taylor.

"Let's hear it," said Hawthorne.

"I'll let Tori do the honors. Her team has done some digging on Walker's time in the military, and on some of the forces that shaped his outlook. Tori?"

"Sure. Thanks, Drake. As I believe you're well aware, Walker spent time in both Afghanistan and Iraq with the Australian Special Air Service Regiment. After interviewing a number of his fellow soldiers, it's clear that he developed a strong friendship with a member of the British Royal Marines, and reportedly with one or two of our own SOF operators.

"The British Marine was a man named Matthew Harrison, a die-hard who appears to have been obsessed with the climate issue. He kept a journal, which we now have, that reads as if he thought of little else. Harrison wrote countless articles and letters, which he sent to dozens of websites and online publications.

"Harrison and Walker were described by some as inseparable, and we believe that Walker's radical views stem at least in part from this relationship. In fact, at one point in his journal, Harrison describes Walker as a 'kindred spirit' and labels him one of the few people he's met who truly 'gets it' with regards to global warming and the urgency for action. Unfortunately, his journal is all we have; Harrison was killed by a sniper in early 2007."

"Interesting," said Morgan. "And what about the U.S. operators he befriended?"

"We're still digging. We actually know of the other friendships through Harrison's journal, but neither name is mentioned explicitly. We've connected with quite a few men who served with Walker; no luck yet, but we'll stay on it. We've also have discovered that Walker made roughly half a dozen contributions over the past five years to a highly regarded non-profit called the Climate Defense Fund. However, the big question remains unanswered: namely, who he later teamed up with to act on his radicalized beliefs."

After a pause, Hawthorne said, "that certainly is the key question." He looked at his watch. "I need to get to another meeting, but this was a very helpful briefing. Please keep at it; I don't think I have to tell you that we need answers here, and we need 'em real fast."

Hawthorne and Morgan thanked the team for their efforts, and made their way out. The door closed, leaving just the four of them in the room.

"Well guys," Taylor said, looking around at the faces of his team, "that was well done. I just wish we were closer to cracking this thing."

They all chatted for a few more minutes, discussing next steps and who needed to finish what reports and send what to whom. Finally, Ellie and Verit left, leaving just Taylor and Tori.

"How are you holding up?" Taylor asked Tori as he closed his notebook and placed it into his briefcase by his chair.

"I'm okay. The sleep deprivation is manageable," she said with a smile. "How about you?"

"Fine. A little tired," he replied, "but we're making progress; this is certainly not the time to take our foot off the gas."

After a few seconds of silence passed, Tori changed the subject. "Drake, I know my job description does not include weighing in on detainee interrogation, but—" Tori stopped, suddenly unsure of whether she really wanted to continue.

"But what?" he prompted.

"Well, it just seems to me that Ryan Walker could tell us everything we need to know to put an end to this nightmare. We've had him for almost a week; shouldn't we have more information by now?"

Taylor really did not like this topic. He was a bit of a boy scout when it came to "enhanced interrogation techniques." In his mind, it was torture, and 99 times out of 100, it was just plain wrong—and notoriously unreliable. Then again, if ever there was a proverbial "ticking time bomb" requiring all available methods, this was it.

"You heard me respond to the Secretary's questions. We will get something out of him, but it takes time. And whether we'll get truth is another question entirely; when a detainee talks under extreme duress, he usually says exactly what he thinks his captors want to hear. And the guy could be just a pawn; he may know only what he needed to know to fulfill his part of the plan."

"I guess that means we'll just have to keep digging," said Tori, trying to sound upbeat.

"Yup. That's exactly what it means." Taylor rubbed his eyes, then looked back at Tori and attempted a smile. A few moments of silence passed. "These hours must be hard on you."

"And on you," she countered.

"But I'm used to being alone. I know you have a life."

"Theoretically," she replied with a dry smile.

Tori and Taylor had never really discussed any intimate details of their lives with one another, but it was hard not to share their basic circumstances given the amount of time they were now spending together. In the past month, they'd grown quite close and more comfortable. Tori had confided in him that, just before joining his team, she broke up with someone that she'd been dating for nearly three years. He just wasn't the right guy, she had concluded—and besides, her commitment to her job made such relationships difficult.

"Tori, just be careful you don't completely sacrifice your personal life for your career," Taylor offered.

"Gee, good point, Drake," she replied sarcastically, almost laughing. "I'll just have to do a better job balancing the fate of millions of innocent people with more nights out with friends."

Taylor smiled, realizing the silliness of his comment. "I guess I meant when this is all over."

"Fair enough. When this is all over, feel free to remind me."

It occurred to Taylor that his admonishment was patently unfair—for several reasons. First, his job at DHS left him with very little time for anything else; as such, there was no reason to think that Tori's situation was any different, especially given the workload he put on her plate. Second, Rachel's death still haunted him almost daily, but had she been his wife while he took on this role, it was entirely possible that he would be as neglectful of his home life as Tori was of her social life. *Then again*, he thought to himself, *had Rachel lived, perhaps I wouldn't have taken this job.*

He looked across the table at Tori, and momentarily stopped thinking about Rachel. Tori had on a white cotton sleeveless blouse and a high-waisted pencil skirt. She was tired and overworked, but—despite the stress—still managed to look quite beautiful. This woman always seemed to come through for him, often with a smile. He appreciated her more than she knew, probably more than it would ever be appropriate to tell her.

The two of them spent more time together than either might with a spouse or significant other—one of the ironies of the workplace. As such, he got to enjoy her company more than any boyfriend ever could. While that was pretty much okay with him, he realized that it probably wasn't fair to her.

"Tell you what," he finally replied, taking her hand in his and giving it a gentle squeeze, "when this is all over, I'm going to force you to take a vacation, and throw in a bonus to boot."

Immediately feeling as if he had crossed a line, he started to pull his hand back, but Tori used her other hand to hold it firmly in place as she looked into his eyes. Her hair was pulled back, but a few blond strands had slipped free, delicately framing her face.

"Deal," she said with a wide smile. "And when this is all over, Drake, we should both put our social lives back on the priority list."

49

The video, comprised of a time-lapse sequence of satellite photos, had gone viral. It looked like an explosion, with the dense clouds of the storm rapidly doubling in size, and the expanding eye forming a crisp cylindrical hole at the center. Looping over and over, the viewer was hypnotized by the fury and power of the rapidly accelerating storm.

On the verge of making landfall, Typhoon Isabel/Benito had, over the course of just 24 hours, gone from a super-typhoon to the largest storm in recorded history.

Teams at PAGASA in Quezon City, at the Joint Typhoon Warning Center in Pearl Harbor, Hawaii, and at the Regional Specialized Meteorological Center in Tokyo were now all cooperating, sharing data and modeling the storm's path. By their calculations, Isabel/Benito was exhibiting 10 minute sustained winds of 194 mph, 1 minute sustained winds of 211 mph, and occasional gusts in excess of 245 mph.

Every one involved knew that they were looking at one of the most destructive forces that mother nature had to offer, and it was still tracking directly for Luzon, the largest island in the Philippines—home to roughly 50 million people.

PAGASA had issued level 4 public storm warning signals to all regions, with authorities calling for the immediate evacuation of all low-lying areas within the capitol city of Manila, and urging citizens to seek refuge, if possible, in steel-reinforced concrete buildings—including schools, which had begun cancelling classes two days prior so that they could be properly prepared for use as evacuation centers. Food, first-aid supplies and medicines had been positioned in and around populated areas for easier access during and following the storm.

Nonetheless, designated evacuation centers quickly reached capacity, with frightened families now being turned away. Stores had been picked clean of emergency supplies, roads were jammed with traffic, and many people had simply nowhere to go, forced to seek refuge in houses or structures that were clearly not capable of standing up to a storm of this magnitude.

Outside of Manila, in thousands of coastal and mountain towns and villages, Filipinos were doing the best they could to reinforce their dwellings, and find the best possible place to hunker down and ride out the storm.

In Ifugao Province, Dabert, Rowena, Ignacio and Myla had tied down their possessions within their hut, and had begun their trek to the shelter within the village.

Rowena had tried very hard to put on a brave face for her children, but she was not succeeding. She was scared, and her eyes were red from crying. She would do anything to keep her little ones safe, but felt completely helpless. The shelter was their only defense, and she would have to accept it. Ignacio and Myla, on the other hand, were wonderful; they gently rubbed her back when they saw tears, and assured their mother that everything would be okay. Dabert was stoic; he just wanted to get through it, and begin dealing with the damage.

Governments from all over the world were already offering to help, but their assistance would have to come in the aftermath, since the point at which supplies could be airlifted in or people out had now passed.

In Washington, FEMA had obtained authorization to ship five million dollars worth of supplies, and send several trained personnel to help with recovery efforts once the storm had passed. But this was a drop in the bucket; if the storm proved as deadly as had been predicted, the United States would be pressured to send 50 to 100 times that amount—and it would require legislation to unlock the required funds.

In truth, however, five million dollars worth was all FEMA could spare at the moment. The agency's resources were completely consumed by preparations for a potential nuclear blast in a major American city. Mobile medical facilities needed to be procured, properly equipped, and stocked with an extensive array of first aid supplies and medicines. These would be necessary to treat many thousands of patients injured by the shock wave, and many more thousands with Acute Radiation Syndrome, resulting from exposure to the fallout. Not to mention the resources necessary to collect and manage the bodies of those who would likely die in the blast.

While the evacuation of Houston had been a logistical challenge, managing this potential crisis was already proving as or more difficult. Preparing for an event in an unknown location, when resources had to be properly distributed across an affected population, was demanding an immense amount of speculative planning. Every major city had to be studied, and a rollout and deployment strategy for each had to be developed. In short, an insane amount of work.

Taylor did not have much spare time with which to contemplate the typhoon either; although the irony was certainly not lost on him. The loss of life, destruction of property, human despair, and regional instability that the storm would cause was horrible, and he suspected that the GOC would find it difficult not to use the typhoon as an "I told you so moment."

The Western media played right into the GOC's hands. While typhoons in the Pacific typically did not get a great deal of attention from U.S. or European news outlets, that changed immediately when it became the largest storm ever recorded.

Suddenly, Isabel/Benito was crowding its way into the headlines right next to the looming terrorist threat. Details were provided on how typhoons and hurricanes form and the ingredients necessary for a large storm to become larger. Extensive discussion took place regarding the connection between high-intensity storms and climate change, and endless conjecture was offered on the storm's track and which areas would receive the worst impact.

As a result, the two events were being conflated in the mind of the general public. The largest terrorist threat ever encountered was now inextricably linked to the largest cyclone on record; the Guardians of Civilization were warning humanity about the imminent dangers of a warming planet, and here was Mother Nature proving the point.

Suddenly, humanity began to feel quite fragile.

50

Taylor's suspicions were correct; the GOC did not let the moment pass unobserved.

It was possible, of course, that the missive had been planned all along; but it was much more likely that—as the media merged these two events—they had sensed a perfect moment to reinforce their message.

The treatise appeared on the web late in the day. It was quickly flagged by Taylor's team and the site was taken down. Within 10 minutes the site was back up using a different hosting provider. Once this was removed, two more identical sites popped up. Then four more. In short, it was useless; not only had the GOC been fully prepared to reestablish the site as often as needed, they had also sent the text to over two hundred media outlets.

It went viral within two hours. Though written in English, it had been translated into over a dozen languages overnight. And by the end of the following day, it was estimated that it had been read by more than two billion people.

In an age when reality television was significantly more popular than the news, and general knowledge of world leaders and events was low and little-changed despite a revolution in information availability, the speed with which the GOC's message was shared and studied by so many people was unprecedented. Perhaps it was simply because no event had so dominated the entire world's population in quite the same way; people felt a visceral need to better understand the twisted minds behind the global panic into which humanity had been plunged.

A message from
The Guardians of Civilization

Our human society is in jeopardy. Though the impacts thus far have been modest, we are on a course wherein our coastal cities, our island nations, our agriculture, our oceans, and our civilization as a whole will experience massive disruption unless we act now.

The GoC does not seek the destruction of anyone else's way of life, or to alter anyone else's values. In fact, our intent is not to change people's lives, but to protect lives from changing. Our goal is simply to force the world to act in its own self-interest: We ask only that developed nations put in place a mechanism to properly address climate change, the most pressing issue of our time.

To date, many nations have experienced greater storm intensity and increased flooding, an increase in droughts and wildfires and witnessed the human and economic costs of each—loss of life, people driven from their homes, crop losses, massive destruction of property, and extreme financial hardship.

But these are just the obvious impacts; over time, we can expect another layer of dangers to surface. The instability brought about by droughts, natural catastrophes, scarcity of water and other resources— all of these cause unrest and lay the seeds for conflict. Conflict begets violence; militaries get involved and wars erupt. Governments are toppled, creating yet more instability. All of which means our world becomes less secure, and as a result, more people are killed and more lives are disrupted.

As you read this, Isabel/Benito, the largest typhoon ever recorded, is bearing down on the Philippines. Science has proven that global warming has brought about higher sea surface temperatures, which equates to larger, more ferocious storms. How many more Isabels will it take for the world to take action on this issue? How many more droughts? How prevalent must wildfires become?

We do not consider ourselves terrorists, but we fully understand why we are seen in that light. If we felt that world leaders and legislative bodies were making steady progress towards the implementation of a solution to the climate crisis, we would not exist. But very little progress is being made; all we've seen thus far are a handful of voluntary agreements that merely suggest the possibility of real action. Time is running out. As a result, we came to the conclusion that we must threaten civilization in order to save it.

The world will question the morality of our actions; we freely admit that our approach is criminal and unethical by definition. We fully understand that, should we be apprehended, we will be punished severely. But know this: The morality of complacency is highly questionable as well. The number of people who will die, and the mass of humans who will be displaced, as a result of the world's inaction on climate will dwarf any casualties or displacement caused by us.

Since the industrial revolution, the world has seen global average temperatures rise by approximately 0.8 degrees Celsius (1.4 degrees Fahrenheit). Because there is a latency between CO2 emissions and their impact on the atmosphere, computer models estimate that temperatures will rise by another 0.8° C as a result of emissions that have already occurred—bringing us to 1.6° C above average.

There has been much debate over how much temperature rise is "acceptable." The current scientific consensus is that we must establish 2° C as the upper limit of temperature change, and do everything in our power to see that this threshold is not crossed. While many believe this limit is much too high (some experts fear it may trigger an irreversible acceleration of ice melt, among other consequences), almost no one who's studied the data believes it is too low.

A decade ago, holding the line at 2° C might have been achievable through a series of steady, serious changes to how we generate, consume and save energy. However, that time has passed; instead, we have allowed continued growth in worldwide emissions, and atmospheric concentrations of CO2 now stand at over 400 parts per million—a level not seen for the past eight hundred thousand years. Unless ambitious mitigation efforts begin immediately, the goal of remaining below 2° C will be unachievable. As it is, inaction on emissions, or "business as usual," will see us usher in a change of 2.6 to 4.8° C by the end of this century; that translates to average temperatures across the globe rising by 4.7 to 8.6 degrees Fahrenheit. Were this to occur—even at the low end of the forecasted range, we would all witness cataclysmic change, and the earth's ability to support our human population, often referred to as the planet's "carrying capacity," would suffer a devastating blow.

Implicit in the figures above is the fact that we now have a "budget" of 0.4° C—the difference between temperature rise already in process and our 2° C limit. Expressed as a measure of actual emissions, this means that global civilization can allow itself to emit only 469 gigatons of additional CO2 into the atmosphere as this century unfolds.

Limiting ourselves to this budget will be extremely difficult, since it will require that we leave approximately 80% of identified fossil fuel resources untapped. This is analogous to getting the manufacturer of a wildly successful product to leave 80% of inventory in their warehouse. We must make sure that the manufacturer doesn't ship it, and doesn't sell it to anyone else; it must remain in the warehouse—forever. Stated plainly, the producers of oil, coal and natural gas will not go for this— and all those who stand to profit from the status quo will resist it as well. This is understandable; very few of us would willingly give away our current or future riches unless obligated to do so.

This is why we must put a price on carbon, and why the exception made for fossil fuels must end. No other industry is allowed to ignore the waste created by their product or service. In most developed countries, a chemical plant is not allowed to dump toxic byproducts into a nearby river; a gas station is not allowed to throw used motor oil down the drain; a hospital is not allowed to throw potentially infectious bio-waste into the nearby landfill. In each case, the company or organization must pay for proper disposal of the waste product, so that it does not adversely impact society—and in each case, there are usually steep penalties for any transgression. In nearly all cases, the costs associated with waste disposal are borne by the provider of the product or service. However, fossil fuels get a free ride; no one bears the cost of CO2; a company or individual can dump as much as they so desire into the atmosphere—with nothing to stop them, and with no costs incurred.

This cannot continue. Society simply cannot allow anyone to deliver a product wherein the substantial hidden costs of that product can wreak havoc on civilization. And for those who would offer that putting a price on carbon is somehow counter to free-market economics, it could easily be said that the exact opposite is true—not pricing the full costs of fossil fuels allows their producers to unfairly manipulate the market in a way that is quite harmful to innovation and competition.

We don't pretend to know precisely how consumers will respond to a tax on carbon, but this much is clear: Use of fossil fuels will drop as the price increases; and alternatives will become more attractive. For those countries with the ability to innovate, this represents a huge opportunity to take the lead in transforming the $6 trillion global energy industry. This is not about solar power, or wind energy, or energy efficiency— though each will play an important role once the cost of fossil fuel is adjusted to reflect its true costs. This is about preventing a catastrophe.

Civilization faces many great challenges. Within any given nation, there are countless issues that must be addressed—many quite serious. Yet very few issues have the potential for such widespread destruction; very few have the ability to decimate the lives of humans and destroy their property on such a massive scale; very few have the power to bring the global economy to its knees.

And most important, very few issues facing human society are so acutely time-constrained. Very few will become unresolvable unless action is taken soon. Yet that is precisely the case. Unless the developed world acts boldly in the very near future to prevent further warming, we will condemn future generations to a life consumed with the problems we have left for them. They will be forced to spend an incalculable amount of money, time and effort cleaning up after our ignorance and inaction. They will pay dearly in both quality of life and in human lives.

We do not wish to harm anyone. Our advance warning before detonating the devices in London, Houston and Novosibirsk were testament to our desire to achieve our goal with no loss of life. However, we are fully prepared to follow through on our ultimatum unless the leaders of the

20 largest developed nations sign a treaty that obligates them to put an escalating price on carbon, and enforces penalties for non-compliance.

The Guardians of Civilization are not dictating a set of binding rules under which humanity will suffocate. We are demanding one single economic price signal that will, if properly and consistently implemented, unleash a new direction in how civilization balances its voracious demand for energy against the critical need to avoid atmospheric changes that threaten mankind's ability to thrive as a species.

We do not seek to be heroes; we are not martyrs. We do not expect history to look back upon us kindly. We wish only that, as this century comes to a close, mankind will have the luxury of looking back with satisfaction, knowing that, when the issue of climate change reached a critical juncture, action was taken and a true calamity was avoided.

After he'd finished reading, Taylor turned and stared out his office window for a long minute or two, looking at nothing in particular. *Who the hell are these guys?* he thought to himself.

He was very angry—for a number of reasons. For starters, he was incredibly frustrated that the GOC had so easily been able to send this missive to the world. He felt somehow responsible for allowing them this outlet—as if he and his team should have been able to hold such information back from the internet. The GOC's communication would inevitably fan the flames of both outrage and panic among the population, which in turn would only make his job harder.

He was also angry at fate—or perhaps at Mother Nature, for timing Typhoon Isabel in such a way that it added fuel to the GOC's twisted mission, quite possibly creating sympathizers among many who had previously seen these actors only as the terrorists they were.

Last, he supposed, he was angry at the treatise itself—for no other reason than that it was well-crafted. There were no crazy statements; no obvious lies; no deceit; no vitriol. Just a logical outline of why the issue they were fighting for was so important.

His team had clearly made progress in their investigation; there was new data on the table, and some pieces were starting to come together. Nonetheless, Taylor sensed that somehow the terrorists had scored a victory, and his team had suffered a defeat.

He leaned back in his desk chair, stretched his arms over his head and rubbed his eyes. *Regardless what these bastards may think,* he told himself, *their ends will never justify their means.*

51

Sophie looked in the rear-view mirror to check on her young son, fast asleep in a makeshift carseat made of pillows and braced by an old suitcase and a flimsy cardboard box containing her few possessions. The box had shifted, and he was leaning over more than she liked—she'd have to stop and fix that soon. But first, she wanted to put her old life behind her. She shifted her eyes and glanced out the filthy back window, sincerely hoping that she was looking at Footscray for the very last time.

She took a right on Princes Highway, crossed the Maribyrnong River, and wrestled with the clutch as the car gained speed. After several attempts and a fair amount of grinding, Sophie got the beat-up sedan into third gear. The car was a 1988 Holden Commodore, a relic that—on a good day—would start on the third or fourth try and just barely get you to your destination. It belonged to her sometimes boyfriend, but was rarely used. The keys had been hanging on a hook by the door of her one-room apartment for months; three days earlier, she'd taken them off the hook, held them in her hand, and hatched a plan.

With two weeks to go before the GOC's stated deadline, Melbourne was slowly emptying out, with residents of Australia's second largest city of over four million people advised to find shelter in the countryside 100-200 kilometers outside the city. She wasn't sure she could make it that far; she was sure the car would die on her at any minute—not to mention the fact that she had very little money, and wanted to spend it on food, not petrol.

Instead of getting on one of the major freeways and heading north or west, she'd decided to head northeast on smaller roads, towards Lake Eildon. It was closer, which meant less chance of breaking down on the way, and it was a place she had dreamed of since childhood. When she was five years old—just a few years older than her son was now, her mother had taken her there on vacation. The lake was in a national park, and she'd never seen such natural beauty; the mountains, the clear water, the wide open spaces of the bush. It had been magical—and now seemed like a good place to restart her broken life.

Her parents had married in their late teens, but her father had left the family shortly after she was born. Sophie never knew him at all. Then, almost two years to the day after her mother died, she received a short letter from him. He had only recently learned of her mother's death, and asked if she was okay.

At first, she didn't believe it; her mother told her that he'd been killed in combat fighting for the Australian Defence Force. By that point in time, however, it was difficult to know when to believe her mother's words—they'd become less and less attached to reality; and as she read the letter, it was clear that this man was who he said he was. But simply the act of hearing from him—from this man she'd never met, yet someone she'd thought about so very often, hit her with unexpected force. She felt as if she'd been punched in the stomach, and was unable to get her wind back. Sophie had shoved the letter in a drawer and tried not to think about it, but it haunted her.

This man had abandoned her and her mother, leaving them entirely on their own. Part of her wanted to write back and yell at him for all the hardship she'd encountered; for her mother's desperate attempts to make enough money to sustain them, and the horrible jobs that had required; for her mother's struggles with alcohol and drugs, and the eventual overdose that killed her. She wanted to scream at him for her son's lack of sufficient food and decent clothes.

But at the same time, Sophie also wanted to see him; she hated her life in the dirty streets of Footscray; she felt so trapped, so alone. In a corner of her brain, she thought that maybe reconnecting with her father might offer a way out—a chance to live a more normal life where feelings of hunger, isolation, and painful concern for her son didn't dominate her every waking moment.

As these opposing emotions raged inside her, the letter sat in her drawer for over a month. Then, another letter arrived. This one was several pages; it talked of his life in the military, and his recent decision to leave; of his anguish over having left them so many years ago; over his desire see her, and to be helpful in any way he could.

Eventually, she was somehow able to put aside her anger— at least temporarily. She wrote a letter back, providing a few details of her life, and noting that she now had a child of her own—his grandson. This led to another letter from him, and eventually to emails between the two of them. Sophie actually started looking forward to her weekly trips with her son to a nearby internet café to check for messages. They finally agreed to talk over the phone, and a few days later he called her and they spoke for 45 minutes. It had started out about as awkwardly as she'd expected, but by the end, they were laughing and sharing stories. Conflicted as she was, he seemed like a good man; she had left the conversation feeling more hopeful than she had in years. They had decided to meet, although details would have to wait; he'd told her that he had some matters to resolve, but would call her again in exactly one week with a definitive plan.

That was two weeks ago; his call never came.

She had tried to call him—several times, but for some reason his number always went right to voicemail. She wrote an email, asking him to respond; then another, infused with some of the anger and resentment that had built up over so many years. But she got nothing in return. It was a day later when she took the keys off the hook and decided that, as life had taught her time and time again, the only person she could trust was herself.

The light ahead turned yellow then red; she put her foot on the clutch and braked as she approached the big intersection at Racecourse Road. She again looked in the rear-view mirror, this time to see that her sleeping son had now fallen forward. Sophie took the car out of gear and pulled the emergency brake, then quickly got out of the car, opened the back door and began reconstructing the supports. As she gently moved him back against the seat, she heard shouting right behind her.

Suddenly, she was shoved from behind, falling on her son, who awoke with a shriek and started to cry loudly. A man climbed in beside her, grabbed her arm with a tight grip and put a handgun to her head. Meanwhile, another man had jumped into the driver's seat. Both doors slammed shut.

"Alright, all set. Let's get out of here!" the man next to her shouted to the driver. The driver lowered the emergency brake and revved the engine, but the car didn't move. "Drive, you ratbag!" The man shouted again.

"It's a bloody red light, you dill! Shut the fuck up!"

Both men looked to be in their early twenties; each wore dirty t shirts with the sleeves torn off. The driver had both sides of his head shaved close and greasy dark hair in between. His scalp was sweating. The man next to her had tattoos covering the arm that held the gun. He looked at her with wild eyes. "You make the wrong move, sheila, and I'll shoot you and your boy without blinking! And shut that kid up now!"

As he yelled, she could feel the spit from his mouth hitting her in the face. Sophie pulled her screaming son close to her side, and stroked his hair. She couldn't believe this was happening.

The light turned green and the car lurched forward, taking a right onto Racecourse Road. As the car picked up speed, the man with the gun jerked his head around to see if there was any police behind them. Seeing none, he turned forward, keeping the gun leveled at her head. A few years ago, even with a weapon pointed at her, Sophie would have given sass right back to these men, but with her son next to her, she remained quiet, just hoping that the two of them would live through this.

Somewhere, deep beneath her fear, was resignation. Her life had been such a shitshow for as long as she could remember, that a part of her thought that being carjacked was somehow expected; a continuing pattern of pain and tragic events that would never end.

Her son had stopped crying, but the two men continued to shout at one another.

"Do you see anything back there?" the driver yelled, "I can't see a bloody thing!"

The man next to her frantically looked back again. As he did, the gun barrel poked her hard just above the ear. She pulled her head away.

The man's knuckles, still holding the gun, smashed into her chin. "I told you not to move, you dumb bitch!" He put the gun to her temple. She closed her eyes, as tears of pain and fear sprang forth, running down both cheeks.

"Up here, just as a I take a left," the driver said.

Keeping the gun hard-pressed against her temple, the man next to her reached over and started grabbing at her son's stomach, who immediately started screaming once again. Without thinking, she pushed him back, only to feel the stinging crush of his knuckles once again beneath her left eye. The man then reached over again and successfully undid the seat belt from her son's lap, then leaned over even further and put his hand on the door handle.

"Now!" yelled the driver.

The car took a hard left onto Boundary Road, throwing them against the passenger door just as he opened it. Mother and child fell from the moving vehicle onto the pavement. Sophie held her son tight, enveloping him as much as she could to ensure that any impact was on her and not him. They rolled several times, each contact with the road causing bolts of pain throughout her body.

The car sped away as the passenger door slammed shut.

The young boy's screams were muffled by the noise of traffic as he lay next to his motionless mother.

52

President Gilman listened patiently to the ongoing argument; it was one he'd heard repeatedly since they'd received the first message from the GOC that there were devices in Houston. Every time it came up, he managed to find some value in the back and forth. But today, he was simply tired of it.

"Dan, the stated deadline is two weeks away," bellowed Bob Baker, the Director of National Intelligence, "and you're arguing to stay on the current course? That makes no logical sense! We've got nothing; our only choice is to aggressively push every asset we've got and use every available means to lean on anyone who might have information. What other choice do we have?"

DNI Baker, responsible for the CIA and the NSA, was a bear of a man. He was in his mid-seventies, but at six feet five and with two decades as a marine under his belt, he was still fairly solid on his feet. He was standing behind one of the couches in the Oval Office, pointing a finger at Secretary Hawthorne as he spoke. Taylor sat at one end of the couch. Across from him and next to Hawthorne was a woman named Andrea McKnight, the newly appointed FEMA Administrator. Both of them had remained silent once the argument erupted.

The meeting was supposed to be a fairly quick, efficient briefing on current intelligence and readiness regarding the terrorist threat, but Baker's presence had sidetracked the meeting almost from the start; there'd been nothing quick or efficient about it.

It was pretty clear to all that there was no love lost between Baker and Hawthorne. After leaving the Marines, Baker had spent years as a field agent in the CIA, and then a decade in administration, including a stint as Director of Central Intelligence. He was a crusty old jar-head, but hadn't slowed down much. Since DHS and the Office of the DNI had overlapping responsibilities, the friction between these two men was almost pre-ordained. The CIA were the supposed experts, having been around since 1947—formed on the heels of World War II. DHS were the new kids; in the CIA's view, their job was to take the collective wisdom and intelligence offered by Central Intelligence, and apply it to the protection of the nation.

It never worked that way. While the public expected the two agencies to collaborate and share information like members of the same team, this was Washington—and the idea of true collaboration was laughable. Everything was politics.

Hawthorne was a little less Machiavellian than most, but not immune. "Bob, for the third time, all I'm sayin' is that, if we strain our network to the degree that you're suggestin', and use the techniques you're advocating, we'll get a whole bunch o' false leads that'll literally waste what little time we've got. Worse, we'll have turned away a lot of valuable assets who may be very important in the future."

"Screw the future!" Baker bellowed. "Avoiding a nuclear blast in a major American city should be our only concern right now. End of story."

Hawthorne looked at Taylor and McKnight, perhaps wishing that neither were present for what he was about to say, then back at Baker. "Bob, let's assume the worst; let's assume that, God forbid, we can't stop these guys, and a nuke is detonated on American soil. If we've squandered all of our assets and sources in the run-up to such an event, we'll have nowhere to turn for answers; worse, we'll have created more enemies who'd like to see the same thing happen again. If, instead, we're more surgical, then most of our sources will still be on our side in the aftermath."

Baker shook his head. "I can't believe I'm hearing—"

"Bob!" Hawthorne interrupted. "We gave you guys carte blanche with Ryan Walker. This man is not just a source, but a known member of the GOC. What'd the CIA get from him?"

Baker was cornered, and didn't like it. "Dan, you know that's a bullshit argument. The man is a trained special ops—"

"Gentlemen!" This time it was the President who interrupted. "I have heard this argument several times, as both of you are aware," he began. "I see both sides of the issue, and truly believe it's not an either/or."

He took a sip of coffee, replaced the cup in its saucer, and leaned back in his chair. All remained silent. The President knew that Baker's hostility stemmed, in part, from the fact that the CIA would ordinarily lead on a terrorist plot of this sort. However, he had been burned multiple times during his first term by a Central Intelligence Agency largely out of control—it was quite intentional that he had asked DHS to take charge of the GOC investigation.

"Dan, Bob: By day's end, I want both of you to formulate a list of specific sources that you believe we should bring in for aggressive interrogation. Then I want you to bring your teams together to review and finalize those lists, and submit the results to me. Are we clear?"

"Yes, Mr. President," Hawthorne replied immediately.

"Yes, sir," added Baker.

"Good. I will then make a determination as to how aggressively we will proceed." The President looked at his watch. "I've got a call in a few minutes, but before we break, I've got a question for Andrea."

"What is it, Mr. President?" McKnight asked.

"I believe your team's initial numbers regarding potential casualties were rough estimates. Have you reworked those?

"We have, sir."

"Give me a quick summary."

McKnight's appointment as FEMA Administrator had been confirmed by the Senate just four days earlier in a rushed vote that acknowledged the immediate need for agency leadership. McKnight had instantly been thrown headlong into a boiling cauldron of issues and deadlines and finger pointing. In her mid-fifties, she was a capable and experienced manager who'd spent eleven years as the Director of the Florida Division of Emergency Management. During her tenure, she'd coordinated the response to several major hurricanes, comprising some of the largest emergency response efforts in U.S. history. McKnight was short and somewhat stout, firm on her feet and very willing to take a stand—but also wise enough to stay the hell out of arguments that did not impact her area of focus.

She looked squarely at the President, her plain, doughy face absent of emotion: "For a single device, we are estimating 10 to 50 thousand dead, and another 300 to 900 thousand with Acute Radiation Syndrome."

"Hmmm. They've gone up?"

"Yes, sir." Everyone in the room received such data with calm objectivity, but only because it was their job to do so. It was impossible to hear such staggering figures without inward horror at the thought of such an occurrence.

"And why such a spread between high and low?" President Gilman asked.

"Well, Mr. President, there are a number of variables: where the bomb is located within a city, how many residents have voluntarily evacuated in advance, the prevailing winds at the time of detonation, and—perhaps most important—the actual size of the device."

"And what do we know about the bomb?"

"I'll let Drake answer that, sir."

He turned to Taylor. "Drake?"

"Mr. President, we got our hands on the first full report from the lab in Guam just yesterday. Assuming that the terrorists were accurate in describing the planted devices as twice the size of what we extracted in Shanghai, we are estimating that the planted devices will each deliver a blast of approximately 10 kilotons."

As it turned out, while there was still no word on the Los Alamos scientists, the one team member that had made it to Guam had been helpful in pushing the lab to provide more detail.

"You'll excuse my ignorance, Drake. I have no idea what that means," the President offered.

"It means, sir, that we would see total destruction of anything within a half-mile radius of the detonation, and severe to moderate damage within a half-to-one mile radius."

"My God." The President closed his eyes for a moment, considering what he'd just heard. He took a deep breath, and slowly exhaled. "And radiation?"

"The radiation cloud would likely extend 20-30 miles from ground zero; anyone within 10 miles would be exposed to well over 1000 rads and would die from the exposure. Within 10 to 20 miles, they would—"

"Tell you what, Drake," President Gilman said, raising a hand to stop him from continuing, "why don't you send me the report and I'll take a look on my own." He was clearly shaken by the data. He stood from his chair and headed back to his desk. "That'll do it for now. Thanks, everyone."

Baker, Hawthorne, Taylor, and McKnight headed for the door in silence. Baker opened it and held it for the others.

"Gentlemen," the President said, as all turned. "Let's find these bastards."

An assortment of nods and "yes sirs" were offered in response, and the group took their leave.

* * *

The President's scheduled call had been initiated, and pleasantries exchanged. "President Wei, you have my word that this conversation will be held in the strictest of confidence, with only myself and my interpreter on the line. May I assume the same is true on your end as well?"

President Gilman waited as his words were translated into Chinese, the response was offered, and translated into English. Given interactions he'd had with President Wei Xiaoming regarding an evolving arms agreement—as well as other recent discussions regarding the terrorist threat, the two had developed a rapport that made conversation a little easier.

"Good. Thank you, Mr. President," said President Gilman. "I'm sure we both read the message from the terrorists that appeared yesterday. I noted with extreme interest that, in reiterating their demands, they did not state that we must sign their treaty; they instead demanded that we sign a treaty placing an escalating price on carbon. Did this subtle change come through in the translation you received?"

Again, he waited for the translated response.

"Excellent. I'm very impressed; I'm not sure my team would have noticed had the text been offered in Chinese." President Gilman waited for the joke to reach Xiaoming's ears, then chuckled along with him when it did. "What I would like to discuss today picks up on our conversation last week: Specifically, I want to explore what you think your government's appetite might be for constructing a climate treaty of our own with a great deal more structure than what we've discussed in the past..."

President Gilman was not at all certain he could ever get U.S. congressional leaders to tow the line on such a strategy, but for now, that was irrelevant. His sole focus was on getting the leaders of the largest emitting nations on board and comfortable with his plan.

His next call was with Mahendra Rafi, President of India.

53

The old motorcycle taxi lay on its side, buffeted by the typhoon's fierce winds. Such contraptions were prevalent in Manila—a primary source of transportation. The machine rattled and bucked, scraping the pavement, held in place by a rusted chain that held it fast to a tree at the edge of a near-vacant parking lot. The canopy over the ancient Kawasaki had been ripped off, unable to withstand the onslaught of wind and water, but the battered and dented enclosed metal sidecar was still attached and in one piece.

As the storm advanced, the tree swayed wildly—until at last it snapped with a crack. The trunk and branches were immediately carried away, leaving the chain just inches from clearing the top of the short, remaining stump. Gust after gust continued to lift the old machine, then drop it unceremoniously back onto the street. Each time the chain climbed a little closer to freedom, violently chafing against its captor. Finally, it rode up just high enough to slip over the top of the stump.

The liberated vehicle wasted no time, first sliding then rolling end over end across the parking lot of one of Manila's supermalls. Despite the Philippines' status as a developing nation, the capitol city had witnessed the construction of dozens of huge malls which had become an integral part of Filipino life and culture.

The taxi, now an unrecognizable tangle of mangled metal and rubber, was occasionally airborne, bouncing up to five feet in the air as it caught the storm's ferocious gusts and gained further momentum.

It moved rapidly across the broad expanse of pavement, and rammed into a pillar holding up the ornate steel and glass overhang that served as the mall's lavish entrance, then smashed into the boarded-up glass doors, cracking the façade. An onslaught of crazed wind and seawater attacked the small opening, reaching wet, wild fingers into the cracks, slowly prying them open. Once the barricade was breached, the water's power quickly overwhelmed the door's defenses, expanding the crack into a sizable fissure, and then pushing them down entirely. Inside, the sound was deafening as water surged into the lobby as a violent, unwelcome guest, sure to remain for many weeks to come.

*   *   *

All across the city, Benito's wrath ripped the roofs off hundreds of thousands of houses and buildings, sucked out the contents within, whirled it all up in a violent cloud of debris, then deposited everything back on the ground as a chaotic layer of rubble across the cityscape.

Despite the call for evacuation, millions had remained in Manila. A foolish few remained by choice, but most had either been turned away at evacuation centers or defeated in their attempt to flee the city by colossal traffic jams. Some were hidden in the interior rooms of schools and what were thought to be the city's stronger buildings, but many more crouched in the cellars, closets or bathrooms of lesser structures.

Early in the storm, one man emerged from his apartment, from which he'd been evicted by rising water, and clung tightly to a streetlight pole—a lone human venturing forth into a great battle between nature and city. Flood waters up to his waist flowed past with tremendous force. Every gust tested his grip on the pole—and tested the streetlight itself, which was now swaying slightly. Finally, the winds and water overcame his strength, and he lost his hold. Trying desperately to regain his footing in the fast-moving flood, his efforts were in vain. The churning waters rejected his bid to reattach himself to another pole or object, and declined even his frantic efforts to keep his head above water. Within minutes, he'd been pulled under, and was now just one more object among millions within the roiling soup of the storm.

As the typhoon gained strength, this man's peril was played out en masse, as people were forced from their homes or hideouts by rising waters. Isabel/Benito had not weakened before making landfall. It slammed into the big island of Luzon with sustained winds exceeding 217 mph. It was now officially the strongest storm ever experienced in human history—and the largest, with a wind diameter in excess of 1,500 miles.

The flooding in Manila was more than just high water in the streets. It was as if the streets had become ocean—and, in fact, they had—as the extreme winds had created a storm surge on par with a major tsunami. White caps could be seen all across Ayala Avenue, while large, rolling swells barreled down Roxas Boulevard. Where they intersected, at the Ayala Triangle in the center of Makati City, the water thrashed violently like a riptide, whipped into a frenzy by angry cross-winds. People screamed in horror as water flushed clean the first and second floors of many of the structures it encountered. Bobbing frantically on the flowing torrents—now as deep as fifteen feet, residents fought for their lives. In most cases, however, the fight was in vain. Their cries were not answered; the storm steadily sapped their strength, and they succumbed to the unrestrained power of the tempest.

Outside the city, the electric grid had collapsed shortly after the storm hit. Poles supporting power lines snapped like brittle twigs, leaving residents all over Luzon—and rescue operations—without electricity. Torrential rains pelted and flattened entire villages, then regrouped on the now-saturated soil like a swarming army, racing down any incline, and sweeping away roads and bridges as if they were unattached to the land.

Large catchment basins atop hills and mountains, used by farmers for irrigation, gave way to landslides, unleashing yet more gushing water down into the populated valleys below. Muddy, turbid flood water pounded on the doors and windows of homes, town halls, schools, and health centers where residents had sought refuge. Many structures succumbed to the barrage, allowing the invading elements to displace their human occupants, and sending countless villagers to their death.

54

In Ifugao Province, the high ground of the mountains was of limited value. Winds ripped over the hillsides, toppling millions of trees. Rains, falling in sheets at rates of up to five or six inches per hour, excavated huge gullies, reengineering the landscape.

Some of the famed rice terraces held firm against the ferocious typhoon; but many others could not. Already weakened by a wetter than average rainy season, and exposed by deforestation, the soil could not process such an influx of moisture, and gave way. Terraces that had served as the economic lifeblood of mountain villages for hundreds of years collapsed as mudslides undermined their foundation.

In the village of Pula, the shelter that Dabert and Rowena had helped to stock and reinforce was holding. Though it was quite small, inside its four walls were over a dozen families—each with barely enough room to sit. The building had originally been built as a modest house, but over the years, it had also served as a store, a school, and a storage shed. It was made of cinderblocks; in preparation for the storm, the windows had been boarded over both inside and out with plywood as a final barrier. Fifteen to twenty additional cinderblocks had been placed on the corrugated metal roof, chained together and lashed down. So far, the extra weight had been sufficient in preventing the roof from ripping off.

Most of the villagers sat quietly or chatted softly to one another, despite the violent noise of the storm all around them. Though the now-windowless room was fairly dark, eyes adjusted and the villagers could make out each other's faces. Rowena and Myla sat together in the corner farthest from the door; Dabert and Ignacio a few feet away.

As the storm hit, Myla had been terrified, screaming uncontrollably. Dabert and Rowena had taken shifts doing their best to comfort her, with other villagers trying to remain understanding, tolerating the added tension of her cries. Eventually, she'd settled down, exhausted by her spent emotions. She actually slept for an hour or two, but was now squirming restlessly in Rowena's lap.

Several hours into the storm, a group of villagers had come by seeking refuge. They had pounded on the door, explaining that their shelter had lost its roof, and that they had no where else to go. After a brief discussion among those inside, the other villagers were allowed in, making the single open room even more crowded, and their supplies less adequate. Water was leaking in through one of windows, the door and through two different holes in the roof—and seemed to be coming up between cracks in the floor as well. All took shifts using a hand pump to pump the water into a bucket, and dump it out the door. Although this prevented water from rising, the floor was now under a half inch of muddy water.

They had now been in the shelter for seven or eight hours, and expected to be there for another seven or eight at least. Without any news or updated information, they had no idea how the storm was tracking, but from what they could hear, it hadn't let up a bit.

Rowena was very tired, her muscles stiff from holding her daughter on her lap. But so far, they were safe, and that was all she cared about. Myla's head lay against her mother's chest, with Rowena slowly stroking her hair.

Myla pulled her head away and looked at her mother. Strands of hair were matted against Myla's forehead; her face was streaked with sweat. Rowena used her thumb to gently wipe under each of her daughter's eyes.

"I have to go to the bathroom, Nanay," Myla said quietly.

"But you just went a short time ago, Myla."

"I know. But I have to go again."

"What kind, iha?" her mother asked.

"Just pee."

"Okay, let's go."

Rowena lifted Myla off of her lap, and then stood up. Dabert looked over with a quizzical look; Rowena motioned with her head to the small water closet.

"Again?" mouthed Dabert. Rowena nodded, rolling her eyes. It actually felt good to get on her feet after sitting for so long.

"Where are they going?" Ignacio asked, who had been sitting in his own chair with his head against his father's shoulder.

"Shhh, iho. They are just going to the toilet," Dabert replied.

Other villagers shifted their chairs slightly to allow the two to pass. The small stall held just enough room for a toilet and a sink. Due to the flooding, the toilet had backed up, and a fresh wave of odor hit Myla and others sitting nearby when she opened the door. She crinkled her nose and looked at her mother.

"Go on, iha," Rowena urged.

The young girl entered the stall, and closed the door behind her.

Rowena stood waiting. She crossed her arms and stretched as best she could while standing in place.

Suddenly, the entire building seemed to shift slightly; Rowena had to take a step to steady herself. She looked quickly over at Dabert, who was saying something to Ignacio. Several of the villagers stood up, one woman screamed. The building then shifted again. Rowena, now terrified, rapped on the stall door.

"Myla, come out of there at once!"

"I'm not done yet!" she replied.

The entire structure then started moving. Dabert dragged Ignacio over to where his mother was standing, then ripped open the door and grabbed his daughter, who had just pulled up her pants. The family huddled, panic-stricken, as the building started to pivot in place. Cracks emerged between the cinderblocks in one corner, then widened, allowing a glimpse of the storm's wrath beyond. Dabert leaned forward, his eyes adjusting to the light and focusing on what he could see outside. He wasn't sure, but it appeared as if a mudslide had caught one corner of the building, and was dragging it along, rotating the structure.

The building stared to buckle; the front door cracked, splintered, then fell away, allowing rain and gusting winds to enter the open room. The villagers screamed in panic; many ran through the door believing the shelter was about to collapse. The doorway was fairly small, and bodies pushed and shoved against one another in an effort to escape. The open door and cracks in the walls had allowed the sounds of the storm—as well as the elements—to rush in—but the screams and cries of the villagers rose even higher, competing with the storm and creating a crescendo of screams and rainfall and crying children and whipping winds. One child had been badly trampled, but had been yanked up into the arms of his fleeing father.

The four of them and one or two other families remained frozen in place. Dabert, Rowena and the children all turned to look as the corner of the building where Rowena and Myla had been sitting crumbled away, leaving a large open rift. Through it, all could now clearly could see a river of mud and trees flowing swiftly through the village center. With openings at each end, the power of the storm surged through the shelter, tugging at their clothes, rain whipping their faces.

Myla started to cry, quietly at first, then hysterically as she watched other frightened villagers pushing and shoving to leave the shelter through the single door. Her mother pulled her daughter to her, and pressed her head against her side. Myla put her arms around her mother, and buried her face in her stomach.

Dabert looked up briefly, realizing that the weighted roof would not hold much longer. He looked at the flowing mud, then back at the door, where 10 to 15 villagers were still waiting to exit. The building then shifted once more, and they could see cracks opening on all four walls. This created even greater urgency at the door, and once again screams and cries were heard as villagers fought to get past one another.

Ignacio clenched his father's shirt. "Are we going to be okay, Tatay?" he asked, looking at his father and squinting to protect his eyes from the horizontal rain. Dabert turned to the faces of his family and, ignoring his son's question, pointed to the far wall and yelled "follow me!"

He pulled them over to the side of the shelter away from the mud slide, and stuck an arm through the widening crack in the wall. He managed to get his other arm out, then a foot. The wall separated further, allowing him to slip through entirely. As the building continued to fall apart, a corner of the roof gave way, and half a dozen cinderblocks crashed down into the shelter just a few feet from where Rowena and the children were standing. "Myla," Dabert shouted, "give me your hand!" He carefully lifted and pulled his daughter out, then his son, and at last his wife.

He pulled them away from the structure as it completely disintegrated before their eyes; the mudslide carrying huge chunks of the structure away. The terrifying shrieks of villagers who had been unable to get out in time could be heard over the raging storm. Myla once again turned to her mother, and buried her face in Rowena's now soaked dress. The little girl was shivering uncontrollably—not because of the rain, which was warm, but as a direct result of witnessing events that, to her, had been unthinkable. Dabert pulled his son's face to his chest as well, so that he would not have to watch the scene unfolding before them.

Several villagers waiting to exit the shelter had been crushed in the collapse, and lay lifeless in the moving mass of concrete and corrugated metal. A number of others were critically injured; one woman, with blood covering her hair and face, was rocking back and forth, embracing what appeared to be a small child. Another man, who had lost an eye and whose left hand was badly mutilated, simply knelt atop the pile, dazed, as the pelting rains washed the flowing blood away from his wounds.

Dabert motioned for his family to hunch down, and he led them further away from the mudslide, eventually having them huddle behind a fragment of an old stone wall. Outside of the shelter, the sound of the storm was deafening. He yelled firm instructions to each of them. "Ignacio, you hold your mother's hand as tight as you can. Myla, come to me." He held out his arms, and Myla hugged him around the neck, as he put one arm around her back, and used the other to put his daughter's legs around his waist with the other. He grabbed Rowena's hand and wrapped it firmly around the waistband of his pants. Speaking to all three of them, he shouted loudly over the storm: "Whatever you do, do not let go."

They left the protection of the stone wall and made their way down a side road of the village. The devastation around them was striking; while the shelter they'd chosen had not been able to stand up to Benito's ferocious winds, it had clearly lasted longer than all the other buildings. The village had been washed clean of virtually all man-made structures; homes, sheds, animal fences had all been whisked completely away, leaving only a barely-visible patch on the ground where these things once stood. Even that evidence stood little chance of survival as water etched away the top layer of soil.

Dabert helped his wife and children over quite a few fallen trees. Each time he did so, he worried that the trees—and his family—might be lifted up and carried away in the process. His plan was to bring them out of the village, and up a nearby hillside to a very small cave, or hollow, where farmers used to store tools for farming the adjacent rice terraces.

The going was slow; they remained very low to the ground—at several points actually getting down on hands and knees when the winds blew unobstructed across their path. After what seemed like hours—but was probably closer to twenty minutes, they reached the bottom of the hill. Although Dabert could make out the terraces above, he could not yet see the cave. But he had lived in the village since birth, and knew the landscape intimately. Although these were not the terraces he farmed, Dabert was confident he could navigate known landmarks to get them to the safety of the cave—provided nothing got in their way. His biggest fear was that it would already be occupied—he knew of no other suitable place, and had no back-up plan to protect his family.

They began their journey upwards. This specific hillside had a set of stone steps, of sorts, that meandered up the side of the terraces. Far from a staircase, it was comprised of rocks wedged into the side of the terrace structure that provided a logical path. Dabert now had Myla on his back, her arms around his neck and legs around his waist. Though he would have preferred to follow his wife and son, they needed him in front to establish the route—so Ignacio was next, with Rowena bringing up the rear.

The hillside itself offered cover from the storm, meaning only that the whipping gusts of wind and rain came at them at 100 miles an hour instead of 200. But the water underfoot alternated between a steady stream and a torrent, making each step a challenge in itself. Dabert had wanted Ignacio holding onto him—and Rowena connected to her son, but the climb clearly required the use of both hands for balance.

Progress was difficult. Dabert did not want to get more than a few feet ahead, and Rowena was obsessively careful with each step she took. The steady roar of the storm was an immense distraction, forcing each of them to apply intense effort just to focus on the task at hand. Worse than the thunderous noise were the objects—projectiles—which the storm threw down the hill. Many of these were inconsequential: small sticks and leaves, or small pebbles. But occasionally, a larger rock or sizable branch or even an entire tree would fly by, missing them only through the grace of fate and the whimsical rules of chaos theory.

Up ahead to the right, Dabert could now see the outlines of a rock formation that he knew was about thirty feet below the cave. At their current pace, he estimated that they could make it in another twenty minutes or so.

Step by step, the family made their way up the hill. Slowly but surely, the rock formation came into sharper focus, and he could now vaguely see the cave itself. Suddenly, he heard his son give a shout.

"Look!" Ignacio cried. All looked up to see a number of felled trees, clumped together, extending over the crest of the hill. Time stood still as the typhoon's tremendous winds pushed the trees, several feet at a time, over the edge.

Once they went, they fell fast, smashing down into the first terrace, dislodging a number of large rocks that came crashing down about ten feet away from where they stood. The wind then caught the trees again, and they rolled over the terrace wall, ripping it open in the process, and allowing all of the water pooled within to rush down the next terrace pool below.

Dabert saw what was about to happen. "Hurry!" he yelled, "quickly, follow me!"

He took a number of steps up the hill, then began climbing away from the steps toward the cave and away from the collapsing terraces. Ignacio followed, with Rowena behind him, but moving slowly.

A new mass of mud, rocks and logs came over the top of the hill, and slid down following the path of the trees. The terraces were now disintegrating from the middle outward, as the mudslide pulled more and more material down the slope level by level. Dabert, Myla on his back, had turned to gauge his wife and son's progress, and realized that Rowena was in danger of being pulled down by the slide.

"Ignacio; your mother!" Dabert yelled. Ignacio turned around and saw the danger his mother was in. He climbed back down several steps to offer her a hand. She reached out and grabbed it just as the rocks beneath her feet gave way. Dabert tried to unlock his daughter's hands so that he could leave her where they were standing and help the others, but she immediately tightened her grip. With no other choice, he started down towards his son with Myla attached. Ignacio pulled with all his strength, but the steps beneath his feet were now starting to come loose as well.

"Dabert!" cried Rowena, wild-eyed and desperate. He arrived just in time to grab Ignacio's arm as the boy started sliding down the hill with his mother. They now formed a chain, with Dabert holding Ignacio holding Rowena. Dabert took a step up the hill, pulling the other two with him. Then another step.

It wasn't clear whether Rowena loosened her grip or if Ignacio could no longer hold on, but with a scream she fell backward into the disintegrating hillside. Ignacio immediately lunged downward to try and catch her, and inadvertently pulled his arm out from his father's grasp. The boy fell after his mother. A horrible scream reached up from the falling bodies. Dabert watched, incredulous, as they quickly slid further down the hill, and merged with the accelerating mudslide.

And that was it. They both were gone, consumed by the massive flow of sliding rocks and mud.

Dabert stood, stunned. His brain was numb; any conscious thought made impossible by a thick cloud of emotion and despair that multiplied within his head until it physically hurt. His muscles twitched instinctively, wanting desperately to lurch headlong into the slide, to save his wife and son—but held back by some inner mechanism that understood futility, that recognized the important and fragile life upon his back.

His eyes hurt, as pressure built; then, an explosion of tears rushed forth, only to be washed away by the pelting rain. He remained frozen, utterly paralyzed by the loss of his family—the loss of his loving and caring wife; his growing son, who would soon have become a man by his side; and the loss of all the years ahead, all of the moments in which the family would work together, eat together, share a house, and feel each other's love.

Dabert felt incredibly weak. The temptation to simply crumple in place and give himself up to the storm that had just so violently ripped his family in half was overwhelming. His life was now of little value; all that he'd built, all that he'd worked for seemed so completely meaningless as he looked down at his lost wife and son.

Little Myla, who had surely heard her mother and brother fall away, pulled herself up on her father's torso, tightening her grip around his neck with her arms and around his waist with her legs. She had not once moved her head to look down the hill. Instead, amid the cacophonous mayhem of shouts and the rain and whipping winds, she had squeezed her eyes shut as hard as she could, and simply clung to her father with every ounce of strength her little body could offer.

Myla's movement reawakened a part of Dabert's brain, forcing him to realize that his life was not entirely his to give away. His daughter was alive, she needed him, and he had to do everything in his power to bring her to safety.

Slowly, painfully pulling his eyes from the spot where he last saw Rowena and Ignacio, he turned and began a careful climb upward towards the cave.

55

Thirty-six hours after the storm had hit, blue sky could be seen between the storm's remaining clouds. The most violent cyclone ever witnessed by civilized man had passed.

But the calming blue skies above were in stark contrast to the near total devastation below. The island of Luzon had experienced damage beyond anyone's expectations. Over a thousand villages had been flattened, the infrastructure that supported them—and connected them—destroyed. The landscape appeared as if bulldozed, with wreckage evenly spread across the ground where homes and fields and plantations and schools and hospitals and businesses had stood just a short time ago.

Mother nature had not spared her own: the deforestation throughout central Luzon was staggering. Most of the trees still standing had been sheared of their leaves, stalks protruding awkwardly up from an unending mass of logs and branches—their fallen brethren. In countless areas, the earth had simply given way, leaving large brown scars where landslides had occurred.

Across Manila, flooding and high winds had left huge swaths of the city decimated, with the majority of structures complete destroyed, and another sizable percentage badly damaged, many well beyond repair. The wreckage was everywhere; the entire city looked like one massive debris field.

A small number of intrepid Filipinos had ventured out, many in boats or on makeshift rafts, to inspect the aftermath. Rescue workers emerged, some doing their best to resupply evacuation centers; others inspecting infrastructure, making decisions as to where power might be restored, and which cell towers might be repaired so as to allow loved ones to find one another.

While the tragic loss of property was visible from every vantage point, the greater tragedy, loss of human life, was still mostly hidden. Within the endless debris, there were hundreds of corpses visible to those surveying the scene, but this was only the tip of the iceberg. It would be days, weeks—even months— before all of the bodies had been found. Initial estimates were that between twelve to fifteen thousand people may have lost their lives in the storm.

But all knew that this was just a preliminary guess.

56

Taylor was seated at his desk, scrolling through photographs of Isabel's devastation, and reading news reports. He was not one to spend a lot of time online—and certainly had plenty of other things to worry about, but the typhoon had dominated the U.S. news cycle in a way that no pacific storm ever had before. Not only was the magnitude of the impact difficult to even contemplate, but the sheer scale and power of the cyclone itself had rewritten the book on what many scientists thought possible.

Of course, in the back of Taylor's mind was the nagging knowledge that such a display of Mother Nature's wrath would inevitably draw more sympathizers from the lunatic fringe to the GOC's cause, and lead many sane-minded voices to advocate for appeasement. Both of which he found infuriating.

Tori knocked once on the sidelight window next to his door and walked in. "Drake. I've got something. I think it could be big." She stopped short and studied him for a long moment. It was clear that he hadn't shaved in a couple of days, and when he turned to look at Tori, the bags under his eyes were pronounced. "Hey, when was the last time you slept?"

"Not important," he replied, managing a meager smile. Tori was a welcome and pleasing sight in contrast to the haunting photographs of Isabel. "What have you got? Please tell me it's good-big and not bad-big."

Tori gave it some thought before responding. "It's big, a little tragic, but it may be a huge opportunity; I'd say good-big."

"Alright, shoot."

"We were just notified by Australia's Secret Intelligence Service that they have Ryan Walker's daughter."

"Daughter? Did we even know he had a daughter?"

"I should have said estranged daughter, but that's no excuse. Somehow we missed it—as did Australian intelligence. Anyway, her name is Sophie Walker; she was carjacked trying to leave Melbourne, and is now in the hospital. Pretty banged up, but they think she'll be okay."

"Holy shit!"

"Wait, it gets better. She has a son—Walker's grandson."

"Wow." Taylor leaned back in his chair, his mind working the angles on how this might play into their investigation.

"Though we don't have all the details, it looks like Walker reconnected with her a month or two before we captured him. I had our friends at the NSA do a quick analysis of their phone records, and it appears that they spoke at least once for nearly forty-five minutes."

"You were right—this could be big. Is she able to talk?"

"She's been in an induced coma for the past 48 hours, but the doctors plan to bring her out of it in the morning—which, for us, is later tonight."

"Tori, do we have anyone we could send in from that part of the world?"

"I can check, but the folks at ASIS seem pretty capable. I'm not sure that shoving our—"

"Tori, Australia's Secret Intelligence Service missed the fact that the guy had a daughter! You're saying you trust them to handle this?"

"Yes, I'm saying I trust them to at least go the first round or two. Besides, Drake, we have no authority to take point on this. She's an Australian citizen on Australian soil."

"Fair enough. We can get recordings of their interrogation?"

"I'll make sure we do—or at least transcripts."

"I want both."

"I'll take care of it; don't worry."

"Good." Taylor rubbed his eyes, trying to force moisture into them. Though a number of thoughts streamed through his mind, one was foremost. "I guess I'll need to head back to the USS Bainbridge and pay Mr. Walker another visit."

"I think that sounds like the right plan," said Tori. "I think if we play this card right, we have at least a small shot at getting him to open up."

"That's what I'm hoping." Ideas and possibilities still flowing through his brain, he absentmindedly looked again at his monitor, and was brought back to the appalling devastation of Isabel/Benito. He stared, then reached his hand to his mouse and flipped through several additional photographs.

"Absolutely horrific," Tori said softly, looking over his shoulder. "I was looking at the coverage earlier. It's almost impossible to comprehend."

"It really is." Tori was leaning in, her face close to his. The fresh, alluring smell of her perfume momentarily distracted and relaxed him, clouding out other thoughts. *Get it together,* Taylor told himself.

"I just wish there was something we could do," she said, pulling her head back and standing up straight.

He smiled grimly. "I think there is; we can catch the bastards behind the GOC threat, and prevent equally horrific coverage of a nuclear blast in some major city."

"Of course. But it's so ironic that—"

"I know, I know," he turned and looked up at her. "It kills me that they are using that storm to make their case."

Sunlight streaming in through the window seemed to illuminate Taylor's green eyes. Tori hesitated slightly before responding. "I can't say I blame them. Isabel played right into their hand."

"It sure as hell did, and I'm sick about it," Taylor said, turning back to his monitor.

Tori placed her hand on his shoulder. "We're making progress, Drake. They may score a few points with their little speech, but we'll get 'em."

As Tori pulled her hand away, Taylor turned to face her again and changed the subject. "Hey, can I run something by you?"

"Sure."

"In my first session with Walker, he was more than willing to talk about the GOC's motivation; in fact, I sensed that you could have probably kept the guy talking for days about anything related to climate." He leaned forward. "I'm not willing to commit just yet, but I'd like your opinion: What do you think about possibly taking Ellie with me for the next session?"

Tori leaned against the door jam, and narrowed her eyes. "I think it could work. You'd certainly have to establish ground rules ahead of time."

"Okay. I'll discuss it with her. Please keep this between us until I do."

"Understood." Tori pushed away from the door jam, and turned to go—then turned back. "You know, Drake, you could always take Nate Verit with you as well. I'm sure he'd love to get more face time with Ellie."

Taylor snapped his head around, and saw that she'd been smiling as she said it. "I suppose I could," he replied, grinning. "But I think if he got too excited by the conversation, we might lose him to the other side."

They both laughed, and Tori headed back to her office.

57

The deadline set by the Guardians of Civilization was now just 13 days away. With all major cities suspect, people had begun to flee urban areas on a massive scale, creating tremendous strain on smaller municipalities and rural towns. Doomsdayists were making final preparations before retreating into their bunkers with righteous resignation. Governments urged calm, but as often as not such advice was categorically ignored in favor of either panic or paralysis.

However, as news emerged from the Philippines, there seemed to be a temporary lull in the pandemonium. The initial death toll released a day after the storm passed had been way off—lives confirmed lost on the island of Luzon now exceeded 35 thousand, with another 60 thousand people reported as missing, and more bodies being discovered every hour.

The size and force of a typhoon did not always correlate to loss of life. Prior to Isabel/Benito, the strongest storm on record had been Haiyan/Yolanda, a category 5 super typhoon with 1 minute sustained winds of 195 mph that ravaged Southeast Asia in 2013, killing over 6,000 people—many of whom were inhabitants of the Philippine city of Tacloban. Whereas

Typhoon Nina, with lesser winds of 155 mph, killed nearly 230 thousand people in China in 1975.

Given the advances in forecasting and communications, it had been hoped that the death toll would be lower. However, Isabel/Benito's huge diameter and punishing winds left many residents of the island with virtually nowhere to hide, while the torrent of water—a record 73 inches of rain over 36 hours—created rushing flood waters not just in cities and low-lying areas, but throughout inland towns and mountain villages as well. In essence, for the duration of the storm, the entire island of Luzon had become a death zone, where survival was determined by several factors—the most important of which seemed to be luck.

While Isabel's status as the largest storm in recorded history had initially grabbed the world's attention, the resulting media coverage of the devastation left in its wake had grabbed its hearts and pocketbooks. Even at a time when large cities worldwide were under a dire terrorist threat, the Philippines received an outpouring of goodwill—including millions of contributions from individuals and generous offers of aid from dozens of countries. All of this was instrumental in getting supplies and resources to those in need. Nonetheless, whatever was sent was not enough. In addition to the rising death toll, over 15 million people had been displaced—nearly a third of the island's population.

For anyone who didn't pay much attention to this part of the world, it was brought home in media reports that the Philippines had steadily become a poster child for the devastating effects of a warming planet. Mean temperatures had been rising significantly faster than the global average. In addition, although there had been an increase in rainfall since the 1980s, the island nation had also experienced some of the worst droughts in its history over the past quarter-century—decimating crops, lowering the water table and resulting in the rationing of fresh water. Experts predicted that future extreme weather would decrease food production and yields, and cause further land erosion. Off the coast, the bleaching of coral reefs was likely to accelerate, resulting in the loss of fisheries—and the loss of tourism dollars generated from the bright blue tropical waters that surrounded the Philippine archipelago.

Unlike the United States and many European nations, where changing weather patterns had so far impacted the lives of only a small percentage of people, climate change in the Philippines was an ongoing battle waged daily by its residents. Surveys indicated that Filipinos rated global warming as a bigger threat than rising food and fuel prices. The issue had become an all-hands-on-deck challenge to government, industry and inhabitants alike; many considered it an "existential threat," arguing vehemently for better storm warning systems, stricter building codes, more evacuation centers and other aggressive adaptation measures.

In the absence of such action, many believed that the Philippines would lose its already fragile hold on a future of economic viability; others believed that, without aggressive investment in infrastructure to protect against the perils of global warming, the island nation might well become uninhabitable altogether.

58

"**D**rake, you do know that I'm a trained interrogator," Ellie reminded Taylor as they approached the helicopter. The wash from the slowing rotors whipped strands of Ellie's long dark hair around her face; she batted them back impatiently. They had just driven from the Nebraska Avenue Complex to CIA headquarters in Langley, Virginia—the nearest heliport to DHS.

"Yes, I do know that—and I trust you, or you wouldn't be here," said Taylor. "But once we're in there with him, it's very important that we don't step on each other's toes."

"You're the boss, and you're in charge. I will follow your lead; I won't head down any path you don't want me to, and I'll shut up whenever you give me the signal."

"Good. Sorry to go back over this again, but we won't have a lot of chances with this guy, and I want to make sure we make the most of it." Taylor looked over at Ellie; he'd gone with his instincts and brought her along, and now hoped like hell it was the right decision.

Once the rotors came to a full stop, the co-pilot stepped out of the H-60 and opened the rear door. Ellie then Taylor climbed in, buckled up and put on their earphones as the he-lo's rotors re-engaged.

They were soon passing over the suburbs north of Washington, DC, heading towards Annapolis. From there, they would head south down the Chesapeake Bay for the ninety-minute ride over open waters to the deck of the USS Bainbridge.

59

Walker looked like hell.

He was no longer in sick bay, having been transferred the previous week to a detention cell, which held only a cot, a sink and a toilet. For the session with Taylor and Ellie, he'd been moved to a separate cabin.

Taylor looked through the small round porthole in the door, and could see that Walker's right eye was nearly swollen shut—his other looked tired and bloodshot. His hair was greasy and disheveled, as was his orange jumpsuit. He sat in a metal chair, leaning back, with his right arm still in a sling and resting on a small, square metal table. His left leg, which appeared to have a fresh cast, was propped up on one of three other chairs in the cabin. His right leg was still in a leg iron, this time shackled to a secure eyelet in the steel plate that comprised the floor.

Taylor had read the reports, and knew that whatever enhanced interrogation techniques had been used on Walker had been unsuccessful. As was the case during their previous session, Walker was initially willing to talk about his views and motivations, but offered nothing when interrogators asked for information on the GOC, and then shut up completely when harsh techniques were employed. As a result, they had precisely zero hard information over and above what Taylor had extracted during his last visit.

A guard punched in a combination on a keypad, opened the heavy metal cabin door, and Taylor and Ellie entered. The sound startled Walker, he quickly pulled his leg off of the other chair and sat up.

"Ryan, good to see you again. Drake Taylor." He extended his left hand; Walker looked at it for a half second, then offered his own.

"I remember you, Mr. Taylor," Walker replied in his native Australian accent. He seemed a bit slow; perhaps just sleep deprived, but Taylor wasn't sure.

"And this is Ellie Alder, a colleague of mine." Ellie said hello and also extended her left hand; she received the same weak, uncertain handshake. She wore a conservative brown pantsuit, while Taylor had on a pair of khakis and a windbreaker, which he took off and placed on the back of a chair.

"It looks like some of your recent visitors may have been a little unfriendly. Let me assure you that our intent today is just to talk."

"That's good to hear."

"I saw that you pulled your leg down as we walked in. Would you prefer to have it up?" Taylor asked.

"I'd like that. Thanks." Walker carefully put his leg back up on the chair to his left. As Taylor and Ellie took seats in the remaining two chairs, the metal legs screeched as they dragged along the floor. Taylor sat directly across the square table from the detainee.

"Looks like you've got a new cast; problems with the leg?" Taylor asked.

"Seems your friends managed to smash the last one. Otherwise, the leg's just dandy," Walker replied. Ellie shot a glance at Taylor—who now wished he hadn't asked.

"Okay, let's jump in. Ryan, I'd like to go back a few years, and ask some questions regarding your past. Would that be okay with you?"

"I suppose so," Walker replied, his eyes listless.

"Let's start with your time in Sydney when you were a kid."

"If you like."

"Tell me about high school"

"Fair dinkum, Mr. Taylor? We're gonna do this?"

"Yes, we are." In truth, Taylor would have much preferred not to do this; but he knew that their only chance of getting anything from Walker was to reestablish a modicum of trust, and let him relax a bit. Therefore, he and Ellie had consciously decided to start by engaging him on topics completely unrelated to the GOC.

Walker sighed. "Alright then. I guess you could say high school was a bit of a blur."

"Did you enjoy it?"

"Not really. Had a few friends, but was pretty much a screw-up."

"Did you do well in school—gradewise?"

Walker chuckled. "Hell no."

"When did you first think about joining the Defence Force?"

"Let's just say the suggestion started popping up when it was clear I was unlikely to attend university."

"Did you want to go?"

"To university?"

"No, the ADF."

"Then? Not one bit; last thing I wanted to do."

"When did you first give thought to actually signing up?"

Walker looked down at the table, and seemed to be recollecting that period of his life. He said nothing for several moments, then lifted his head up and looked at Taylor. "I'm not sure. I made so many bloody mistakes back then; seems like enlisting was the only way out."

"Ryan, when we chatted a week or so ago, you noted that joining the ADF was 'the best bloody thing you ever did.' Yet later in our conversation, you made it awfully clear that you were quite disillusioned by your life in the service. Help me understand that."

"Pretty simple, really. My life was a total mess before joining the army; enlisting saved my arse. And for quite a few years, it was the best family I'd ever had—actually, the only real family I ever had. It wasn't that I soured on the SAS; I became totally disenchanted with the bloody wars we were fighting. They were bullshit."

Taylor put a hand over his mouth and cleared his throat.

Ellie leaned forward. "You mentioned family; what prevented you from having a close relationship with your parents?" she asked.

Walker turned to Ellie, not entirely sure what she was doing there, but still willing to talk provided no one was demanding information on his GOC colleagues. "That's an easy one. My father was an alkie. My mother was nice enough, but when Dad would drink and get rough with me, she'd pretend to ignore it. I could never forgive her for that."

"I know a little something about that," Taylor interjected, but offered nothing more.

"So when did you leave home?" Ellie asked.

"It was a gradual process, I suppose. As I got a little older, I started spending more and more nights with my mates, and eventually just stopped coming home."

"Did you get your own apartment?"

"Not for a while—pretty much wore out my welcome with my friends' parents, but I think they understood. It wasn't until I had a steady girl that I got my own place."

"Did you have a job then?"

"Yeah. I did construction, mostly roadwork. We'd cut up a street, dig a hole, replace a pipe or some such, then patch it up. Bloody hard yakka."

"Yakka?"

"Tough work."

"The girl—was this the one you married?"

"Yeah." Walker sighed. "Quite a sheila; a real bludger."

"Sorry?"

"Oh. Always looking for a handout. Didn't do a damn thing to help herself."

"Any regrets that you didn't try to stick it out?"

"In the marriage?"

"Yes."

"Blimey, no. I got out of that as fast as I could. We got married for all the wrong reasons, and fought constantly. I really don't think it would have been much good for either of us if we'd kept it going."

There was a knock on the door. Taylor got up and walked over to see an officer waiting. A guard opened the locked cabin door from outside, and he stepped out, holding it behind him to prevent it from closing.

"Yes?" he asked.

"Mr. Taylor, you have a call from Secretary Hawthorne. He says it's urgent."

Taylor was annoyed. He looked back at Ellie and Walker through the glass, considering whether to leave them, pause the interrogation, or have the officer tell Hawthorne he'd call him back. "Did you tell the Secretary I was conducting an interrogation?"

"Yes sir. He insisted on speaking with you."

Taylor thought about it some more, and stuck his head back in. "Ellie, I have an important call I have to take. Please carry on without me." Ellie nodded her understanding. Taylor let the cabin door close and lock behind him as he followed the officer down the passageway, nervous about leaving her in charge.

Ellie used his departure as an opportunity to switch gears; she didn't think anyone was ready for the finale just yet. "So Ryan, when did you become so interested in climate change?" she asked, hoping her nervousness was not evident to the detainee.

"There was no specific event, but while I was fighting in Afghanistan and Iraq, I started to give thought to how many wars we were going to fight in the future, and how many more of my comrades were going to die for questionable causes."

"It was your belief that the wars in Iraq and Afghanistan were questionable?"

"It sure as hell wasn't the defeat of fascism." Walker tilted his head and looked at Ellie. "May I ask you a question?" he asked.

Ellie was a bit taken aback, but only for a second. "Sure— no promises that I'll answer, but go ahead."

"Do you know what percent of coalition casualties occurred while protecting fuel convoys?"

"Actually, I think I might. Something like 1 soldier killed for every 24 convoys? Which I believe, in Afghanistan at least, translates to 35% of all army casualties."

This time Walker was a bit taken aback, but Ellie didn't give him a chance to respond. "I also know that one U.S. marine combat brigade uses over half a million gallons of fuel per day; that our military's operational energy bill was over $11 billion in 2010; that fuel accounts for half of the supplies carried by our armed forces; and that the logistical tail created when we move all that fuel to the front makes us very, very vulnerable."

Walker was clearly impressed; Ellie silently congratulated herself for finally reading Verit's thesis two days prior.

"But that's all about energy, Ryan. Definitely related to global warming, but a different beast."

"Is it? I'm not so sure. All of that energy—consumed by both the military and everyone else—will put more soldiers in harm's way than anyone could have even contemplated just a decade or two ago. The wars may be regional or global; they may be about water, about refugees, or about oil. But no matter how you slice it, there will be a shitload of armed conflict as a result of fossil fuels and their impact on civilization."

"I don't entirely disagree with you," Ellie responded, "but I certainly don't condone threatening half of the world's population with nuclear mayhem as the solution."

Walker let this go. He slowly lifted his left leg with his right hand, adjusting its position on the chair; it was clearly causing him pain. When finished, he looked back at Ellie.

"It's Ms. Alder, right?"

"Yes," Ellie replied.

"Have you ever been to Australia?"

"I have not."

"My country is in deep trouble, Ms. Alder. When I made my way back there after leaving Iraq, I was amazed. Iraq was hot, damn hot. But you know what? Australia isn't much better. My home town of Sydney has seen high temperatures of nearly 115 degrees—in a coastal city! Not long ago, in Oodnadatta, north of Adelaide, it was reported that motorists couldn't fuel their cars because the petrol would bloody evaporate before it entered the tank. Eight of the hottest ten summers on record have occurred since 1990—our meteorologists have added two new colors to our weather maps just to keep up."

"Ryan, I'm actually quite familiar with the data. I know a lot more than I'm letting on about how that heat translates into wildfires and higher storm intensity. I truly understand Australia's predicament, and fully appreciate that what we've just seen in the Philippines is symptomatic, but—"

"What about the Philippines?"

Ellie scolded herself for her carelessness. Her brain raced to come up with an evasive response, but faltered.

"What happened in the Philippines—a typhoon?" Walker guessed.

She thought about ignoring the question, but their strategy depended on building relationship and trust. "Yes, a typhoon," she admitted.

"A big one?"

"Yes, fairly big," she lied, wanting to move on. "But Ryan, any impact it might have had was lost in the media circus of your group's nuclear threat," she lied again.

"Ms. Alder, with all due respect, your media doesn't give a damn about typhoons in the western Pacific. Neither does your government, for that matter."

They care about this one, Ellie thought to herself. "Fair enough. But Ryan, have you given any thought to the panic you're causing?"

Walker turned his head away, tired of the conversation before it started. "People should be panicked, Ms. Alder—by the man-made threat they helped create."

She sensed that this would not be a fruitful path, so decided that, with or without Taylor, this was as good a time as any to play their trump card. "I assume you anticipated that people would flee major cities in advance of the GOC's deadline?"

"That did occur to me."

"People are moving out of cities en masse, and it's not pretty."

"I'm sure it's mayhem, but—"

"Ryan, let me tell you a story."

He was silent, so Ellie continued. "Several days ago, a young woman prepared to leave her city apartment. She loaded the car, put her toddler in the back seat, and began the journey to somewhere she thought would be safe." Ellie paused to make sure she had Walker's attention. "But given the growing lawlessness out there, things didn't quite go as planned. The woman and her son had made it only a few blocks when a couple of thugs attacked her car at a stoplight, carjacked the vehicle, and dumped the woman and child out the side door as they drove away."

Walker looked at her without saying anything, looking neither interested nor bored by her story. It wasn't clear whether he had any idea of what he was about to hear.

"You with me so far?"

"I'm with you, but I really don't see—

"Ryan," Ellie said forcefully. "The city they were fleeing was Melbourne. The woman's name was Sophie."

She watched as the features of Walker's face went slack. "That's right—Sophie Walker, your daughter," she said, "and the toddler was your grandson."

Walker stared—not at Ellie, but at the picture she'd just painted for him. She remained silent, and saw tears start to form in the corners of his eyes.

Ellie quietly grabbed her bag, Taylor's briefcase and windbreaker, and walked to the door. She signaled the guard, then turned back to Walker. "They're both alive, Ryan. But what happens to them from here on out, and whether you ever get a chance to see them, is entirely in your hands."

The guard opened the door, and Ellie walked out.

60

"I don't understand, Drake; back up a bit. You're saying this general wanted us to end up with the nuke? Why?" Ellie suddenly felt very confused and somewhat out of her league.

"We don't know why; that's what we have to find out." He leaned into the speakerphone. "And Tori—"

"I'm on it, Drake. I've already drafted the paperwork to have our team take command of the lab in Guam—including the nuke, and to hold the lab manager and his staff for questioning. As soon as you get it signed by the Secretary, we're good to go."

"Tori, let's not waste any time; send it to him directly, noting that you've talked to me."

"Will do."

"And what about the guy we sent over there?" Taylor asked.

"Yup. He'll be in my office in an hour."

Taylor and Ellie were in a private cabin on the Bainbridge, with Tori looped in through a secure satellite connection. The call from Hawthorne had indeed been urgent; the Secretary had just heard from the Chinese Minister of National Defense that an officer in the People's Liberation Army, a General

Sheng, had committed suicide. The general left behind a cryptic note confessing that he'd allowed himself to be blackmailed into helping the U.S. gain control over the Shanghai operation.

"Drake, are we going to get a copy of the note?" Tori asked.

"I'm not sure."

"Did it say who blackmailed him, or what they had on the general?"

"I don't think so, but these are the right questions, Tori. Let's catalogue them and send the list to Hawthorne, so he can work them with the Chinese, or direct us to someone we can work with on our own."

"Got it."

He paced back and forth in the small cabin, thinking through the various puzzle pieces, trying to get them all to fit together in his mind—but they refused to cooperate.

"Tori, let's add a few items to the list: We need to know whether General Sheng ever had contact with anyone in the Australian Special Air Service, or with anyone in the British Royal Marines—especially that guy Walker befriended..."

"Harrison," said Tori.

"Right, Harrison. Also—and we can do this ourselves—let's find out if our SOF teams have conducted any joint exercises with the Chinese over the past decade, and see if we can determine whether Sheng was involved in any way."

"Got it."

Taylor shook his head. "The answers are out there; let's push hard on this stuff."

"Understood, Drake," said Tori. "Half my team is now sleeping at the NAC; no one's letting up."

"Good. Tori, you have my authorization to bring in dinners, offer car services, laundry services—hell, even a masseuse. Whatever you think will make everyone feel valued, and keep them fully engaged."

"Thanks, Drake. They'll appreciate that."

"Okay. Ellie: Let's focus on Walker. Where do things stand?"

"Well, I can't attest to his current state of mind, but his reaction to the news regarding his daughter and grandson was visceral; it hit him hard. I think he's ready for the next step."

"Alright, let's get to it. Tori, I'll call you as soon as we're out."

"Sounds good; I'll be here."

61

The black Town Car sped along the Whitehurst Freeway, finally slowing as it approached the light at M Street in Georgetown.

"So, what's on your mind, John?" Bob Baker asked, after they'd covered various other topics—including the Redskins, the weather, and the useless meeting they'd both just attended at the State Department. Morgan had asked if he could ride back to McLean with Baker so that they might discuss a sensitive issue.

"Well, this is a fairly delicate matter," Morgan began. The car turned right on M, and then took an immediate right onto Key Bridge.

"Fire away. Nothing happens in this town without a little broken glass," Baker offered. "What's the issue?"

Morgan paused briefly, looking out his window at the Potomac below. He turned back to Baker. "One of my analysts has uncovered some information indicating that Drake Taylor may have been compromised."

Baker stared at Morgan. "What?" he asked. "What the hell do you mean by 'compromised'?"

"It appears as if he's been withholding data critical to the investigation, and may, in fact, be a sympathizer."

Baker said nothing for a moment, studying Morgan's face. "When you say 'sympathizer,' you mean you actually believe he's working for the Guardians of Civilization?"

"I'm not sure if he's actively working for them, but I do believe that he may support their cause. As such, his investigation may not be as vigorous as it should be."

"John, this is an awfully big accusation you're making. What's your evidence?"

"Were you aware that Taylor and the GOC detainee, Ryan Walker, served together in Afghanistan?"

"No, I was not. Walker's Australian—he's SAS, isn't he?"

"Yes. Walker and several other SAS commandos actually saved Taylor's life during Operation Anaconda in Afghanistan."

"When was that?"

"2002."

"Was this in any of Taylor's reports?" Baker asked.

"I don't believe so."

"Did they know each other at the time, or communicate thereafter?" Baker asked.

"We don't know. We're trying to find that out."

Baker was more than a little surprised, but knew full well that all of this did not constitute real evidence. "What else have you got?"

"I'm guessing you're aware that he hired Ellie Alder, an ex-ecoterrorist, to consult on the investigation?"

"Yes, I did know that. What of it?"

"Did you know that she met with Alan Stewart?"

"Who's he?"

"A convicted ecoterrorist who did time for blowing up an abandoned building."

Baker absorbed this; his eyes narrowed on Morgan. "Was the meeting documented?" he finally asked.

"Not to my knowledge."

"And you know this how?"

"Stewart is connected to a woman named Bella Knobloch, another known terrorist who'd been under surveillance by some folks at the DIA. There's a theory that she may somehow be connected to the GOC. Phone records indicate that, both before and after the meeting with Ellie Alder, Stewart spoke with Knobloch—each time for more than 10 minutes. We think Stewart may have passed on intelligence he received from Alder regarding the investigation."

Baker was clearly bothered by what he was hearing, but he'd also been in the intelligence game for a long time, and knew better than to jump to any conclusions based on circumstantial information. However, he was also a political animal through and through; he was no fan of Dan Hawthorne, and more than a little pissed off that the President had put DHS on point instead of the CIA. Hearing that Taylor was under suspicion didn't exactly upset him.

"One more thing," said Morgan.

"What?"

"This is still a little murky, but we have reason to believe that the nuclear device extracted from Shanghai was a fake, that Drake Taylor knows it, and that he's withheld this information from Hawthorne, the President, and the entire intelligence community."

"Holy shit." Baker was shocked. If that was true, it was huge. "What's your source?"

"The lab manager in Guam, responsible for analyzing the nuke, suggested as much to me over the phone last night. For some reason, he clammed up as soon as he said it, and wouldn't elaborate. I'm going to talk to him again tonight."

"Why didn't you have him taken into custody?" Baker asked.

"On what grounds? He was trying to tell me something, but clearly got cold feet. Attempting to force his hand could shut him up forever; my instincts are to have him come around on his own."

Baker's brain was moving quickly. If everything Morgan had told him was true, then there was clearly enough here to raise the issue with the President—he sure as hell wasn't going to take it to Hawthorne. But it was a very big if. "John, are you willing to put everything you've told me in writing, and to stand behind it personally?"

"Absolutely," Morgan replied firmly.

"Good. I'd like to get something from you as soon as possible, including any updates from your man in Guam."

"Understood. Give me 24 hours; I'll have it hand-delivered."

"Perfect." Baker turned to look out the window, his mind still churning on the implications of all this.

"You know, it just occurred me that—" Morgan stopped himself. "Actually, never mind."

"What?" Baker asked. "Tell me what you were going to say."

"Well, it's speculation, but if Taylor did put a lid on the bomb analysis in Guam, then the disappearance of those two scientists from Los Alamos may have been his doing as well."

"Holy shit," Baker repeated.

62

"You're saying I'll get to see her face to face?" Walker asked.

"You have my word," Taylor confirmed.

"Alone?"

"I can't guarantee that."

"Can the boy come along as well?"

"Don't think that'll be a problem."

There was a long silence as Walker gave serious thought to what was being offered. His decision could have a transformative impact on his daughter's life. No one had threatened to harm Sophie or her son if Walker didn't cooperate; in fact, they'd done the opposite. The deal was that, if Walker refused to cooperate, she'd be delivered right back to the Footscray area of Melbourne, where she'd resume her miserable, hardscrabble life—and he'd never see her or be allowed to communicate with her ever again. However, if he offered up what he knew, she'd be given a decent job, a nice apartment in a prosperous neighborhood with good schools nearby, and—painfully important to Walker—he would be able to see her up to four times a year.

Putting the deal in place had been quite an undertaking. Taylor and Tori had to work it through senior levels of the Australian government and the ADF, then through key members of the U.S. administration as well. Once again, Secretary Hawthorne had to battle the CIA, who felt that this was capitulation; given time, Central Intelligence was sure their team could break Walker without the need for any such concessions. Taylor argued to Hawthorne behind the scenes that they couldn't spare any more time; he also offered that, if Walker didn't go along with this plan, then the CIA could take full and complete control of Walker's interrogation from here on out. Eventually, Hawthorne prevailed, and Taylor and Ellie scheduled another session with Walker to see if they could pull this off.

They were back in the same cabin, sitting around the same stark metal table. Only this time, Walker had been given a shower and a fresh jumpsuit, and seemed more alert than he had hours earlier.

"How do I know you'll keep your end of the bargain, Mr. Taylor?

This was exactly the kind of question Taylor wanted to hear Walker ask. They were very close to getting him to talk. "Ryan, on my honor as a fellow soldier, I promise you that your government and mine both agreed to these terms, and that I will personally see to it that they are upheld."

"And what if you decide my information isn't enough?"

"We've already covered this; if your information materially advances our investigation, then we'll honor the deal. But if, at any point in time, we discover that you've lied or withheld information, then the deal's off."

Another very long silence. Taylor was tempted to fill the void with persuasive arguments as to why Walker should cooperate, but he sensed he'd be better off letting the Australian convince himself.

Unfortunately, despite being told to remain quiet, Ellie couldn't resist injecting a plea into the silence. "Ryan, you said yourself that the world is already thinking differently about the need to address the climate crisis; in a sense, you've already succeeded."

Walker's silent deliberation came to an abrupt end. "Pardon my language, Ms. Alder, but that's bullshit and you know it." came Walker's immediate reply. "There are still plenty of powerful people with their heads buried deep in the bloody sand. I don't think for a minute that we've managed to wake them up. But we will—I promise you that."

Taylor was furious at the distraction; he crossed his arms, giving Ellie the agreed upon signal that she was to stop talking. She ignored it.

"I don't disagree that there are many, many heads still in the sand," Ellie shot back, "but you and I both know that any major action on this issue is going to happen only when the people demand it—when the deniers run out of constituents and have nowhere to turn." Somehow, Walker was listening, and Ellie continued. "There's something I didn't tell you during our earlier session; the typhoon that hit the Philippines wasn't just big, it was the largest typhoon in human history—"

"Ellie!" Taylor said sharply, imploring her to shut up.

"Drake, he needs to hear this!" she responded, but kept her focus on Walker. "Between the GOC's threat and a death toll of over 35 thousand on the island of Luzon, this world has had a crash course on the dangers of climate change. If you blow up multiple cities and kill half a million people, you are going to turn a rising tide in precisely the wrong direction."

Ellie's face was red. "Ryan, I know a little something about this. Believe it or not, before I entered counter-terrorism, I was an activist with Earth First! The impact your group has had is already the envy of the eco-terrorist community; you've generated more awareness than anyone could have imagined was possible. If you care as deeply about this issue as you say you do, then you must realize that following through on your plan is probably the very best way to undue all of the awareness and momentum that you've generated."

Yet another silence—this one so complete, Taylor could again hear the creaking of the ship echoing through the metal hull. But Ellie wasn't quite finished.

"Please listen to me: If you detonate nuclear devices in major cities, you will hand back to the deniers all of their previous constituents and then some. You will empower them with everything they need to block a meaningful solution for decades to come. Please don't allow that. Help us put a stop to this now and you'll not only better serve the cause that drove you to act, you'll secure a promising future for your daughter and grandson."

Taylor studied Walker, who seemed to be giving full consideration to Ellie's heated remarks. He was beyond angry that Ellie had ignored his signal; in his world, she'd disobeyed a direct order. She was also selling past the close, offering her thoughts just when Walker was about to take him up on the offer. To Taylor, Ellie seemed much too sympathetic with the GOC's position. However, as he looked at Walker, who was looking down at the table deep in thought, he still wasn't sure whether her sympathies had helped or hurt their objective.

Slowly, Walker raised his head and looked Taylor in the eye. "Okay, I'll tell you what I know. I just hope it's enough."

63

President Gilman had quietly made significant progress in hatching a new home-grown carbon treaty to replace the one that the Guardians of Civilization had sought to ram down the world's throat.

After a difficult start, he had successfully engaged President Wei Xiaoming of China and President Mahendra Rafi of India, and the three—after much deliberation, were finally nearing consensus. Initially, the U.S. President had told no one on his staff of the ongoing effort; but as the document evolved, he carefully selected a small team to help him think through a few of the stickier issues. Key among them was a senior member of his Council of Economic Advisors, and his Secretary of State—one was a top economist to help devise a simple, workable framework; the other a seasoned diplomat who could help him sell the treaty to other world leaders.

China's willingness to engage was not unexpected. The country had undergone incredible environmental growing pains as it gave birth to a burgeoning middle class with a voracious appetite for energy. In many cities, air pollution was reaching levels of 1,000 micrograms per cubic meter—40 times greater than what World Health Organization considered safe.

Add to that the recent and somewhat predictable finding that even minor air pollution was now a known carcinogen, and the threat became that much greater.

Parents were now putting masks on their children even when indoors, and severely limiting their time out of doors. Cities all across China were using lotteries and auctions to determine who could purchase and register new cars, since the number of vehicles on the roads was a prime contributor to air pollution and the very expensive health crisis it created. Making matters worse, a recent MIT study indicated that roughly half a billion Chinese—located in a region that had used coal almost exclusively to heat their homes—had seen their life expectancy drop by a staggering five years because of coal-related smog. The country's citizens were increasingly well-educated and outspoken on the issue of air quality; some were actually leaving the country over the dangers it presented to them and their families. As a result, the issue was already a top concern within the leadership. Convincing China to move beyond the voluntary cap that they'd agreed to in 2014 required less persuasion than Gilman had expected.

India was in a similar situation. Outdoor air pollution was the country's fifth-largest killer, after high blood pressure, indoor air pollution (caused primarily by cooking fires) and health issues related to smoking and poor nutrition. One recent study by the Health Effects Institute noted that, in 2010, outdoor air pollution contributed to over 620,000 premature deaths in India, up from 100,000 in 2000. In other words, the problem was bad and getting much worse.

The treaty now emerging could help both countries address these critical issues, while ensuring that all developed nations within the G20 followed suit. The plan called for all participating economies to levy an upstream tax on fossil fuels. This meant that the tax would be imposed and collected as coal, oil or natural gas passed from the original producer to the next entity in the supply chain—typically a shipper or importer, a pipeline, a refiner, or a utility. As such, tax collection would be limited to a smaller number of parties, and thus simpler to implement.

The tax itself was structured as a fee per ton of CO2 emitted by the burning of any given fossil fuel. The cleaner the energy source, the lower the fee. In this fashion, different fossil fuels could easily be segmented according to the CO2 emissions they generated—even allowing for the substantial variations in different grades of coal.

How the tax receipts would be utilized within any given country remained unspecified; each nation would have to decide that for themselves. In the United States, President Gilman very much preferred the notion of tax-shifting, where the revenue derived from the carbon tax would be offset by a reduction in the federal income tax or payroll tax, with some funds held back to ensure that any individuals or business unfairly impacted could receive appropriate relief.

Although the President was incredibly pleased by the speed with which the U.S, China and India had reached near-consensus, he knew full well that convincing the other G20 nations to follow the lead set by the world's three largest emitters would be no easy task. However, given the alternatives—direct compliance with the GOC's demands, or the potentially devastating cost of inaction—he thought he at least had a fighting chance. Of course, whether he could get the congressional leadership bought into his strategy was another question entirely, but that would come later.

The next challenge was trickier, and was for the most part a crap shoot: getting the GOC to accept this treaty in place of their own, and to stand down from their threat of nuclear mayhem.

64

Taylor was not altogether surprised. He'd suspected for some time that there was something fishy about the device. "Ryan, you're absolutely certain that the nuclear device was fake?"

"One hundred percent certain. I was there when we planted it. Think about it, there was no reason for us to use an actual nuke—even those of us at the bottom of the food chain knew that there was no plan whatsoever to detonate the damn thing. It was all about establishing credibility for the threat to come."

Suddenly, a big chunk of the mystery fell away. It was now crystal clear why the nuke ended up in Guam and not in the hands of the Chinese, and it was also clear that the team now in charge of the device was complicit—quite possibly along with those involved in getting it there. Last, it confirmed that the experts sent from Los Alamos had not been victims of some random crime, they'd likely been abducted—or worse.

Taylor was standing in a corner of the small cabin on the Bainbridge, rolling up the sleeves of his white button-down. Ellie sat at the table across from Walker, taking notes. The session was also being recorded.

On the heels of Walker agreeing to take the deal and tell them what he knew, Taylor had briefly excused himself and Ellie, sought out a private cabin for the two of them to talk, and then had let her have it. He did his best to remain rational and controlled, but he was absolutely furious that she'd engaged Walker against his wishes and broken the rules they'd established. He was tempted to fire her right then and there, but decided to stop short, stating emphatically any further breach of trust between them would indeed result in her parting ways with the investigation and with DHS.

Ellie was suitably contrite. She accepted his anger, knowing she deserved it. She confessed that she'd allowed the emotion of the moment get the better of her, and promised not to misbehave again—or else accept the fate that Taylor had outlined. Thereafter, the two of them had put the incident behind them, and returned to question the detainee. And they were at last getting the results they were after.

"And what do you know about General Sheng?" Taylor asked Walker.

"I only heard the name once. I assumed he was our guy on the inside in China."

"That's it? That's all you know?"

"That's it. I think you're going to find I don't know half as much as you'd like me to."

Taylor kept firing questions one after another, pacing back and forth in the cramped room. "Were the special ops teams who removed that device working with the GOC?"

"I'm not entirely sure. Other than Sheng, I don't think so."

"Who built that device?"

"I have no idea."

"Alright, let's come back to Shanghai in a minute," Taylor said. "Were you involved in setting the explosives in Houston?"

"No."

"Okay. How about London?

"Nope. I had nothing to do with it."

"Novosibirsk?"

"Yes, I participated in that operation."

"Tell me about it."

"Not much to tell. We set the charges over the course of two nights. Fairly straightforward job."

"Are you trained in demolition?"

"No, not specifically. I more or less assisted," said Walker. "I was also the driver," he added a bit sheepishly.

"What kind of car was it?" Taylor asked, knowing the answer but wanting to hear it from Walker.

"It was a, um… Oh, what the hell was that thing?" Walker asked himself.

Taylor waited patiently.

After a second or two Walker pulled it from memory. "It was a Lada minivan."

"What color?"

"Tan. Or beige, I suppose."

"Alright. Let's talk about your colleagues. How many men in total?"

"There were five of us."

"All military?"

Walker hesitated. "I'm not sure. We were all given strict instructions not to discuss our backgrounds with each other, so I never asked directly, but…" Walker trailed off.

"But what?" Taylor persisted.

"Well, I'm guessing the answer is yes."

"What makes you think so?"

"Our training, our discipline. We all instinctively knew how to put together and execute an operation—and those instincts come from experience."

"Nationality?"

"Again, I'm not entirely sure. Two guys had slight accents—I want to say eastern Europe, but the other two were definitely American."

"Are you sure of that?" Taylor abruptly stopped pacing and looked intently at Walker.

"Sure as I can be without having looked at their passports. You Yanks have a pretty distinct swagger about you."

"What were their names?"

Walker looked tentatively at Taylor. "I've got mostly first names, and some are nicknames."

"Let's have 'em."

"Right." Walker extended a finger for each name as listed them off. "Sandman, Trevor, Wolf and Grable."

"Grable?"

"Yeah. He was the team leader. That's actually his last name. His first name was Terry—but that's the only full name I've got."

"Which of those four were American?"

"Wolf and Grable."

Taylor began to pace once more, his tall, powerful frame making the room seem even smaller. Walker followed his movements with weary eyes.

"Okay. How about weapons?" Once again, Taylor thought he knew the answer but wanted to hear it from walker.

"We all carried Mark 23s and one guy had an MP5."

"An MP5?" Taylor had only known about the pistols, but wasn't aware of any submachine guns. He strode over to his briefcase, while still keeping the conversation going. His thoughts were firing rapidly; it finally felt like they were getting somewhere "Did you use that thing?"

"No. Strictly insurance in case it all went to hell."

He pulled a legal pad from his briefcase, flipped a few pages until he had a clean sheet, and scribbled a note. It instructed Ellie to call Tori and arrange to have everyone involved in the Shanghai extraction taken into custody immediately for questioning.

He ripped the page out of the pad, and handed it to Ellie. "I need you to take care of this."

She read the note quickly, and looked back at Taylor. "Sure. I assume you mean right now?"

"Yes, please." He tried to say the words politely, masking his residual anger.

"Okay." She got up from her chair, walked to the door and knocked on the glass. The guard let her out.

"So, Ryan," he continued, "tell me how you were recruited."

"When I was in Iraq, I had a good mate named Matt Harrison. The man knew more about the shit we're in than anyone I'd ever met. He was a walking encyclopedia of how our actions are going to bite us in the arse."

"Regarding climate change, you mean."

"Of course, but—well, let's just say he knew a lot about a lot. It was through Matt that I got to know Terry Grable."

"In Iraq?"

"Yeah. Terry was nowhere near as knowledgeable as Matt, but he was radical. He was fed up, and sick of watching his country spend a trillion dollars on a senseless war—while it refused to spend a dime on an issue that was going to impact everyone on the planet. A couple years after I disappeared, I sought him out and reconnected. He nearly freaked out when he learned I was alive. A while later, he asked me if I might want to get involved in a crazy plan to save civilization, and I jumped on it."

Taylor was mildly incredulous. "You're saying that Grable asked if you wanted to help him threaten civilization with nuclear bombs and you were all in? Just like that?"

"No, mate. The plan came together over the course of a few months. It wasn't clear when we started exactly how it was all going to work. He was dealing with some fairly powerful people, and as—"

"What powerful people?" Taylor demanded.

"The blokes who supplied the weapons, the guys with big bickies." Walker noticed Taylor's quizzical look. "Oh, sorry. The guys with the money, who financed the whole thing."

"And who were these guys?"

"Damned if I know, Mr. Taylor. They certainly weren't idiots; the only one who'd ever met them was Terry. Absolutely all communication went through him."

"And you know absolutely nothing about their identities—no details, no names, nothing?"

"Nope. Though I did overhear a phone conversation Terry had one day, and I thought I heard him call someone 'Jack,' and another guy 'Seej,' but I don't even know if that was them."

"What kind of a name is 'Seej'?" Taylor asked, as he made some notes on his pad in Ellie's absence.

"I don't have a clue. It might not even be a name. Look, I want to see my daughter, and I don't want to feed you any bullshit that's going to screw that up. Those names probably mean nothing."

Taylor let it go. "Alright, so now for the big question: Where are the devices?"

"You mean the nukes?" Walker asked.

"Yes, what cities are they in?"

"Blimey, I haven't a clue."

"Ryan, you were a key member of the team. You fixed the charges in Novosibirsk, and planted a nuke in Shanghai—"

"A fake nuke, Mr. Taylor."

"So be it. If you guys didn't plant the other devices, who did?"

"There were two teams, Alpha and Bravo. We were Bravo, responsible for Novosibirsk and Shanghai. The other guys did Houston and London, and planted the nukes. We were never given any information about their operations, and they were supposedly in the dark about ours. The only bloke who might have been briefed on both was Terry."

"And how do we find him?"

"You don't. That guy was a bloody ghost. During an operation, he could disappear and reappear while he was standing next you. After Shanghai, we were all given instructions to leave no trace. If it hadn't been for that bloody fuckin' knife, I'd have disappeared as well."

Taylor looked at Walker, took a deep breath and slowly exhaled. He sensed that the man was telling the truth, but he also knew that some people were masters at misinformation.

"Alright, Ryan, let's call it a day. I assume you'll have no problem providing answers to these and other questions under polygraph?"

"Of course not," Walker replied. "Mr. Taylor, I'm dead serious when I tell you that I want to see my daughter. What I told you today is the truth."

"Okay."

"So when can I see her?"

Taylor shook his head. "Ryan, are you serious? I'm a man of my word, but shit, give me some time to work what you've just told me. I need to convince a few folks that you're truly cooperating before anything is going to happen."

Walker looked a bit despondent. Taylor really didn't have a hell of a lot of sympathy for the guy, but he definitely did not want the man to rethink his decision to talk.

After grabbing his briefcase and knocking on the door, he turned his head back. "Ryan," Taylor offered, "please trust me. I believe you've told me the truth today. Just give me some time and I'll make damn sure you get to see your daughter and grandson as we agreed."

Walker nodded his understanding, and Taylor took his leave as the guard opened the door.

65

It was a big, beautiful sunny day. The sky above was bright blue, and the air was relatively dry. When Dabert looked up, he was filled with hope; when he brought his eyes back down to earth, that hope seemed to dissipate quickly.

He was almost finished rebuilding his family's hut, although rebuilding was probably not the right term for it. Dabert had salvaged what he could—including pieces of the old structure, and various other logs and hewn beams, and built a hut that was roughly half the size of the original, with fewer creature comforts. His primary goal was simply to put a semi-permanent roof over the heads of him and his daughter.

Around him was total chaos. The village, the forest, the terraces all looked as if they had been pounded from above with a giant club. Debris was literally everywhere, both man-made and natural—trees, brush, clothes, pots and pans, pieces of corrugated metal roofs, all mixed together with drying mud and blanketing everything in sight. The forest was strewn with fallen trees as well, ripped from their roots by the voracious 200 mile per hour winds of Typhoon Benito. The terraces had fared no better, decimated by the rushing water and pervasive landslides. Although Dabert had heard rumors that the damage in some areas was only moderate, in and around Pula it was heart-wrenching. The retaining walls, built hundreds or even thousands of years prior, and repaired and patched by generation after generation, were now no longer walls at all. They were not much more than piles of rocks and mud, spread across the hillsides, a far cry from the lush green, beautifully layered pools that had been the primary source of food for the Kalanguya for centuries.

It had been five days since the storm had subsided. Two days ago, Dabert and half a dozen men from the village had spent an afternoon sorting rocks and preparing to rebuild a terrace beginning at the top of one hillside. After six hours of back-breaking work, they had cleared an area no larger than the footprint of a medium-sized hut; as the men walked down the hill and back to the village in the fading afternoon light, the clearing and the small stub of a wall that they had constructed was hard to even notice amid the chaos of trees, rocks and mud. It was not lost on any of them that restoring the terraces would take not months, but years—perhaps even decades. What they would do for food in the interim was still an open question.

Since the storm, and the tragic loss of Rowena and Ignacio, little Myla had not said a single word. She ate little, and mostly slept; when she was awake, she would wedge herself into quiet, dark places. Occasionally, Dabert could get her to sit next to him, and to lean her head against his chest as he stroked her hair. He thought he could feel her relax a bit at these times, but she still didn't speak, and he was never really sure what she was thinking or feeling.

Had it not been for her, he may well have crawled into some hole as well—staying there until hunger, thirst or the elements took him away. The pain in his heart was agonizing. The vision of Ignacio, his little iho, and Rowena, his precious wife, falling back into the mudslide played itself over and over again in his mind, each time causing an explosion of pain in his chest.

But Myla had survived. Although the death of his wife and son seemed a wound that could never heal, he still had a beautiful daughter who needed him—perhaps now more than ever. He had a responsibility to put a roof over her head, and to ensure that she was well-fed and cared for. Focusing on simple tasks that would serve his daughter's basic needs was the only way he could wrench his mind away from his despair.

Dabert put the final roof support beam in place, using a peg-in-hole system to anchor it, then using twine lashing for extra strength. After he tied it off, he gave it a firm shake to test its strength—good and solid.

He turned around and looked for his daughter. She had been sitting in the corner formed by the wall of the hut and the front step, but she was now nowhere to be seen. He walked around the hut, but still did not see her.

Ordinarily, there was not much of a view from their home. The forest surrounded them like a cocoon. But after the typhoon, so many trees had been ripped down and washed away that he could see a considerable distance in several directions. His eyes scanned the stubble of fallen and standing matchstick trees, looking for Myla. Finally, as he shifted his search from one forest opening to another, he saw her. She seemed to be digging next to the root ball of a large fallen tree about fifty meters away.

He quickly set out in her direction, keeping an eye on her as he walked. When he reached her, he quietly took a seat on the fallen tree and watched her dig with her hands.

What are you digging for, iha? Dabert asked.

His daughter said nothing. She kept digging, occasionally stopping to use her muddy fingers to push the hair in front of her eyes behind her ear.

"Can I help you dig?" Dabert finally asked. He knelt down beside her and began scooping dirt away as well. They did this for a while, eventually creating a fair-sized hole, or bowl, in the hardened mud.

Then, Myla stopped digging. She tucked her hair behind her ear once more and sat back on her knees, looking at the hole. She didn't move for several minutes, and as Dabert watched her, his heart ached for his daughter, her pain, and for the loss they'd both endured. He loved her so much, and to see her so damaged by the death of her mother and brother was harder than anything he'd ever experienced. His throat ached with emotion; his vision blurred from the tears that pushed themselves out of the corners of his eyes.

At last, Myla turned to him, and looked up into his face. Her eyes began filling with tears as well.

They stared at one another for half a minute, until at last Myla spoke. "I want to go look for them, Daddy. Can we? Please?"

Dabert's tears came more forcefully. He wiped his eyes with the sleeve of his shirt, and waited several seconds for his throat to relax before speaking, but also to figure out how best to answer his daughter's plea. "They are gone, iha. The storm took them from us."

She began to cry, but was determined. "I know, but I want to find them."

Dabert offered a small smile as tears now poured down his cheeks. He reached forward and lifted little Myla in his arms, and brought her close. As he put his arms around her, she hugged him with all of her strength. They cried together for some time, sitting by the small hole they had dug next to a fallen tree in the storm-tossed forest.

After both had grown quiet in each other's arms, Dabert pulled her gently away by the shoulders and looked into her eyes. "Myla, you can look for them, and I will help you. But we may have to do it a little bit at a time, and may have to wait until areas around the village have been cleared. Is that okay?"

Myla nodded tentatively.

"You and I—we're going to be okay. What happened was horrible, and I know it hurts very much. But we must stick together. I don't want to pretend it won't hurt tomorrow, or the next day, or the day after that, but I promise you that, in time, it will hurt a little less, and then a little less after that. Do you understand?"

Again, she nodded without saying a word.

Dabert put her back on her feet, stood up, and led her by the hand back down toward their hut. Dabert had been a good father, but had never been a mother. *I will have to learn how to be both*, he thought to himself as they entered the clearing next to the cooking area.

He looked down at his daughter, who looked back up at him. "I love you Daddy," she said quietly.

He scooped her back up in his arms and walked towards the door of the hut. "I love you too, iha. So very much."

66

The gate beeped, and a waist-high glass partition swept open. Armed guards watched the man enter—along with other IT professionals both coming and going, and raised no alarms. The system indicated no breach of security.

It was around 10 pm, and as the man walked up a carpeted flight of stairs, he could see through the lobby's large plate glass windows the dark outlines of scaffolding which once served as test beds for space shuttle rockets. He approached a steel reinforced door, swiped his access card, punched in a code, and heard a heavy click as the door unlocked. He pulled it open and entered the large, air conditioned room; it hummed with over a thousand blade servers, each processing massive amounts of DHS data.

The sprawling facility in Mississippi, just a few miles from the Gulf, was nestled within the Stennis Space Center, where generations of rocket engines had undergone testing in preparation for various NASA missions. In nearby communities, it was once said that if you want to go to the moon, you first have to go through Hancock County, Mississippi.

The Department of Homeland Security had selected a giant building on the Center's campus as the site for one of their largest data centers. DHS maintained some of the biggest national security data repositories in the world, and was in the process of consolidating over forty-five such centers down to five. Critics noted that such consolidation would place too much information behind too few targets, while those defending the decision countered that it would bring all DHS data within a smaller perimeter that would be easy to control and protect.

The second floor of this specific data center was tasked with running dozens of internal applications for the agency, all facilitating the productivity of DHS personnel, and tracking their activities.

The man held the door for a woman leaving the room; she nodded her thanks. Due to the immense amount of work involved in constructing, outfitting, and now debugging the data center, there was a steady stream of workers in all parts of the facility day and night; most of them were contractors, employees of one of several enormous consulting firms that now ran large segments of federal government operations, especially within the intelligence community. As he entered, the man noticed only a handful of people—one young man in a far corner troubleshooting a server rack, with tools and computer gear littering the aisle, and two others seated side by side and chatting casually at one of the data stations.

He turned left, and walked past several aisles before turning right and heading for an unoccupied data station halfway down. He took a seat.

He entered an employee code, and waited. The computer verified his code, and asked for a password. He provided the string of numbers, symbols and letters and waited again. Seconds passed. He heard someone walking down the aisle, but remained focused on the screen in front of him. They passed by and kept walking. Finally, the computer came back, indicating acceptance of his password, and granting access to the specific applications his employee code permitted.

The man took a deep breath, and entered a special programming key to access the program that governed this specific application, then made two small changes to its timestamp subroutine. He then proceeded to make the database changes he had carefully memorized in advance. When he was finished, he reset the subroutine and logged off, knowing that, while it was impossible to completely hide his tracks, the timestamp on his changes would no longer correlate to the current time—or to the video of his presence within the building. Thus, the database changes would look real, while the act of changing the underlying program would be a veritable needle in a chronological haystack.

He exited the server room, walked down the stairs, back through security and out to the parking lot. Once he'd gotten himself onto Highway 607, he removed his mustache and goatee, black-framed glasses and wig, placing them in a small bag on the passenger seat. In few minutes, he'd be on Interstate 10, heading North and away.

67

The wall looked like it could have been a collage created by a class of energetic third graders. Up close, however, there was a clear method to the madness. Faces, names, locations, weapons, devices, organizations and events were all represented by labels, articles and assorted pieces of paper.

Now that Taylor and his team had something to go on, the challenge was to leverage this new information to identify other pieces of the puzzle. The goal was to create a link chart and see if they could reach any conclusions that previously would have been impossible.

They were back in the dingy conference room near Taylor's office. The table had been tilted on its side and leaned against the far wall, and most of the chairs had been shoved against it or into the far corners. The night before, Sherry had gone out to buy self-adhesive corkboard tiles, and covered the wall in preparation for the exercise. It was not lost on them that other intelligence organizations, such as their well-budgeted brethren in Langley, probably had entire office suites properly equipped and dedicated to this purpose.

The building was playing its usual games, and—despite the thermostat's call for AC—the room was about 80 degrees and quite stuffy. They'd opened the windows for a time, but realized that it was more humid outside than in. Ellie and Verit were using pushpins to affix the last few items into place; Taylor was standing off to one side, taking it all in. Ellie was sitting in a chair nearby.

Taylor looked down at a legal pad on which he had about a dozen pages of notes. He flipped forward two pages, then another, then looked up. "Okay, here's where I want to start." As Ellie and Verit both took seats, he walked over and pointed to an area labeled *Shanghai*. "Tori, tell us the status of the team responsible for extracting the nuke from Shanghai."

"Okay. We now have four of the six SOF operators in custody, as well as the two helicopter pilots. The other two operators are on assignment, due back to base tomorrow. Their COs have been notified that each is to be confined upon their return, with no outside communication."

As a veteran SOF operator, Taylor knew full well how difficult it would be for a team to take one of its own into custody. Worse, the humiliation of the suspected operator would be devastating.

"Have we cross-referenced the dates of the operators' missions with the placement of devices in London, Houston, Novosibirsk and Shanghai?"

"We have," Tori replied, "I just received the classified mission schedules before coming here."

"And?"

"And all of them are accounted for on each of the dates in question—the same for the pilots," she said somberly.

"Shit," Taylor muttered under his breath. So he had given orders that—at least temporarily—had damaged the careers of fellow operators. Most likely all for nothing.

Tori quickly understood his response. "Drake, we had no other option; bringing those men in was the only course of action."

"Yup. I know," he said with a sigh. "Since we have them, let's put each under a polygraph, and make sure everyone checks out."

"Will do," said Tori.

"And in the list of questions, be sure to include whether they're familiar with any of the names that Walker gave us."

"Got it," Tori said, jotting it all down in her notebook.

"Now, how about the Chinese. Are they looking into whether their Snow Leopards have alibis for the dates in question?"

"Supposedly, yes." Tori replied, "but we really will have no way of verifying on this end. Let's just say that they're not exactly opening their kimono in response to our inquiry."

Taylor laughed gently. "Isn't a kimono Japanese, not Chinese?"

Tori grinned. "I have no idea. Isn't it both?"

Ellie glanced at Verit, catching his eye, and smirked at their bosses' flirtation. Verit smiled and rolled his eyes in response.

"Anyway, moving on," Taylor continued, "anything on General Sheng? Did we get a copy of his suicide note?"

"We did not. The Chinese seem to be very reticent to share anything related to Sheng. I think it's mostly pride and posturing, but it's hard to say."

"I'll ask the Secretary to work it." Taylor added a note to his pad. "How about any joint exercises between the U.S. and China?"

"Not much to speak of. In 2012, we conducted a joint anti-piracy drill in the Gulf of Aden, and completed a disaster-relief exercise in Chengdu, but that's about it."

"Let's find out who was involved in the piracy drill. If any of our Special Operations Forces participated, let's get a list of names."

"Got it."

"Alright, let's keep going here." Taylor pointed to Shanghai, then moved his finger due east to a clump of papers and photos. "We know something's rotten in Guam. Tori, last night you implied that the lab manager had agreed to cooperate. Have we gotten anything from him yet?"

"Yes. His name is Greg Kingsley, and he was interrogated yesterday shortly after being picked up. He's confessed to knowing the device was fake, and to falsifying the report he sent us." Tori grabbed her computer from her bag, and opened it on her lap. In a moment she had the file she was after. "Apparently, the other analysts in the lab were scared to death of this guy. He was in charge, and didn't let anyone else near the thing."

"So Kingsley hid the fact that this thing was fake from everyone else?"

"Looks that way. Bear in mind that this was a small lab created specifically to handle this device." She stared at her screen, taking in the pertinent facts. "There was just Kingsley and three analysts working beneath him."

"Okay, but who did this guy report to?" asked Taylor.

Tori scrolled down, scanning the file. "Hmmm. Doesn't say. I'll find that out."

"Please. And what about the guy you sent over there."

"Yeah, well, that's a little embarrassing. Let's just say your instincts to get nuclear experts in there were well-founded."

"Was the guy in cahoots with the lab manager, or just incompetent?"

"It looks like the latter. The guy swears he received a full briefing on the device, and even witnessed two different alarms indicating that trace amounts of uranium had escaped from the containment vessel they were using."

"The alarms were bullshit?"

"Yup. In fact, once Kingsley was taken into custody, two of the remaining analysts actually proved that the alarm system had been re-programmed. They also confirmed that the device contains no nuclear material whatsoever. It was all a bluff."

"Unbelievable. But why? What was Kingsley's motivation?"

"It looks like he was a fellow believer in the cause—and it appears some money helped convert him. He received twenty-five thousand dollars in an offshore account shortly after the device arrived in Guam."

"And who gave him the money."

"He claims he had one contact, and only knew his first name."

"Which was?"

Tori looked up from her laptop. "The contact's name was Jack."

"Holy shit, Walker was right," said Ellie, looking over at Taylor.

He nodded. "We need to talk to Kingsley as soon as possible."

"He's in the air as we speak," said Tori. "Due to arrive at the Naval Station in Norfolk, Virginia sometime tomorrow morning."

Taylor walked over to the conference room phone and dialed his assistant, Sherry. He asked her to arrange a helicopter to take him to Naval Station Norfolk tomorrow at 0900, then hung up the phone and turned back to the board. "Tori, one last question on Kingsley—does he know anything about the pair of scientists from Los Alamos?"

She again scanned the file on her laptop. "No. He claims he knew they were coming, but that this guy Jack took care of it. That's apparently all he knew."

"Wow. Okay, if you could have someone summarize that file for me, so I can read it before I head to Norfolk."

"Yup, done," Tori confirmed, making another note in her book.

"Let's move on to the names that Walker gave us."

"Ellie and Nate took point on the research," said Tori.

Taylor looked at the two of them and broke into a smile. "You guys get all the fun stuff."

"Yeah, well, I learned a hell of a lot about databases," Ellie offered, "but Nate's the IT geek. I'll let him present."

Verit shot Ellie a friendly smirk as he stood and walked over to the far right hand side of the cork-board wall, where a list of names and photos had been posted. "So, I wish we had more to report, but here's what we've got." He quickly rearranged a few items, and continued. "Walker gave us six names: Sandman, Trevor, Wolf, Terry Grable, Jack and 'Seej.' He also told that us that he firmly believed Wolf and Grable were American. I'll start with what we do know: Terry Grable, pictured here," he pointed to a photo of a sandy-haired, square-jawed soldier in camo fatigues, "has an impressive record of successful missions in both Iraq and Afghanistan with the 24th Special Tactics Squadron, a unit of the Air Force Special Operations Command."

"Hold on," Taylor suddenly felt sick to his stomach. "You're telling us that Terry Grable, an integral member of this terrorist organization, previously served in the U.S. Special Operating Forces?"

Verit hesitated, realizing that he hadn't fully considered how Taylor would take this information. "Yes, sir," he said softly. Verit looked back at the board, which included a summary of Grable's military career. "He served for nine years."

Taylor pinched his eyes shut with his thumb and index finger. No one in the room spoke. Finally, Taylor looked back at Verit. "Nate, isn't the 24th Special Tactics Squadron the Air Force component of the Joint Special Operations Command?"

"I believe so. I found a reference or two indicating as much, but I couldn't confirm it."

Taylor smirked. "Of course you couldn't. They try very, very hard to make sure you can't. Please continue."

"Grable was born and raised in Dayton, Ohio. Both his parents worked in the Aerospace industry; his father served in the Air Force. There doesn't seem to be any trigger event or point in time when he veered from what appears to be a fairly conservative upbringing, but there is this." Verit pointed to a printed web page posted on the wall. "Two years, ago, Grable donated a surprisingly large sum—over two thousand dollars—to the Climate Defense Fund. You may recall that this was the same organization supported by Walker."

"Nate, I don't know a lot about the CDF," said Ellie, "but I do know that the founder and executive director is supposedly a bit of a nut case. Could these guys be involved somehow?"

"It's a good question. I looked pretty hard at that, but don't believe so. The Director definitely has a reputation as an eccentric, but he's also incredibly well-respected, as is the CDF board of directors. Plus, his schedule is very public; the guy gives an insane number of speeches all over the world. I'll do some further digging, but I don't think he's involved."

"Okay, let's move on," said Taylor.

"Well, Other than a stellar military career, including various medals and an honorable discharge, Grable does not leave much of a footprint. Little is known about his companions while serving, and his file offers strangely little in the way of personal information."

"Just the way he likes it, I'm sure," said Taylor.

"I guess so. After leaving the service, Grable spent about two years in Cincinnati, where he rented a small apartment and then disappeared. No record of employment while he was there, and when he vanished he left behind no debts or creditors—a clean slate."

"Walker referred to him as a ghost; sounds like the shoe fits," said Ellie.

"I wish we had more—oh, there is one more thing." Verit lifted a piece of paper outlining Grable's service record, and pointed to the sheet beneath. Don't think this means anything, but a year and a half ago, Grable spent three months in Washington at the Pentagon on loan to the Office of the Undersecretary of Defense for Policy."

"Huh," commented Taylor, clearly intrigued. "What was the nature of the assignment?"

"Umm," Verit studied the sheet. "I'm not sure."

"And who did he work for, or with, while he was there?"

"I don't know, sir. I will find out."

"Tori, doesn't John Morgan report to the USD Policy?"

"Give me a sec." She tapped at her laptop for several seconds, took a look, then tapped some more. "Yup," she confirmed, looking over at Taylor. "Looks like Special Operations and Low-Intensity Conflict does fall under Policy."

"Interesting. Maybe Morgan knew the guy and can help us. I'll look into that." He made another note on his legal pad. "Okay, Nate, what about the other names?"

"Well, since we believe Wolf is also an American, I ran it with and without an e attached through all of our service databases, and came up with forty-three soldiers who served in either Iraq or Afghanistan. The next step—which I should have complete by tonight—is to correlate their service dates and locations with Walker, Grable and Matthew Harrison. Assuming we get a few hits, I'll begin running them down immediately."

"Good. And the others?" asked Tori.

"Sandman and Trevor will both be very difficult. For starters, you'd be shocked at just how many soldiers have the nickname 'Sandman'; and Trevor is a whole lot more common than I expected as well. Both will take some time. One thing I can report concerns 'Seej.' It looks like it's occasionally used as a nickname for a nickname—specifically, 'Seej' may refer to someone who goes by CJ."

"Huh." Taylor was intrigued. "And what did you get back when you plugged that into your database query?"

"Roughly eight hundred and twenty candidates. But I should be able to bring that down by doing the same correlation with dates and locations."

Taylor rolled this over. "So the masterminds behind this horrible plot are named Jack and CJ…"

"I think we should call that a best guess, and nothing more," Tori quickly offered.

"So be it. But a best guess is a hell of a lot better than a random guess," he replied with a grim smile.

68

An assistant led the two men forward in the aircraft. The protocol for most of those on board was quite simple. Each individual had an assigned area, from which they could move aft as they pleased, but they could not move forward of that area without an escort.

Bob Baker and John Morgan were stationed in the senior staff compartment, which allowed them access to most of the tan-carpeted areas of the plane—including the combination conference and dining room, as well as all of the blue-carpeted areas designated for guests and reporters.

Two Secret Service agents stationed in the corridor nodded their permission to pass as they were led to the door of President Gilman's office by an aide and announced.

"Gentlemen, please have a seat," the President instructed, just finishing up a final edit of the remarks he would be giving shortly. The aide closed the door behind him, leaving the three alone together.

This was the only slot available in the President's calendar for the next several days, so Baker and Morgan had opted to ride along on Air Force One for a trip to Chicago so that they might discuss the situation with him face to face.

They sat quietly as they waited for the President's attention. After a minute or two, he put his pen down, squared the document he'd been editing and put it neatly in a corner of his desk, pressed a button on his phone and asked the individual to swing by his office for a sec, then looked up at Baker and Morgan.

"So Bob, I understood from your email that the two of you want to discuss Drake Taylor. Is that correct?"

"Yes, Mr. President."

There was a knock on the door. "I'm sorry, hold on one sec," President Gilman said to the two of them. "Come in."

A young woman entered and the President handed her the speech. "Gina, here's the final; you might have Gail take one last look before it gets uploaded."

"I will, Mr. President," Gina replied. She took the document and left the office, closing the door once again.

"Alright, so what's this all about?"

* * *

John Morgan presented to the President the circumstantial evidence that he had offered to Baker several days prior regarding Ryan Walker and Operation Anaconda; the connection between Ellie Alder, Alan Stewart and Bella Knobloch, and phone records implying that secrets were passed at their meeting; and the suspicion that the nuclear device extracted from Shanghai was fake, and that Taylor knew it.

The President had listened calmly thus far, without any noticeable reaction, but finally asked a question. "John, you said it's suspected that the Shanghai nuke was fake, why hasn't this been confirmed?"

Morgan took a deep breath. "Well, sir, that was our next step, but yesterday at approximately 1300, the lab manager in Guam, his team, and all of the SOF operators involved in the extraction were detained on Taylor's orders. I have reason to believe that he took this action specifically to cover his tracks, and prevent the truth from coming to light."

The President looked at Morgan for several long seconds, many thoughts flowing through his mind. The first was simply that, if what he was hearing was true, it would not only complicate his evolving strategy for dealing with the crisis, it would probably derail it. The next was that Taylor had been extremely reliable in sending daily reports to both him and Secretary Hawthorne—but the President had yet to read yesterday's or today's, so what Taylor may have already reported was an unknown.

"I find this deeply troubling. But while the evidence is compelling, it doesn't strike me as conclusive. Do you have a report detailing all of this evidence?"

"Yes we do, Mr. President." Morgan pulled a classified folder out of his bag and handed it to President Gilman. "But there's one more thing."

"Go on."

Morgan deferred to Baker. "Mr. President, I had a member of my team look at Taylor's communications. Just yesterday, we discovered phone records indicating that Taylor contacted Walker well in advance of his capture."

The President's eyes narrowed. "How far in advance?"

"One conversation about nine months in advance, another six months in advance, and another three weeks in advance," Baker replied. "Each of the calls occurred at precisely the same time of day, and each was made on the first Tuesday of the month."

"You're absolutely sure about this?"

"We are, Mr. President," Morgan confirmed.

President Gilman ignored Morgan's comment and looked directly at Baker. "Bob, you've personally looked at all of this evidence and stand behind it?"

"I do, sir," Baker said firmly.

The President was stunned, but he was not one to show emotion or think out loud in such situations, especially when he knew the friction between the Office of the DNI and DHS. Furthermore, he was not going to try and resolve this with Baker and Morgan present. He needed time to think.

His deskphone beeped, and he hit a button. "yes?"

"Mr. President," said an aide, "we will be landing in three minutes. We're running a bit late, so we will be leaving immediately for the Pritzker Auditorium."

"Got it. Thanks." He released the call.

"Mr. President," said Baker, "we would like to further investigate, but I did not want to proceed without your knowledge." He had phrased his comment in such a way as to inform President Gilman of his intentions rather than ask for permission.

This was not lost on the President. "Bob, all of this bears further exploration, but I want you to be damn careful about moving forward on unproven allegations. Am I clear?"

"Yes, Mr. President."

"And I want daily reports on this," he said, pointing a finger at Baker while once again all but ignoring Morgan, making it known who he was holding responsible.

"Yes, Sir," replied Baker.

"Thank you both," President Gilman said, looking at his watch and indicating that the conversation was over.

"Thank you, sir," they both replied a little clumsily.

After they'd departed, the President hit another button on his phone, then proceeded to button his top button and straighten his tie.

"Yes, Mr. President?"

"Gina, see to it that Dan Hawthorne is in my office waiting for me when we return from Chicago."

"Yes, sir."

69

As a civilian, Ellie Alder had never seen a military installation so large in her entire life. In truth, few ever got the chance.

She'd been asked by Taylor to come along for the interrogation of Greg Kingsley. If this guy was indeed as committed to the cause as Walker, Taylor needed someone along with better knowledge of the GOC's cause than himself. He also thought it might offer Ellie a chance to redeem herself. She had promised him that she'd be on her best behavior.

Naval Station Norfolk, the largest naval complex in the world, was tasked with ensuring the operational readiness of the U.S. Atlantic Fleet. The base supported 75 of the Navy's roughly 285 ships. And with 134 aircraft, its Air Operations unit conducted approximately 275 flights per day—or one every six minutes.

Their helo had landed at Chambers Field, affording a bird's eye view of the massive installation as they approached. Ellie counted four aircraft carriers, three destroyers, and an assortment of other battleships as they passed over the Station's four miles of waterfront.

The brig, or prison, where Kingsley had been taken, was no longer on the base. A new prison, officially called Naval Consolidated Brig Chesapeake, had recently been built nearby. This facility replaced not only the brig at Norfolk Naval Station, but one at Quantico and Camp Lejeune as well. It was not a prison for the general public; it was a military prison. As such, it held inmates who had violated the uniform code of military justice.

Despite having read the interrogation report from Guam, and studying the man's background, Kingsley was not exactly what Taylor or Ellie had expected. He was a small man, about five foot five, with delicate features, dark hair and penetrating brown eyes. He wore thick, tortoise shell glasses which made his eyes appear larger. When he spoke, his words and sentences were extremely precise—with regards to both word choice and diction.

They were seated in a large cell designed for meetings between inmates and their lawyers, with walls on three sides, locked prison bars on the last, and a guard posted outside a few yards away. They sat at one end of a rectangular steel table, bolted to the floor, each of them in a steel chair. Kingsley sat at the head, with Taylor and Ellie on either side. They had worked their way through a few preliminary topics, mostly as a warm-up, and Taylor decided it was time to get down to business. "So, Greg, tell us how you got yourself into all of this. What drove you to perpetrate a nuclear hoax from your perch in Guam?"

"Well, I certainly wouldn't describe myself as the perpetrator," Kingsley said pointedly. "I was pretty close to a pawn in the grand scheme of things."

"But what motivated you to get involved in the first place?" Ellie asked.

"Well, I'm a scientist. While my specialty is weapons technology, I am very much a student of other scientific subjects, one of which is the warming of our planet due to the consumption of fossil fuels."

Taylor rolled his eyes out of view of the detainee, thinking *I really didn't come down here to listen to more speeches from righteous environmentalists.* But Ellie kept him talking. "I think a lot of us are pretty frightened by the issue, but that doesn't mean we want to hold the world hostage," she said. "What caused you to cross the line?"

There's the pot calling the kettle black, Taylor thought to himself.

"That's a good question," said Kingsley. "It certainly doesn't look like the right course of action from where I'm sitting now." He paused, giving it all further thought. "Actually, I take that back. If confronted with the same choice, I think I would probably head down this same path all over again—even knowing that I might end up in precisely this predicament."

This caught Taylor's attention. "Why? Because you think that this plan to threaten civilization is really going to have some positive impact on the debate?"

"I know it's having a positive impact, Mr. Taylor. I'm sure you've all read the newspapers, and spent time looking at various reactions in the on-line world. As one would expect, there are plenty of people calling for our heads, but there's also a growing number of people who understand that, without action on this issue, we are condemning ourselves to something far worse than what the Guardians of Civilization might inflict. Most important, a carbon tax is no longer some mysterious vehicle for solving the problem. People now understand what it is, and are finally discussing it on the merits."

Taylor realized his patience had waned; he wasn't sure he could stomach another self-righteous diatribe. "And you're willing to give up your life just to move the needle on public awareness?" Taylor asked incredulously.

Kingsley sighed. "Yes, I suppose I am," he said. "You know, at this moment in history, humans are on a collision course with the natural world that supports them. Our man-made reckoning is approaching, and the very best time to mitigate its worst effects is right now."

Taylor shook his head, and took a deep breath, trying not to explode. "When this guy Jack approached all of you, did he offer you a choice of two pills, and you took the red one?" he offered, a little too sarcastically.

This time, Kingsley seemed annoyed. "I didn't need a pill, Mr. Taylor. The reality of our predicament is startlingly obvious. I really don't think that it requires much mental horsepower to see that we are on a highly unsustainable course, and that humanity has precious little time before we enter unknown territory."

Ellie agreed with every word, but also knew full well that a detailed discussion on global warming was not the reason for their trip to Norfolk, and that Taylor wouldn't take much more of it. "Greg, we understand the issues, but we're not here to debate—"

"This is not a debate," he stated emphatically. "As we approach a rise of one degree Celsius, we are already starting to see irreversible changes in our weather patterns, in our oceans, and in our quality of life. By the time we hit two degrees Celsius—"

"Greg, enough!" Ellie demanded, surprising even herself with her impatience. Taylor had essentially stopped listening, but perked up upon hearing his colleague's firm command.

"This is very important to me," Kingsley said earnestly. "I need to present the reasons behind my complicity."

"Fair enough," Ellie replied, "but I think we get the gist. We've got a lot to cover here."

Kingsley was momentarily silent, but looked wholly unsatisfied. "Just hear me out, so you can at least appreciate my motivations. That's all I ask."

Taylor ignored the man's plea. "Greg, who else at your lab in Guam knew that the nuclear device was a fake?"

Kingsley said nothing, and stared at the floor in front of his chair.

Taylor looked at Ellie, then back at Kingsley. "Tell you what: If I let you finish your little tirade, will you then answer my questions?"

Kingsley looked up and answered in a measured tone. "I will, Mr. Taylor. Since I was given scant information to begin with, I don't mind offering up what little I know. However, it's extremely important to me that you and others understand why I chose to cooperate with the Guardians of Civilization in the first place."

Taylor was mildly incredulous. "All right then. Have at it." He had no idea whether Kingsley would uphold his end of the bargain, but it would at least give them a modicum of leverage.

"Okay," said Kingsley, "it's very important that you appreciate where we're headed here." He cleared his throat as Taylor leaned back in his chair. "At two degrees Celsius, insects—no longer held in check by cold winters—will migrate northward in large numbers, killing off forests necessary to support the food chain on most continents. Most of our tropical coral reefs will be lost to bleaching and ocean acidification, decimating an ecosystem critical to the ocean food chain. At three degrees Celsius, the Arctic will become completely ice-free all summer long, turning what was a global ocean refrigerator into a heat sink—and greatly accelerating further warming. The Amazon rain forest, often referred to as the lungs of the planet, will start to desiccate, or dry up. Snow caps on the Alps will all but disappear. Glaciers in the Himalayas and elsewhere will disappear, eliminating the primary source of potable water for well over two billion people. The West Antarctic ice sheet will approach total collapse, accelerating sea level rise, and creating literally hundreds of millions of refugees."

Kingsley paused, noticing that his small audience had yet to shut him down. "I'll end with this: The heat-trapping power of methane is over twenty-five times greater than that of CO_2, and there are many billions of tons of it locked in the frozen shelf of the Arctic Ocean, the Antarctic, and in the permafrost of the Siberian tundra. Warming over the past century has already started to cause this methane to escape into the atmosphere. If this accelerates, the prospect of reaching four degrees of warming or beyond will become very real; the global economy will be decimated, and mankind will find itself living on a inhospitable and unrecognizable planet.

"All of this is not opinion or conjecture," Kingsley continued, "it's well-documented scientific projection, based upon an increasingly large mountain of data. That is why I agreed to get involved in this GOC scheme." He looked directly at Taylor. "Perhaps you could say my motivation is to give a red pill to all of civilization."

Taylor stared at Kingsley, having inadvertently absorbed more of his tirade then he'd intended. After a moment or two, he shook it off and looked down at his notes. "Alright. A deal's a deal; now I want some answers."

"Ask away," Kingsley said softly.

70

Taylor paced back and forth in the cell, reading questions from a yellow legal pad as Ellie took copious notes. Kingsley had been true to his word; for the past twenty minutes, he'd been entirely forthcoming in response to Taylor's queries.

"Who else at your lab in Guam knew that the nuclear device was a fake?" he asked.

"No one. I will admit that I'm known as somewhat of an autocratic manager, and I was insistent that I was the only one who conducted hands-on analysis."

"How did you convince the visitor from Washington that it was real?"

"With all due respect, he was not the sharpest tool in the shed. A few false radiation scares and he wanted nothing to do with the device. It was, as they say, a piece of cake."

"And how did you stop the two scientists from Los Alamos from coming to your lab?"

"I have no idea how their visit was halted. I was scared to death of their planned arrival; I knew that there was literally no chance that I would be able to pull the wool over their eyes."

"You do have an idea," Taylor insisted, glaring at the man. "Who stopped them from coming?"

"My contact—a gentleman supposedly named Jack, said he had taken care of it. I asked him how, but he wisely ignored the question."

Taylor zeroed in on the name immediately "Tell me about Jack."

"I never met him."

"You must have talked to him numerous times. Tell me about him."

"I'm not sure what to say."

"Well, what was his voice like? Did he have an accent? Did he use any phrases that stood out?"

Kingsley thought for a moment. "Well, he was very confident. No accent, but he was not shy about swearing. He seemed to have lots of resources at his disposal."

"Speaking of resources," Ellie interjected, "You received twenty-five thousand dollars after the nuke arrived at your lab. Was everyone paid for their involvement?"

"That money was not for my involvement. I participated because I believed that this would make a difference."

"Alright," said Taylor, getting frustrated, "then what was the money for?"

Kingsley hesitated, then responded: "My mother."

"Your mother?" Taylor asked with an obvious note of disbelief.

"Yes. She's eighty-six, and lives alone in Corvallis, Oregon. It became very clear as all of this was unfolding that she had reached the point where she needed full-time care. I told Jack that I would have to take a leave of duty to address the situation, but he insisted that I stay put. He offered the money so that I could arrange to have someone stay with her at home."

Ellie took these details down in her notebook. "You know we will corroborate this, right?"

"Of course," he replied quietly.

"Did you ever meet or work with any other GOC members?" asked Taylor.

"No."

"Were you involved in any way with Houston or Novosibirsk?"

"No. In fact, I found out about both incidents through the news."

"How is that possible?" asked Ellie, "You did what you did blindly, without knowing the full plan?"

"More or less, yes. I was told that the GOC would demonstrate its capabilities—and prove to the world that it was quite serious—without any human casualties, and that no one would be harmed whatsoever if a carbon treaty was signed."

"And you actually thought that a signed treaty was likely?"

"I'm not sure," said Kingsley. "But now that we all know the GOC's endgame, do you really think that world leaders will stand on pride and allow nuclear devices to be detonated in their cities? No, they will sign the treaty—if for no other reason than to buy themselves some time."

Taylor looked at Ellie, and back at Kingsley. He'd never even considered the possibility that any leader would do such a thing, and—up until that very moment—he didn't think anyone else had either.

71

As the helicopter rose out of Chambers Field, and gained speed and altitude for the journey back to DC, Taylor adjusted the microphone attached to his earphones.

"Well, that was a complete and total waste of time," he said to Ellie, who was wearing a similar set-up.

"Yes, I suppose it was. But I've got to say, I'm amazed by just how committed these guys are."

"Not sure I follow. Both Walker's and Kingsley's willingness to talk strikes me as indication that their commitment to the GOC is pretty fragile. In fact, they seem to prize righteousness over silence and a well-executed plan.

"Perhaps. I could be wrong, but I think Walker opened up because, in addition to wanting to see his daughter and grandson, he truly believes that detonating a device might undo what he thinks they've accomplished—the positive awareness they've generated. And Kingsley, holy cow; that insistence on finishing his lecture blew me away. I guess that's what I mean by committed."

Taylor turned and looked out the helicopter at the water below. After a minute or so, he turned back. "Ellie, let me ask you a question."

"Sure."

"Was everything he said back there true?"

"How do you mean?"

"About the effects of each degree of warming. Is that accurate?"

Ellie bit her bottom lip, and considered her response. "I'm afraid so. The earth is a pretty complicated system, so there could be lots of checks and balances that we don't yet know about, but there are also a number of highly sophisticated computer models that are all starting to align. What he told us is well supported by scientific research."

"I'm not sure I realized..." Taylor trailed off.

"Realized what?"

"Realized the stakes, I guess."

Ellie smiled slightly, and raised her eyebrow. "Wow. I think I might tear up."

They both laughed.

"Don't get your hopes up, Ms. Alder, I'm not about to quit my day job and become an eco-freak."

"Probably a good thing; I'm not sure you have the right temperament for it," Ellie responded, relieved that the tension between them had diminished. She hadn't realized how much his trust and respect meant to her until she'd damaged it.

"I think that's probably true. And I'll tell you this: I truly believe that the GOC has its head up its ass if it thinks—"

"Mr. Taylor," the pilot interrupted, breaking into their channel. "You have a call from Washington. May I put it through?"

"Yes, by all means."

"Stand by," the pilot instructed, flicking several switches on a console between him and his co-pilot.

Taylor heard a click. "This is Drake Taylor."

"Drake, it's Tori. Where have I reached you?"

"Somewhere over the Chesapeake Bay. What have you got?"

"Well, it's a bit sensitive; is this a secure call?"

He looked at a small communications panel on the partition in front of him, but had no idea how to work it. He tapped the pilot on the shoulder, who then patched into Taylor's earphones.

"Yes, Mr. Taylor."

"Lieutenant, I just wanted to ask if this call was secure."

"Yes, sir. You'll notice the light on your comm panel is now yellow. When I switch myself out, it will go green, indicating a secure connection, provided your colleague is on a secure phone."

"Got it. Thanks."

"No problem. Out."

The pilot switched out of the call, and Taylor watched as the light turned back to green.

"Alright, Tori. Shoot."

"First, just a heads up. I just saw Sherry, and apparently Secretary Hawthorne wants to see you immediately upon your return. I think she just sent you an email."

"Okay. Know any details?"

"No, but Sherry implied it was important. Anyway, not why I called you."

Taylor waited for her to continue. He looked over at Ellie, who was looped out of the conversation, and looking out her window.

"Umm, this is a bit tricky," Tori began.

"Spit it out."

"Well, Nate Verit has been digging into the names supplied by Walker. He's tried all sorts of schemes with various names, but one database query was significant. He looked at everyone currently serving in the U.S. military with the initials C.J., and then subtracted anyone below second lieutenant, assuming that we were dealing with someone higher up in the ranks."

"And?" Taylor prompted.

"He narrowed it down to a hundred and seventy-five targets, then began correlating their service records with those of Grable. He found connections between Grable and three officers, but after further research, one rose to the top."

Taylor's impatience was returning. "Who is it, Tori?"

"Lieutenant General Charles Jerrick, Commander of the Joint Special Operations Command."

"Oh my god," Taylor muttered in shock. "What are the connections?" he asked, keeping his voice calm.

"Grable and Jerrick served together on seven different operations as operators, and then Grable served under Jerrick for eleven more," Tori reported. "Also, it turns out they were fraternity brothers at Ohio University."

Taylor was dumbfounded. First Grable, now this. It infuriated him. *These assholes took an oath to defend the Constitution of the United States against all enemies, foreign and domestic,* he said to himself, *and now they threaten the whole fucking world with nuclear mayhem?* Nonetheless, he remained calm, fully aware that the evidence Tori presented was far from conclusive. But as his brain began processing recent events, some pieces began clicking into place. That Jerrick had hand-picked the team for the extraction in Shanghai wasn't that unusual, but the fact that he had taken direct ownership—actually flying to China and overseeing the operation from the deck tower of the USS George Washington—definitely was.

Or was it? Taylor asked himself. *This was, after all, one of the most important operations Jerrick had ever managed.* "Tori, what about phone and email records?" he finally asked.

"Drake, I didn't dare take that step without your approval."

"Yup, nor should you have. I'll work this with Hawthorne as soon as I see him." Taylor was lost in the implications of all this. "Anything else, Tori?"

"No—actually yes, one more thing: I just got word that a full search of Kingsley's living quarters turned up a secure satellite phone that is clearly not government issue. We're sending it to the lab now for analysis."

"Good. How much will a phone like that tell us?"

"Not sure. It could be useless, depending on how clever they were. There are certain encryption protocols they could have utilized that could make it very hard for us to discern what other phones were involved—or even when the calls took place."

Taylor had little interest in understanding the finer points of telephony encryption, and moved on. "Okay. Tori, do me a favor and discreetly track Jerr—" Taylor cut himself short, realizing that using Jerrick's name in front of the pilot and co-pilot was ill-advised. "Track our new suspect's whereabouts. In fact, see if you can get me his movements and schedule since we pulled in the Shanghai extraction crew. If you're right, and he's behind this, that should have spooked him; let's see if it impacted his behavior."

"Will do. I should be able to pull that off without triggering anyone's attention."

"Good. And Tori, have your team put together a list of anyone who served with him, or under his direct command, more than half a dozen times. In fact, let's sort the list by frequency of common missions."

"Okay, Drake. That'll be fairly easy."

"Okay. And needless to say, let's make sure this stays between us. Please make sure Verit says absolutely nothing to anyone."

"I've already covered that with him," Tori responded patiently.

"Good. Also, I'll need a written summary of all of this before I meet with Hawthorne. Can you have that ready for me in thirty minutes or so?

"Not a problem. Want me to meet you in the main building?"

"No need. I'll just swing by the office."

"I'll be here."

Her voice sounded a bit sharp. Taylor realized just how often he barked orders at this woman, but now was not the time to deal with it. "Great. See you then."

Taylor looked at the comm panel as Tori disconnected and all lights went off. His mind returned to what they'd just uncovered. *I can't believe that after all this, it's coming back to our own goddamn people*, Taylor mused, feeling very anxious to get back to Washington.

72

Upon his arrival back at the Nebraska Avenue Complex, Taylor went to his office before heading over to see Secretary Hawthorne.

He had only just dropped his briefcase and sat down to do a quick email scan when Tori walked in.

"Here you go." She handed him a thin folder, and leaned against the corner of his desk.

"Great. Thanks." He drew in a breath and ran a hand over his head. "Tori, I know I've been awfully demanding lately—and I know that I'm not always that polite about it. I just..." He trailed off, looking away, unsure how to continue.

Tori's gaze softened as she studied him; he looked exhausted. She put a hand on his arm, forcing him look at her. "Drake, you don't have to apologize. But thank you. For the record, I don't consider your style impolite—I find it efficient. I think I'd get awfully impatient if you surrounded every request with pleases and thank yous."

Taylor's mind had gone blank the moment she'd placed her hand on his arm. They looked at one another in silence for several seconds, the afternoon light setting her face and dark blue eyes aglow. Suddenly, out of nowhere, Rachel's face flashed in his mind and he looked down at the forgotten folder in his hands.

"This…" he began, awkwardly holding the folder up. "This has everything we discussed?"

Tori lamented the moment's passing, but found his clumsy discomfort endearing. "It does," she replied, a gentle smile on her lips.

"Great. This is terrific, work, Tori," Taylor offered, regaining his composure somewhat. "Not quite a smoking gun, but definite progress."

"We're getting there," Tori said, pushing herself away from his desk. "Hey, before you run, two updates from our session yesterday. First, the polygraphs of the SOF operators from Shanghai all came back clear; I guess that's both good news and bad news, but no help. Second, we now have the names of those involved in the Gulf of Aden piracy drill; it turns out that Colonel Sheng was presiding for the Chinese, and—get this—none other than Charles Jerrick was in charge of our side."

"You're kidding me. Is that in here?" Taylor asked, opening the folder and skimming the report.

"It is. On the last page," Tori instructed. "For the record, ASD Morgan was there as well."

"He was involved in the piracy drill?"

"He's listed as an observer. When you reach him to ask about Terry Grable's stint in the USD Policy office, you might ask about how much interaction Sheng had with Jerrick and other operators during the drill, and whether Sheng and Jerrick met previously to plan the effort. I looked for a record of any meetings, but couldn't find anything."

"I certainly will; I left a message for Morgan to call me." Taylor closed the report and placed it in his briefcase.

Sherry popped her head in next to Tori. "Drake, glad I caught you. Apparently there's been a change in plans. Instead of meeting in the Secretary's office, you are to head directly to the White House. I just called for a car."

"The White House? Where am I going once I get there?"

"The Oval Office. I'm assuming the Secretary will be meeting you there."

"Sherry, are you sure of this?" Taylor asked.

"Yes, I'm sure. The Secretary's office just called."

Taylor furrowed his brow, and looked at Tori, who shrugged her shoulders. "Don't look at me!"

"Are you going like that?" Sherry asked, looking at his shirt.

"Like what?" Taylor looked down and noticed a small coffee stain to the left of his tie. "Really? You think that's noticeable?" Tori covered her mouth to hide a grin.

Sherry answered indirectly: "You've got a few minutes before your car gets here; there's two fresh shirts in your bottom drawer." She reached for the door, ushered Tori out, and started to swing it shut behind them to give her boss some privacy.

"Sherry, before you go," Taylor called out. She swung the door back open. "Could you call John Morgan's office and ask if I can meet with him early this evening?"

"His office just called as well," she replied. "In fact, I told them that you were heading to the White House, and that you'd be reachable around six. I'd be happy to set that up as a meeting."

"Great. Thanks, Sherry."

"Don't mention it. Now get changed!" she ordered with a smile, and closed the door.

Sherry and Tori walked back down the hall together, making small talk.

"You know," Sherry said, "John Morgan's secretary is hysterical," Sherry noted. "She has me in stitches every time I talk to her."

"How long has she worked for him?" Tori asked.

"I'm not sure—a year or two at least," Sherry said, "but I laugh just listening to her." She lowered her voice to a false whisper. "I shouldn't be telling anyone, but she calls him 'Jack the Ripper'"

Tori stopped and turned. "She calls him what?"

"Shhh," Sherry admonished playfully with a finger to her lips. "She calls him 'Jack the Ripper,'" Sherry repeated, again in a soft voice. "I guess it's some old high school nickname she discovered."

"But why Jack? His name's John," Tori asked, somewhat stupidly.

"I don't know," said Sherry. "Maybe he was called Jack when he was younger. Pretty common."

Tori stood, frozen, her mind thinking through the possibilities.

"You okay?" Sherry asked.

"Um, yeah. I'm fine. Just remembered something I have to do."

"Alright. I'll see you later," Sherry said, turning to head back to her desk. After a few steps, she turned back. "But please pretend I never said anything. I'm sure Morgan would be furious if he ever heard her say it."

Tori watched her go, then walked back to Taylor's office and knocked on his sidelight. He had stepped out of sight on the other side of the door. "Come in."

Tori opened the door and closed it behind her as Taylor was tucking in a new shirt. Taylor was about to make a suggestive joke, but stopped short when he saw Tori's expression.

"Drake," she said, her face a little pale, "I think we may have just found another big piece of the puzzle."

73

Taylor held one hand in front of him, made a fist, then spread his fingers wide and observed the slight trembling of his fingers. He brought his hand back to his lap and took a couple of deep breaths to steady his nerves.

He wasn't sure why he'd been called to the White House, but that was not the source of his anxiety as he sat in a waiting area outside the Oval Office. When Tori had returned to his office to relay her conversation with Sherry, Taylor at first pushed back; this was not a smoking gun, it wasn't even circumstantial evidence—it was a minor coincidence.

Tori was insistent. Though admitting that it was indeed circumstantial, she highlighted the fact that both "Jack" Morgan and Jerrick were both with Colonel Sheng in the Gulf of Aden, and that Terry Grable had spent three months working in the office of the USD for Policy—precisely where Morgan worked as well.

As Taylor thought about it, other minor coincidences came to mind. He remembered Morgan waving off the fact that the Chinese had allowed the U.S. to control the Shanghai operation, chalking it up to the politics around an upcoming arms deal. He also recalled Morgan becoming quite defensive when he heard of Taylor's efforts to send additional experts to the lab in Guam, and managed to resolve it by agreeing to handle it himself. Then, Morgan had been dismissive regarding the notion that there might be something suspicious about the disappearance of the Los Alamos scientists on their way to Guam, when it seemed perfectly logical to think they might be connected.

Realizing full well that he should probably wait for the Secretary's permission—but doubly concerned that time was rapidly running out, he authorized Tori to search all internal databases for phone calls or emails between John "Jack" Morgan, Charles "CJ" Jerrick and Greg Kingsley. Grable and Walker were left off the list since neither had active U.S. government phones and accounts.

As Taylor left for the White House, Tori dug into the task, but found absolutely nothing. This was a little surprising in itself, since Morgan and Jerrick had good reason to communicate, at least on occasion, and ten days ago Morgan had specifically agreed to contact the lab in Guam—meaning Kingsley—on Taylor's behalf.

As Tori had suspected, the data on Kingsley's phone indicated multiple calls, but the numbers involved and call logs were heavily encrypted. It could be days or even weeks to descramble, and the end result might still be gibberish depending on which encryption algorithms were used.

However, it was when Tori grabbed Nate Verit and they utilized the agency's location tracking tools that the real surprises surfaced. The technology was quite simple, and had been utilized by various agencies for some time. All cell phones register with all nearby cell towers every couple of minutes; this allows them to receive and place calls, and for the cell network to manage traffic and ensure optimal signal quality. It also allows, through a process known as multilateration, for the phone's location to be determined by calculating the signal strength between the device and all of the towers within its vicinity. As long as the phone is in the on position, its location is trackable, whether the user makes or receives any calls or not.

Actually pulling up the data and then comparing locations could be incredibly laborious, but a new tool had been developed which relegated the heavy lifting to a software application. Once they plugged in the names of the three individuals whose locations she wished to compare, it came back with any instances where any two of the three shared the same location.

Despite the fact that Morgan and Jerrick had no record of ever talking to each other via their government-issued cell phones, they, or at least their phones, had indeed been in the same location—three times in the past year. Once at or near Morgan's office, once in what looked to be an administrative building at Fort Bragg where Jerrick was stationed, and the last just a month ago on a Fort Bragg golf course.

Tori and Verit then considered whether they might have turned off their phones in advance of other meetings, or perhaps even turned just one of their phones off. She queried the system to list all locations where each man's phone had been turned off, or back on. *Nothing.*

Tori then had an idea. Thinking that maybe these guys would proceed to a remote or secluded location to contact each other using private, secure satellite phones, she had Verit formulate a complicated query that first instructed the system to subtract the 25 most common locations for each of the three men, and then to provide any points in time where two phones were at uncommon locations simultaneously. In essence, they were asking the application to tell them whether any two of their targets were both in strange, abnormal locations at the same point in time—using the locational data from their dormant phones.

"Yes!" Verit exclaimed, pumping his fist as the system came back with several dozen such hits between Morgan and Jerrick, and another ten or so between Morgan and Kingsley. As they began to map and study the list, it was clear that something strange was going on. During one instance, Jerrick was right next to a pond off of Honeycutt Road near Fort Bragg while Morgan was in the middle of Virginia Highlands Park; they both appeared to begin moving away from each location at exactly the same time. In another instance, Morgan was back in the same park, while Kingsley was roaming the woods next to the base in Guam. Once again, Morgan started moving out of the park at the same time that Kingsley started heading back to his lab.

"Tori, this is genius. I never would have thought of it," Verit said as they continued to study the data.

"And I never would have known how to pull it off without your help," she replied, ruffling his disheveled hair. "But we're not done yet; we need to package up what we think we've got and get it to Drake as soon as possible."

They documented the instances that seemed obvious, and Tori crafted an email summarizing their findings. She then sent it off, and contacted Taylor just as he was approaching the White House to make sure he read it on his phone before the meeting with Hawthorne and the President. He did so immediately.

As he sat and waited outside the President's office, he was cognizant of the fact that his evidence was still far from conclusive. But he also felt that he had no choice but to make his boss and the President aware of what his team had found.

It unnerved him to think that he was about to implicate two well-respected members of the U.S. Defense establishment as suspects in one of the worst terrorist plots the country had ever confronted. He pulled a handkerchief out of his pocket and wiped his forehead, then again squeezed his hands into fists to see if he could stop them from shaking.

At last, the door to the Oval opened, and the Secretary of State emerged, closing the door behind her. She nodded at Taylor as she headed out, and he nodded back; they'd never met. He looked at his watch impatiently and realized he'd only been waiting ten minutes.

74

It had now been 20 minutes. *Not a long wait to see the President of the United States,* Taylor thought to himself, but he remained incredibly restless—every minute seemed like five.

A phone rang. The President's personal secretary, working at her keyboard outside the waiting area, picked it up.

"Oval Office," she answered. "Yes. Yes he is... I believe so, yes." She wheeled her chair back and caught a glimpse of Taylor, smiled at him, then moved her chair back to her desk.

"Yes," she said, then listened. "I would suppose so. It sounds like I have no say in the matter." Another pause. "Yes, sir, I understand fully. Goodbye."

The call wasn't any of Taylor's business, but he didn't understand why she'd looked over at him mid-call. It could have been his nerves, but something about it seemed a little off.

After she'd hung up the phone, she got up from her desk and poked her head into the alcove where Taylor was seated. "Mr. Taylor, I'm sure it won't be much longer," she assured him.

"Great. Thank you," Taylor replied. She left, and he heard a door close behind her, leaving him alone in the secretary's annex. He sat in silence for another minute or so.

Through the open door of the alcove he could see one of the two french doors that opened up onto the portico. The marine stationed outside suddenly put his hand to his ear, clearly listening to some kind of communication. Shortly thereafter, a group of uniformed officers appeared; Taylor couldn't see how many.

Curious, Taylor stood and walked to the door of the alcove, and observed as two officers took positions facing one french door, and then two more on the other. Their weapons were drawn.

"Holy shit!" Taylor muttered under his breath, wondering what the hell was going on. Before he had time to give it further thought, the door to his left opened and five officers entered the office. Two held positions guarding the exit, and three advanced to where Taylor was standing.

"Drake Taylor?" one of them asked.

"Yes, that's me," Taylor replied, now totally confused.

"We need you to come with us," the officer stated flatly.

"Come with—? I'm waiting to see the President," Taylor offered. "At his request."

"I'm sorry sir. We have direct orders to take you into custody."

"Custody?" Taylor barked in disbelief. "I don't understand."

"Mr. Taylor, I need you to cooperate," the officer stated.

"This is ridiculous!" Taylor growled, trying to make sense of the situation.

"Please put your arms behind your back, sir," the officer commanded. His voice was calm, but the knuckles on his weapon turned white with tension.

Taylor's stomach clenched. *What the fuck is going on here?* He took a deep breath, and tried hard to remain rational. "Look, this is clearly some kind of screw-up, officer. I'm sure a phone call or two—"

The officer, who seemed to be in charge, cut him off: "Mr. Taylor, please put your arms behind your back." Taylor stood motionless, unable to comprehend the unfolding situation.

One of the other two officers grabbed Taylor's left shoulder, and started to turn him around, but Taylor instinctively rotated his forearm and knocked the man's hand away.

Taylor regretted it immediately. He didn't like being manhandled, but he knew his reflexive response would only make matters worse.

In a flash both men had turned Taylor around and slammed him against the wall, with one of his arms raised behind his back to a very painful position. His muscles flexed, testing the hold. If he'd wished to, he could have given them one hell of a fight, but despite his confusion and racing heartbeat, he realized that these guys were nearly as well trained as he was, and with eight men in total, he wasn't likely to prevail. More important, he was in the goddamn White House, and the best way to untangle this obvious mistake was with calm logic.

"Look," Taylor began through gritted teeth, "this is obviously the result of some misunderstanding. If you'd just allow me to make a phone call, I'm sure we—"

"Mr. Taylor," the officer interrupted aggressively, placing handcuffs on his wrists, "we have orders to bring you in. Once in custody, I'm sure you'll have an opportunity to contact counsel."

"Counsel?" Taylor was incredulous. He couldn't, for the life of him, understand how this could be happening—right outside the Oval Office, no less.

After a thorough patdown, the two other officers swung Taylor around, and he could see that the two by the door had advanced and now had weapons lowered and trained on Taylor's torso. Taylor noted that all of those present had an arm patch declaring that they were members of the U.S. Secret Service Uniformed Division.

Established in the early 1920s as the White House Police, the Uniformed Division had evolved considerably over the decades. It now comprised three branches: one tasked with protecting the White House complex, one focused on foreign missions, and one providing security for the Naval Observatory, where the Vice President's residence was located.

For most of its existence, it had reported into the Department of the Treasury, but in 2003, it was reassigned to the Department of Homeland Security. Taylor was well aware of this last fact, and the irony was not lost on him.

"You gentlemen do know that I'm an undersecretary within DHS?"

"We do, sir," said the officer who had first placed a hand on his shoulder. He said nothing more, and it was clear that Taylor's DHS credentials bought him precisely nothing.

They each took an arm, and began leading him out of the office.

"Wait," Taylor said in an calm, even voice, "my briefcase is in the waiting area. I would appreciate it if one of you could grab it and bring it with us."

The officer who appeared to be in charge looked at one of the guards and signaled with his head for him to retrieve the briefcase. The man found it, placed it on a chair, and took some time to search it for weapons or explosives before bringing it out of the waiting area. Once that was accomplished, the two men with lowered weapons took position behind Taylor and, with officers holding each of his arms, they began moving towards the door.

Taylor was fuming. He had been minutes away from presenting his findings to Hawthorne and the President, and quite possibly on the verge of breaking the terrorist threat wide open, and now this. They moved out through the open door onto the portico, and took a right. The marine stationed at the door closed and locked it behind them as they proceeded along the portico, and down onto a path which curved along the back end of the Rose Garden.

This is ludicrous, Taylor thought as he marched like a prisoner, with arms cuffed behind his back. He reflected on his decades of service in the military; the loss of Rachel in Afghanistan; the lonely life he now led as a man completely devoted to his job—all of the sacrifices he'd made for a government that was now putting him in custody like some common criminal. *What have I done to deserve this?*

As they approached another path to the right which led to the White House swimming pool and, beyond that, a parking area where Taylor assumed a car was waiting, someone behind them called out. Taylor had not heard what was said. He started to turn around, but was yanked back to a forward facing position.

"What the hell is going on here?" the voice said clearly, now closer. Taylor was well aware whose voice it was.

75

The officer in charge, now facing Taylor and the man who'd just called out to them, replied: "My apologies, Mr. President, we certainly didn't mean to bother you. Rest assured, we have everything under control."

"Good to hear, officer, but please tell me what it is you have under control," said President Gilman.

"We have orders to take this man into custody, sir. We'll be out of your way momentarily."

"Drake is that you?" the President asked.

"Yes, Mr. President," Taylor said, his back to the man; he was both incredibly embarrassed and tremendously relieved.

"Officer, bring Drake Taylor back to my office," the President instructed.

The officer looked increasingly uncomfortable standing in front of Taylor. "Mr. President, we have orders—"

"Do it now," President Gilman commanded sharply.

The train of Secret Service officers turned and headed back to the door of the Oval office with Drake Taylor in tow. The President instructed the marine stationed outside to permit the two guards holding Taylor and the officer in charge to enter. All remaining guards were instructed to wait outside.

The President directed his first question at Taylor: "Drake, what the hell is going on here?"

"I wish I knew, sir. I was waiting outside your office to meet with you and Secretary Hawthorne, when these officers entered and took me into custody. I have absolutely no idea why."

The President looked Taylor squarely in the eye. "Drake, you're saying there is absolutely no reason that these men might have for detaining you?"

Taylor needed no time to think. "No, Mr. President, I assure you, this is definitely the result of some mistake or misunderstanding."

The President maintained eye contact with Taylor for a few seconds, then nodded, and turned to the officer in charge. "Officer..." he trailed off, prompting the man for his name.

"Officer Pinney, sir."

"Officer Pinney, who gave you the orders to take Drake Taylor into custody?" the President asked in an even voice.

"The orders were confidential, sir, I—"

"Pinney, who gave you the orders?"

"Ahh, the orders were issued by the Director of National Intelligence, Mr. President. Bob Baker."

The President seemed to consider this for a moment or two, then turned and walked toward his desk. "Release Mr. Taylor immediately," he said.

"Mr. President?"

"You heard me, officer. Release him."

"But I have direct orders—"

"Pinney, are you a fool, or just play-acting? The Secret Service reports to who?"

"We are a unit of DHS, reporting to the DHS Secretary."

"That is correct, and who does he report to?"

"He reports to you, Mr. President."

"Correct again. Now take these goddamn cuffs off of Drake this instant or every one of you will be collecting unemployment within 24 hours."

"Yes, sir." Officer Pinney nodded to one of the guards, who proceeded to unlock Taylor's cuffs. Taylor rubbed each of his wrists—not because they hurt, but more to rub off the feeling of having been captive.

"Now," President Gilman instructed. "You may post one guard outside this office—whether that's you or a member of your team, I don't care. When Drake and I are done, I will let that individual know how we will be handling the situation." He paused. "Is that clear?"

"Yes, Mr. President," Pinney said quietly, "I will remain and send my team back to base."

"Fine. Make it so."

Pinney turned and started to herd his fellow officers back out the way they'd come.

Before they reached the door, Taylor spoke: "Ahh, Officer Pinney? My briefcase?"

The officer with the briefcase handed it back to Drake, and the three of them departed; the marine on guard closed the door.

President Gilman and Drake Taylor were alone in what suddenly seemed a very quiet Oval Office.

76

"You okay?" the President asked, walking over to a sideboard and pouring two glasses of water.

"Yes, sir. But I'll admit to being more than a little confused."

The President handed him a glass, keeping one for himself. He gestured for Taylor to take a seat, then walked behind his desk and sat down as well.

"Tell me how your investigation is proceeding," President Gilman said, "I've been reading your daily reports, and this news about Jerrick is downright shocking—not to mention disgraceful."

"I very much agree, sir." Taylor was still reeling a bit from what had just occurred, and was a little surprised at President Gilman's desire to dig in to the business at hand as if nothing had happened, but such was the President's prerogative. "I'm afraid, however, that it gets worse."

"How so?"

"Well, while we don't have hard evidence just yet, we have reason to believe that John Morgan is involved as well."

The President said nothing. He leaned back in his chair and seemed to fix his eyes on Taylor as he took in this news.

After an uncomfortable silence, he finally responded: "Drake, I know I don't have to tell you that these accusations, starting with Terry Grable and now including the JSOC commander and an Assistant Secretary of Defense, are not easy to take. If your suspicions prove correct, it could turn this country on its head."

Taylor shifted uncomfortably in his chair. "That point is not lost on me, Mr. President. And while I will be the first to admit that our evidence remains mostly circumstantial, I do believe that our suspicions have merit."

"Alright. Walk me through what you've got," said President Gilman, "and please, only facts."

"Mr. President, what about Secretary Hawthorne? Was he suppose to be joining us?"

The President glanced at a small, gold clock on his desk. "He should be here, but I don't have time to wait. Dig in and we'll brief him when he arrives, or you can meet with him later."

"Yes, sir."

Taylor brought the folder out of his brief case and carefully relayed to the President all of the evidence that they'd recently uncovered, including the connections between Jerrick and Grable; Jerrick's insistence on personally running the Shanghai operation; the drill in the Gulf of Aden; and Grable's assignment in Morgan's department.

Taylor then pulled out his phone, retrieved Tori's email, and offered the President an overview of what she and Verit had just discovered through their location tracking efforts.

After hearing Taylor's summary, the President sighed. "Drake, give me your phone."

"I'm sorry, sir?"

"Give me your phone," the President repeated.

Taylor handed him his phone. The President picked it up and held it. "Drake, if I were to have this device analyzed, would I find that you communicated with Ryan Walker before he was apprehended in Costa Rica?"

Taylor was flabbergasted. "No—no, Mr. President. Why would you think that?"

Ignoring Taylor's question, President Gilman continued: "And do you know a man named Alan Stewart?"

"Umm, I'm not sure, sir." The name was familiar, but it took Taylor a moment to recall why. "Yes, now I remember. Alan Stewart is a contact of Ellie Alder's, a woman on my team that we recruited from the LAPD. She and another young analyst met with Stewart not long ago. I do not know him personally," Taylor explained. Then added, "as you may recall from some of my reports, Ellie has quite a few contacts in the world of eco-terrorism. We ruled Stewart and a number of others out at this point; they simply lack the sophistication required for this kind of threat. Can I ask what this is about?"

Taylor felt as if the earth had opened up beneath him and he was falling into a hole. He had come to the Oval Office with a sinking feeling about incriminating American colleagues; he now had a sinking feeling that somehow the tables had been turned.

The President sat without saying a word, looking at Taylor, and tapping a finger against his cellphone which he now held in his hand.

The silence was almost unbearable. He wanted to ask a hundred questions—number one of which was why the fuck Bob Baker would issue orders for his arrest. He wanted to explain to President Gilman why any belief that he was culpable—in anything—was absolutely crazy. But he did neither. He met the President's eyes, and waited.

Finally, President Gilman leaned forward. "Drake, yesterday morning, on my way to Chicago, John Morgan and Bob Baker briefed me on evidence that implicated you as a sympathizer, if not a co-conspirator, in this terrorist threat. They claimed to have phone records clearly indicating that you and Walker had communicated multiple times in advance of his capture."

Taylor closed his eyes, realizing that the odds of prevailing in a truth war against the DNI and a top defense official were poor at best. But when he reopened them, the President continued: "I didn't believe it then, and I don't believe it now. I don't know how Baker figures into this, but I'll tell you something I probably shouldn't: I don't like Morgan and never have. Thought he was a bad hire when we appointed him, and don't trust him as far as I can spit. He sat in front of me yesterday on Air Force One listing a number of facts that you had supposedly covered up. However, last night, after catching up on your daily reports, it was clear that you had provided ample detail on each and every one of them, including what you just said about Alan Stewart. Does he receive those reports?"

"Actually, I offered to loop him in, but Secretary Hawthorne rejected the idea; he wanted to keep that information on a short leash within DHS."

"There's a shocker," President Gilman said sarcastically, "our enlightened intelligence community at work. I'll say this: Hawthorne's inability to share may have saved your ass. And I'll also tell you this, Drake: I don't think you have Morgan yet, but I think you're on the right track."

Taylor couldn't believe what he was hearing. He felt like a yo-yo, plunging from one extreme to another.

"There is one issue, here," the President noted. "The phone calls to Walker." He held up Taylor's phone. "I'm going to keep this and have it analyzed by a different intelligence agency. If the phone records were manipulated, I'm going to find out how—which may not be easy given how many goddamn people have access to them. You're also going to submit to a polygraph. Any problem with that?"

"Of course not," Taylor replied.

"Drake, we now have less than eight days to stop the Guardians of Civilization from detonating devices in cities across the globe. If that happens, and hundreds of thousands of people die as a result, it will be our fault for not trying hard enough. Are we clear on that?"

"We are, sir."

"Good. Because you now have precious little time to find the evidence and round these bastards up."

"I'm well aware of that, Mr. President."

"One last thing. I'm going to assign a Secret Service agent to you."

"Mr. President, that's really not necess—"

"It is, for two reasons. First, assuming you're right about Morgan, and I think you probably are, things could get ugly; second, even a president needs to cover his ass. This guy's job will be both to protect you and to watch you—at least until we clear up the phone records and conduct a polygraph. Fair?"

"Yes, Mr. President," Taylor replied, still a little dizzy from the afternoon's unfolding events. "Are we talking about Officer Pinney?" Taylor asked, turning his head toward the french door outside of which Pinney was standing.

"That idiot?" The President joked, smiling. "No, one of my guys. Top notch. I think you'll like him."

Behind Taylor, there was a knock, and the door opened. "Mr. President, Secretary Hawthorne is here," his secretary announced.

"Thanks, Carol. Send him in. And Carol—could you ask Agent Clasby to join us if he's available?"

"Yes, sir."

Hawthorne entered, immediately apologizing. "I'm awfully sorry, Mr. President. Our plane was forced to sit for an hour on the tarmac in Dulles like a fat sow on hot day in July. I still have no clue why."

"Well have a seat, Dan. I think we have to catch you up on a few things, and make some decisions on next steps."

77

So far, it had been one hell of a day—but it wasn't over yet. As the Cadillac headed out Connecticut Avenue, Taylor's new phone rang just as they passed the National Zoo. It was Tori; he'd reached her just before leaving the White House, and she was calling him back. He looked at the device given to him by the President's secretary, found the right button, and answered the call.

"So are we all set?" Taylor asked without a greeting.

"We are," Tori confirmed. "As requested, I processed the paperwork for accessing Jerrick and Morgan's email. We're downloading the data into our system as we speak."

"Thanks, Tori."

"You know, of course, that we're not likely to find much on their DOD computers. They'd be idiots to use those for anything related to the GOC plot."

"I'm aware of that. I still want to go through them with a fine tooth comb."

"Understood. I'll call you if we find anything."

"Okay, I should be back at the NAC within ten minutes or so."

"Got it."

Taylor hung up the phone, and looked at the man sitting next him. "So, I'm not entirely sure how this works," he began. "Should I assume…?" Taylor trailed off.

Secret Service Agent Tom Clasby knew exactly what was being asked. "Should you assume that you can trust me as you go about your business? Yes, absolutely," Clasby stated firmly. "I will reveal nothing that I observe or overhear except to the President. "With that one exception, I will treat everything I see and hear to be confidential and privileged information."

Clasby was not a large man, but seemed extremely solid, as if his body was somehow more densely packed than the average mortal. He had short, reddish hair and gray eyes. Not young, not old; Taylor suspected he might be in his mid-forties. It was clear that he was very comfortable in his own skin, and in his job.

"Alright," said Taylor, "that seems workable."

"Good. Just remember, Mr. Taylor, I will do whatever is necessary to protect you, but at the same time my job is also to monitor your activities and whereabouts at all times."

Taylor smiled and shook his head. "Yup, I get it. Seems crazy to me, but I understand the situation."

"Well, it's new territory for me as well."

Taylor was now heading back to his office after what had could only be described as an emotional roller coaster ride. However, after final discussions with President Gilman and Secretary Hawthorne, he now had sufficient resources, and unambiguous authority.

Now all he needed was enough evidence to make a move.

78

President Gilman wrapped up the call. He was very, very close. Working with his Secretary of State, he now had China, India, and 15 other members of the G20 on board—every country, in fact, except Italy and Turkey, who were both holding out in hopes of getting their way on unrelated issues. The President had already put wheels in motion to address their requests, and expected them to join the group's consensus within 48 hours.

Ironically, Saudi Arabia, Canada and Brazil, three countries endowed with tremendous fossil fuel resources, had been early supporters of the plan. Leveraging their endorsement had been instrumental in convincing others.

Of course, the huge question lingering in everyone's mind was whether the treaty that President Gilman had put forth would placate the Guardians of Civilization. It was not the GOC's document, and differed substantially with regards to timeline and economic penalties for non-compliance, but it was definitely a binding treaty on emissions, with a carbon tax as its central tenet.

By effectively spurning the GOC's document and taking independent action, President Gilman had walked a fine political line. He could honestly state that the G20 would not be acquiescing to the GOC's demands, but would nonetheless be taking prudent action on a timeline of their own choosing. From the start, it was very clear that very few world leaders had an appetite for completely "giving in" to the GOCs demands, yet each and every one of them was petrified at the prospect of a nuclear device detonating in one of their major cities.

The G20 signatures that President Gilman hoped soon to have in hand signified that the leaders would commit their best efforts to drive for full approval by their respective governments. The President knew that this could take months, or even years—but the GOC had only asked for a commitment by the leaders of the developed world; they knew as well as he did that trying to get legislative or parliamentary approval in advance of the deadline would be pure folly.

The risks to the U.S. President's approach were threefold. First, the plan would inevitably be attacked by many, including some portion of the U.S. House and senate, as a form of appeasement. President Gilman and the G20 leaders would be perceived as caving in to the demands of terrorists. Second, the new treaty would be attacked on the opposite front as "non-compliant," essentially inviting the Guardians of Civilization to carry out their nuclear threat. He fully expected these reactions, and while he was unsure whether he could overcome the appeasement argument, he was confident that that the non-compliant camp would be shouted down rather quickly.

However, there was a third possibility that worried him greatly; it was really a combination of the first two. Since President Gilman's plan would be signed by G20 leaders and did not represent a full commitment by G20 governments, its success might ultimately boil down to politics. If the majority of legislatures, parliaments and citizens circled the wagons in support of the plan, then the argument could be made that real action was being taken, and the President calculated that the GOC would allow the new treaty and back off their threat. If, however, there was immediate and vocal opposition from legislatures and parliaments, then there was a distinct possibility that the GOC would decide that their demands had not been met and they should carry out their threat.

President Gilman and the staff he'd brought into the process were mildly astounded by the fact that the effort had yet to leak. There had certainly been speculation, and a few media outlets seemed to have bits and pieces of the story, but it never metastasized into a full-blown exposé. One reason for this was obvious; there was just too much other news to report.

Civilization was essentially eroding. With just eight days before the GOC's deadline, people all across the globe were now fleeing large cities in droves, and casualties resulting from this exodus were mounting. Looters were now running rampant in increasingly empty cities; incidents of road rage were increasingly common as urban refugees made their escape; and those living outside of cities were defending their property from invading city-dwellers with everything they had. Law enforcement did its best to preserve order, but was ultimately impotent, as events overwhelmed the systems that normally maintained the veneer of a functioning, civil society.

In the midst of this, President Gilman and other G20 leaders were doing what they felt they had to do: find a solution to the crisis that would alleviate the threat while alienating the smallest possible percentage of the electorate that brought them to power.

79

"Wow," said Verit, as he subconsciously spun his pen around his thumb. "This guy really gets around."

"I know, right?" Ellie nudged him and pointed at the wall. "Look at this. He actually went to the Kentucky Derby last year. Who actually does that?"

The five of them—Taylor, Tori, Ellie, Verit and Agent Clasby—were in the cleared-out conference room looking at a wall now more cluttered than ever. Much of the previous session's material had been pushed off to the side, and a new set of photos, itineraries, locations and emails now covered the corkboard from floor to ceiling. The morning sun was blasting through the windows, once again making the room incredibly warm.

They were now looking at the goings on and extra-curricular activities of John Morgan, having just gone through a similar exercise for Charles Jerrick.

The journey into Jerrick's background had not yielded much, in large part because there wasn't much to yield. The man appeared to eat, sleep and breathe the military, and was rarely anywhere but on a base, in meetings at the Pentagon, or directly involved in a sanctioned operation. The one exception made perfect sense: Jerrick seemed to have attended nearly every single seminar, briefing, or event in and around Washington that involved the military and its connection to climate change. His one-time CO and current mentor, a four-star General named Hank Hothroy, was the designated leader of a non-profit military advisory board of retired generals and admirals who all supported aggressive action by the United States on the issue.

Verit had seized the opportunity to explain that this advisory board of extremely well-respected and decorated U.S. military leaders had caused quite a stir when they declared their view that global warming was a serious threat to America's national security. They referred to it as a "threat multiplier," noting that it was already increasing instability in volatile areas around the globe. Left unaddressed, the group stated unequivocally that it would dangerously stretch U.S. military resources as more and more trouble spots demanded more and more interventions by U.S. military personnel.

While the group offered a number of recommendations for how the nation should address the issue, it was very clear from Jerrick's emails that he was a big believer in bigger, bolder action. Just six months ago, in a late-night missive to Hothroy, Jerrick had strongly urged the retired general and the board to use whatever means necessary to convince congress of the critical need for action, including a board-led drive to get active soldiers and officers from all branches of the armed forces to unite in support of such action. This, of course, went directly against long-held policies, and Hothroy appeared to have been somewhat taken aback by Jerrick's stance—so much so, in fact, that their email exchanges became fairly cool thereafter.

However, as they studied Morgan's movements and interactions, it was a whole different ballgame. Morgan travelled extensively—both for his job and to areas and events that were clearly part of a very active social life.

"Unfortunately," said Tori, sitting in the back and staring at her laptop, "there doesn't seem to be the same connection to climate change that we found with Jerrick." She tapped away at her keyboard, coaxing the emails she'd downloaded to offer up answers. "In fact," she declared, "there doesn't seem to be a single mention of it anywhere."

"That seems hard to believe," Taylor offered. While he was well aware that the evidence on Morgan was flimsy, his instincts were dead certain that Morgan was somehow involved—and that his run-in with the uniformed division of the Secret Service had something to do with his team getting a little too close to the truth. "Tori, you're saying that, of all the seminars and briefings that Jerrick attended, Morgan did not go to any of them?"

"Not a one," she replied.

"Keep looking," said Taylor, feeling increasingly anxious to find more incriminating evidence. The President had been quite clear, and Taylor had agreed: If they moved on Morgan with insufficient proof, the guy would likely shut up and offer nothing at all. They needed something to hold over him, and they didn't have it yet.

Ellie was standing at the board, flipping through a few pages that were tacked under the label *Locations.* "Check this out," she said, without turning her head from the documents she was studying. "As Morgan travels to a number of different destinations, there's a number of instances where our tracking files do not have him landing at major airports. In other words, his starting point in several cities appear to be small airports or even no airport—which could, I guess, be a helipad."

"And these are private trips, Ellie?" Taylor asked.

"They seem to be."

Taylor turned. "Tori, can you work your magic on this? Search for anything that might indicate how he's getting from A to B."

"On it," she said.

"Ellie, are you seeing any common locations?" he asked. "Any place where Morgan seems to be going multiple times?"

"Hmmm." Ellie flipped through several pages. "Yes," she concluded. "It looks like he has repeatedly visited a spot in the Blue Ridge Mountains, and another on Chappaqu—" she stopped. "The print-out is a bit smudged, so I can't read the full name, but it looks like it's part of Martha's Vineyard." Tori walked to the back of the room to get her laptop.

"I think you mean Chappaquiddick," said Agent Clasby, offering the first spoken words since he'd been introduced to everyone at the start of the meeting an hour ago, and causing all to turn and stare at him awkwardly. Clasby just shrugged. "I serve presidents, and happen to know Martha's Vineyard fairly well." He smiled confidently and offered nothing more.

"Thank you, Tom," said Taylor, smiling slightly and now on a first name basis with his protector. Clasby just waved a hand subtly as if to say *don't mention it.*

"So," Tori announced, "I think I just found out how he's getting around major airports. He seems to have a close friend in Francis Vermeer."

"The Francis Vermeer?" Verit asked.

"The very one. There are quite a few emails here discussing trips together, each involving logistics regarding both his private jet and helicopter."

"That seems like a mismatch," said Taylor. "Why would Morgan be hanging around with one of the richest guys on the planet?"

"I think you mean why would Vermeer be hanging around with him?" said Verit.

"Fair enough," Taylor acknowledged. "But that just seems odd to me."

Francis Vermeer was the Chairman of Isis Therapeutics, one of the most successful biotech companies in existence. For over two decades, the company had been on a roll, offering one blockbuster drug after another. It was estimated that the man's net worth was north of 30 billion dollars. He was famously private, but also known, on occasion, to give away lavish sums to causes he cared most about.

"And no surprise," Ellie announced, now seated in back with her computer on her lap, "The coordinates on Morgan's tracking sheet place him squarely on Vermeer's twenty-seven acre compound on Chappaquiddick."

"So what does that tell us?" asked Taylor, speaking as much to himself as the others.

"I'm not sure," said Tori, "but here's another little nugget: None of those trips on Vermeer's plane or helicopter were reported as gifts."

Taylor shook his head, and sighed. "Great. So we've got him on violating the gift policy. Not exactly the damning evidence we were looking for." He looked at his watch. "You guys can keep going here, but I've got an appointment." He looked at Tom Clasby, who looked at his watch, then turned to grab his coat off his chair.

They both knew that Taylor was due at Secret Service headquarters for his polygraph. He was actually looking forward to it. He certainly did not enjoy undergoing polygraphs—they were uncomfortable and unnerving; however, he wanted to put the previous day's events, and the stain of perceived complicity, behind him.

"There's a lot here, Drake," said Tori, "I'll have my team dig in and explore all of it. We'll find some actionable evidence."

"Alright. Thanks, Tori. But let's go further: if these guys are using private satellite phones to plan this whole thing, then we need to get our hands on those devices. Based on what we've got so far, can you draw up the paperwork for a search of Jerrick's and Morgan's cars and apartments, and get Hawthorne to sign off?"

"Consider it done." Tori closed her laptop and stood up. "I actually have to head out as well—I've got a meeting with the new FEMA Administrator."

"Andrea McKnight?" Taylor asked as he grabbed his suit coat and briefcase.

"Yes. She wants an update on our efforts to see if it might help her better target FEMA resource deployments."

"Huh," he replied, wondering why McKnight wouldn't have reached out to him directly. Since she was appointed, they had been in a few meetings together on a handful of occasions, and had developed somewhat of a rapport.

Taylor and Tori walked out of the conference room back toward their offices, with Agent Clasby quietly falling in behind. Ellie and Verit remained.

"I don't think I have anything for her," said Tori. "We don't exactly have any intelligence on device locations at this point."

"No, but if we can be helpful in any other way, let's do it," he said. "At this particular point in time, I'd say she has the worst job in Washington."

"Next to yours, you mean."

Taylor laughed. "Yeah. Next to mine."

As they approached Sherry's desk, they noted that Andrea McKnight had already arrived, and she and Sherry were chatting. She wore a dark gray pant suit which—though not exactly stylish—conveyed an air of competence.

"Andrea, good to see you again," Taylor said warmly.

McKnight looked up. "Likewise, Drake," she replied. "And Tori, good to meet you." She extended her hand as Tori returned the greeting.

"You come all the way over to our humble DHS campus and you don't even tell me you're coming?" Taylor teased.

"Well, I had a sense that you had enough on your mind. Plus, it was a scheduling issue. I had to be here for some other meetings, and you seemed to be unavailable."

"True," he replied, looking again at his watch, "just heading out. Everything okay with you?"

"You know that's a loaded question," McKnight replied. "Things are pretty hectic."

"I'll bet."

"We've got a lot of ducks in a row, but we're a long way from where we need to be."

"What are the big issues at this point?" he asked.

McKnight paused to give to give the question some thought. "Well, probably how and where to most effectively stage our resources, the trickiest of which are the ARS medications."

"ARS?"

"Acute Radiation Syndrome," she replied. There's a new drug available that can mitigate a fair amount of the cell damage that occurs following moderate radiation exposure, and we need to make some decisions quickly on where to stage it. It's a little finicky to move around, and needs to kept at low temperatures at all times."

Taylor sighed, giving momentary consideration to the concept of ARS drugs and to the horrendous catastrophe that might result if he failed in his efforts. "To be honest I am totally focused on finding the bad guys; I don't even want to contemplate what it would mean if we don't."

There was an awkward silence. "I'm afraid I don't have that luxury," said Andrea.

"No," he replied, as they exchanged a serious look. "No, I guess you don't."

80

"You made a total fool out of me!" Bob Baker bellowed, nearly poking the side of Morgan's head with his index finger. "Do you know how bullshit the President was?"

"I assume he was fairly angry," Morgan replied quietly.

"Good fucking assumption. I'll tell you, Morgan, you truly screwed the pooch on this one," Baker said. "I'm not sure you'll be able to recover from it." He paused, briefly, then added, "Hell, I'm not sure if I can recover."

"Director Baker, I am incredibly sorry if I—"

"Sorry won't cut it, I'm afraid," Baker shot back. "Virtually all of the so-called evidence you gave me was fully explained in reports that Taylor had already given the President. You made me look like an idiot!" Baker turned his head and looked away. "And you have the balls—and the incredibly poor judgment—to have Taylor apprehended as he's standing outside the goddamn Oval Office! When I said you could use my authority to make the arrest, I assumed you'd do it in a somewhat less conspicuous fashion!"

Baker had a loud voice to begin with, but everything he had to say on this occasion was at two or three times his usual volume. They were standing in a small room in the basement of the CIA's massive facility at Langley. Baker had demanded that Morgan meet him there. At first Morgan assumed it was to further discuss the evidence and how best to proceed, but now it was crystal clear that Baker had called the meeting for the express purpose of ripping him a new one. It did not appear that Baker cared one way or the other as to whether anyone could overhear.

After several moments, Morgan calmly broke the silence. "I realize I should have been much more vigilant regarding what Taylor included in his daily reports, but the fact remains that he made calls to Ryan Walker well in advance of his capture. Even if the other evidence doesn't—"

"Oh for chrissakes!" Baker interrupted Morgan again, pulling his phone from a holster on his belt, and angrily bringing up an email. He read from the small screen: "regarding the calls to Walker, an IT specialist…" he stopped, realizing he had the wrong section of the message, and scrolled down several times. "Here it is: …the calls made by Drake Taylor to Ryan Walker do indeed appear in the system, but there are clear irregularities with how the data is formatted. Further investigation will be required…" He scrolled down a few more times, then returned his phone to his belt. "I think you get the gist. The bottom line is that there seems to be a strong possibility that the calls were inserted into the record." Baker stared at Morgan, who refused to look back. "What the fuck is going on here, Morgan? Is this all political? Do you have some kind of vendetta against this guy? Whatever the hell it is, I want no part of it."

"I understand."

"Yeah? Do you?"

The question hung in the air, and Morgan chose not to answer it. It was very apparent that the conversation had come to an end.

* * *

Morgan felt a little beaten up as he sped along the GW Parkway back towards the Pentagon. Getting taken to the mat by Baker was clearly not pleasant, but he had it coming.

Up to that point, Morgan felt he'd done a fairly good job of managing the flare-ups, ensuring that Jerrick only knew what he had to know. His usual philosophy was: if he could take care of it, then no one else need be the wiser or need get involved, and morale remained high. However, at this juncture, he felt he had no choice but to at least issue a warning.

As he passed Fort Marcy Park, Morgan reached into the glove box and pulled out his satellite phone, dialed the unlock code, punched in the number, and put the phone to his ear.

Jerrick picked up after three rings. "Jack, I've got about three minutes; let's make this quick."

"Where've I reached you?" Morgan asked, attempting a bit of small talk.

"Jack, I've got very little time here. What is it?"

Jerrick's demeanor was much sharper than usual, but Morgan ignored it. "Well, nothing specific. I just wanted to let you know that Drake Taylor seems to be making decent headway in his investigation. As we'd discussed, it may be time for us to vanish."

Morgan heard what he thought was a sigh on the other end of the satellite call. "You there?"

"Yes, I'm here. What do we know about Gilman's efforts?" Jerrick asked.

"I've only received a few bits and pieces, but it looks like he is indeed working towards some kind of an agreement. Beyond that, I have no specifics."

"Well at least there's that," Jerrick offered.

"CJ, we are proceeding very close to our original plan," Morgan said. "However, as we knew it would, the shit is hitting the fan, and these guys may be fairly close to uncovering who's involved. You should think seriously about disappearing."

Again, a long silence from Jerrick. Finally, "It's just not that simple, Jack. I've got a lot going on here. Good men involved in critical operations. I can't just drop the ball."

Morgan's tone caught an edge. "CJ, I would strongly suggest you do exactly that. If they figure this out, and you're apprehended, things will get ugly very quickly—for both of us."

"And there it is," said CJ, a sarcastic tone now infiltrating his words "Jack Morgan: always looking out for the other guy."

"That's not fair!" Morgan shot back. "The whole purpose of this call was to warn you about—"

"The whole purpose of this call is to make sure that I don't put you in jeopardy by getting caught," said Jerrick. "Well don't worry about it, Jack; no matter what happens to me, I'm not going to be turning anyone in."

Morgan knew damn well that such assurances were not enough, but he also knew that he'd get much farther with a carrot than a stick. "Look, I promised you that, when this was over, I would ensure that you could live a comfortable life, and I mean to keep that promise."

"Yeah, well I've been giving that a lot of thought," said Jerrick. "I'm not entirely sure I want your help."

Jack's tone once again soured. "Oh, and why is that?"

"Because I'm not sure I trust you, Jack. I have no idea what enables you to make that promise, and I'm not sure I want to know."

"CJ, where is all this animosity coming from? Is something going on that you're not telling me?"

"Perhaps I should ask you that question."

"What the hell does that mean?"

"Well, Jack, for starters, a few days ago, Wolfe told me that you had ordered him and two other operators to kidnap a couple of scientists from the Honolulu International Airport."

Morgan paused briefly, deciding how best to respond. "CJ, I did order that operation, and here's why: If those scientists had made it to Guam, we would have been badly exposed."

Morgan added, "in doing so, I saw no reason to loop you in—it only would have made you an accomplice."

"An accomplice," CJ repeated incredulously. "We hatched and executed a plan to threaten civilization with nuclear devices, and you're worried about my complicity in tying up one loose end."

Morgan wasn't quite sure what to say, so remained silent.

"What else aren't you telling me, Jack?"

"CJ, What's gotten into you?"

Jerrick changed the subject. "So how close is Drake Taylor to figuring all of this out, and how much time do we have?"

"I can't say for certain. I have a plan to stall Taylor, but I would still strongly suggest that you wrap things up and make yourself scarce within four to five days, tops."

"And your plan for Taylor, it's 'need-to-know' only?"

"CJ, what do you want from me? I'm busting my ass to shore up this whole effort and prevent it from unraveling! I don't need your crap!"

"I guess not, Jack. And I don't need yours. Thanks for the warning."

The line went dead, and Morgan realized he'd driven several miles past his exit.

81

Ellie, Tori and Verit were all clustered in Tori's office, discussing whether their circumstantial evidence on John Morgan was nothing more than coincidence.

"I'm just not sure we have anything on the guy with any substance whatsoever," said Ellie. "I mean, you look at Jerrick, and his one-man crusade on the issue of global warming, then combine that with other evidence, and it makes for a solid case. With Morgan, we're falling short."

Tori frowned. "You're right, Ellie."

"I don't think so," said Verit. "The locational data is strong. That couldn't possibly be coincidence."

"Nate, it's entirely circumstantial. We need something tangible," said Ellie.

"No, she's right, Nate," Tori added. "Dig deeper into his personal emails, and see if there's any cryptic language between those he's interacted with the most over the past year. Maybe he's using some kind of code to set up meetings and calls."

"Alright. There's a new program I can use—it's designed to look for uncommon phrases and non-sequiturs. Should speed the process." Verit pushed himself away from the wall against which he'd been leaning and started to head out.

"You know, Nate," Ellie offered, "you might see if Morgan's buddy, what's-his-name Vermeer, has any links to climate change—or to any of the other actors involved. Those two still strike me as an odd couple."

"I'll take a look." Somewhat dispirited, Verit walked out the door.

"Ellie," Tori instructed, "We ran an analysis of all special forces operators who've served with or under Jerrick, and came up with this list." She handed Ellie a single piece of paper. "I'll email it to you as well. I'd like you to do a locational analysis on each of these folks in conjunction with Jerrick. It's quite possible that, just as Morgan, Kingsley and Jerrick all seemed to be in strange places simultaneously, the same might be true with Jerrick and these men."

"By strange places, you mean any unusual location where both might be communicating via a secure sat phone?" Ellie asked.

"Precisely. Enlist Nate's help if you need it."

"Okay." Ellie got up from her chair. "By the way, did we get anything off of Kingsley's phone?"

"Yes and no," answered Tori. "Since we only have the one phone, it's hard to draw conclusions—but we did confirm that the analysis we did the other day was accurate: When Kingsley's regular cellphone showed him wandering in the woods by the base in Guam, timestamps show he was talking on the sat phone at the same time. It all matches up with Morgan's movements, but it's just not enough."

"Tori, what is enough?" Ellie asked. "If there's even a chance these guys are behind this, and there's seven days left before the deadline, shouldn't we just bring them in?"

"I hear you, Ellie. But the logic is, if we've got nothing on them, there's no good reason for them to open up. We could use harsh techniques, but if by chance we've missed the boat, we'd be torturing senior members of the military—and U.S. citizens to boot. Bottom line: we need more. Hawthorne just authorized us to search for Jerrick's and Morgan's sat phones. If we can get our hands on them, we should have pretty good corroboration."

82

Agent Clasby, who'd been sitting patiently just outside the soundproof room on the fifth floor of Secret Service headquarters where Taylor was holed up, dropped the magazine he was reading back on the stack, and stood up. He put clasped hands behind his head and stretched his torso to the left and right, and brought each leg briefly to his chest.

He then looked at his watch; Taylor had been in there for over an hour. He walked twenty feet down the hall, turned around, and walked a short distance in the other direction.

Finally, the door opened, and Taylor emerged; he put his briefcase on a chair and gave a nod to Clasby as he put on his suit coat. He pulled his phone from the inside breast pocket and powered it on, having been instructed to turn it off during the polygraph. Fairly quickly, the phone popped up a number of priority messages noting that Tori Browne had called repeatedly.

"How'd it go?" Clasby asked as he approached.

Taylor looked up from his phone. "It went well. I assume the full results will be sent to my boss and the White House, but I'm guessing I won't be tried for treason after all." They both chuckled.

"Good to hear," said Clasby, picking up Taylor's briefcase and handing it to him. "Ready to go?"

"Thanks. Yes, all set," Taylor replied, still slightly uncomfortable at having someone assigned to him.

They took the elevator to the lobby, signed out, and headed outside to their waiting car, with Taylor scrolling through accumulated emails as he walked.

The driver of the Cadillac was leaning against the vehicle and stood when he saw the two of them exit the building. He opened the rear passenger door. "Here you are, Mr. Taylor."

"Thanks," he replied, looking up only briefly before getting in. The door closed behind him.

"Where's the car that brought us here?" Clasby asked the driver.

"It had a mechanical problem and had to return to base, Mr. Clasby. I was sent to pick you up instead," the driver replied, walking around to the driver's door without offering to open the other rear door for Clasby.

"Why wasn't I notified?" Clasby asked, pulling out his phone and remaining on the curb next to Taylor's door.

"I don't know—you sure you don't have a message?" The man asked, not slowing down as he opened the driver's door to get in.

"Drake. Out of the car. Now!" Clasby commanded, opening the door and forcefully grabbing the shoulder of Taylor's suit coat.

Taylor sprang out of the car, and the driver did the same, quickly turning to point a Ruger suppressed .22 handgun directly at Clasby's chest. Both men froze.

Though it was clearly Taylor this man was after, the driver knew that Clasby was definitely armed, while Taylor was probably not. Taylor wasn't used to being helpless when guns were involved—and he didn't like the feeling one bit.

"Get behind me," Clasby said firmly under his breath.

"Tom, I—"

"It's not a request," Clasby cut him off calmly, without emotion. Taylor did as he was told, feeling powerless.

"Hands up, Clasby," the driver warned.

Tom Clasby made a quick decision. To go for one of his weapons would likely draw the driver's fire, meaning Clasby would take one in the vest—or worst-case, the head. Either way, he'd be out of commission and Taylor would be a sitting duck. Instead, knowing Taylor's history, Clasby slowly raised his hands—but he didn't stop when his hands were on either side of his head; he continued raising them until his arms were straight up in the air and slightly forward, pulling his suit coat awkwardly upward as well.

The driver narrowed his eyes, trying to understand the Secret Service agent's somewhat strange method of compliance with his command, but chose to ignore it. "Alright. Taylor, get in the car," the driver instructed. Neither of them moved. Taylor seemed to be frozen, unsure how to proceed. "Taylor, last chance. You have five seconds to get back in the car, or I take out your protector here. After that, I have no qualms about putting a bullet in you as well."

"Do it, Drake," said Clasby, staring straight at the driver.

Taylor fully understood the meaning of Clasby's instruction, and took a deep breath. He'd only have one go at this.

"Okay, take it easy, I'm getting back in the car," Taylor said to the driver. As he leaned down to reenter the vehicle, he reached his hand behind Clasby's back and seamlessly pulled a SIG Sauer P229 from the agent's now exposed back holster. Then, in one fluid move, he slid into the seat, glanced at the chamber indicator, aimed the weapon and rapidly fired three shots through the front side window into the driver's abdomen. The driver stumbled backward and fell to the ground, clutching his stomach with his free hand; blood seeped through his fingers.

Upon hearing the first shot, Clasby had leapt over the trunk of the car, and as the driver landed, he kicked the weapon out of his hand, rolled the man over, and put zip cuffs on both his hands and feet.

Taylor approached. "That was damn good thinking, Tom. Shit, at first I had no idea what you were doing with that weird reach for the stars thing."

"Well, I'm awfully glad you figured it out, Drake. Nice shooting," Clasby pulled the driver to his feet as the man winced in pain. His pale blue shirt was drenched deep red over his stomach. Clasby turned him so he was facing the trunk, then pushed him over so he was now bent at the waist with his chest on the car.

Taylor walked over to pick up the driver's weapon.

"Don't touch that!" Clasby barked. Taylor pulled his hand back and turned, half expecting to see the agent holding a gun on him—after all that had happened of late, Taylor truly had no idea which end was up. But Clasby had only raised his hand. "Drake, the last thing we want, at this point in time, is your fingerprints on a strange weapon. Come and hold this asshole while I get it."

Taylor stood and walked towards the car. "That's probably a good call."

They switched positions, and Clasby retrieved the gun with a handkerchief, carefully removed the clip, and placed gun and ammunition in separate pockets of his coat. Then he looked up at Taylor and laughed gently. "I really can't believe this guy had the balls to pull this off directly outside Secret Service Headquarters."

As if on cue, the door of the building burst open and several armed agents came out to assist, weapons drawn.

"It's okay, guys," Clasby said, pulling his badge. "The Sundance Kid and I seem to have this situation under control."

83

Verit emerged from the shower, grabbed a towel, dried his hair, wrapped the towel around his waist, and went back into the bedroom to turn on the radio.

Business news. *Just as well,* he thought, heading back to the sink to shave. Verit considered himself a news junkie, of sorts, but of late it had gotten rather monotonous, filled with non-stop stories of tragedy from the Philippines—and horrible crime stories about people treating each other badly in their mad rush to get the heck out of the city. And not just Washington—the stories poured in from cities all around the world.

It had started to gnaw at him. The ceaseless drone of bad news was a constant reminder that he and his colleagues had yet to find the perpetrators and put an end to the panic.

He lathered his face with shaving cream as the anchorwoman ran down the results from the previous day on Wall Street. The stock market was not faring well in all of this. The mayhem and madness that now dominated urban life had, not surprisingly, badly upset the markets.

"In total, the Dow dropped another 92 points yesterday, with losers outstripping winners three to one," the voice on the radio announced. "One bright spot was Isis Therapeutics, which gained three and a half percent, reaching an all-time high of 271. The S&P was also down for the sixth straight session, finishing the day..."

Verit froze. He looked at his half-shaved face in the mirror, grabbed a washcloth, and hastily removed the remaining shaving cream. He rushed back to his bedroom, opened his laptop, and spent the next ten minutes researching his suspicion. His hunch was confirmed.

Adrenaline now pumping through his veins, he hastily got dressed, threw his laptop in his bag, and ran out the door. He needed to learn more, and that required getting at information only accessible from inside the DHS firewall.

84

Morgan pulled into the Pentagon's sprawling South parking lot and drove up towards the reserved section. Parking policies at the Pentagon were arcane. There were multiple 50+ page documents outlining who could park where, yet virtually everyone sought to get around the rules. At the top of the food chain, however, it was fairly simple: parking permits were allocated to individuals based upon the square footage they occupied within the Pentagon itself.

Morgan, therefore, was in the clear. As an Assistant secretary of Defense, even his top staff merited parking spaces—though much further away from the entrance than his own.

He pulled into his spot, turned off the car, grabbed his bag and hopped out. As he walked toward the building, he pressed the lock button on his key fob and put it in the front pocket of his bag. He passed some poor sap in a GMC Yukon holding a map of the Pentagon complex, and walked on.

Five minutes later, as Morgan entered the building, the man in the Yukon folded his map and put it on the passenger seat next to the jamming device. He got out of the vehicle, walked over to Morgan's BMW, opened the driver's door, and hopped in.

By jamming the frequency used by Morgan's key fob to lock the car, the device prevented the signal from reaching the vehicle, leaving the car unlocked as Morgan had walked away. Once inside the car, the man tried the glove box, noted that it was locked, then did a quick search—looking under the seats and in all open compartments. Nothing. He then pulled a small case from his vest pocket, extracted a tool, picked the glove box lock, and opened it. Bingo.

Meanwhile, 320 miles away in North Carolina, a very similar scenario played itself out in a parking lot at Fort Bragg.

85

"Here he is—our boss, the special ops bad-ass!" Ellie exclaimed as Taylor entered the room. Everyone laughed and cheered for a few seconds; Tori scanned him head to toe, making sure he was truly unharmed.

Taylor smiled, but he was already tiring of the attention. First of all, it was simply embarrassing. Second, though he had never been at liberty to discuss it, the previous day's incident outside of Secret Service headquarters was fairly mild in the context of the many extreme situations he'd confronted with the 75th. Last, with just six days remaining before the GOC's deadline, his sense of humor was drying up.

The team, with the exception of Verit, was assembled in Secretary Hawthorne's conference room. After the foiled attempt to abduct Taylor, it was decided that he and his team should receive additional security, and the Secretary's suite was perhaps the most secure spot on the NAC campus. They had been instructed to abandon their building and would now be working out of an open area near the secretary's office. Furthermore, another agent had been assigned to help Clasby, who was now responsible for the entire team.

"Okay, folks," Taylor said, holding up a hand, "I appreciate the accolades, but we've got a hell of a lot to do here, and I want to get to it." Everyone quieted, and Ellie looked a little sheepish. He realized he'd shut her down, but wanted to dig in—especially after losing several hours the night before to paperwork and debriefs related to the shooting. "Over the past thirty days, this team has done some excellent work, and I want to thank you—and all of your people—for putting in ridiculously long hours. Unfortunately, as everyone here knows, it's simply not enough. We seem to be getting very close, but so is the GOC's deadline. The bottom line is this: I don't care how long it takes, but we are not leaving this room until we've got the evidence necessary to begin rounding up the sons of bitches responsible for the panic out there. As I've said before, well-supported suspicions won't do it; we need enough evidence to show these bastards that we've got 'em."

Taylor paused and looked at each face in the room to make sure they understood, then frowned. "Tori, where the hell is Verit?"

"He sent me a text early this morning saying he might be late," said Tori, picking up her vibrating phone.

"Goddamn it, I wanted everyone here at eight am sharp. Did I not make that clear in last night's e—"

"Drake?" Verit said from the doorway, a little out of breath, and looking more disheveled than usual. "I'm sorry for being a few minutes late, but I think I've got the goods on Morgan."

"Meaning what?" Taylor asked.

"Meaning we have a money trail that makes it pretty clear what Morgan's up to," Verit replied.

"And as of about ten minutes ago," Tori interjected, reading a text that she'd received as Verit appeared, "we now have both his and Jerrick's sat phones."

* * *

"So every time Isis lands a new contract for Radivene," Verit explained, "Morgan's account receives a payment."

Verit had started at the beginning, noting that after he'd met Andrea McKnight as she was leaving the NAC yesterday, Tori had mentioned the whole issue around the staging of ARS medication. When he heard on the news this morning that the stock of Isis Therapeutics was rising when the rest of the market was tanking, he jumped online wondering if by chance they were one of the sources for the medication. It turned out that they weren't one of the sources—they were the sole source.

Radivene, as the drug was called, was designed to help victims who'd experienced heavy doses of radiation. Normally, such exposure would trigger the death of critical cells, making the victim highly susceptible to infection and internal hemorrhage. Radivene, using what was known as cytokine therapy, leveraged a cocktail of different biological formulations to help reconstruct the victim's blood cells without requiring cell transplantation. It had initially been seen as an important discovery but only a modest moneymaker, most helpful in the aftermath of nuclear accidents like Fukushima, Chernobyl or Three Mile Island.

However, on the heels of the terrorist threat to detonate nuclear devices in three major cities, the drug was suddenly in great demand. Governments from all over the world had placed multi-billion dollar orders, and Isis had scrambled to keep up with demand. Meanwhile, the company's stock had soared.

As Verit learned all of this, his next hunch concerned Morgan's relationship to Isis Chairman Francis Vermeer. It didn't require a huge intuitive leap to wonder whether Morgan might somehow be profiting from all of this. Utilizing the new FinCEN portal developed by the Treasury Department for researching financial crimes and the movement of money into and out of terrorist organizations, Verit discovered three offshore accounts in John Morgan's name.

"And what are we talking about here, Nate? How big are the payments?" Taylor asked.

"Very big," Verit replied. "At this point, John Morgan appears to have received over eighty-five million dollars." He spun his pen around his thumb as if for emphasis.

Everyone in the room was stunned by the figure. Ellie whistled softly.

"Just want to make sure I heard you; you said eighty-five million?" Taylor asked.

"Yes. Eight Five—and that's just the accounts we've discovered thus far; there may be more."

"That's a shit ton of motive," Ellie said emphatically. "I can't believe that these fuckers would threaten the world just for money. It's disgusting. And Isis is making these payments? That seems awfully brazen to me."

"No," clarified Verit, "the money is most definitely not coming from Isis. It's coming directly from Vermeer."

"We're sure of that?" Taylor asked.

"Well, we've got a clear, verified trail for several of the payments. They originate at one of Vermeer's Swiss accounts, travel through another Swiss bank, and end up in Morgan's account. We don't have a trail for all of it, but I've asked the guys at Treasury to lend a hand; we should know a lot more over the next twenty-four hours."

A few seconds passed as everyone digested all that they'd just heard.

"Damn. Incredible work, Nate. Well done," said Taylor.

"Thanks." Verit tried to suppress a smile.

Taylor looked more closely at Verit. "Nate, I don't want to embarrass you, but why does it look like half your face is shaved and the other half isn't?"

Verit's face turned deep red as he touched a hand to each cheek. "Well," he explained, "I was shaving when the Radivene connection occurred to me. I guess I didn't want to waste any time."

Taylor grinned. "That's what I call dedication." He clapped Verit on the back, after which Ellie winked at him and gave him a quick hug. Verit flushed even deeper, clearly pleased by the attention.

The moment passed, and Taylor looked over Tori. "Alright, then. That's definitely enough to pull in Morgan, but what about Jerrick?"

Tori, who'd been monitoring her laptop ever since she'd gotten the news on the satellite phones, pored over recent messages, and found one that offered the information she was after. "It looks like they've downloaded the contents of both phones, and put them back where they found them. It appears they haven't yet—" She stopped herself, and skipped down in the message. "No, I'm wrong. They're estimating having a report for us by three pm this afternoon, but can confirm that the two phones have been in direct contact well over a dozen times."

"Excellent," Taylor said. "Alright folks, listen up. We've now got what we need to bring Morgan and Jerrick in, but we need to harvest every nugget possible from all the data we've generated here. The more we've got, the more pressure we can apply to these guys to call off the threat. We also need to dig in and try to identify as many other players as possible, so we can round them up as well."

"What about Vermeer?" Verit asked.

"Don't worry, Nate. He's on the list. But I want both Morgan and Jerrick in custody before we take any action on Vermeer." He looked around at the faces in the room. "I know this goes without saying, but I'm going to say it anyway: all of you need to treat this information as top secret; do not share it with anyone that is not directly working with you on a related activity. Is that clear?"

Everyone around the room offered a muted yes or simply nodded.

"We are now damn close to cracking this thing," Taylor continued. "As I said earlier this morning, I'm well aware that I've asked a lot from you, but right now I need to ask for a lot more.

All of you need to double-down and leverage our progress, and get everybody who works for you or with you to do the same."

He grabbed his brief case and prepared to head out. At the door, he turned back to the team. "What we do in the next few days will determine whether hundreds of thousands of people die, or return to their normal lives. It will also determine whether we emerge as scapegoats or heroes. Personally? I'd prefer the saving lives/hero option. Let's get it done."

As he finished his pep talk, he looked directly at Tori, as if to say *I really need you to drive all of this home.* She immediately understood the implied message, and gave him a smile as she subtly nodded her head in response. *You are an incredible woman,* he thought, hoping that this message would transmit as well. Her smile broadened.

Finally, Taylor turned and left the conference room with Agent Clasby. His next task was to brief Secretary Hawthorne and get the required authorization and resources to finish the job.

86

Morgan's BMW pulled out of the Exxon Station on Leesburg Pike and took a left.

Tori was beside herself. As Morgan had left the Pentagon, the GPS signal from his car had cut out, leaving her and the FBI team in charge of his capture completely blind. Miraculously, the signal had reappeared about fifteen minutes later at a gas station in Idylwood. Three FBI units had immediately converged on the signal and were now discreetly following the vehicle as it headed north on the Beltway.

Why Morgan hadn't been apprehended at the Pentagon still baffled Tori. There had been a huge kerfuffle over who had responsibility for making the arrest; the FBI insisted they would handle it, while the DoD Police would not budge in asserting that they had exclusive jurisdiction over the Pentagon complex. The fact that this argument was unfolding as the GOC's stated deadline was now just 72 hours away was incomprehensible.

Finally, the FBI decided to take Morgan into custody at his apartment or at the first stop he made after leaving the Pentagon, since no one wanted a car chase if it could be avoided.

Taylor had wanted to be in Washington as this went down, but the President, hosting a special meeting of G20 leaders at Camp David, had asked for a private briefing. Taylor, Secretary Hawthorne, and Agent Clasby had taken a helo to Frederick County Maryland earlier in the day. The briefing had just wrapped up; the President was pleased at the progress, but was now doubly insistent that they finish the job and put an end to the threat. Since the status of Taylor's efforts directly impacted how President Gilman would play his discussions with world leaders, he'd asked to receive updates every four hours—or as soon as there was any substantive change in status.

Taylor emerged from Aspen Lodge, Camp David's main meeting facility, and immediately called Tori.

"How'd things go with Gilman?" she asked.

"It went well," Taylor replied, but he was now somewhat impatient to tie up all loose ends. "Tell me where we are with Morgan."

"I gotta say, Drake; the bureaucracy in this town is hard to believe. We're now tailing Morgan in his BMW, and should have him in custody shortly—but I'm sick over the fact that we should have had him an hour ago."

"You mean the shoving match between the FBI and DoD police you mentioned earlier? It is amazing, but after a couple of decades in the military, it hardly comes as a surprise." Taylor steered them back to the topic at hand. "Where is Morgan now?"

Tori pulled up the application on her laptop that was monitoring the GPS signal. "Let's see, looks like he's just gotten on Interstate 270. Now that we allowed him to fill his tank, he could go all the way to Pittsburgh," she lamented.

"Alright. Keep me posted. As I know you're well aware, I want to see him as soon as we get him get back to DC."

"I am well aware, Drake," Tori said patiently.

"Okay, good. I just have to finish up here with the Secretary, and I'll be heading back."

*   *   *

The BMW got into the right hand lane, and took Exit 10 off of I-270. The three FBI units followed, each carrying four agents apiece. Though it was the middle of the day, traffic was fairly heavy as more and more people had made the decision to leave the city in advance of the deadline. Many cars were stuffed to the gills with luggage and belongings—some had gear tentatively roped to the roof.

Morgan took a left off the exit and headed east towards Gaithersburg. Kat Stenson, the FBI Special Agent in Charge, was in the passenger seat of the lead car. She picked up the radio and confirmed their location with dispatch, then addressed her team: "Alright folks, get set. I'm guessing our opportunity is coming very soon." The BMW turned right onto a smaller side street. As Kat's car made the turn, another car pulled out of a parking lot, separating her from Morgan. A 12-year veteran of the Bureau, she remained calm, and checked the small laptop installed above the center console. Even if they temporarily lost line of sight, the GPS would allow them to track closely behind. She looked in the side mirror to see units two and three round the corner and fall in behind.

Morgan took a left, as the car behind him went straight, leaving Kat a clear view of her target. The BMW continued for several blocks, then took another left. The neighborhood had an eerie feel to it, with most driveways empty and no signs of life in well over half of the houses—yet more signs of people getting the hell out of Dodge in advance of the GOC deadline.

After two more blocks, Morgan signaled and pulled into the driveway of a small yellow ranch. A young woman in a striking red cocktail dress, who'd obviously been awaiting his arrival, came out of the house with huge smile across her face.

"Alright, team, let's take him," Kat barked into the radio.

All at once, the three FBI units screeched into position behind Morgan's car and 12 doors opened simultaneously; 12

agents drew weapons and assumed a crouched position as Morgan emerged from the driver's seat.

"Both of you, hands up!" Kat yelled. They both complied immediately, as the young woman's smile contorted into a look of pure fear.

Kat looked closely at the BMW to see if there were any additional occupants. None. They certainly hadn't seen any while in pursuit. Her mind raced, wondering what had gone wrong. The car was clearly Morgan's; the license plate matched, and the GPS was accurately signaling it's location. But the man who'd just emerged from Morgan's BMW was 20 years younger, 20 pounds lighter, and definitely not John Morgan.

"Driver, close your door slowly and put your hands on the top of the car," said Kat. He did exactly as instructed. Kat looked at the young woman. "Tell me who else is in the house."

Tears were now running down the woman's face, taking recently applied mascara along with them. She was clearly petrified. "It—it's just me and my mother."

Kat drew a deep breath. She was furious at this turn of events. She looked back at the driver. "What's your name?" she asked him.

"It's Sal, Salvatore Petrangelo."

"And where did you get this car, Sal?" Kat inquired sternly.

"I rented it, officer. I'm taking my girlfriend out for a special date, and I wanted to impress her with a nice ride," he replied. At this, his girlfriend started crying uncontrollably, and brought one hand to her face to wipe away the tears. Kat would ordinarily have demanded she raise her hands, but the woman's dress was so tight it was pretty clear she wasn't packing a weapon—while the heels ensured she wasn't going anywhere quickly.

"What do you mean, you rented it? From whom?"

"From some guy on the web. Through a car rental website; it's totally legit!" Sal insisted.

"Did you meet 'this guy'"? Kat asked.

"Yeah, I just picked it up. We'd agreed to meet at a gas station in Idylwood."

Kat shook her head. They'd been played. She motioned for two agents to cuff both Sal and his girlfriend, then instructed three other agents to check the vehicle. They holstered their guns and moved into the driveway, carefully inspected the interior of the BMW, and popped and inspected the trunk.

After a few minutes of further discussion, an inspection of the house, a look at the rental contract—which was, in fact, legitimate—and identification from all at the scene, the agents uncuffed the young couple and Kat returned to her vehicle to make the unpleasant call to DHS.

After explaining what apparently had transpired, Tori was at first incredulous. "Agent Stenson, did any of your units actually see the driver when you picked up his trail in Idylwood?" she asked.

"I'm afraid not. Using the GPS, we actually fell in behind the vehicle as it approached the onramp to I-495," explained Kat.

Tori was despondent. *They'd been inches away from capturing the ringleader of the GOC, only to let him slip away—all because of a bureaucratic, territorial pissing match over arresting authority at the Pentagon.*

Then she snapped out of it, rapidly forming a tasklist in her head for what needed to be done next.

"Agent Stenson, we'll need that vehicle back here for immediate analysis. Please make sure that nothing is removed."

"I'll see to it," Kat replied, and the call ended.

Kat then chatted privately with Sal Petrangelo. Without offering any detail, Kat explained to him that this had been a case of mistaken identity, and asked him a number of additional questions about his brief interactions with Morgan at the gas station. She also informed him that the car would be immediately impounded, and gave him her card so he could contact her for reimbursement.

Sal groaned. "You don't understand, officer. I need that car." He leaned in a little closer and spoke very softly so no one else would hear him. "We're going downtown for dinner tonight and I'm going to propose to my girlfriend."

Kat smiled, somehow refreshed by the fact that life continued despite lunatic threats from terrorists.

"Congratulations," she replied earnestly. "But you'll have to make do without the car. I'm sorry."

Having somehow bounced back from having twelve agents point weapons at his torso and head, Sal now turned away, deflated that his evening was unraveling.

"Tell you what," Kat offered, realizing the trauma they'd injected into these two young lives, "when you contact me for the rental fee, send me your dinner receipt as well. This one's on us."

Sal's face lit up, and a broad smile emerged. "Are you serious?"

"I am, Sal," Kat replied, hoping like hell that a free dinner would suppress the nightmare lawsuit that could well have resulted from the day's events. "By the way," she added, "I'm sure you're aware that terrorists are threatening major cities; you're not at all worried about that?"

"Naw," Sal replied. "My dad says we can't let ourselves get pushed around by terrorists. As soon as we do, they win."

87

"He rented out his fucking car?" Taylor yelled. "I don't believe it; I don't believe those assholes let him get away."

Taylor was standing outside the Camp David Field House near the helipad with Agent Clasby. Given the comings and goings associated with the President's meeting of G20 leaders, there was a backup and the helicopter that was supposed to take him and Clasby back to Washington was only just now approaching to land.

"Tori, we need to get on top of this right away. For starters, we'll need any video footage available from that gas station—"

"I've already contacted the security firm, and we should have it within minutes."

"Good. Next, now that the element of surprise is clearly gone, we need to move on Jerrick immediately. I know we wanted Morgan first, but—"

"Drake, I've already been in touch with the FBI. Jerrick is currently scheduled to give a presentation to a veteran's group starting in about five minutes. Say the word, and we'll take him."

"Do it." Taylor offered silent thanks to whatever higher power had placed Tori by his side.

"Okay. Let's hope this goes better than the last."

"No shit. Tori, the question is where the hell Morgan went. Have you started to formulate a list of possibilities?"

"I have three members of my team doing nothing else. But if he knows we're after him, his destination will likely become very unpredictable."

"Agreed. But we have to start somewhere." Taylor looked up to see Bob Baker walking his way. "Hey, Tori, I need to go. I should be in the air shortly and back at the NAC within an hour or so. If you get your hands on that footage, I think you know how to reach me."

"I do," Tori confirmed.

When Taylor hung up, Baker was nearly upon him. "Drake, I wanted to have a word with you."

"Of course, What can I do for you, Director Baker?" Taylor asked politely, somehow managing to quell the urge to drop the guy to his knees.

"Please, call me Bob."

"Alright, Bob. I will." *Though I'd rather call you Dick*, Taylor thought to himself.

"Drake, I'm sure it's much too little, much too late, but I wanted to apologize for jumping the gun in response to Morgan's suspicions. Getting accosted by the Secret Service inside the White House had to be a horrible situation, and I fear it was entirely my fault."

Out of the corner of his eye, Taylor saw Agent Clasby suppress a small smile. He wanted to tell Baker just how incredibly humiliating it had been, and castigate him for his gullibility, but realized it would get him nowhere. Instead, he focused on Morgan's whereabouts. "I appreciate it, Bob. But please forgive me for changing the subject: I know you've been read in on Morgan's involvement in all of this. An FBI effort to bring him into custody just went south; given your interactions with him, would you have any idea where he might hide out?"

Taylor heard the sound of an incoming helicopter; it grew louder as it appeared over the treetops and started to descend.

"Gosh, Drake, I don't," Baker said, leaning in towards Taylor to be heard over the noise. "Morgan and I never got particularly close. Truth be told, he's not a very likable guy. You know, I knew his father quite well, may he rest in peace. Now he was a great man; I shudder to think what he—"

Taylor didn't need to hear this man's ruminations on Morgan's father. "Bob, this is my ride back to DC. If you think of anything, let me know," he replied, nearly yelling as the helicopter landed. He nodded at Clasby who ducked and went around to the other side of the helo. Upon getting the signal from the pilot, they both opened the doors and stepped up and in.

Taylor was about to shut the door, when Baker ran up to him through the wash of the blades, and motioned that he had a thought. Taylor bent back down to listen.

"Morgan's father hated Washington," Baker yelled. "He used to escape to a cabin in the Blue Ridge Mountains every chance he got. I wonder if that cabin still exists."

At first Taylor had no idea what the old man was talking about, but then he realized what Baker was suggesting. He nodded vigorously to indicate that he understood. "Thanks, Bob. I'll check that out," he yelled back.

Baker nodded in return and moved away from the helicopter. Taylor closed the door and buckled in as the machine rose back into the air.

88

The Palladian Ballroom was standing room only. The main event, an awards gala honoring those whose actions had positively impacted the lives of soldiers and veterans, would not occur until the evening. It was to be held in a much larger ballroom in a different part of the hotel.

Years earlier, shortly after the Association of Veterans from Iraq and Afghanistan had been founded, the gala was launched as a singular bash for which many traveled long distances to attend. Its popularity, however, caused the organization to expand the it into a two-day conference, with talks and presentations by military and civilian leaders bracketing the star-studded event.

Ironically, the number of attendees skyrocketed even as the wars in each country had started to wind down. This was, in part, a result of more soldiers becoming veterans, and more politicians wishing to pay their respects to those who'd served. It was also due to simple nostalgia; as more time elapsed, the desire on the part of veterans to reconnect grew exponentially, turning the conference and gala into a massive reunion.

Commander Jerrick's presentation, titled *Climate & Conflict in the 21ˢᵗ Century: A Rising Storm*, had definitely drawn many interested vets, but Jerrick knew better than to think they'd all shown up for him. He had cleverly lobbied to be slotted on the heels of another session that he knew would be a big draw— *Life, Liberty, and Maximizing Your VA Benefits.*

Jerrick walked to the podium, retrieved the remote control for his presentation, and then stood quietly, waiting for the audience of about 500 to settle down. He was wearing his dress uniform, featuring a fairly impressive array of awards and decorations.

Knowing that many in the audience had fairly limited knowledge of the topic, he began with the basics:

"Climate change is a very complex phenomenon, but conceptually, it's fairly simple. Greenhouse gasses, foremost among them carbon dioxide, build up in our atmosphere, forming a blanket, of sorts, which prevents solar radiation that reaches our planet from reflecting back into space. The thicker the blanket, the more heat that gets trapped, and the greater the average rise in global temperature."

Jerrick flipped through a number of slides which visually depicted the mechanics of global warming.

"There is nothing new here. This phenomenon, along with significant changes in global temperatures, has occurred throughout geologic history. Just recently, in mid-2013, researchers from Stanford University took a close look at major climate events or transitions that have taken place since the extinction of the dinosaurs—including our emergence from the most recent ice age. During that period, temperatures increased between 3 and 5 degrees Celsius, similar to what scientists tell us could occur by the end of this century." He paused for effect. "So, there you have it: we've seen this movie before— what's the big deal?

"Well, the big deal is this: The Stanford Scientists observed that that the earlier changes in global temperature occurred over a period of 20,000 years, whereas we will likely see a similar change occur over a span of just decades. When this type of disruptive change occurs over millennia, animal and plant species are at least offered some time to adapt; when it happens within a single century, adaptation for most living things is not an option. In fact, the Stanford researchers found that the rate at which global temperatures are changing is up to one hundred times faster than anything the Earth has experienced in over sixty-five million years. And that is a very big deal.

"So there's the context. Let's now focus in specifically on how the issue might impact our nation's military. In 2008, in response to a bipartisan request from Congress, the National Intelligence Council, or NIC, prepared what is called an Intelligence Community Assessment of the security challenges presented by climate change."

Jerrick pressed the button on his remote and a new slide began populating with the official seals of numerous government agencies.

"The Assessment was a collaboration between 16 intelligence agencies, including the Central Intelligence Agency, the Federal Bureau of Investigation, the Defense Intelligence Agency, the Office of Naval Intelligence, the State Department's Bureau of Intelligence and Research, and various other organizations within the U.S. intelligence community. The report was also informed by outside experts and allied partners.

"Though the full, 58-page report was classified, a basic summary was made public. It's conclusion? Climate change poses a very real threat to national security.

"According to the Chairman of the NIC, the report looked at the national security implications through 2030, and concluded that changing weather patterns could contribute to political instability, disputes over resources, and mass migrations of regional populations. It noted that climate change would have wide-ranging implications for national security because it will aggravate existing trouble-spots, serving as a 'threat multiplier' in regions where governments are already unstable, such as Sub-Saharan Africa, the Middle East, and Central and Southeast Asia.

"Then in 2012, the Secretary of State, increasingly concerned about how a warming planet might impact the geopolitical landscape, asked for an assessment of global water security. In response, another Assessment was prepared, once again leveraging the effort and input of 16 intelligence agencies. The new Assessment offered the following summary of its key judgments, and I quote:

"'During the next 10 years, many countries important to the United States will experience water problems—shortages, poor water quality, or floods—that will risk instability and state failure, increase regional tensions, and distract them from working with the United States on important US policy objectives. Between now and 2040, fresh water availability will not keep up with demand absent more effective management of water resources. Water problems will hinder the ability of key countries to produce food and generate energy, posing a risk to global food markets and hobbling economic growth. As a result of demographic and economic development pressures, North Africa, the Middle East, and South Asia will face major challenges coping with water problems.'

"However," Jerrick noted emphatically, "despite these two definitive Assessments, each involving many thousands of hours of effort from some of our nation's best and brightest analysts, the United States—save for one voluntary agreement with China—has yet to display any global leadership on this issue. In major climate talks held in Kyoto, Bali, Copenhagen, Cancun, Durban, Doha and Lima, our nation has dropped the ball on an issue that could directly threaten our security as a nation."

Jerrick allowed his statement to hang in the air. For years, he'd been convinced that, when and if the military came to the conclusion that global warming imperiled our national security and argued for action, then the balance would finally tip.

He'd been wrong.

The military had made it clear—repeatedly—that this was a critical issue, and yet somehow politics had shouted down such concerns, offering nothing in return. In fact, Congress had actively worked against them, denying the military the funds and resources necessary to implement new energy technologies that would not only reduce their emissions, but also shorten the troops' "logistical tail" in wartime and save lives.

Jerrick couldn't understand why the military's well-researched conclusions were not carrying the day. In response, he did the only thing he knew how to do: he tried harder. Using every spare minute available, he worked vigorously with an array of different groups to advance more research, promote new voices and reach new audiences—but progress was elusive. In fact, there were many days when it seemed as if the issue had lost ground instead of gained.

"This much is clear," said Jerrick, looking out on the assembled crowd of veterans, "the frequency and severity of droughts, floods, fires, storms, and other events are on the rise."

He began pressing his remote in a rhythmic fashion, pulsing through slide after slide of devastating, real-world images of recent extreme weather events and the horrible toll they'd taken on people around the world.

"When this is combined with a global population that has nearly quadrupled—yes, quadrupled—in the last 100 years, you have a recipe for extreme cultural stress. From a national security standpoint, we will witness substantial geopolitical instability in numerous regions—regions where climate-induced events will far outstrip the ability of the impacted society to manage an appropriate response.

"One example close to home: As storms in the Caribbean worsen, countries like Haiti and Cuba will experience more frequent humanitarian disasters. The United States will likely be forced to confront the possibility of massive migrations from these countries to our shores—or find itself providing tremendous levels of aid to offset such an eventuality.

"In short, U.S. military intervention for missions involving humanitarian assistance and disaster relief will grow rapidly. This will strain our forces, and will require an ever-greater expenditure of dollars and resources. In many regions, the large-scale disruption caused by climate-related events will lead to political violence—which, in turn, will undermine governments and may then require other kinds of U.S. military action.

"In numerous hotspots around the world, particularly in Africa and Asia, natural disasters can weaken governments and allow the wrong elements to gain strength; worst case, these areas will become breeding grounds for terrorists. By way of illustration, consider the African nation of Mali. Hard-hit by droughts, shrinking rivers, and a resulting decline in agricultural production, the government was overthrown by Al-Qaeda-linked militants in 2012, who leveraged the country's increasing instability. While it would be inaccurate to say that climate change caused this overthrow, it is quite clear that it multiplied the existing threat.

"Another example played out in 2010, when severe wildfires in Russia led to a dramatic decrease in grain output. In response, Russian grain exports were reduced, and the world witnessed a sizable spike in grain prices. This, in turn, raised the price of basic goods throughout the Middle East, and was believed by many analysts to be a significant contributor to the uprisings associated with the Arab Spring.

"Although a warming planet will not often be the direct cause of any given conflict, there is little doubt that it will serve as a potent catalyst for instability. In other words, a conflict that might not have justified U.S. involvement might now intensify to the point where a U.S. response is required.

"Even with regard to well-developed nations, a warmer world will serve to heighten tensions and make relationships more complex. For example, in the Arctic, scientists now consider it a near-certainty that we will witness the vanishing of summer sea ice by the middle of this century. The Northern Sea Route and the Northwest Passage will become areas of contention between major powers, as each seeks to dominate the area for shipping and oil exploration. Although the likelihood of armed conflict is low, the situation will inevitably create tensions between the U.S. and other nations, which may then play themselves out on other fronts."

Six months earlier, Jerrick had become completely discouraged—and angry. He was furious that a monstrous locomotive was barreling down the track aimed directly at the livelihood of billions of people worldwide, yet neither the United States, nor any other major economic or military power was willing to take a stand and call for real action.

When Morgan first approached him, Jerrick considered the plan deranged, and he waved it off. There was no way in hell he was going to sell out his country and sign on to a terrorist plot. But as denial and take-no-action rhetoric within the U.S. ratcheted up—while the science only grew more and more confident, he started thinking differently.

By chance, he'd happened to come across the writings of a modern-day philosopher named Roderick Davidson, an Oxford-trained authority on the ethics of war and conflict who posed a simple question: Is it possible for the immorality of a terrorist act to be outweighed by the good that such an act achieves?

Jerrick wrestled with this. If, in fact, a plan such as Morgan's was the only way to wake the world up and lead developed nations to act on an issue that threatened the very livelihood of humanity, then was it—could it possibly be—justified?

He didn't know the answer, but he did know this: As Commander of Joint Special Operations Command, his job was to send men on missions where identified targets would be taken out, or "neutralized"—occasionally with some amount of "collateral damage," meaning that innocent lives were lost in the process. Conceptually, the cause was just; the United States had a right to defend its citizens from both real and perceived threats. But he knew full well that the moral justification for quite a few of these missions was vague at best. JSOC was one of the sharpest spears in the U.S. armed forces, and one of the most powerful tools the country had in combatting terrorism. Its actions were authorized by the chain of command and an invisible army of lawyers—but the truth was that, while JSOC units often walked a fine moral line, most believed that any questionable acts on their part were far outweighed by the good that they achieved.

After much contemplation, Jerrick came to look at Morgan's plan through a similar lens. The moral imperative of acting in the face of climate change was, once he thought it through, more definitive than his day job. As such, with more than a little apprehension, he signed on and began helping Morgan recruit the required team.

Jerrick continued with his presentation. On the screen, he began clicking through beautiful, high-resolution images of America's coastal cities. In the back of the ballroom, there seemed to be some kind of commotion, but it seemed to resolve quickly.

"Global warming does not threaten the viability of a country as large as the United States. However, its effects can kill or endanger large numbers of people, cause civil disorder, and damage critical infrastructure."

The images then switched to images of devastation wrought by hurricanes that had hit the U.S. mainland over the past decade. Jerrick listed each storm as he advanced the slides: "Jeanne, Charley, Frances, Ivan, Katrina, Rita, Wilma, Ike, and Sandy. While the impacts of climate change extend well beyond hurricanes, the rising intensity of these storms, in combination with rising sea levels, remains one of the most dangerous domestic threats we face."

Off to Jerrick's right, two police officers entered the ballroom and stood quietly. He didn't think much of it, and continued.

"Nearly 50 percent of Americans—over one hundred and fifty million people—live within fifty miles of the coast. A number of years ago, a NASA simulation that combined a modest forty-centimeter sea-level rise by 2050 with storm surges from a Category 3 hurricane found that, without new adaptive measures, large parts of numerous American cities would be inundated, resulting in significant damage to infrastructure and dwellings, and causing a substantial blow to regional economies. One of the cities modeled in the simulation was New York; NASA's model anticipated that flooding would occur throughout much of southern Brooklyn and Queens and portions of lower Manhattan. Sometime after this simulation was completed, Hurricane Sandy very effectively confirmed NASA's projections.

Jerrick crossed the screen, stopped, and turned to face the crowd. As he did so, he noticed three more policemen standing by the other entrance. This gave him pause. They did not seem to be taking any action, simply standing by the entrance. Were they there for him? Morgan had warned him that DHS may be on to them; had this incredible adventure suddenly reached its end-game in the Palladium Ballroom of the Omni Hotel? The officers were all looking at him, but then again, so were the other five hundred people in the room.

Jerrick wasn't sure what was going on, and really had no way to find out, unless he wanted to stop his presentation and ask someone—or try to leave. However, since he'd already made up his mind some time back that he would not run from his actions, he decided to simply carry on. If they stopped him, so be it. But if not, he'd finish his presentation.

"For obvious reasons, many of our military bases are also situated in coastal regions. Severe storms can also impact—or even undermine—our national defense resources."

Jerrick heard rumblings from the audience. He casually looked left and right, and noted that half a dozen fully armed SWAT agents had now joined the police officers at each entrance. It seemed increasingly clear that his time had come, but he was determined to finish.

Pressing the button on his remote, he now displayed a series of photographs of storm damage to various military installations.

"For example, Homestead Air Force Base in Miami, the home of the U.S. Southern Command, suffered intensive damage from Hurricane Andrew in 1992, and never reopened. Pensacola Naval Air Station was shut down for nearly a year on the heels of Hurricane Ivan in 2004. The truth is that our nation's military might has been and will continue to be impaired by the adverse impacts of rising sea levels and more intense storm activity.

"Overall, the U.S. military manages property in all 50 U.S. states as well as 40 other countries around the world. These facilities are valued at nearly $600 billion—"

A SWAT agent had walked calmly to where Jerrick was standing, and very quietly informed him that he was under arrest. Jerrick had the foresight to cover his lapel microphone with his hand as the man approached to ensure that the agent's words were not conveyed over the sound system.

"Well, folks," Jerrick said without missing a beat, "a situation has arisen that requires my immediate departure. I apologize for having to cut this short."

There was an awkward silence as he removed the microphone from his coat, pulled the wire so it disconnected from the transmitter clipped to his belt, and left both on a small table near the screen. He followed the agent out of the ballroom, and quickly found himself surrounded by a bevy of armed guards as he was handcuffed and led from the building.

89

This time, Taylor knew the drill. "Tori, hold on a sec." He looked up at the communications panel, and watched the light go from yellow to green as the pilot switched himself out.

"Alright, we're secure. What have you got?" Taylor asked.

"First the good news: We have Jerrick in custody."

As he heard Tori say the words, Taylor felt a huge weight leave his shoulders. He quietly pumped his fist. "Excellent. That is great to hear."

"No fight, no fuss. Looks like he had decided he wasn't going to run. If you're back in time, you'll have the first crack at him; otherwise, we're recommending that General Williams, Commander of the United States Special Operations Command, take a shot. The thinking is that chain of command may still mean something in Jerrick's mind."

"Not a bad idea. You know that I served under Hank Williams during my time in the 75th."

"I didn't know that," Tori replied. "Think he's the right guy for the job?"

"Right enough," said Taylor, "certainly better than letting the CIA guys beat the crap out of him. But Tori, I think I still want the first crack. Let's have Williams meet with Jerrick after me."

"Okay, I'll make sure that's understood."

"Good. Are they taking him to Langley?"

"I believe so, yes."

"I should be there within an hour."

"Alright," said Tori, "now the bad news. We've been analyzing the video footage from the gas station; Morgan must have scoped it in advance, and knew to stay away from any cameras. We can clearly see his BMW leaving with the kid in the driver's seat, but there's no footage of Morgan leaving."

"Goddamn it!" Taylor barked, feeling the weight crawl back up his spine. "So we've completely lost him."

"Not necessarily. There's a little more to it. A white Toyota Corolla is shown leaving the gas station about five minutes after the BMW. It appears as if there's only the driver in the car, and he's wearing a hat, but we think—"

"It's Morgan?" Taylor asked impatiently.

"No, we think it's Terry Grable."

"Wow. There's a twist. But you said he's alone in the car?"

"I said he appears to be alone. Given the camera angle, it would be easy for someone to crouch down and go unseen."

"When will you know if it's Grable?"

"Our video guys are enhancing it now, and we've fed them every known image of Grable that we've got. I'm guessing we'll have confirmation within the hour. The car was rented two days ago from a Hertz outlet in Tyson's Corner using fake identification."

"Any video footage from available from Hertz?"

Tori sighed. "Nope. Nothing. And the alias used is not one we've seen before—whether by Grable or anyone else."

"So what's next?"

"Well, we've put out a BOLO on the car, but given how clever Morgan has been, I'm guessing they'll switch the plates."

"Can't we include a description of Grable?"

"Oh, we did, and also noted that the plates could be from any state. But all that means is that we're about to get barraged by possible sightings."

"Did you limit the area?" Taylor rubbed his eyes, thinking of other possible actions they could take.

"Of course, but we're talking a late model Toyota Corolla here—not exactly an uncommon vehicle. As I noted earlier, we're also finishing up a list of possible hide-outs, but I'm not hopeful that Morgan would be stupid enough to use a known or linked location."

"That reminds me, for the reasons you just mentioned, this may not be useful, but Bob Baker just told me that Morgan's father had a cabin somewhere in the Blue Ridge Mountains."

"Okay, I'll make sure that police departments in that area are given a special heads-up."

"Anything else?"

"Nope."

"Alright. Tori, thanks. You're the best. I'll call you once I get to the CIA."

"Talk to you then. Be safe, Drake."

*   *   *

Twenty minutes later, Taylor was chatting with Clasby as the helicopter made its way south. From spending every waking hour together for the past several days, the two had become friends, and Taylor had confided details of the situation to a man whose opinion he now trusted—and whose discretion was unimpeachable.

They were kicking around the topic of Morgan's whereabouts, when the pilot clicked back in and notified him of an incoming call from the same party. Taylor didn't wait for the green light.

"Tori, what's up?"

"Drake, miracles do happen. I acted on Baker's Blue Ridge tip right after we hung up, and an off-duty police officer just made Grable and Morgan as they passed through Afton, Virginia."

"You're sure?"

"Positive. He was clever enough to take a stealth photo with his iPhone."

"Incredible. Nice to get lucky once in a while. Where's Afton?"

"Right off Route 64—on the Blue Ridge Parkway."

"Did the officer pursue?"

"He is tailing them, but from a distance. I've already notified the FBI. They're assembling a SWAT team and should be airborne with 30 minutes."

"Half an hour?" Taylor asked. "Out of Quantico?"

"Yes. They told me they can be on site in 70 minutes."

"You mean the cabin?"

"Yes."

Taylor leaned forward and signaled for the pilot to open the call up to everyone on board. The pilot leaned forward, hit two switches and nodded over his shoulder.

"Tori, what are the coordinates of the cabin?"

"Hold on a sec." She worked her laptop for a few seconds, and listed the GPS coordinates. She then added, "it looks like it's right near a place called the Sugar Tree Inn," she added.

The pilot looked back at Taylor. "I know roughly where that is—right near where the Parkway hits Route 56."

"How long would it take us?" Taylor asked.

The pilot gave it a moment's thought. "We're fairly close. I could have you there in about ten to fifteen minutes."

Taylor looked over at Clasby. "This is where Morgan is headed. You up for this?"

Clasby just smiled calmly and gave a steady thumbs up.

Taylor looked back at the pilot. "Let's do it."

"Drake," protested Tori. "This is insane. There's two of you. Wait for the SWAT team."

"And let this bastard slip away again? Not a chance."

"Drake, I can't let you do this." There was panic in her voice.

"Tori, I'll be fine. As you may recall, I have a little training." He looked at Clasby, then the pilot, realizing this conversation was public.

"Drake, Grable and his team killed two policemen in cold blood in Shanghai. He'll have no qualms taking on you and Clasby. Please don't do this," she pleaded, "I don't want you to get hurt—or worse." The panic in her voice had now devolved to tears.

Taylor was somewhat taken aback by this uncharacteristic surge of emotion. "Hey, don't get upset," he said softly, trying to comfort her. Clasby looked away to give him at least the semblance of privacy. "Tori, if these guys got away because I held back, I'd never forgive myself." Then, in a quieter voice, "I'll be okay. Clasby and I will be careful, and when—"

"Drake, please, please don't do this!" Tori said, her voice cracking.

Taylor drew a breath and exhaled. "Tori, I have to," he said firmly, tapping the pilot on the shoulder and silently giving him the signal to proceed, "and I'm going to need your help."

The helicopter banked hard and rerouted towards the mountains, as the pilot began punching in the coordinates.

Taylor braced himself. "For starters, we're going to need a place to land away from the cabin."

90

Terry Grable was not a happy camper. "We should be over the Atlantic by now," he said to Morgan.

The original plan had been to begin their journey eastward as soon as possible. Their plan was to cross the Atlantic, make their way to Jakarta, and then part ways. They chose Indonesia since it was a sprawling archipelago of nearly 20,000 islands, with millions of places to hide—and a country with no extradition treaty with the U.S.

Morgan, however, had insisted that they pass through the Blue Ridge so that he could grab a few items from his cabin. He'd first told Grable that the items were sentimental: mementos—including a photo of his parents—that he wanted to take with him into exile. But when Grable pushed back, outlining the risk they were running to go anywhere near his cabin, Morgan had come clean: in the cabin was a laptop that could incriminate members of the GOC.

At this, Grable was enraged. First, he couldn't believe that Morgan had been so careless as to leave such an item in an unsecure location; second, he was bewildered as to why he'd left its retrieval to the last minute. Nevertheless, he now realized that the trip to the Blue Ridge was non-optional.

Forty-five minutes after leaving the highway, they left the Blue Ridge Parkway and veered north onto the Tye River Turnpike. Shortly thereafter, they took a left onto a dirt road called Lodge Trail. After passing the Sugar Tree Inn, the road turned left, and Grable slowed the car.

"How much further to the cabin?" he asked.

"Next one up on the left—maybe 50 yards," Morgan replied.

Grable stopped the car.

"What are you doing?" Morgan asked, "the driveway is right up there," he said pointing.

"Thanks," Grable responded dryly. "Might be worth taking a quick look to see if anyone's beaten us to it." Grable reached behind him and grabbed his bag. He pulled out a Beretta 92FS, pulled the slide, checked the chamber, and decocked the gun. He then took a 15-round magazine out of the bag's side pocket and inserted it into the grip. He handed the gun to Morgan.

"You know how to use this?" he asked simply.

"Yes, of course," Morgan replied, taking the gun. He was telling the truth—more or less. Though he'd received some weapons training, it was a long time ago, and it had been a few years since he'd actually fired anything; he'd certainly never handled this specific pistol. But he didn't particularly want a lesson right now. He wanted to get the damn laptop, and get the hell out of there.

Grable pulled his own gun from his shoulder holster, checked it, and put it back. He then took a small pair of binoculars from the bag, and jumped out of the car.

He closed the door and stuck his head back in the driver's window. "You should stay with the car. If there's any trouble, don't be afraid to use that," he said, motioning to the gun, "or at least fire a shot in the air so I'll know something's up."

Morgan nodded.

With that, Grable crossed the dirt road, and slipped down the embankment and into the woods.

Morgan looked at his watch, then pulled out his phone to check emails. Nothing. They hadn't had service since leaving the highway. Morgan thought about his new life: no emails, no worries; a life of pure luxury—albeit completely removed from anything he'd known previously. Although incredibly stressed and anxious by the goings-on of the past month, he was very much ready to start over.

After several minutes, Grable returned to the car and announced all clear. He put the car in drive and headed up to the cabin.

* * *

Taylor and Clasby had instructed the pilot to come in low from the east. Working through Tori, they'd arranged to meet up with the off-duty cop who'd been following Morgan and Grable, a local named Levi Zeldin, on the north-bound side of the parkway in a clearing across from a christmas tree farm. Zeldin had assured Tori that the area would be hard to miss from the air, and once on the ground it was less than a two-mile drive to the Sugar Tree Inn.

The pilot came in low and landed the helo in a large field. The foliage was only just starting to turn, and with leaves on the trees and a headwind, Taylor hoped the sound wouldn't carry. Zeldin was waiting for them, leaning against his car at the landing site. He was a short, stocky man, about five feet eight, with shaggy brown hair and a horseshoe mustache.

As Taylor and Clasby exited the helicopter and made their way towards Zeldin, he approached them with big smile and hand outstretched. "How're you guys doin'? The name's Levi Zeldin."

Taylor introduced himself and Clasby, and Zeldin gestured to his vehicle. As they walked to the car, Taylor couldn't help but notice just how pristine it was.

"What year is that, Levi?" Clasby asked, "looks like a '78."

"Awfully close. It's a '79."

Clasby whistled. "She's beautiful."

The car was an old, vintage Chevrolet Monte Carlo, black with red pinstripes, and an all red interior. The chrome wheels gleamed in the afternoon sun.

"Thanks," Levi said, smiling.

Taylor hopped in the front seat, Clasby in the back. As Zeldin climbed into the driver's seat, he removed a weapon from the back of his jeans and placed it on the center console behind the gear shift. As he started the car, Taylor felt obliged to ask a couple of questions.

"Levi, the two men you've been following could be quite dangerous. You're not obligated to assist, but we could sure use your help. You ready and willing to lend a hand?"

"Hell, yeah, Mr. Taylor. Your assistant Tori briefed me on the situation, and frankly, I'm itchin' to help."

"Alright, great," said Taylor. "And please—call me Drake," he added, having never entered a firefight with any member of his team calling him *Mr. Taylor.* "Next question: By any chance would you have an extra weapon?"

"I sure would." Zeldin pulled some keys from his pocket, then reached in front of Taylor to unlock the glove box. He pulled out an older Smith & Wesson pistol and handed it to Taylor.

Though it had been a while, muscle memory kicked in as Taylor rapidly checked the weapon over—pulling the slide to inspect the chamber, and popping the magazine to check available rounds. "I think this'll do it. Thanks."

They pulled off the shoulder and began discussing their approach. Looking at a detailed topo map that Tori had forwarded to Taylor's phone, they decided not to follow Morgan and Grable's route, but instead go straight on the Blue Ridge Parkway to a point where they could easily move through the woods to Lodge Trail Road and the cabin. If by chance Morgan and Grable had heard the helo, they might be looking towards the road for any approaching vehicles.

Taylor instructed Zeldin where to pull over. They got out of the car and went over their plan once more. Taylor reemphasized that, if at all possible, they wanted both of these guys alive, but most important was Morgan. Absolutely no head or torso shots—the guy may well be the only one who could actually put an end to the GOC threat. He showed Zeldin and Clasby a few photos of each man that Tori had forwarded as well. Once everyone was clear on their targets, they headed into the woods.

* * *

The wide, pine floor boards creaked rhythmically as Morgan and Grable entered the log cabin. It smelled of a time long, long ago—a pleasing mixture of wood smoke, crisp autumn air, leather couches and thick wool blankets. The 200-year-old structure looked to be as sturdy as the day it was built. Grable temporarily put his impatience on hold, allowing the place to calm his nerves. He walked over to the stone fireplace and studied a cracked and faded but vibrant painting of a river running beside a mountain.

He stared at the painting, a rich and entrancing vision of America as a wild frontier. The landscape drew him in, and his mind was transported back to his childhood, to carefree summers as a boy when he'd travel with his family to what was then the wilds of southeastern Ohio. He began to contemplate the long journey he'd taken over the past decade—from patriotic soldier hell-bent on protecting the free world, to a very different kind of soldier fighting for a very different cause. Grable fully realized that his views were seen as radical by others, but it was crystal clear to him that he had merely latched on to a critical truth earlier than most.

Somewhere in the mayhem of war, it had become increasingly apparent to him that the developed world's grinding determination to reshape everything in its path was a dead end. He could no longer remember when it happened, but his perspective had been transformed, and it was now painfully obvious to him that civilization was simply fiddling as Rome burned. He didn't know all the answers, but of one thing he was absolutely sure: mountains and streams and meadows and swamps and animals and insects and even fossil fuels buried deep within the ground weren't simply resources for man to use as he saw fit, they were all part of a system that, once off kilter, could easily spiral out of control. In short, mankind's appetites were leading to its own demise.

"Nice painting isn't it?" Morgan asked, breaking Grable's trance and causing him to flinch a bit. "The artist is a guy named George Beck, a Brit who came to the U.S in the late 1700s. Apparently, George Washington bought one of his paintings, and hung it in Mount Vernon. Beck knew my great-great-grandfather, and gave him this one as a gift. Probably worth a fortune. I keep meaning to have it appraised; I could probably buy a condo in Georgetown for what it's worth."

Grable shook his head at Morgan's comment, but decided keep his mouth shut. He turned around to see Morgan flipping through a stack of papers at a small, antique writing desk, pulling out a few as he went.

"You almost ready?" Grable asked.

"Yup. Pretty much," said Morgan. He took the extracted papers, squared them on the desk, and put them into a bag he'd brought in from the car. He then went to a cabinet, pulled out the laptop they'd come for, and placed it in the bag as well.

"You're taking that with you? We should destroy it."

Morgan tensed. In addition to a number of emails that could incriminate the GOC, there was also a file on the laptop containing all of the numbers he would need to access his offshore accounts. If that got destroyed, then he would have a hell of a time trying to get to his money.

"You're probably right," Morgan finally replied. "I just need to grab a few old files off it before we do. I can do that in the car."

Grable seemed satisfied. "Okay. Let's get outta here." He walked towards the door.

*   *   *

Taylor, Clasby and Zeldin had found the cabin with very little trouble. Taylor had gone around to cover the opposite side, and would signal once he was in place. They would then close in on the cabin from each side, and Clasby would take the front door.

Suddenly, the door opened, and Morgan and Grable emerged. Morgan closed and locked the door behind them, and the two men started down the porch steps.

Clasby turned to Zeldin. "Levi, you need to go get your car—now," he whispered. "Bring it around and block the driveway, or give chase if they make it out of here."

"Got it. Back in a flash," said Zeldin, and he was gone.

Grable must have heard Levi's footsteps and turned. He immediately pulled his gun, pointing it generally in Clasby's direction, but couldn't yet see precisely where the sound had come from.

"Jack, get in the car!" Grable yelled.

Morgan started jogging towards the Corolla. Taylor, determined not to let them make it to the vehicle and escape, opened fire, taking two shots at Morgan. The first missed the mark, but the second grazed Morgan's thigh, causing him to fall and drop his bag. Grable turned on a dime and fired in Taylor's direction. Ducking behind a tree, Taylor heard the bullet whiz by.

Now it was Clasby's turn. He took careful aim, and fired, catching Grable in the arm. Clasby could see the splatter of blood as the bullet hit. Without missing a beat, Grable turned back, fired twice at Clasby and ran for the car. Meanwhile, Morgan had grabbed his bag, and found his way to the driver's seat.

Taylor no longer had a clear shot through the trees, and had to be careful with just seven bullets left in the gun. He quickly crept forward towards the driveway.

Clasby, however, unloaded. Moving up a small rise, he took out the front passenger window, then the rear window. He then aimed for the tires, but Morgan had started the car, and as Grable jumped in the passenger door behind him, he gunned it, sending a spray of gravel back towards the cabin, and the Corolla accelerated up the driveway towards the road.

Taylor and Clasby broke from the trees and converged, giving chase as they ran up the driveway after the car. Taylor taking careful shots; Clasby, now with two guns drawn, continued to aim for the tires.

Grable, well-braced in the back seat, aligned the front and rear sight of his weapon on Taylor's chest. Just before he pulled the trigger, Clasby hit the mark, sinking a round into the right rear tire and causing the car to drop and swerve. Grable's shot went wide.

The distance between the car and its pursuers nonetheless increased. The Corolla reached the top of the driveway and went right, back towards the main road.

*   *   *

Pushing hard on the Monte Carlo's five liter, small-block V8, Levi Zeldin roared up the Tye River Turnpike and took a left on Lodge Trail Road at about 60 miles per hour. As he passed the Sugar Tree Inn, he saw the white Corolla heading towards him. Both cars accelerated, assuming the other would blink. But neither did.

Zeldin, however, clearly remembered Taylor's instructions. Recognizing Morgan as the driver, he pulled the car slightly to the left and jammed the emergency brake just before impact. The Monte Carlo went into a sideways skid as the passenger side of the vehicle rammed into the front left corner of the Corolla.

The massive collision sounded like two trains colliding, decimating the peaceful tranquility of the Blue Ridge Mountains. The Monte Carlo went over on its side, literally bouncing over the Toyota and rolling two more times as it lumbered off the road and down the embankment. The Corolla skidded off the opposite side of the road and hit a large oak tree.

As both cars finally came to a stop, the quiet returned.

Though half the size and weight of the Chevy, the Toyota's crash cage held, and all air bags deployed, leaving Morgan and Grable stunned, but alive. As each came to, slowly realizing what had happened, Grable turned around in the back seat to see Taylor and Clasby running up the road towards the car. Finding his weapon, he took careful aim out the open back window and fired. Taylor was knocked off his feet, twisting to his left as he fell in the dirt.

Clasby immediately returned fire, forcing Grable to duck back down.

"Drake, you okay?" Clasby asked, holding his gun and gaze on the back of the Corolla. He dropped the magazine out of one weapon and reloaded. Then did the same with the other.

"I'm fine," Taylor replied, getting back up. "The son of a bitch got me in the shoulder."

"Alright. How are you on ammunition?"

"I think I've got four or five rounds."

"That should do it. Can you take the left side?"

"Yup. Got it covered."

As they walked cautiously toward the vehicle, Grable twice popped back up to fire, and was forced back down each time by a prompt response from each of Clasby's weapons.

When they were about fifty feet from the car, Morgan and Grable made a break for it. Grable, limping badly, made it out of the vehicle and around to the front, with the car as cover. Morgan headed directly into the woods.

"I've got Morgan!" shouted Taylor, darting off the road after him.

Morgan had a head start, but Taylor was gaining fast—he could see Morgan up ahead through the trees, a bag in one hand and a gun in the other. The pain in Taylor's shoulder was intense, but he'd had to work through much worse in the past, and he knew that letting this bastard disappear was simply not something he could allow.

* * *

Clasby and Grable were now locked in a close range gun-fight.

Crouching at the rear of the Toyota, Clasby had Grable pinned behind the oak tree which was now embedded in the car's engine compartment. With a clear view through the vehicle, he ensured that Grable's only option was to slowly use up his ammunition with blind shots.

They exchanged fire for a minute or more, until Grable's gun offered up an empty metallic click.

"Shit!" Grable shouted. There was silence.

"Throw the weapon out onto the road," instructed Clasby. More silence.

"How do I know you won't just kill me?" Grable asked.

"I want you very much alive, Terry. Throw the gun out and clasp your hands on top of your head."

"I'm not sure I can do that. My arm is pretty bad."

"Do the best you can."

Grable threw his gun into the road, and slowly emerged from behind the tree, with one arm on his head, the other held awkwardly against his chest.

Clasby moved forward towards the gun, holding his weapon and his eyes squarely on Grable. He squatted, and looked down for just a split second to pick it up. As he did so, his heart sank; his brain processed the last two images, and he realized he'd made two critical mistakes: the gun on the road was not the gun that had just been firing at him, and it was Grable's injured arm above his head, meaning his good arm was free.

* * *

As Morgan and Taylor moved further into the woods, the density of the trees and brush increased, slowing both men considerably. Taylor could see and hear Morgan huffing and puffing less than twenty feet in front of him. Though he had several clear opportunities to take Morgan down, he chose not to use his weapon for fear of inadvertently killing the man most important to his investigation.

Morgan entered a small clearing, and increased his pace. Seconds later, Taylor entered the clearing and sprinted after him. After closing the gap to less than five feet, he lunged, grabbing Morgan from behind and bringing both men crashing down to the ground.

Morgan's bag and gun went flying forward into the underbrush. Morgan wriggled forward, trying desperately to reach the weapon, but Taylor stabbed his knuckles into the side of Morgan's rib cage, snapping one or two ribs and eliciting a shriek from Morgan, who then ceased struggling, but continued to gasp for oxygen as each breath brought fresh waves of pain.

Now kneeling above his prey, Taylor grabbed Morgan by the shirt and wrenched him over onto his back. "Alright, John. This game is over."

"My… oh fuck, it hurts." Morgan was clutching his chest. At first, Taylor thought it was simply his broken ribs, but then he realized that the man's breathing was short and rapid.

Then he stopped breathing altogether.

* * *

Clasby sprang back towards the vehicle, but it was too late. Grable opened fire. The first shots hit the road underneath Clasby's airborne body, sending up puffs of dust. The third caught him in the stomach. He landed on his back, blood pouring from his side. Wincing in pain, he pulled his gun around only to see Grable standing above him, who took another shot, blasting the gun out of Clasby's hand and putting a hole in his palm. Clasby recoiled, pulling the hand to his side.

Grable then held the gun pointed at Clasby's head.

"I really have no interest in killing you, buddy, but I don't think I have a choice here."

"You do have a choice, Grable."

"No. I wish I did, but I really don't." He manually pulled back the hammer on his pistol with his thumb and re-aimed the pistol. "Sorry about this."

A single shot rang out.

*   *   *

Taylor continued administering steady compressions. "Don't even think about dying on me, you asshole."

Some decent color had returned to Morgan's cheeks, and he had resumed breathing. Taylor wanted to check Morgan's bag a few feet away for a sat phone or, ideally, some aspirin, but he suspected both were a long shot, and he knew that continued CPR was the best possible way to save this jerk.

Finally, Morgan regained consciousness. He blinked several times; his eyes rolled in their sockets, then focused on Taylor.

"Welcome back, John. Can you tell me where you are?"

"I—I'm in West Virginia." As he said it, he looked away, suddenly realizing his circumstances.

"And where are the nukes?" Taylor asked pointedly.

"There—" Morgan suddenly convulsed, and Taylor immediately got off of him and turned him onto his side as he vomited. "Oh, shit. I feel like hell," Morgan managed to utter before falling unconscious once again.

Taylor gave thought as to what to do next, and decided that getting Morgan out of the woods was probably his best bet. The man was breathing, and still had color. But without real medical care, it was a crap shoot as to whether he'd live through this.

Taylor grabbed Morgan's bag, noting the laptop inside, popped the magazines out of both weapons, and threw all of it in with the laptop. He then carefully put Morgan over his shoulders in a fireman's carry, and slowly started walking back out of the woods.

*   *   *

The body slumped on the dirt road, a single bullet hole in the forehead.

Clasby stared at the trickle of blood running down the side of Grable's face and into his thick sandy blond hair. He sat up and looked across the road, and saw a broad smile push Levi Zeldin's horseshoe mustache out towards his ears.

"Nice shot, officer," Clasby deadpanned, smiling in return.

"Thanks," Zeldin replied in a somewhat gravelly voice. "I thought so."

They both heard the noise. Two FBI helicopters crossed overhead, and several police cars, sirens blaring, were speeding towards them down Lodge Trail Road.

91

Huddled with the Prime Minister of Turkey in the sun room of Aspen Lodge, President Gilman noted the incoming high-priority text. He excused himself, picked up the phone, punched in a code, and read the message from Taylor.

Pleased as he was by the capture of Jerrick and Morgan, he still didn't have any assurance that the threat had been eliminated; therefore, nothing had changed with regards to his meetings with G20 leaders. They still had to conclude the business at hand. The good news was that they were very, very close.

The proposed interrogation strategy that Taylor had sent to him and Hawthorne seemed logical; he thought carefully about the potential downside, but couldn't come up with much. He quickly tapped out his approval, sent the message, and put the phone back on the table.

Two days prior, he'd allowed himself to think for the first time that they might capture the men behind this thing before the deadline. That had now been accomplished. If they could locate and deactivate the devices, then this whole nightmare would finally come to an end.

Unfortunately, that remained a big if. As he considered the group of presidents and prime ministers now at Camp David, he knew he had no choice but to drive forward as forcefully as possible, since the lives of untold millions still depended upon their progress.

92

"**T**his is not a goddamn negotiation!" Taylor yelled. "Where are the fucking nukes?"

"I don't know!" Jerrick yelled back.

Taylor lost his patience. Standing behind his seated detainee, he grabbed him by the hair and slowly pushed his face into the table. "I don't believe you," he said flatly, and let go.

They were in an interrogation room at CIA headquarters in Langley. Taylor's left arm was in a sling, his shoulder still painful, but on the mend with no broken bones. After the previous day's events, he'd wanted to question Morgan, and to do so, as they say, with extreme prejudice. But Morgan had undergone a double-bypass and was currently in intensive care at Walter Reed; he would not be in any condition to talk for some time—possibly not for a day or two.

"Look," began Jerrick, "like any SMU, it was all based on a need to know."

Taylor was incredulous. "Wait a minute, you're telling me you saw this as a Special Mission Unit? Are you out of your mind?"

Taylor's last question was quite serious. SMUs were not widely publicized, but most senior operators knew they existed.

A Special Mission Unit was a covert action team, often assembled to take on and neutralize transnational threats involving weapons of mass destruction. Typically, they were clandestine black ops, meaning they were paid for out of a "black" budget that was never seen by the public and received extremely limited congressional oversight. To imply that the GOC engaged in such an operation was to state that it was, to some degree, authorized. Taylor knew better.

Hearing no response, he persisted: "Jerrick, are you telling me you operated under the belief that this was a bona fide SMU?"

Jerrick said nothing.

Taylor grabbed Jerrick's hair again and put his face right next to his. "Answer my question."

"The answer is no."

"No, what?"

"No. I knew our actions were not backed by the chain of command," Jerrick responded. "Once the plan started to take shape, I demanded that Morgan show me proper authorization. When it became very clear that there wasn't any—and never would be, we all had to decide whether to proceed without it."

"Authorization? Did you really think that someone in the chain of command would authorize an operation that directly threatened U.S. citizens?"

"Look, we both know that the CIA has done some pretty crazy stuff over the years."

"Yes. In other countries, to other governments—and hopefully we've learned some lessons as to just how much interference is appropriate."

"I heard you served in the 75th," said Jerrick. "Which tells me that you know full well that what you just said is crap."

"Maybe so, but this operation is as harebrained as it gets."

"Is it? We're both well aware of the U.S. government's involvement in assassinations, overthrows, and broad-based surveillance. I would hold that the justification for much of that is weak compared to the justification for action on climate. I don't think you truly understand the stakes—"

"The stakes?" Taylor roared, "what about the stakes of detonating devices in urban areas?"

"You know as well as I that our military is overextended as it is," Jerrick shouted back, "unless we act on this issue, and act now, we will find ourselves mired in more conflicts than we can handle—either that, or we'll stand on the sidelines as country after country, region after region, falls into a state of instability and civil war. The Philippines may well survive Typhoon Isabel, but most developing countries won't be so lucky; they'll quickly fracture into—"

Taylor had no patience for the man's diatribe. "Jerrick, do you have any idea as to the full repercussions of your actions here?" he shouted, barely able to contain himself. "Millions— no, make that billions of people around the world are terrified right now. They've uprooted their families, their lives, and are running away from a threat that you've imposed on them. Hundreds of people have lost their lives as a result of the chaos. These are people that you and your team essentially killed; they would not be dead otherwise. Furthermore, you've turned your own government, including the military, upside down. You've basically spit on the constitution that you swore to serve and protect, and you've forced your commander-in-chief to abandon his priorities in order to deal with a crisis that you personally created."

Taylor watched as Jerrick looked away, unable to look him in the face. He wondered if by some small chance his words had penetrated this man's arrogant shell.

He paced towards the two-way mirror in front of the table, then turned back. "Let me ask you something, Jerrick," he began, "your buddy Jack Morgan—do you see him as equally dedicated to the cause?"

Jerrick finally looked back at Taylor, at first a little unsure of the question. "Yes," he offered tentatively, "in his own way. It was Morgan who worked to finance the operation."

"Ahhh, yes" Taylor responded, "Morgan was the money guy." This was precisely the path he wanted the conversation to take. "And where do you suppose ol' Jack got his hands on the funds?"

"Our operation was funded by private individuals. People who believe this is the most important issue facing civilization," Jerrick said firmly, though he sounded like he was trying to convince himself as well as Taylor.

"Is that right? And who are these generous individuals?"

"I can't tell you that," Jerrick said, looking away again.

"I'm going to go way the fuck out on a limb here, and guess that the reason you can't tell me is that you don't have a clue."

Jerrick said nothing.

"What if I were to tell you that at least one of the funders was an industrialist who stood to profit handsomely from your little adventure."

"I would guess that any number of people stand to profit— that does not necessarily mean that their funding is tainted."

Taylor shook his head. "Jerrick, just how much due diligence did you do before jumping into this foolish scheme? Or did you blindly accept whatever Morgan told you?"

Jerrick once again remained silent.

"Do you think it's possible that Jack Morgan profited off of the GOC's threats?"

Jerrick looked at Taylor, clearly interested in hearing more, but not wanting to break ranks. "What do you mean by that?" he finally asked.

"Exactly what it sounds like. Do you think that Morgan might have been in this for the money?"

"What money? The money he secured was used to pay for our operations," said Jerrick, starting to look a little confused.

"I'm sure some of it was. You don't think he kept any for himself?"

It was clear Jerrick wanted details, but he refused to allow himself to play Taylor's game. "Look," Jerrick stated, "if you're about to tell me that Morgan skimmed some money off the top, that doesn't in any way change my view that what we did was justified—the world needs to focus on this issue now, and we forced that to happen."

Taylor was not going to take Jerrick's bait either—and he was intent on making damn sure that Jerrick knew just who he'd gone into business with. "I guess you could say he skimmed some money off the top, if by that you mean he enriched himself to the tune of nearly a hundred million dollars."

Jerrick's head turned sharply towards Taylor. "That is bullshit!" he said pointedly, "I don't believe a word of it."

"No? Well, we've uncovered offshore accounts clearly proving that Morgan has amassed a fortune of well over eighty-five million dollars," Taylor replied calmly. "And there's probably a whole lot more that we have yet to find." He paused. "Want to know where it came from?"

Jerrick's expression made it very clear he did.

"It came from Francis Vermeer. All of it. And the quid pro quo is pretty damn simple: every time his company received a major order for Radivene, Morgan received what looks a lot like a commission."

"Radivene?"

"A new medication for treating Acute Radiation Syndrome. In short, it looks like the Guardians of Civilization served as a front—a profit-making engine for Isis Therapeutics. As nations around the world prepared for a nuclear detonation, they ordered over twenty billion dollars worth of the stuff."

Jerrick squinted at Taylor, trying very hard not to show his emotions. "I don't believe you," he repeated.

"Well," Taylor said, pulling his phone out of its holster and working to pull up some information, "Take a look." He held the phone on the table in front of Jerrick; it showed a staggering rise in Isis stock over the past three weeks. "I think you're probably well aware that most stocks haven't been doing so well lately."

Jerrick leaned forward and stared at the graph.

Taylor continued: "We also have concrete evidence that Morgan made extensive use of Vermeer's jet and spent time with him at his estate on Martha's Vineyard."

Jerrick sat very still, looking straight ahead.

"In short, it looks like you and your team got played," Taylor said. "Whether you believe it was for a just cause or not, once this gets out, the GOC will be viewed as nothing more than a bunch of greedy terrorists."

"But that's simply not true!" Jerrick shrieked.

Taylor knew that this was a man who commanded some of the best trained men in the U.S. military, and oversaw hundreds of operations, both successful and catastrophic. Getting upset was clearly not in Charles Jerrick's MO, but right now he was damn close to losing it over even the possibility that the GOC's mission would be viewed as self-serving.

"But it is true, Jerrick," Taylor said calmly, "Joe Sixpack out there in America—or, for that matter, Russia, Australia, China or Brazil—is going to hear the connection between the leader of the GOC and one of America's top industrialists, and come to an obvious and logical conclusion: this whole crisis was driven by nothing other than greed. As soon as that happens, the level of cynicism towards your precious cause will quintuple overnight, and there won't be a snowball's chance in hell of any climate treaty ever being agreed upon by the G20."

Jerrick put his face in his handcuffed hands. Taylor's phone buzzed; he quickly viewed the incoming message, and couldn't help but smile at the irony. He tapped Jerrick on the shoulder and showed him the top part of the message. "We just apprehended Vermeer."

Jerrick read the message and looked away.

Taylor spoke slowly and directly. "Jerrick, where did you plant the nuclear devices?"

He turned and stared back at Taylor. "I—I can't tell you that."

"You can, Jerrick."

"No, I can't. It's no secret that the leaders of the G20 are assembled at Camp David at this very moment, engaged in a discussion on whether to comply with our demands. I am not going to remove the threat and let them walk away from that discussion."

"Then I guess I'll have to hand this interrogation over to my heavy-handed friends in the CIA. Not sure they can get you to talk, but it doesn't look like I'm getting anywhere." He started walking to the door; Jerrick stopped him.

"Look, Taylor: I'm not an idiot. When I committed to this plan, I knew that I was most likely sacrificing my career and possibly my life. The threat posed by those devices is all I've got left. I'm not just going to hand it over to you—or the to the CIA.

"I think you're overlooking a simple reality, Jerrick: once we announce that we've captured the leaders of the GOC, and expose the motive that drove the nuclear threat, there isn't a government on the planet that is going to implement a carbon tax. Just ain't gonna happen."

Jerrick put his head back in his hands. Taylor took a deep breath, and prepared to play the ace he'd been hiding up his sleeve—for which he'd needed the President's approval.

"Let me ask you this, Jerrick: Would it change your mind if we were to agree not to release the information on Vermeer and Morgan?"

Jerrick looked up at Taylor with bleary eyes, and considered the question for some time. "Why would you do that?" he finally asked.

"That's easy—to prevent the loss of innocent lives. It's not as if I'm offering you a get out of jail free card."

Jerrick continued to stare at Taylor, his mind mulling over the end-game, and how to best to pluck some shred of victory from the probable jaws of defeat.

"Look at all of this from another angle," Taylor offered, recalling Ellie's advice to Walker. "Since you launched your threat, there is not a person on the planet who has not been barraged by a near constant stream of climate change data and projections. You've succeeded in generating worldwide awareness of this issue that no one would have thought possible.

"Combine that awareness with the high likelihood that the storms, droughts and wildfires of the past few years will continue, and I'd say you've moved the needle considerably. But I'd also guess that once the public knows that Morgan made out like a bandit, that needle will snap back pretty quickly."

Taylor laid it out for Jerrick. "How about this: Tell me where the nukes are, and I'll guarantee you that the world will continue to think that the GOC is bunch of foam-at-the-mouth fanatics, and will never be told that the whole plan was driven by money."

Jerrick leaned forward on his elbows, looking down at the table as he gripped his head between his cuffed hands. Taylor decided to keep quiet and let him think.

Half a minute went by, neither of them moving or saying a word. Finally Jerrick looked up.

"Okay."

"Okay, what?"

"I'll make that deal."

"A wise decision," Taylor said, extending his hand. "Tell me where the devices were planted, and you have my word as a fellow soldier that the Vermeer connection will remain a secret."

The two men shook hands, but Taylor didn't let go.

"Well?" pushed Taylor.

Jerrick sighed heavily. "There aren't any devices."

Taylor's hand squeezed tighter on Jerrick's. "Bullshit."

"Think about it," Jerrick continued, "there was no need. We sure as hell weren't going to detonate any nukes. This was never about harming anyone; it was always focused only on waking people up. London, Houston, Novosibirsk, and Shanghai were all to establish credibility. All we needed was for the world to believe the threat was real—and it appears we succeeded. After you got your hands on Kingsley and realized the device in Guam was fake, we thought you might figure it out."

Taylor was speechless. He stared blankly at Jerrick, and slowly let go of his hand.

93

"You look like hell, boss," Sherry said with a smile as she handed him a cup of coffee and carefully inserted a granola bar into his left hand—which remained in a sling.

"That may be," Taylor said, smiling in return, "but I haven't felt this good in weeks." As Sherry walked out, he placed the coffee down on the table with his one good hand, ripped open the energy bar with his teeth, and ate half of it in a single bite.

He had been up all night, having gotten a call late the previous evening that Morgan would likely be conscious and available for questions at around midnight. It turned out to be closer to 3 am when Morgan finally came to, but Taylor was there, and he did not treat the convalescent with tender loving care.

He ripped into Morgan, telling him what they knew when it made sense to do so, and threatening him in ways that evoked maximum anxiety. The doctors objected, but Morgan didn't give a shit. He told the staff that they were welcome to kick him out if Morgan had another episode or lost consciousness, but that otherwise he wanted to be left alone.

On the heels of his near-death experience, Morgan was frail and scared. When Taylor threatened to pull him out of the hospital and toss him in a cold cell, Morgan reacted viscerally, setting off an alarm of some sort on one of the dozen devices to which he was attached. For an hour and a half, Taylor battered the Assistant Secretary of Defense, until he'd coughed up names and confirmations of key elements of the GOC plan. It was only when Morgan's voice was barely audible, his energy faint, that the doctors finally insisted he finish his questioning after the patient got some rest. Taylor acquiesced; for the most part, he had what he needed.

On his way back from the hospital, Taylor had given Tori a head's up that he wanted the team assembled by 7 am. She said she'd take care of it, but did not let him go without a lecture. She told Taylor that what he'd done was reckless, irresponsible and illegal. Furthermore, she noted, it was inconsiderate—to all those who cared for him, making it clear that she counted herself foremost among them.

Taylor didn't feel particularly guilty about putting himself in harm's way, nor apologetic about taking the situation in his own hands. In fact, it felt good to get his hands dirty again—especially when there were decent odds that the FBI would have arrived too late to ensure the capture of Morgan and Grable.

But the fact that he'd been inconsiderate, that got to him; he hadn't felt like anyone had cared about his welfare for a long time. Tori's honesty awoke something inside of him, and as he hung up the phone he was determined to act on it.

This was going to be another long day. After meeting with the team, he had to catch a helicopter to New York at 8:45. He stopped briefly at his apartment for a four-minute shower and a change of clothes, then headed over to the NAC. As requested, the group was assembled in the Secretary's conference room when he arrived.

"So Tori, why don't you start us off. Do we think that there is still any reason at all to believe that the supposed devices actually exist?" he asked.

Without being told anything about the conversation between Jerrick and Taylor, Morgan had independently confirmed
that the planted devices were nothing more than a bluff—simply a means for ensuring that the world took action. Of course,
as far as Morgan was concerned, taking action meant nothing
more than stocking up on Radivene.

Taylor had relayed this information to Hawthorne and the
President, and the White House had subsequently prepared an
announcement that the threat posed by the Guardians of Civilization had been neutralized, and that the President and other
world leaders would make a public announcement later that
day at the United Nations.

"Myself, Nate and three other members of my team have
been at it since you called me at five am. We've been through
everything on Morgan's laptop, and also performed locational
analyses of everyone involved, and we have not located any data
to suggest operations in any other major cities."

"Not only that," Verit added, holding a piece of paper in
his hand, "but one of the encrypted emails we took off the laptop was a message from Morgan to an account we believe to be
Jerrick's. In it, he insists that Jerrick oversee the Shanghai operation personally, noting that, and I quote, 'if the world gets a
close look at that device, the entire deception would be at risk.'
That could certainly be taken as an admission that nuclear devices were a pretense."

"Can I see that?" Taylor asked, reaching for the piece of
paper containing Morgan's email message. Verit handed it to
him and he read the full message. "Do me a favor, Nate," he
said, handing it back, "work with Tori on a short memo outlining what you just told me, and get it to Hawthorne." Taylor
turned to Ellie. "Now, let's talk about Vermeer. I got your email
last night, but why don't you provide a quick summary of your
interrogation."

"Sure. So I spent about two hours with Vermeer last night,"
explained Ellie. "The guy is damn smooth, and didn't offer
much. He claimed total ignorance of a broader operation, and

explained away the payments to Morgan as compensation for an off-the-books consultant who was helping to secure contracts with foreign governments. He claims Morgan insisted that he be paid under the table."

"You buy that?" Taylor asked.

"Not sure. The guy may be a billionaire, but he's also sleaze-ball. As far as being in on the GOC conspiracy, I'm guessing he's telling the truth—but that may be only because he didn't need to know. The good news is that Morgan's laptop gives us ample evidence to prove that Vermeer appears to have broken a dozen laws or more in funneling the money to offshore accounts."

"Is that your opinion or a lawyer's?" Taylor asked.

"I'm afraid it's only mine. And given that he can drop tens of millions on his own defense, putting him away won't be easy."

"Agreed. I assume it'll all come down to getting these guys to roll over on each other. I'm glad that's not my job. Okay, what else?"

"There's this," Tori interjected, scrolling down through her email and opening one from last night. "It appears that yesterday afternoon, two scientists from Los Alamos were mysteriously dumped out of a van on the side of a dirt road east of Haleiwa, Hawaii."

"Are they okay?" Ellie asked.

"Yup, apparently. Looks like the FBI has 'em, and notified us once they learned that the two were originally headed to Guam."

"I'll be damned," Taylor said, shaking his head. "That, of course, brings us to accomplices. Tori, where are we regarding the names Morgan gave me this morning?"

"Nowhere, to be honest. We'll dig into that immediately."

"Those guys will disappear into the woodwork faster than we can blink—that is, if they haven't already."

"Understood, Drake. I'll put it at the top of the list."

"Thanks, Tori." He held her gaze for several long seconds, finding it hard to break away.

Finally, Taylor turned to the rest of the people in the room. He felt his face flush a bit, but didn't really give a damn. "Hey. Thank you. All of you. Thanks for all of your incredibly hard work, and for all of the contributions from everyone on your respective teams. We did it, goddamn it."

His words seemed to unlock hidden smiles from everyone in the room, and he replied with a crooked grin, his eyes sparkling.

"From the start, this really didn't look like it was going our way," he continued, "there were some agonizing, frustrating weeks there when I seriously thought we were miles away from breaking through. But due to your persistence, your insights and hunches, and your dogged efforts day in and day out, we untangled this thing, and put the bad guys behind bars."

His eyes were irresistibly drawn back to Tori, who was trying unsuccessfully to keep tears from leaving her eyes and flowing down her cheeks. He had a sudden urge to hold her in his arms in celebration of their hard-won victory, to kiss away her tears. Without further thought, he dropped his briefcase, walked over and embraced Tori with his one good arm. She threw her arms around him in return. Once again, the image of Rachel briefly flashed in his mind, but then vanished—and all he could think of was how much this woman meant to him, and how much he wanted to kiss her. Tori seemed to read his thoughts, and pulled him tighter.

After a few moments, each pulled back, and they shared one last glance before Taylor turned and put his good hand on Verit's shoulder, and then on Ellie's arm. "You guys have all been awesome," he gushed, looking at each member of the team. "In a day or two, after everyone's caught up on work and sleep, let's all go out for a celebratory dinner at the most expensive fucking restaurant we can find. Deal?"

The group replied with loud cheers, giddy smiles on everyone's faces. He looked again into Tori's eyes. *And you and I will do some catching up of our own*, his eyes whispered silently to hers.

He grabbed his briefcase. "Alright, I'm off. Be sure to watch Gilman's speech. You may see me somewhere in the background, trying to keep my eyes open." His team laughed as he turned and left the room.

For the first time in a very, very long time, Taylor felt whole. He felt hope.

94

New York City looked like Mardi Gras.

As Taylor took a cab uptown from the Manhattan Heliport to the UN Building, he was riding on air. Thoughts of Tori, along with the success of their investigation made Taylor feel as if he were going to burst. And it didn't hurt that people were celebrating his success everywhere he looked. The White House had shared the news with leaders of the G20, and it had been released to the public shortly thereafter.

The reaction was immediate—and worldwide. Major cities all across the globe collectively breathed a massive sigh of relief. There were spontaneous parties and parades in the streets, as billions of people all over the planet came out in force to celebrate the end of the cataclysmic threat that had weighed them down for the past month. Many carried signs; some were patriotic, some religious. Some were righteous in response to a major victory over terrorism. As Taylor came off FDR Drive and headed west on 42nd street, he saw a young woman in her 20s with a sign that read: "GOC and Climate Change: One down, one to go!" He shook his head, wondering how it would all play out.

The global economy had taken a sizable hit from the mass migration of people out of urban centers—and away from their jobs. There was a critical need for the developed world to get back to work, back to the companies and organizations that produced products and services and drove the engine of the civilized world. But it was crystal clear that no such thing would happen today. This was a moment of triumph; a moment to feel a tremendous weight being lifted off the psyche of humanity. Taylor felt absolutely euphoric.

Once off the FDR, the cab slowed to a crawl amidst the crowds of people, but for Taylor, it was incredibly gratifying. It was not lost on him that this was, to a sizable degree, a celebration of his team's hard work and eventual success. No, the nuclear devices that had instilled fear in so many were not real, but the menace of a small group of individuals blackmailing the rest of the world very much was. That menace had been stopped—through his efforts, and those responsible would now be brought to justice.

Eventually, the taxi pulled into the entrance off of United Nations Plaza. Taylor clumsily paid the cabbie using just his one good arm, hopped out, and made his way inside through the throng of people.

95

As Taylor entered the General Assembly Hall, he felt overwhelmed.

During the entire trip up from Washington, he'd been excited and honored to have been invited by the President to witness his speech at the UN, but now, once inside, he felt like such tickets were going cheap. The place was absolutely packed. He'd been told he'd be met by an aide at the front of the Hall, but as he looked down towards the gleaming gold backdrop emblazoned with the UN insignia, it became very clear that it was going to take quite a while to get there.

Nonetheless, Taylor patiently and politely made his way through the crowd, his injured arm getting bumped and jostled a few times in the process, until he'd at last reached the front row. As he tried to turn the corner and head towards the podium, a guard stopped him and requested credentials.

He looked around at those assembled—representatives from 192 nations—and realized that almost every one of them was wearing a badge of some sort around their neck. He handed the man his DHS identification, but somehow suspected it wasn't going to get him very far.

The guard looked quickly at his DHS badge, then shook his head. "I'm sorry sir, this area is only for—"

"It's okay, Charlie, Drake Taylor is on the list," said a young woman in a sharp beige suit, who approached from behind the guard.

The guard flipped a page on a clipboard he was holding, found Taylor's name and checked it off. "So he is. You should have said so, Mr. Taylor!" the guard said cheerfully, then motioned for him to pass.

"Mr. Taylor, I'm Gina Karmel, special assistant to the President."

"Nice to meet you, Ms. Karmel," he replied, pleased to have been rescued.

As soon as they passed by the guard, the crowd thinned considerably. And as Taylor looked around, he recognized a number of world leaders engaged in conversation around the podium. Turns out his ticket wasn't so cheap after all.

"The speech will be starting any minute. If it's okay with you, I'm going to take you to your position immediately."

"My position?"

"Yes," she replied, "the President has requested that a handful of key people stand behind him during the speech, you among them. I'm sorry, I thought this had been explained to you. Would that be alright?"

"To stand behind the President?" Taylor asked.

"Yes," she confirmed.

"Sure, that would be—I'd be happy to."

"Great. Follow me."

She led Taylor around to a small set of steps that brought him to a platform behind the podium.

"What did you do to your arm?" she asked, making small talk.

Taylor looked down at his arm and realized he had yet come up with a stock answer for explaining the sling. "Oh, I… I was in a fight, actually" he said, wishing he'd offered something less dramatic.

"A fight?" she asked incredulously, clearly implying *Aren't you a little old to be fighting?*

"It's a long story."

"Might be interesting to hear it sometime," she smiled, "I assume the other guy looks a lot worse?"

"Yes, I think you could say that," he smiled back.

As they walked towards the center of the platform, Taylor saw Secretary Hawthorne off to one side, chatting with half a dozen top security officials from several other nations, some of whose faces Drake recognized.

Gina Karmel pointed to an X on the floor. "You'll be standing right here. And as I noted, the President will be starting very shortly."

"Okay. Thank you."

"My pleasure," she replied. She reached in her pocket and handed Taylor some kind of pass. "One last thing: the President would like you to join him after the speech. He'll be in Meeting Room D. This pass, along with your DHS ID, will get you in to see him."

"Alright, got it." *And a backstage pass to boot,* he thought to himself.

"If you need anything else, just ask Charlie—the guard. He'll know how to locate me."

"Great. Thanks again, Gina."

"Good to meet you, Mr. Taylor." She shook his hand, then proceeded across the platform and back down the steps. He placed the pass in the pocket of his suit coat.

Hawthorne had seen Taylor, and was walking across the platform, arms outstretched. "Drake!" He embraced Taylor carefully, making sure to avoid his bad arm. The two had traded a dozen emails over the past 48 hours, but this was the first time they'd seen each other in several days. "Well done—outstandin' effort! I don't have to tell you jus' how proud I am of what you've pulled off here."

"Thank you, sir."

Hawthorne turned and introduced Taylor to several of the other people on stage, making sure to note Taylor's lead role in the U.S. pursuit of the terrorists. A chime sounded, and everyone in the Hall took their seats—that is, those who had seats. Taylor could see that there were several hundred people standing at the back and down the aisles on either side. Those on stage all took their assigned spots.

A door opened down next to the stage, and President Gilman emerged. He skipped up the steps, nodding to those assembled, and walked to the podium.

96

President Gilman looked out over the crowd, and up towards the back of the auditorium.

"Mr. Secretary General, Mr. President, fellow delegates, ladies and gentlemen: I am extremely pleased to report that early this morning, as I and other leaders were gathered at Camp David, it was confirmed that the threat posed by the so-called Guardians of Civilization had been neutralized."

The General Assembly, not known for spontaneous applause during speeches given by world leaders, erupted into an immediate standing ovation. President Gilman, those standing behind him, and the U.N. officers seated behind them, all joined in. Although the U.S. President's pronouncement was certainly not news to anyone present, the combined nations of the world did not witness many moments in history when such a large swath of humanity all shared in a common triumph; the jubilation expressed on the heels of his words represented both a celebration, and an outpouring of relief after nearly thirty days of agonizing stress and uncertainty.

"The pursuit and apprehension of those responsible involved many nations, many agencies, many heroes. Some of those whose organizations were pivotal in bringing the GOC to justice stand behind me this afternoon. I think we owe them a debt of gratitude."

The Hall exploded once again into loud applause, the President joining in.

"Allow me, if you will, to call your attention to one man within our own Department of Homeland Security who played a central role in identifying and bringing to justice those who sought to do us harm: Undersecretary Drake Taylor."

The crowd roared yet again, and Taylor, goose bumps forming on his arms and neck, suddenly felt a little dizzy. He raised his good hand up briefly, and looked at back at the President, who offered a smile and a firm nod. As his flushed face started to cool, he thought of Tori, wishing she could be here—not only to see this, but also to share the credit.

The crowd quieted, and President Gilman resumed.

"The scourge of terrorism has been present for most of human history, and it is likely not something that we will ever fully eradicate. But our recent efforts reinforce a fundamental truth: Whenever anyone or any group causes or threatens bodily harm to innocent people, civilized nations will rise and up and do everything in their power to hunt down the perpetrators and see to it that they never cause or threaten such harm again.

"We have determined that the Guardians of Civilization were an unusual terrorist group, comprised of extremely well-trained individuals from a number of countries—including the United States. While additional details will be forthcoming in the days ahead, certain specifics will remain confidential in order to protect sources and methods. In this case more than others, it is believed that revealing our techniques and details regarding the organization we've uncovered would potentially jeopardize the effectiveness of our intelligence apparatus.

"As we all know, this was a new form of terrorism. No less heinous, given the nuclear threat under which we have all been living for the past four weeks, but very different in its approach. The GOC's primary goal was not to cause loss of life; instead, the group sought to blackmail humanity into addressing what it perceived as the most critical issue of our time. During this crisis, the world had no choice but to gain a better understanding of this phenomenon. In the Philippines, we witnessed the full wrath of Mother Nature in a warming world. The typhoon that claimed nearly forty thousand lives broke so many records that it is difficult not to see it as a precursor to more intense storms yet to come. The global media, while not always focused and not always accurate, offered everyone within range of a newspaper or electronic device a near endless stream of information on climate science and related impacts.

"Since the GOC threat emerged, I and a sizable number of world leaders have been in close contact. As the deadline approached, we gave extensive consideration to what would constitute an optimal response. As you might expect, we covered all possibilities, and at the end of the day we came to the conclusion that, despite the tremendous stakes, we would not—we could not—acquiesce directly to the terrorists' demands.

"But arriving at this conclusion was not easy—for two reasons. First and most obvious, refusing to comply with the GOC's demands would put at risk millions of human lives. Second, refusing to comply would, in all likelihood, delay substantially the point at which developed nations do take action on this important issue. Fortunately, with the leaders of the terrorist group in custody and the nuclear threat eliminated, the issue of how best to respond to the GOC threat has become moot. But this in itself raises a different question: Since it is clear that any action we now take would not be in response to any terrorist demand, what action, if any, is appropriate?

"Over the past 72 hours, as the likelihood of capturing the terrorists before the stated deadline steadily increased, I and other leaders of the developed world engaged in a very serious discussion around this very topic, and we arrived at the following conclusion: The world must act."

The audience within the hall let out a mixed reaction, which included scattered applause in conjunction with numerous gasps and more than a few jeers. Taylor, standing behind the President, showed no visible reaction, but was somewhat taken aback. At first blush, President Gilman's announcement seemed like a betrayal; after tirelessly pursuing the GOC, and fixating on the prevention of their attempted blackmail, it seemed he was acquiescing after the fact—handing victory to the GOC after Taylor had secured their defeat.

But Taylor had come to trust President Gilman, and had, as much as anyone, received a crash course in the seriousness of the issue. As he gave it further thought, he decided that that the President's strategy was quite clever—and extremely courageous.

Looking out on the audience and oblivious to Taylor's thoughts behind him, President Gilman had fully expected a varied response—both here at the UN and across the globe, but he had made this decision, had expended substantial effort to bring other leaders on board, and was now fully committed. Up to this point, he had certainly not made action on the climate a signature goal of his administration. But the number of weather-related natural disasters that he had been forced to deal with during his six years in office was two or three times that of any previous American President. He knew damn well that this issue was inserting itself into the U.S. agenda whether he or anyone else liked it or not.

"I'm sure that, like me, many of you have an instinctual desire to shun the issue that drove the GOC. Billions of people around the world experienced paralyzing fear as a result of their actions; it's only natural that we should want to avoid acknowledging their stated cause in any way—let alone see this cause advanced. I strongly urge you to suppress such instincts. Windows of opportunity for nations to bind together and act as one are few. The world's increasing complexity ensures that new issues push others off the stage with astonishing speed. If we let this moment pass, there is no telling when such an opportunity will come again.

"So let us, for the moment, push the GOC threat aside and consider this: Changing the climate is the largest thing that mankind has ever done. We have witnessed tremendous achievements in human history: the great pyramids, the invention of electricity and the internal combustion engine, landing a man on the moon. However, none of these compare in scope to the fact that we have actually altered the atmosphere of the planet on which we live, changing the behavior of its many natural systems in the process. Unlike all of the others, this was unintentional, a negative result of our other achievements and certainly not something to be proud of. Unlike the others, it is something that threatens our future, and something we must expend significant effort to address.

"Fortunately, the effort required is miniscule in comparison to the centuries of hard work that built our industrial civilization. There will be no call for us to make dramatic sacrifices in our way of life, or for rising nations to accept lesser dreams in order to accommodate a future with fewer emissions. Members of the G20 have collaborated on a treaty of our own, comprised of a simple price signal—a carbon tax—that ensures that the price of fossil fuels will no longer ignore the harmful impacts caused by their consumption. The plan, which we will be releasing today, calls for all participating economies to levy an upstream tax on each ton of CO_2 emitted through the combustion of fossil fuels, with each nation free to allocate the proceeds from this tax as they see fit. This proposed treaty is, we believe, well-crafted and comprehensive, and it has the support of every single leader of the world's twenty largest economies. Collectively, we represent 90% of global GDP, two thirds of the world's population, and approximately 85% of global fossil fuel emissions. Nonetheless, a long road lies ahead. In the coming weeks, the treaty will be debated vigorously by the legislative bodies of many nations—those of the G20 and, I hope, those of many other countries represented here today. I welcome an honest, informed deliberation.

"However, as we begin the process, let us all be cognizant of the fact that this plan is not experimental; we are not entering new territory. Around the world, more than a dozen countries and many states and regions have successfully implemented a price on carbon. While their path was not without obstacles, not one of them witnessed the collapse of their economy or a downward drop in their standard of living. In fact, many industries within such regions now have much greater market certainty; the investment horizon for energy-related investments is longer and less confused—both of which give businesses an advantage in driving new efficiencies."

President Gilman paused, and took a sip of water from a glass placed within the podium. He looked to his right and silently acknowledged President Wei Xiaoming of China, who had emerged from the waiting room and was patiently listening to the end of his remarks. After Wei would be President Mahendra Rafi of India. This troika of the world's largest emitters, President Gilman hoped, would make it crystal clear that the stars had aligned, and that this initiative had considerable momentum.

"Let us look at this day as one of celebration, when the world apprehended the perpetrators of what could have been a tragic human calamity. Let us also look upon this day as a turning point, a juncture in time when we finally came together as one to address what many have called the most pressing challenge of our time.

"The opportunity to come before you today was fortuitous. I'm extremely pleased that our successful capture of the terrorists coincided with the annual coming together of nations within the General Assembly. But this is more than just a venue—it is precisely the right body in which to launch a global treaty. The nations represented here must take this torch and carry it forward, so that all people in all corners of the world may benefit from a future that avoids the worst consequences that we might otherwise bring upon ourselves.

"We have a long road ahead, with many miles to go before we may rest in the knowledge that a solution is in place. I look forward to making this journey with all of you, and to celebrating once again as we reach our destination. Thank you."

The Secretary General came down from the upper dais and shook the U.S. President's hand. As he then moved on to the podium to introduce the Chinese President, Wei Xiaoming climbed onto the stage and greeted President Gilman warmly.

The path was set.

97

The three VH-60N Whitehawks streamed over the Hudson River, gaining altitude for the trip back to Washington.

Within one of these helicopters, an aide handed the President a glass of sparkling water, and one to Taylor, then took a seat aft next to a Secret Service agent also on board. Following the speech at the UN, Taylor had met up with President Gilman, as requested, and the President had asked him to ride with him back to DC on Marine One.

"Cheers," said the President, holding up his glass. "To you and your team for bringing the GOC to justice."

"Thank you, sir. Cheers," said Taylor, taking a sip and placing the glass in the holder next to his seat. There was a brief moment of awkward silence. "That was a very impressive speech, Mr. President."

"Thanks, Drake. Did it surprise you?"

"A little, but I very much respect your decision to move ahead. I think you're right; an opportunity like this may not present itself for some time."

"Well, that was my calculus. I certainly never thought I'd be the 'climate change president,' but you build your hand out of the cards you've been dealt."

Taylor smiled. "You know, I used to say the same thing to my team out in the field when an operation took an unexpected turn."

"Although in my case the stakes are little less dire."

"Sir?" Taylor didn't understand. *This is the President,* he thought, *how could the stakes get any higher than that?*

"If I screw up, Drake, there's a political price to pay. When a Ranger screws up, he could get his head blown off."

"Very true," Taylor agreed, chuckling. Another few seconds passed. Taylor decided to change the subject. "So I wanted to ask you a question, Mr. President. You said nothing during your remarks about the capture of Morgan and Jerrick, or about the fact that the nuclear devices were a bluff; how would you like us to play it—with regards to what we say and what we don't?"

"How do you think we should play it, Drake?"

"Well, that's a political question. I don't think it's mine to answer."

"I'd certainly agree that it's not entirely your decision, but I'd like to hear your thoughts."

Taylor glance out the window of the helicopter to buy a few seconds of thought, then looked back at President Gilman.

"Well, Mr. President, I think this is a bit tricky."

"It is indeed."

"I guess the first issue is whether or not to inform the public that the operation was led by two of our own. While it would be nice to simply tell the truth, I'm not sure we would be well-served in doing so."

The President said nothing, waiting for Taylor to continue.

"If the world knew that a senior leader of our Special Operations Forces and an Assistant Secretary of Defense were behind the plot, it would undermine our credibility and the trust that people have in the United States."

"It certainly would."

"The second issue," continued Taylor, gaining confidence from the President's apparent agreement, "is whether to release the fact that there never was a nuclear threat."

"And?"

"Well, the problem there is that, as soon as it becomes clear that the world fell for a bluff, then a lot of bad guys out there might get ideas about holding the world hostage around whatever cause floats their boat—which would be a total disaster."

"Not to mention the fact that it would make your life miserable," President Gilman joked.

"That it would, sir."

"Drake, I think you nailed it on both counts. I'm not sure exactly what the final story will be, but we've probably got forty-eight hours or so to figure it out."

"I'm not sure it's my forte, Mr. President, but let me know if I or my team can be helpful."

"Thank you, Drake. I may take you up on that." The President sat back in his seat, leaning on an elbow and supporting his chin with the thumb and fist of his left hand. "Let me run something else by you, Drake."

I could get used to this, Taylor thought to himself. "Yes, Mr. President?"

President Gilman stared at Taylor for a moment. "Bob Baker will be stepping down from his role as Director of National Intelligence."

Taylor suddenly felt a chill run up his spine, wondering where the hell this was going.

"I'm going to nominate Dan Hawthorne to take his place," the President continued, "and I was wondering whether you might be interested in being considered for DHS Secretary."

Taylor froze. A number of thoughts raced through his mind, the first of which was whether he was even remotely capable of doing the job, and the last was whether he'd ever find another second-in-command as good as Tori Browne, since serving as her boss would soon, he hoped, be a violation of the agency's anti-fraternization policy.

"It would be an honor to be considered, Mr. President," he finally managed to respond.

"Good," President Gilman said firmly. "Then I'll add you to the shortlist," he said, smiling. "You understand of course, that this is a cabinet position, and any appointment would require a confirmation hearing."

"Yes, of course," Taylor answered, but the whole thing still seemed ridiculously surreal.

"That said, given your recent success in stopping the GOC, I'm guessing the committee would fawn all over you."

The aide who'd handed them each water at the start of the flight reappeared from behind Taylor's seat. "Mr. President, you have a call from the Secretary General."

The President furrowed his brow. "That seems a little odd," he remarked. "Excuse me, Drake," he said, picking up the phone by his seat and taking the call. "Mr. Secretary General" the President said warmly.

Taylor listened as the two conversed, but was quickly lost in thoughts of his own. He had only just started to accept that the nightmare of the past month was over, when suddenly he's on Marine One with the President, and is under consideration to head DHS. *And not only that, I'm falling in love with the most beautiful and intelligent woman I've ever met,* he thought to himself. It all seemed absolutely crazy. If someone had told him a few weeks back how all of this would have unfolded, he wouldn't have believed a word of it.

The President finished his call and put the phone back in its cradle. Taylor forced himself back to the moment at hand.

"Well," said President Gilman, "it would appear we've got a tailwind."

"I'm not sure I know what you mean, sir," Taylor said.

"The Secretary General was just calling to say that he will do everything in his power to support the U.S. and other nations as the treaty moves forward. He wanted me to know that over a hundred countries will likely be signing on, and that the vast majority of delegates will be quite vocal in helping our congress and other legislatures to understand that this is the moment."

"How difficult do you think it will be to get Congress to support it?" Taylor asked.

"I think it will be damn near impossible, Drake," the President replied, grinning. "But in my experience, just about everything that's truly important looks that way at some point or another."

Taylor smiled in response. *Tell me about it*, he thought to himself.

Epilogue

The vehicle lurched to the right as its front wheel hit a large pothole. Several people groaned, but the overcrowded bus kept its steady pace down the mountain. Myla's small hands were pressed against the window as she stood on her seat, eyes wide. She had never been outside of her village, and her mind was rapidly processing every new thing she saw along the way. Dabert sat beside her, his arm protectively around her waist in case she lost her balance. The journey from the village of Pula in Ifugao Province to Manila was just over 200 miles, but the terrain made for slow going—it would take well over 7 hours to get there.

Leaving his village had been one of the most difficult things Dabert had ever done; he felt as if he was giving up on everything he had worked so hard to build. The truth, however, was that there wasn't much left—the storm had destroyed just about everything he held dear. As Myla had, very slowly and painstakingly, emerged from the dark recesses of her shock and despair, Dabert had forced himself to confront the fact that raising his daughter among the devastation of their old life was not in her best interest—and it was not particularly good for him, either.

The pain in his chest still was still almost unbearable when his thoughts turned to Rowena and Ignacio—which occurred a hundred times a day. The family's compromised hut, the devastated rice terraces, the battered village, and the entire landscape were all constant reminders of the loss that he and Myla had suffered.

Although leaving Pula had been heart-wrenching, Dabert knew that the village that they'd known before Hurricane Benito would likely never return. Hundreds of villagers had already fled, leaving very little manpower to rebuild; any sense of community that had existed previously was lost, now just a hazy, warm memory of family and neighbors living a simple but rich life together away from the bustle of civilization. He had fought with his conscience over the decision; whether to keep his daughter in the place where she was born and raised—even if it was only a shell of its former self, or thrust them both into a complete unknown, a new world in which they would live a new life with very little resemblance to anything they'd ever experienced.

Of course, Manila was a mess as well—but reconstruction meant that there would be lots of jobs. Dabert had corresponded with a family that had left Pula several months prior. He was encouraged that they had managed to find employment and a small apartment that they could afford with what they were making. They offered to help him and Myla get settled. As he spent much of his day struggling just to feed the two of them, he realized that the choice was obvious.

The bus lurched again, this time seeming as if it might actually tip over. A passenger in the seat behind them shrieked, but the bus slowly rocked back and proceeded slowly ahead. Myla, frightened, sat down next to her father and huddled in his arms. Dabert looked down at his daughter, and gently stroked her head. After a minute, Myla shifted, and looked up into his eyes. "Daddy, why do we have to leave home?"

Dabert studied his daughter's face; they had discussed this many times, and Dabert had patiently responded each time, explaining that the storm had made life in Pula very difficult, and that they had a to start a new life in a new place. This time, he smiled and simply said "this will be a wonderful adventure, Myla. You will see; there are buildings in Manila as tall as the tallest trees in the forest, and amazing machines that will make our lives easier."

She looked back at him, seemingly trying to pull confidence from his words, then buried her head in his chest. He gave her a hug and kissed her forehead.

In truth, Dabert could not offer his daughter confidence, since he was nearly as frightened as she, and had no idea what they might encounter in Manila—he had only been to the city once in his life, some fifteen years prior. He had heard that the city had grown a great deal since then, but also knew that the storm had turned large parts of it to rubble. In the back of his mind was his greatest fear—that Manila, in its current state, would prove to be a poor choice for raising his daughter, and that he and Myla would be forced to journey once again to another country in search of a suitable place to live.

* * *

"I'm already on it. I'll have it on your desk tomorrow morning," Tori assured her boss.

She ended the call as the car came to a stop outside her townhouse. She grabbed a few files lying on the gray leather seat next to her and placed them into her bag. She looked up as she unbuckled her seatbelt and reached for the door handle.

"Tom, I have an early meeting tomorrow. Let's say 6:30 am?"

"Absolutely Ms. Browne. See you then," the driver replied.

"Thanks." She got out of the car, and walked up the steps to her front door. It was a warm summer evening, but a faint scent of autumn was in the air. A mild breeze ruffled the sleeves of her white cotton blouse. As she rustled in her bag for her keys, the door swung open wide; Taylor stood in the doorway, with a wide warm smile.

"Surprise!" he said.

Tori's face lit up with delight. She dropped her bag on the stoop and melted into Taylor's arms. "Drake! I didn't expect to see you until tomorrow night" she exclaimed, looking up into his deep green eyes.

He embraced her warmly and gave her a long, lingering kiss.

"I missed you," Taylor said, holding her tightly in his arms.

"I missed you too," she replied, laying her head on his chest.

They stood for a moment, Taylor lightly caressing her hair, as the warm breeze flowed over and around them. Finally, he leaned down and grabbed Tori's bag.

"I wrapped up early, and hitched a ride home on a State Department flight," he explained as they walked inside, his other hand on the small of her back.

I'm delighted you did," she said. "I was looking for a good excuse to take a break from work tonight."

"Happy to oblige," he replied with a mischievous smile.

Drake Taylor and Tori Browne had become a known power couple within the U.S. Intelligence community. After Taylor had been confirmed as DHS Secretary, Tori had been recruited into the CIA as Deputy Director for Intelligence. Their schedules were chaotic, and finding time for one another was a constant challenge, but after living together for nearly a year now, the spark between them had blossomed into a warm, glowing fire that showed no signs of diminishing.

The world had evolved noticeably since Drake had accepted the President's nomination. World leaders had been largely successful in rallying their lawmakers and citizens around the treaty put forward by President Gilman and leaders of the G20. A number of the largest developed nations, including India, China, Germany, France, the U.K., Mexico, South Africa, Saudi Arabia, Canada, Japan, Brazil and Turkey had all formally approved the treaty, with a number of other nations about to follow suit. However, one critical country was still a holdout: the United States.

Despite President Gilman's best efforts, those opposed to the treaty had dug in, spending vast amounts of money to lobby legislators and convince Americans from all walks of life that signing on would devastate the country's economy, destroy the American dream, and lower quality of life for all. While this campaign to hold back the tides of change did not persuade a majority to stand fast against Gilman's treaty, it succeeded brilliantly in enabling a now vocal minority to block passage—and even to block consideration—of the treaty within the halls of congress.

Taylor grabbed two glasses from a cabinet in the kitchen, and began to uncork a bottle of wine. Tori approached from behind, wrapped her arms around Taylor's waist and squeezed firmly. Taylor put the bottle and corkscrew back on the counter, and turned to hold Tori in his arms. She looked up at him with a warm smile, and they shared another long kiss. As their lips finally parted, he looked down into her dark blue eyes.

"I'm awfully glad I found you," said Taylor.

"I'm awfully glad we found each other," she replied with a broad smile, standing on her toes to give him another kiss.

With Tori in his arms, Taylor often found himself a bit overwhelmed. He never expected to find love again, and yet, here was this warm, intelligent woman, more beautiful to him now than on the day he realized he was falling in love with her. Lightning had struck twice.

She let go and wandered to the fridge to begin excavating the ingredients for dinner, while he turned back to the bottle of wine.

"So how was the trip to Miami?" Tori asked, as she put a bag of lettuce and couple of bell peppers on the counter, then returned to the fridge. "Did you see Andrea?"

"I certainly did—in fact, I spent most of the day with her. She seemed very tired to me; I don't envy her position."

Tori turned and looked at Taylor with a raised eyebrow. "I think many would say the same of you and me."

Taylor laughed gently. "Fair enough."

Andrea McKnight, still serving as head of FEMA, had been called upon to take point in gathering data and helping to explain to the American public the extent to which inaction on climate could seriously jeopardize the country—from flooding in coastal cities to extreme weather in the plains states, to droughts and insect infestations in agricultural regions. At the same time, she still had to do her job; the meetings with Taylor in Miami were focused on preparations for a hurricane forming in the South Atlantic and headed for Florida.

"So what's the latest on the storm," Tori asked, cutting open a bright yellow pepper.

"Not good," said Taylor. "It now looks as if it will hit about 20 miles north of Miami, and there's a 50-50 chance it'll pick up speed and become a cat 2."

"Yikes."

"Yikes, indeed. Possible wind speeds of 98 to 105 miles per hour. It could be a real mess. But—as usual—Andrea's team is doing a great job."

As Taylor and Tori worked to prepare the meal, they talked at length about the storm, the battle for public opinion, and of how many more cataclysmic events would be required to bring America around and secure passage of the treaty. Eventually, as they finally sat down to a candle-lit dinner, conversation moved from work to weekend, and on to other topics.

It wasn't clear how or when the country would step forward to meet the challenge that climate change presented. Politics and human behavior were unpredictable. This much, however, was certain: Mother Nature had now become the most powerful lobbyist of all on this issue, and no amount of money from any opposing group stood a snowball's chance in hell against her power. Given time, she would provide all of the evidence necessary to overcome even the most steadfast dissent.

End.

About the Author

In his everyday life, Nick d'Arbeloff works as an agent in the clean energy revolution, working to transform our energy infrastructure in the face of climate change and finite fossil fuel supply. He lives in Massachusetts.